Brady's senses were regrouping like a school of fish after a shark had swum through it. Gradually, Adonis's face came into focus. Brady was struck by how much he'd aged since they met just a few of days ago. His features were drawn and his eyes had a deranged cast, underscored by deep black shadows. Brady spoke again, slow and deliberate.

"Crackhead told me all about you. Said to say hi.*"*

"How is Crackhead?"

"Having a bad life. Blames you."

"That's a good one. Throw Crackhead in a pit with eleven snakes and you got a dozen snakes."

Gulf Stream Press
Fort Lauderdale, Florida

This is a work of fiction. Names, characters, places, and incidents are products of the author's imagination and/or used fictitiously. Any similarities to actual events, locales, or persons living or dead, is purely coincidental.

ISBN: 13: 978-1482601534 (paperback)
ISBN: 10: 1482601532 (eBook)
Library of Congress Control Number: 2008939415
CreateSpace Independent Publishing Platform
North Charleston, South Carolina

Proudly manufactured in the United States of America.

Gulf Stream Press
Fort Lauderdale, Florida

Where a cool breeze blows and a warm sea flows.

*Dedicated to my wife,
Donna*

Brady's Run

Joseph Collum

Bradys Run

CHAPTER ONE

THE MOONLESS MORNING was so black even the shadows seemed to cast shadows. A tall, sleek figure glided lithe as a cat through the inky stillness, a duffel bag slung over one shoulder and two five-gallon canisters in either hand. In the distance he could hear waves lap sleepily onto a beach and palm fronds whispering in the breeze. The sounds were normally pleasing to him, but at that moment his mood was dismal as a swamp. *Why the fuck am I here?*

The trespasser moved through a swinging wooden gate into the courtyard of the Pelican's Nest Motel. The pitchdark air felt bleak and ominous on his skin, like night-ocean water. He darted around patches of pink neon light cast by the lazy blinks of a *Vacancy* sign and ducked beneath a staircase. Standing stock still, he waited for his irises to adjust to the black velvet shadows. The motel was asleep. His only witnesses were a pair of stars winking overhead, watching down like a barn owl from the rafters. For an instant he smelled perfume, then recognized the thick saccharine scent of jasmine. The stench reminded him of flowers rotting in a graveyard and he fought off momentary nausea. Then the answer to his question came to him. He was here for one reason. *Money.*

The black-clad man bounded up the stairs and moved along a rail overlooking a swimming pool and thatched tiki bar. The second floor was unoccupied. It was October, still the slack season. Fort Lauderdale had not yet been besieged by the perennial parade of snowbirds flocking there in search of restoration from the surf, sand, and sun. When he reached Room 15 he set down the containers and duffel bag and knelt facing the door eyelevel to the knob.

The latch was an archaic pin-and-tumbler, a rotating cylinder composed of several pairs of pins that kept the knob from turning when locked. Simple and ridiculously easy to pick. He removed two small gadgets from his pocket. One resembled a tiny hockey stick, the other a hooked device, like something dental hygienists use to scrape plaque off teeth. He inserted the hockey stick, a tension wrench, into the lower portion of the keyhole and applied light torque, turning it to the right as far as it would go. Then he slid in the dental pick and twisted until he felt the pins lift. The door gave a dull report and sighed open.

He stepped inside, drew the drapes closed, and flipped on the television. The screen flickered to life, giving him enough light to see it was a garden variety Florida motel room, bright and airy and clean as a new car. He compared the Pelican's Nest to the dingy room he rented, with its Salvation Army décor and reek of disinfectant. *Rat's Nest.* The TV was tuned to the Weather Channel, the sound just loud enough to hear.

"Now for the 4 a.m. update on *Hurricane Phyllis.*" The intruder stopped to listen. "As it bears down on the Yucatan Peninsula, *Phyllis* is shaping up to be a storm of historic proportions. The National Hurricane Center reports that a hunter aircraft has flown into *Phyllis's* four mile wide eye and measured winds of one hundred fifty miles per hour. Barometric pressure is a record low eight hundred eighty two milibars, an astounding one hundred points below this time yesterday. At this point the storm track is quite wobbly but all indications are it will hit the island of Cozumel and nearby Cancun within the next twelve hours." *Poor Mexicans.* The weatherman droned on. "Computer projections indicate that after *Phyllis* passes the Yucatan she will loop north and east and gain strength as she heads toward South Florida."

The interloper smiled to himself. Good for business. He lowered the sound and opened his bag, like a surgeon preparing to operate. He lifted out a hotplate and set it on a small white rattan table. Then he removed a stack of newspaper, crumpled the pages, and spread them around the room while his mind wandered away from *Phyllis* to the motel's owners. He'd been watching them clandestinely for a week. Old bald guy and his younger blonde wife. She was a little long in the tooth but, from a distance, her face looked good and her body seemed fit and firm. *Nice rack. I'd hit her.*

He pulled a hand auger from the bag. Soundless, he bored holes in the baseboards on the left and right sides of the room and threaded plastic tubing through each. The five-gallon containers were made of blue plastic. With little effort, he lifted one and attached the spout to the flanged end of the tube on the right and tilted the jug. The smell of gasoline permeated the air as the liquid spilled into the adjacent room. He repeated the process on the opposite wall. The remaining fluid he splashed on the beds and walls, as casual as if he was watering flowers. Then he set the second canister on the hot plate and switched the burner to high. He flipped off the television, opened the drapes, picked up his duffel bag, and slipped from the room, silent as fog.

Five minutes later, he was sitting in a stolen car a half block away. Still as a statue, he stared into the blackness, stony eyes locked on Room 15's big plate glass window, silently counting down. *Three, two, one…*

An orange fireball erupted followed by a dull *whomp.* He held his breath, watching flames climb the walls inside the room. Black smoke began to billow from the white door jamb. The fire spread quickly into the rooms next door. Then the picture window facing the courtyard burst. Tongues of flame broke through the roof and licked at the black sky. Red sparks danced in the air like a swarm lightning bugs. Within minutes the entire second floor of the Pelican's Nest was ablaze. He heard someone shout.

"Fire!"

Like a gust of wind, a robed man ran into the courtyard. The bald motel owner. He stared at the second floor for a moment and then began pounding on doors.

"Fire," he hollered. "Everyone out."

Guests rushed into the night, some dressed in pajamas and nightgowns, some wrapped in blankets. The motel owner ran to the wall behind the tiki bar and grabbed a garden hose. He twisted the nozzle and tried to douse the flames, but the water pressure was too feeble to reach the roof. He abandoned the hose and picked up a bucket, plunged it into the swimming pool, and raced up the staircase. He heaved the water at the blaze. He might as well have spit. Finally, the man ripped off his robe and beat at the fire. The arsonist watched from the street, captivated by the drama he had ignited, admiring his victim. *Old codger's got balls.* Then he saw a woman dash up the stairs, the blonde wife, breasts bouncing inside her yellow robe like desperately beating hearts. She reached her husband and wrestled him away from the flames.

Sirens were soon wailing and the darkness was replaced by flashing lights. Two red ladder trucks roared up. Firefighters quickly attacked the flames with high pressure streams of foam retardant. But too late. The building was burning like a tinderbox.

Crackhead would be proud. The arsonist snorted, the stolen car's engine thrumming smoothly at idle. Crackhead! That pervert would be cranking his shank a hundred miles an hour right now.

The first police squad car screeched to the scene. It was time to go.

Brady's Run

CHAPTER TWO

MAX BRADY KNEW he was dreaming but could not tear himself from his foggy netherworld. It was a bright, unblemished morning. He was padding on foot across the Brooklyn Bridge. Happy. Content. Basking in the memory of her the night before. Soft. Rapturous. Ravenous. Then, with no signal, no warning, no chance to stop time, no way to alter events, his world exploded. He screamed into his cell phone.

"Get out, Victoria. Get out."

"Max, it's so hot."

"Listen to me."

"My God!" she cried. *"People are jumping."*

"Victoria. Get out. Crawl to an exit and get out now."

"Max, I love you. Don't ever forget."

The phone clicked and went dead and he heard nothing but a hiss. A deafening, unbearable, eternal hiss. Brady heard screams and looked up. The blue sky was filled with red fire, black smoke, and falling bodies. In that instant he knew. Knew without thinking. His life had forever changed.

A giant cloud engulfed him and he gasped awake. Drenched in sweat, he was overcome by a profound sense of relief. *It was a dream! Just a dream!* Brady closed his eyes and rolled to the far side of the bed.

He wanted to caress her silky skin and feel her soft flesh, still warm with sleep. He reached out and reality stabbed him like a dagger. She wasn't there. She hadn't been there. Not for years. Only the nightmare that pervaded his sleep like an endless film loop.

Brady lay in the dark trying to get his bearings. *Where am I?* It took several seconds. *The boat.* He rolled from the bunk and staggered naked onto the deck of his schooner, the *Victoria II*. A crescent moon hung in the black western sky like the half-open eye of a sleeping cat. To the east, the first indigo bars of dawn began to purr reveille.

He plunged over the side of the boat, slashing through a layer of mist into chilly blackness, tripping shrill alarms that speared his sensors like ice picks. Suspended in limbo, Brady held his breath for a long moment, fiercely trying to retrieve his fast fading apparition. But, as ever, she swam off like a diaphanous white vapor, turning only to whisper. *"Don't ever forget."*

He hissed to the surface and gasped for air. Day was fast eclipsing night. Treading water, he watched the silhouette of a sprawling Spanish hacienda emerge against the illumining sky like a latent image materializing in a dark room. Victor Gruber, his friend, landlord, and owner of the house, wouldn't be awake for another hour. Brady clambered over the transom and stepped onto the dock, his mind still clouded by the dust of his dream. A shower nozzle protruded from one of the pilings. He turned the spigot and cold water gushed onto his head. A bar of soap sat atop the piling and he lathered himself, then rinsed, and ducked into the schooner's cabin. Moments later he was back on deck in a pair of ragged khaki shorts, high-topped black sneakers, and white T-shirt with a skull-and-crossbones on the back. Printed in black over the left breast pocket were the words *Sea Shanty*.

Brady traipsed through Victor Gruber's dew-drenched lawn, grass blades lashing his bare ankles like chilly spears. The only sound was the chirrup of morning warblers awakening in hidden roosts. An old green Schwinn was leaning against the side of the house. He pushed the bicycle onto Siesta Lane, pedaled to the end, then steered east beneath a catena of royal palms lining Las Olas Boulevard like silent sentries.

After a few blocks he reached the Las Olas Bridge and accelerated up the steep arch as an untroubled titanium sky spread before him. He glanced to his right at a small half-moon bay where a dozen sailboats were resting at anchor and reached the crest just as the golden glare of the sun's aurora broke over a placid Atlantic Ocean. A small flotilla of cargo ships floated benignly on the horizon. Fort Lauderdale Beach was a barrier island bordered by the sea to the east and the Intracoastal Waterway on the west. Brady peered south down the Intracoastal. It was lined with mammoth luxury yachts docked as far as he could see. He wondered, as he did every morning. *Who the hell owns those things?*

Then he turned north and a jolt of electricity shot up his spine. A thick plume of black smoke was spiraling in the sky. For an instant, he wondered if he was still trapped in his nightmare. A car whizzed by, rattling the drawbridge's steel grate. He touched the railing and it was cold. Brady decided he was awake.

With alarm bells shrieking in his brain, he raced down the bridge, his eyes riveted on the dark pillar. At the bottom he tacked left and pumped hard, his dread surging the closer he got. Brady turned the corner at Playa del Sol and his heart sank. The Pelican's Nest Motel was a smoldering shell.

The street was a helter-skelter of fire trucks and thick hoses strewn like spaghetti across the asphalt. Dozens of people milled about like war refugees, many wrapped in blankets, faces painted with numbed expressions, some streaked with tears. Dazed, they watched firefighters douse what remained of the motel. The red barrel-tile roof was caved in and water percolated from the second floor straight down to the first like a monsoon on a black forest. The straw thatch of the tiki bar was scorched and the swimming pool looked rancid as a toxic waste pit.

Brady spotted a white and blue police car and pushed his bicycle over. A cop was scribbling in the front seat. A woman sat next to him. He reached through the open passenger window and squeezed her shoulder. She looked up and a chill stole through him. Olga Klum was a striking woman with a narrow fine-featured face, short white-blonde hair, and translucent blue eyes. She normally looked far younger than her fifty years but now her eyes were red-rimmed and her face was puffy and haggard, as if she'd been transformed like an actress in a special effects film.

"Are you okay, sweetheart?"

Olga wore a yellow robe and a white scarf was wrapped around her head. Her eyes flooded with tears.

"Oh, Max." A sob escaped from deep inside her. "It was terrible."

"It's okay, Olga." He caressed her cheek with the backs of his fingers. "Everything's going to be fine."

"What are we going to do?"

"Don't worry right now. Trust me."

The policeman leaned over from the driver's seat. "Excuse me, sir, can you give us a few minutes?" Then he looked up and recognition crossed his face. "Oh, hi Mr. Brady."

Dan Mason was a young patrolman. He had a dark tan, close-cropped black hair, and thick Popeye forearms. The beach was his beat and Brady had known him for him for a couple of years.

"No problem, Dan. Just checking on my friends. Is Gunther okay?"

The patrolman pointed to an ambulance across the street. The back door was open and a burly bald man lay on a stretcher while a paramedic bandaged his right hand.

"He was burned trying to put out the fire," Olga said, a trace of a German accent in her inflection. Tears were streaming down her cheeks. "He couldn't stop it, Max. It was too far gone. It was just awful!"

Brady patted her shoulder again. "Olga, I'm going to call Victor. He'll want you and Gunther to stay at the house as long as you need to."

Olga looked up at him and swiped soot-smudged fingers across her wet face. "Thank you," she whispered.

Brady negotiated his bicycle over the snarl of hoses to the ambulance, watching Gunther Klum as he approached. Pathos swelled inside him. Gunther was one of those men with a grizzly bear countenance but the temperament of a teddy bear. He and Olga had migrated from Germany to Fort Lauderdale thirty years before, bought the Pelican's Nest, and lived an idyllic life ever since. Now their business, and their home, was a charred heap. Grief was etched on Gunther's ash-caked face, deepening the engraving carved by age.

"Are you alright, Gunther?"

It was one of those reflexive questions people ask at times like that, knowing the other person is far from okay. While the medic wrapped his

Joseph Collum

hand, Gunther looked at Brady. His bloodshot eyes crinkled and his thin white lips curled into a wan smile.

"If by alright, Max, you mean alive, yes, I'm alright. A few minor burns. Nothing that won't heal."

Gunther was seventy years old but, like Olga, normally looked much younger. He seemed to have aged twenty years overnight.

"What the hell happened, Gunther?"

"I don't know, Max," he said, his accent thicker than his wife's. "I heard an explosion. By the time I got to the door flames were coming from the roof. They spread so fast. Thank God it's the slow season. The upper floor wasn't occupied. I roused everyone, then grabbed the hose and did what I could. The fire trucks were here in five minutes, but..."

Gunther's voice trailed off, his bleary eyes gazing out at the gloomy black carcass of his ravaged motel.

"What could have caused such an explosion, Gunther?"

"Nothing," said Klum, slapping at the sky with the back of his good hand. "There are no gas lines. We didn't have anything combustible lying around. No paint or fuel cans. Not even a propane tank for the barbecue. Nothing volatile that could have caused this."

Gunther looked at Brady for several seconds, deep in thought.

"Max," he said gravely, "I don't think this was an accident."

9

Bradys Run

CHAPTER THREE

ADONIS ROCK'S EYES swept the immense green canopy monopolizing the airspace over Jack Del Largo's front yard.

"Magnificent tree," he said.

"Pain in my ass," said Del Largo. "My wetback gardener smuggled his entire goddamn family across the goddamn Rio Grande with the money I pay him just to blow the goddamn leaves."

They stood side-by-side staring up at the monster trunk, two men stamped from vastly disparate molds. Del Largo was short and pear-shaped, with twitchy dark eyes, a mangy thatch of brown hair, and love handles that hung over his belt like fleshy saddlebags. Adonis was tall and resplendent with blonde locks cascading onto tawny granite shoulders showcased in a black tank top T-shirt.

"I can take it out for you," Rock said, assaying the tree with a swift calculating eye.

"No thanks."

"I'll give you a good price."

"I got enough on my plate right now," Del Largo said, waving at Adonis to follow.

"Let me know," Adonis said, still eyeing the tree.

Del Largo lived in a sprawling eight decade old mansion on the riverfront at Sailboat Bend, a snug, leafy slice of old Fort Lauderdale. Legend had it Al Capone once wintered in the house. Del Largo had spent a gold mine remodeling the coral-hued edifice, with its russet tile roof, dramatic arched Castilian windows, and sumptuous pool looking out over New River. The place fetched *oohs* and *aahs* from passing boaters.

The man of the house was reaching for the handle when the front door burst open, nearly knocking Adonis off the stoop into a thorny bed of bougainvillea. A gangly beanpole of a woman blew out of the house like a cyclone, a Virginia Slim dangling from her lips, shoulder blades protruding like pubescent breasts from the wrong side of her body.

"Jack!" she said, not noticing the visitor. "We've got to decide on the menu."

"Jesus, Marla," Del Largo groaned. "Not now."

"Maine lobster crepe with a dill hollandaise," Marla said, ignoring his peevish tone. "Or lobster mango canapés on crisp Asian toast?"

"Sounds delicious."

"Miniature Beef Wellington or smoked duck confit over endive with mandarin orange?"

"What the hell is *confit*?"

"Oh, Jack!"

"This goddamned wedding is gonna bankrupt me," Del Largo said. "I thought the bride's family is supposed to pay for this shit."

"For god's sake, Jack, they live in a trailer."

Del Largo's face reddened. "The band alone is costing me twenty grand. I should be getting the Rolling fucking Stones."

"Jack! Your language!"

Marla whirled around and saw Adonis for the first time. Her eyes grew round as capital *O's*. She extended her hand to him.

"Marla Del Largo. And you?"

"Adonis Rock," he said, not sure whether to shake her hand or kiss it. *What the hell.* He bowed and gallantly pecked her paw. Marla's face lit up like a callow girl being fawned over.

"Adonis," she said. "How fitting."

Jack Del Largo felt like puking. He knew his wife was a sucker for sweet talkers and hand kissers. He also knew she had succumbed to the charms of more than one lothario. He'd never confronted her, just as she had never challenged him. Infidelity was an unspoken reality between the Del Largos. *Ask me no questions, I'll tell you no lies* was their recipe for nuptial bliss. The bottom line for Marla, he knew, was the bottom line. Lucre had always trumped lust. If she had to choose between a blue-collar caveman like Adonis Rock and a roly-poly plutocrat like himself, Del Largo knew she'd opt for the mansion, the Mercedes, and the A-list friends every time.

"He's a tree-trimmer," Jack said.

Disappointment altered Marla's face. "Tree trimmer?"

"I prefer arborist," said Adonis.

"Oh," she said and the spell was broken. Then her eyes brightened like hundred-watt lightbulbs. "Are you here to cut down that nasty old... what is it anyway? Oak?"

Adonis stared at the Del Largos, trying to camouflage his incredulity. *They don't know.*

"I told Jack, er, Mr. Del Largo, I'd give you a good price to take it out."

"Can you get rid of it before the wedding next week?" Marla said.

"No problem. Two day job."

"Oh, Jack, do it."

Del Largo glared at Adonis like his mouth was filled with mustard. "How much?"

Rock turned . He folded his arms and stroked his chin and surveyed the tree again with a contemplative air. From taproot to tree top the gargantuan hardwood stood at least one hundred feet tall. It's trunk was thick as a Scud missile. He did some quick arithmetic and felt a tremor in his gut. He would normally charge five thousand dollars to take down an oak this size and haul away the timber. But this wasn't an oak.

"Three," he said.

"Hundred?"

"Thousand."

"That's highway robbery!"

Adonis looked at him with keen indifference. "Most tree services would charge you six grand," he said, trying to sound blasé, as if he and greed were total strangers

"Jack!"

"No way, Marla. This wedding's already costing me a hundred grand."

"Jack!"

"No, Marla! That's final." Del Largo turned and lumbered toward the doorway. "Come on, Adonis."

"Wait, Jack. What about the first course? Wild mushroom herb ravioli with white truffle sauce or apricot ginger pan-seared sea scallops over seaweed salad?"

"Jesus, Marla!" Del Largo said, waving his hand dismissively. "You decide!"

He led Adonis through an antique cedar door with iron grilles and a postigo window. Inside the house they proceeded down a long arched hallway with red brick walls. The floors were polished black marble. The furniture was hand-carved Mexican. Scallop-backed benches, mesquite armoires, big red ceramic Tamalero pots. Del Largo's study overlooked the swimming pool which, at that moment, was occupied by a young blonde woman in a white bikini floating face up on a raft, displaying an immense pair of breasts that pointed straight at the sky and, to Adonis's practiced eye, did not appear to be the work of Mother Nature.

"Raymona," said Del Largo. "My future daughter-in-law. She might be trailer trash, but she's a primo piece of ass."

"Your son's a lucky man."

"Not really. Hate to call his wife-to-be a derogatory name, but it rhymes with *rich*. I give them three years."

"Why pay a hundred grand for a wedding then?"

"Because Marla's a bitch too. I don't throw a chichi wedding so she can show off for her society friends and it'll cost me five million in alimony."

"Sounds romantic," Adonis said, suppressing a grin.

Del Largo shot him a malevolent look, then stepped to a wet bar in the corner. He splashed brown liquid from a crystal decanter into two short glasses and handed one to Adonis. Del Largo plopped heavily into a black leather swivel chair behind his desk and motioned his guest to the seat across from him. A wooden humidor sat on the desk. *Spanish cedar*, thought Adonis. Del Largo lifted the lid and retrieved a foot-long stogie.

"Cohiba?" he offered. "Straight from Havana."

"No, thanks."

Del Largo clipped the cigar cap with a mini-guillotine, flicked a butane flame beneath the tip, and puffed until it glowed crimson. He took a drag and then opened the top drawer of his desk and extracted a manila envelope.

"Twenty-five large," he said and tossed it to Adonis. "In tens and twenties, as agreed."

Adonis downed his whiskey in a single swallow then rose to his feet and tucked the envelope into the back waistband of his denim shorts.

"Nice doing business with you, Jack. Let me know if you change your mind on that tree."

Del Largo calmly expelled a blue smoke ring. "Sit down," he said. "I got something else."

Adonis looked down at him, hesitant, wondering what *else* Del Largo had in mind. He shrugged and sat again, relishing the feel of the cash-stuffed envelope stabbing him in the lower back. Del Largo dipped the tip of the Cuban cigar in his glass, lifted it to his mouth, and let a few drops of bourbon drip onto his tongue.

"If another motel burns down," Adonis said, "it's gonna get hot around here – no pun intended."

Del Largo leaned back, palms and forearms turned upward on the wings of his chair, appraising Adonis like a big, flaccid, cigar-smoking swami.

"Not a torch job." He flicked off the ash with a chubby finger. "I'm talking about a *removal*. And I don't mean trees. Gotta problem with that?"

Adonis watched the fat man exhale another cloud of smoke then rest his head on the pillow of flesh beneath his chin. He'd met Del Largo a month before through Dantrelle Peppers, his former cellmate at Citrus Correctional. Dantrelle had been doing a five-year bit for armed robbery. It was no secret in population that a Fort Lauderdale lawyer named

Jack Del Largo had connections at the Parole Board. Dantrelle paid him twenty grand and was sprung two years early. In August, Del Largo called him out of the blue. Dantrelle was living in Islamorada, working on a drift fishing boat. They arranged to meet in the gift shop at the Snapper Creek Service Plaza on the south end of the Florida Turnpike. It was a sweltering day. Jack was slurping his second fresh-squeezed orange juice when Dantrelle arrived.

"O.J.?" Del Largo said. "I'm buying."

"Nah," said Dantrelle. "Acid reflux. A cold Yoo-hoo would hit the spot, though."

They walked outside and sat at a picnic table in the speckled shade of a shaggy ficus tree. Dantrelle swiped his soiled angler's shirtsleeve across the wood slats sending several bird pellets flying.

"Feathered fucking rats," he said, setting down his Yoo-hoo. "Whadya need, Jack."

"A favor."

"Anything for you."

"Know anybody who can burn a building?"

"Donald Rockwell," Dantrelle answered without hesitation. "Learned from the best."

"Who's that? The best, I mean."

"Ever hear of Crackhead Corrales?"

"Drug dealer?"

"Fire bug. A dang legend. Never caught."

"Why don't I just hire this Crackhead?"

"He's in prison."

"I thought you said he was never caught."

"Not for arson. Shot some mobster over in Tampa. On the shelf now."

"Shelf?"

"Death Row. Donnie was his apprentice. Kid did eighteen months on a coke rap. Last I heard he got his gate money and was back out on the bricks. Moved down around your neck of the woods. Changed his name to Apollo or some shit. Was trying to make it as a model. Guy's cut like a fucking Greek god."

Del Largo used his contacts to track down Donald Rockwell, who was going by the name Adonis Rock. The lawyer hired him to torch the Pelican's Nest. Now he had *something else.*

"Depends on the money," Adonis said. "*Removal's* a whole 'nother thing. It'll cost you a shitload more than a fire."

"How much?" said Del Largo, blue smoke billowing from his nostrils.

Adonis thought for a moment before deciding on a figure. "Fifty."

"That's about what I had in mind."

"Plus another ten, for a long vacation."

"Now you're trying to fuck me."

"Like I said, things'll get hot. I'll need to get out of town for a while."

"That's bullshit!"

Adonis shrugged and stood up again. "That's my price. Take it or leave it."

"Okay, okay. I'll take it. But sixty's final. Deal?"

"Deal."

Del Largo scribbled a name and address on a piece of paper, handed it to Adonis, and hoisted himself out of his chair.

"Don't do anything until I give you the green light. *If* it happens, it'll be on short notice."

Del Largo stepped to the study door and opened it. Marla was standing there with an upraised hand poised to knock and a startled expression on her face.

"Jack! You scared me," she said and held up a menu. "Seared arctic char with pineapple crab salsa, or carved porcini encrusted beef filet with mashed Yukon potatoes?"

Del Largo turned to Adonis and rolled his eyes. "I'll be in touch. You know the way out?"

"Or," Marla went on, "petite filet mignon atop croutons with lemon butter shrimp…"

Adonis retraced his steps through the hallway arches. He had just turned a corner and was heading toward the front door when he collided with a blonde in a white bikini. The centerfold from the pool. Dripping wet. She turned a pair of dewy brown eyes up at him and inhaled sharply, like a swimmer come up for air.

"I'm *sooo* sorry," she said with a molasses twang.

He looked down and saw two prominent damp spots on the black T-shirt just below his ribcage. "Don't apologize. I enjoyed it."

She smiled and emitted a sultry laugh. "Oh, you did, did you? And who might you be?"

"I *might* be a Hollywood movie star. Or I *might* be a United States Senator."

"Movie star, maybe. Senator, I don't think."

He extended his right hand. "Adonis Rock. Arborist."

"What in the world is an arborist?"

"Just a guy who trims trees. I was giving Mr. Del Largo an estimate."

"Raymona," she said and shook his hand.

"Very nice to meet you."

"Well, Adonis Rock," she drawled, "you can trim my bushes any old time."

"Trees."

"Un-huh," Raymona said and let the tip of her tongue take a languid lap around the contour of her full pink lips.

She brushed past him and strutted down the hallway. Halfway to the end she reached back and tugged the white draw string, liberating her bikini top as she vanished through a doorway.

Adonis shook his head. *Three years may be a stretch!*

Bradys Run

CHAPTER FOUR

MAX BRADY WHEELED south on the beach road letting the salt air wash away the stench of Gunther and Olga Klum's cindered dreams. Summer's sauna season was over and the October air had a zesty bite. It was one of those sunny, serene days when it felt good to be alive, if you let it.

Wavelets were spooling onto the sand like tongues of liquid gold while a pod of dolphins bobbed languidly just off the beach. A pelican tilted low over them, then soared high and nose-dived into the sea, emerging seconds later with a breakfast fish thrashing in its bill.

Brady marveled at the metamorphosis Fort Lauderdale had undergone since he was a kid. Back then it was the Spring Break mecca, overrun by a locust-horde of college kids oozing hormones and Coppertone. An orgy of wet T-shirt contests, pillaged hotels, beer brawls, and cops carting rowdy students off to jail. *"Come for vacation, leave on probation!"* was the town's unofficial motto. A perfect place for a boy to go through puberty.

After Brady went away to college – not to return for more than twenty years – the city's ruling class abolished the beach party and went upscale. Students were evicted and wrecking balls razed the seedy dives along A1A. A concrete canyon of condos and luxury hotels had risen in their footprints, and many more were in the offing. He counted a dozen gantry cranes perched like giant praying mantis in the sky along the ocean. In an hour the air would be filled with dust and the rat-tat-tat of jackhammers.

For now, though, the beach was a placid paradise. Vendors were setting out lounge chairs and jet skis on the sand beneath a throng of spindly coconut trees, their green fronds clapping like long slim fingers in the timorous breeze. Brady steered along a low white wall curling the length of the beach, past water gazers, sun bathers, rollerbladers, and brown-skinned joggers with iPods plugged in their ears like stethoscopes. In the distance, he could see downtown skyscrapers jutting up like a cardboard movie set. Brady braked in front of *Sunny's* and leaned the Schwinn against a palm tree.

A smiling young woman with long golden hair stood on the sidewalk, serving tray in hand and flawless figure on full display in a red thong bikini, red western boots, and red cowboy hat.

"What's the story, mornin' glory," she said.

"Just trying to break even, Sunshine."

Sunny Regan was the siren of Lauderdale Beach, a phosphorescent personality whose tiny bistro raked in a small fortune serving omelets and turkey wraps to tourists. But the main attraction was Sunny. Visitors paid five bucks to take pictures with her in her distinctive outfit standing in front of the red canopy sign over her door: *"Sunny's – Tastes great and its goooood fer ya!"*

Brady took a seat at an umbrella table a few feet from a young mother and father with two squirming little boys.

"The usual?" Sunny said.

"I'm feeling kinda untamed today. Make my toast rye instead of wheat."

"Max Brady, you are too wild."

She scribbled his order, stopping twice to adjust the strap of her scant top. Walking inside, she looked back at him over her shoulder, forcing Brady to keep his eyes on hers.

Two tables down an elderly man was reading *The Miami Herald.* His tanned skin was cracked as old leather and his long withered neck protruded from his shoulders like a tortoise from its shell.

"Morning, Max," he said without raising his eyes. "Don't enjoy my company anymore?"

"Morning, Jonas. Didn't want to disturb your reading."

"Nonsense." Jonas cleared a spot in the shade. "Come sit."

He moved to Jonas Bigelow's table just as Sunny emerged through the double French doors beneath the red canopy bearing a steaming cup of coffee. Brady saw lust flare in the old man's milky blue eyes, then fizzle like a spent roman candle.

"Now, Jonas," Sunny said, wagging her left forefinger at him, "don't start ranting at Max. He wants to enjoy the beautiful day and eat his breakfast without you harping about politics."

Brady looked at Sunny and they both shrugged. Silencing Jonas, they knew, was like trying to muzzle the sea. Brady held up his cup and pointed at it.

"Best java on the beach."

"Can't beat it with a stick," Sunny said.

She turned and sashayed through the French doors and past three high-top tables littered with morning newspapers. She didn't look back this time and both men eyeballed her every step until she'd disappeared behind a pair swinging kitchen doors. Jonas raised his cup to Brady.

"Finest fanny on the beach," he said, his eyes twinkling.

"Jonas, I'm shocked. Seventy-five years old. What would Betty do if she heard you talk like that?"

"I wouldn't live to see seventy-six," he said, and they laughed.

But the good humor was fleeting. Brady noticed Jonas's jaws clench, then heard the sound. Heard it before he saw it. A roar announcing the arrival of the day's first giant cement truck. It thundered past them and raced down the beach road spewing a foul trail of acrid gray fumes in its wake.

"God damn them," Jonas said. "Greedy bastards! All they see are dollar signs."

Bigelow and his wife Betty owned the Coral Reef, one of a colony of mom-and-pop motels clustered in the central beach area. Jonas and a band of innkeepers and activists were fighting tooth-and-nail to stop the incursion of the immense high-rises that were dwarfing their properties.

"They're destroying the beach, Max. The breezy character is vanishing. They're turning us into a Vegas Strip on the ocean."

Brady nodded wordlessly, his rote response to Jonas's perpetual tirades.

"I know you don't want to get involved, Max," Bigelow said, his voice rising, "but we need a good lawyer."

"Ex-lawyer," said Brady. "Besides, Jonas, I've got enough problems of my own. I wouldn't know what to do with yours."

Jonas waved a hand at him in disgust. "Talking to you is like banging my head on the wall."

"Don't knock it. Did you know head banging burns two hundred calories an hour."

"It's not funny, Max. You grew up on this beach. You know they're destroying it. You should be up in arms more than any of us. If we don't stop them those buildings are gonna be around longer than dinosaur turds."

"Times change, Jonas. The world changes. Buildings go up. Buildings come down," he said, thinking: *Yes, buildings do come down.*

"That's a bunch of applesauce, Max."

For a long moment Brady studied the cantankerous old man. Jonas was like a crazy uncle at Christmas dinner – prone to rant and rave, but Brady was as fond of the curmudgeon and his wife as he was of the Klums.

"Jonas," he said, "something terrible has happened."

An anxious expression took hold of Jonas's wrinkled face. "What? Did someone die?"

"No. Not that bad. But the Pelican's Nest burned down this morning."

"Oh, God, no! How are Olga or Gunther?"

Brady filled him in on the fire, Gunther's burns, and that Olga and the *Pelican Nest's* guests were unharmed.

"Damage?"

"Total."

"Goddamnit," he blurted. "What happened?"

"Don't know. Gunther doesn't think it was an accident."

"Arson?"

"I haven't spoken to the fire marshal, but it could be."

"Damn them."

Brady shot a confused look in Jonas's direction. "Them? Them who?"

"Max, I know you think I'm a conspiracy nut, but I don't believe in coincidences. The city's trying to squeeze us out. The mayor and his cronies are handing out building permits on silver platters for those monstrosities at the same time they jack up our taxes and try to crush us with fines. They're doing everything they can to run us off. Now they're burning us out."

Sunny came out with Brady's breakfast in time to catch the tail end of the conversation.

"Fire?" she said, setting the plate in front of him. "Where?"

"The Pelican's Nest," Jonas said.

"No!" She clapped a hand to her mouth. "What about Olga and Gunther?"

"They're fine," Brady said and repeated what he'd told Jonas.

Sunny's eyes moistened. "Those poor people."

"They were burned out," said Jonas.

"I think you're jumping to conclusions," Brady said.

"Really, my friend? Let me tell you something. Greed and corruption are as powerful forces of nature as gravity. These bastards will stoop to anything to get rid of us."

Tears streamed down Sunny's cheeks. The beach community was a close knit group. Most of the small motel, restaurant, and shop owners knew each other. Like Brady and Jonas, the Klums were morning regulars at her sidewalk cafe.

"I'll put plates together for Olga and Gunther," she said. "Jonas, can you drop them off on your way home?"

"Absolutely, dear. That's very thoughtful."

Sunny whisked back inside, a sense of purpose in her step, neither man watching her this time.

Brady considered the old man closely. "Jonas, do you seriously believe the fire is part of some plot?"

"Max, this beach isn't all sunshine and bliss. The politicians and developers are in cahoots. We're like little Davids fighting Goliath."

Bigelow threw his newspaper on the table, jumped to his feet, and strode defiantly to his bicycle, his step as peppy as a vigorous man half his age.

"Those sons-a-bitches ain't gettin' away with this," he said.

Sunny came out and put a bag of food in his bike basket and gave him a peck on the cheek.

"Give 'em hell, Jonas," Brady called out as Bigelow rode off down the beach.

"Goddamned right I will," he shouted back, raising his right fist in the air. "Those bastards are gonna wish they'd never heard of Jonas Bigelow."

Bradys Run

CHAPTER FIVE

BRADY FINISHED BREAKFAST, left Sunny a handsome tip, and pushed his bike a half block to the Sea Shanty. The Shanty was a no frills beach bar for people with sand between their toes. The sign on the door said it all: *No shoes, no shirt, no problem!* It had an L-shaped teak bar, a dozen wooden stools, and six small tables. The walls were adorned with pirate flags, ship lanterns, a 16th Century Seminole dugout canoe, and Brady's old *Dewey Weber* surfboard. There were photographs of his late parents, John and Mary Brady, Duke Kahanamoku, the legendary father of surfing, and an old black man with a black-and-white monkey perched on his shoulder.

On the outside wall facing the beach was a small courtyard enclosed on three sides, with a coral waterfall, several palms, a big twisty banyan tree, and a beach sand floor where patrons could dig their feet in, sip beer in the shade, and watch the waves roll in across the street.

Brady switched on one of three televisions hanging from the walls and clicked to the Weather Channel, listening while he checked his ice bins and emptied the dishwasher.

"We have the 9 a.m. National Weather Service bulletin on *Hurricane Phyllis*," said a female meteorologist standing in front of a satellite map of the Caribbean. "The center of the storm was located near Latitude

18.1 North, Longitude 84.7 West, or about two hundred fifteen miles southeast of Cozumel, Mexico. Maximum sustained winds remain near one hundred fifty miles per hour, making *Phyllis* an extremely powerful Category Four hurricane on the Saffir-Simpson Scale. After passing the Yucatan and making an expected turn north toward Cuba and southern Florida she is likely to gain intensity."

Another storm, Brady thought. *Just what we need.*

He spent the next hour preparing the days fare. Cuisine was strictly pub grub. Boiled shrimp, shucked oysters, chicken wings, and the house specialty, gumbo. He made a fresh batch daily, dicing fish, chicken, shrimp, sausage, and okra, dumping it in a giant pot, and sitting it over a low flame on the gas stove.

Then he slipped on a pair of size thirteen New Balances and set off on his *bikini run*. Based on the carrot-and-stick theory, it involved following the trail of sandy-bottomed girls lazing on the beach, giving Brady the momentum to finish his daily six-mile jaunt with relative ease. The sun vibrated overhead as he jogged down A1A sniffing an olfactory stew of salt water, sunscreen, and deep-fry clams boiling in oil at *Beachcombers Grill*. Further down, construction sites were in full swing. Lunchpail Lotharios in hard hats, scaling scaffolds, pouring concrete, and directing a steady stream of wolf-whistles at girls on the beach.

Brady turned left at Playa del Sol and trotted to the smoldering remains of the Pelican's Nest. The place looked like carnage from a military attack. Only one fire truck remained. Three firefighters were sifting through the debris while another wielded a hose, drowning the few remaining smoky spots. Black water dripped from blistered roof beams and fell like sluggish tears on the twisted ruins of the first floor then seeped into the grim morass that had been a swimming pool.

A few onlookers gawked from across the street, but the Klums were nowhere in sight. Brady had called Victor Gruber who, as he expected, insisted Gunther and Olga stay with him. Victor's manservant, Charles, had apparently fetched them in the Bentley.

"Busy morning?" Brady said to a tall man with a grimy face.

Captain John McCarty turned and grinned. Brady had known him since he opened the Shanty. At the time, McCarty was head honcho at the beach fire station. Now he was a Fort Lauderdale fire investigator. He had honest brown eyes and a boyish face betrayed only by a sprinkle of pewter that dappled the brown hair scaling his temples, like a harbinger of middle-age. McCarty was wearing knee-high yellow rubber boots and latex gloves. Three silver paint cans dangled from his fingers.

"Heard you were here earlier, Max," he said. "Didn't see you."

"Didn't want to get in your way, John. I was more concerned about the Klums."

"Damned shame."

"Whatcha got?"

McCarty held up the silver cans. "Collecting samples. Bedding, plaster, pieces of furniture."

"Figure out what triggered this thing yet?"

McCarty opened the back door of a red Fire Investigation Unit van and set the cans inside. "The run-off water has a rainbow sheen. That usually indicates the presence of an accelerant, probably a petroleum distillate."

"Such as?"

"Could be mineral spirits or turpentine, but my bet is gasoline. One cup of ninety octane properly packaged can be as explosive as four sticks of dynamite."

"Any idea how this was packaged?"

"The answer's up there in the ashes," McCarty said, pointing to one of the fire-gutted rooms on the second floor. "At the source I found pieces of melted plastic. Blue. Seems to be from some sort of canister. Gave it the sniff test. Smells like it might have been a fuel container. Costco and Home Depot sell them by the thousands."

"Arson?" Brady said, palming beads of sweat off his forehead.

"We found a charred hotplate in the same room. It might have been used to ignite the accelerant. I won't know for sure until we run this stuff through a gas chromatograph flame ionization detector."

"Ouch," Brady said. "You're hurting my brain."

"Sorry, Max," the fire investigator said with a tired grin. "We're gonna do some tests."

"Seems like of a crude way to start a fire."

"Crude but effective. When the accelerant explodes flames spray in every direction. By the time our trucks got here the place was burning faster than my ex-wife's cooking. Beyond gone."

"Any suspects?"

Brady expected to hear McCarty say *"too early to tell."* But the investigator hesitated. The look in his eyes made Brady wonder if he already had a perpetrator in mind.

"Arson's tough," he said, a slight smile cracking his sooty face. "Countrywide, we get a half-million a year. Less than one-in-five result in arrest."

"Good non-answer answer," Brady said, but didn't press further. Some secrets, he knew from experience, were best left untold.

McCarty slammed the van door closed. "The guests look clean. Mostly tourists here for a week in the sun. Your friends the Klums don't seem particularly suspicious."

"I can vouch for them, John."

"Owners are always the prime suspects. I interviewed them. They seem genuinely distraught. I didn't detect any signs of deception. They appear to be comfortable financially. They said the place was turning a healthy profit. Motel wasn't for sale. No new insurance policies. No apparent motives."

"Firebug?"

"Pyromaniacs burn out of obsession. Often sexual. This looks like a pro."

"Why would a professional arsonist torch a little mom-and-pop motel?"

"That, my friend, is the million dollar mystery," said McCarty.

"Probably more like two or three million."

"You tell me. You're the cop."

"Ex-cop."

"Well, give me a call if you think of anything."

"Likewise. Drop by the Shanty for a beer."

"Better yet, a beer and bowl of gumbo."

"You're on."

Bradys Run

CHAPTER SIX

JACK DEL LARGO WADDLED up the gangplank and onto the deck, stopping to catch his breath and wipe driblets of sweat from his florid brow. He scanned the yacht, thinking: *Someday I'm going to have a boat like this.* His dream was to sail to a tropical island, live on fruit and fish until he was skinny, and nuzzle a native girl under a coconut tree. *Like Van Gogh or Monet or one of those French fucks.* His wife Marla was not part of the fantasy.

"Welcome aboard the Shangri-La, Mr. Del Largo."

The voice was velvety and slightly breathless. Del Largo looked up and gulped for air again, his extra chins jiggling like rooster wattle. Tiffani Bandeaux had that effect on men. Del Largo patted a hanky over his forehead and let his eyes feast on her. Nearly six feet tall, Tiffani had a ravishing physique, jade eyes, and satiny auburn hair that hung down to her buttocks. She reminded him of a thoroughbred racehorse raring to run. *Scratch the native girl,* he thought. *I'll take Tiffani.*

"Tiffani, my dear, you are a walking aphrodisiac. I would love to take you on a Caribbean cruise."

Del Largo leaned over and kissed her hand as gallantly as a three hundred pound man could, reminding himself of Adonis Rock bussing Marla's hand only an hour ago.

"Would your wife be with us?" Tiffani said in a confidential tone laced with an inflection of possibility.

"Oh, no, dear," said Del Largo, hopeful. "It would be just us."

"Won't she mind?"

"Who's gonna care a hundred years from now?"

"I'm sorry, but Mr. Steele forbids his employees from consorting with business associates."

"Mr. Steele need not know."

"Mr. Steele knows everything."

Del Largo suppressed a grin. *If that preening cocksucker knew everything, he wouldn't need me.*

"In fact, Mr. Steele knows you're here now," Tiffani said. Del Largo looked at her, wondering if she was reading his mind. "He's in the main salon. Would you like a drink?"

"Do fish like water? *Chopin* on the rocks."

It was not yet noon but Del Largo's appetite for spirits was ravenous, no matter the hour. He'd already had a whiskey with Adonis. He could soak up vodka like a dry sponge. Tiffani moved down the companionway with the grace of a Spanish dancer. He followed, his belly quivering like a vat of marmalade, his eyes fastened on her perfect teardrop derriere encased in snug white slacks, gasping involuntarily when he realized she wasn't wearing panties.

Bandeaux's flawless lines and majestic symmetry made her a superb match for the Shangri-La. The yacht was a gleaming two hundred twenty three-foot three-decker, navy blue hull, scads of teak and brass, five staterooms, formal dining room, theater, discothèque, gym, Jacuzzi, two jet skis, a twenty-foot Chaparral dinghy with twin two hundred horse power Mercury engines, and a Bell 427 helicopter on deck.

They entered the salon and found Sherwood Steele stretched out on a buff leather chaise lounge. Steele was as long and lean as Del Largo was short and fat. He had a deep oily tan and a tongue of bottle-black hair lacquered into a *V* over his forehead. His most striking feature was a pair of barren black eyes that reminded Del Largo of a shark.

"Jack, come in," Steele said in a gravelly voice, without getting up. "Sit down."

Tiffani handed him a bottle of vitamin water and, to Del Largo, a tumbler of vodka.

"Will there be anything more, Sherwood?" she asked.

"Tell Hendricks to have the bird ready in thirty minutes."

Prick's got more flunkies than Trump has girlfriends, Del Largo thought, smiling to himself, knowing Steele conducted business like he'd read the instructions on a box of Donald Trump Cereal. Trump's brand was *Trump.* Steele's was *Shangri-La.* It was on everything he owned. His boat, his hotels. *I wonder if it's tattooed on Tiffani's ass,* he thought and his breath quickened at the notion of Bandeaux's naked bottom.

Steele turned to face him, his white teeth flashing a mirthless smile. "How we doing?"

"Making headway," Del Largo said, savoring his day's second infusion of firewater.

Steele's black shark eyes bored into him. "I don't want to hear *headway.* I want to hear *mission accomplished.*"

"We're going as fast as we can, Sherwood. I don't want to raise red flags. We've got some holdouts."

"What's this holdout shit? Isn't that why we're paying our friends a fucking fortune?"

"Well, Sherwood, our friends haven't been earning their money."

Steele glared at the lawyer. "What do you mean, you fat fuck!"

Del Largo felt his face burn and hoped it hadn't turned scarlet, like it used to when he was a tubby kid being humiliated by the bullies on the playground. Sherwood's cruel eyes were trained on him, demanding to be met. Del Largo averted his gaze to the ice cubes melting in his glass. Steele jumped to his feet, his jaw muscles bulging like rubber balls.

"Look at me!" he snapped.

Powerless to resist, Del Largo turned his head feebly toward Steele's unctuous face. Sherwood, he knew, was a tyrant by nature, but he normally kept tight rein on his Pavlovian instincts, rarely raising his voice, preferring to administer his malice with cool calculation. Osama Bin Laden showed more emotion during videotaped death threats.

"You're supposed to be the most connected lawyer in Fort Lauderdale," Steele said, sneering down at him. "I pay you a lot of fucking money."

"Sure, Sherwood, sure you do," Del Largo said, squirming. His chair groaned beneath him. "And I work hard for you. You know I do."

"I only know results and I'm not getting them. Everything's riding on this deal. If it doesn't happen soon, I'm going down. Hard. And if I go, you're coming with me. And so will our *friends*."

"Don't worry, Sherwood. We're gonna get it done. It's gonna be okay."

"Follow me," Steele ordered and stamped from the salon.

Del Largo labored to his feet and plodded after him down a passageway carpeted with white llama skin shaggy enough to hide a Shih Tzu. *Guy's ice,* he thought. *Leveraged to the ears and still living like the Sultan of Burundi, or Brunei, or wherever that fuck's from.*

They entered a cabin. At the center of the room sat a large scale model of Fort Lauderdale Beach, with an ersatz blue Atlantic bordered by white beach and every hotel and motel between the ocean and the Intracoastal. At the center of the display a black sash had been wrapped around a four square block tract like a cummerbund. Inside the demarcation line, yellow patches covered three-quarters of the parcels. Red squares overlaid the rest. Inscribed in gold letters over the ocean were the words *Shangri-La Resort – Fort Lauderdale.* Steele gazed down with an incandescent glow in his black eyes.

"Don't you understand what I'm trying to accomplish here, Jack?"

"Of course I do, Sherwood."

"The Shangri-La is going to be the most opulent hotel complex in Florida. And the largest. It's like I'm trying to build a goddamned mountain. I cannot afford obstacles. I can't afford delays. I need these red parcels to turn yellow by yesterday."

Del Largo pointed to a red square on Playa del Sol. "This'll be yellow soon, Sherwood."

"The smoke?" said Steele. Jack nodded. "What makes you think so?"

"No brainer. It's an older couple. Germans. They'll collect a boatload of insurance. If they try to rebuild, our friends will throw roadblocks in their way. Make it clear to them reconstruction will take two years minimum. Maybe three. They'd be crazy not to sell."

Steele stared at him. "Get it done."

"This is the domino we've been waiting to fall, Sherwood." Del Largo forced himself to keep eye contact with Steele's predatory glower. "With them gone the others will cave."

"They better," Steele said and smiled.

Del Largo felt his blood curdle. Sherwood Steele's smile was as telltale as a diamondback's rattle. The lawyer knew from experience that when he bared it he was coiled to strike.

"Now, who's next?"

Brady's Run

CHAPTER SEVEN

IT WAS A PERFECT day for Brady's bikini run. Puffy white clouds sailed like glorious clipper ships across a pristine sky. A cool breeze was blowing in off the ocean like a refreshing tonic. And the sand was dotted with plenty enough flat-belly girls to get him to one end of the beach and back.

Brady hit the Elbo Room at Las Olas and sprinted the last block. Breathing hard, he shucked his shoes and T-shirt and waded into the tranquil sapphire surf. He laved the sweat from his body then dove head-long and swam with a powerful stroke, not stopping until he reached the basketball courts across from Bahia Mar Marina a half-mile down the beach. He floated in knee deep water for long minutes and let the waves wash over him like children's laughter before finally stumbling from the ocean. Sandpipers skittered out of his path leaving tiny hieroglyphs in the wet sand. Brady doodled back up the beach, skipping stones and catching up on his people watching. Two little girls tossing crackers to a flock of seagulls chittering in midair above them. A group of Latino men strumming guitars and drinking cerveza while they grilled pork under a coconut tree. Their women lazing in the shallows, vigilant eyes on a gaggle of naked toddlers chasing each other ecstatically in the sand.

A small propeller plane caracoled overhead towing a banner bal-lyhooing *Ladies Night* at the Blue Martini Lounge. Brady crossed the beach to a sidewalk shower and rinsed the salt from his skin. He retrieved his New Balances and T-shirt and flopped across the street on bare wet feet the size of clown shoes. A half-block off the beach road he ducked into a doorway and sprang up three flights of stairs to the roof of the same building that housed the Sea Shanty. The instant he stepped inside, a female voice rang out.

"Getting a little gut, Brady?"

Rose Becker was proprietress of the Papillon Gym. Brady smiled. Rose was quite an eyeful. Long pitch black hair, eyes blue as the Gulf Stream, the physique of a fitness maven. And wholesome as an apple.

"Gut?" he protested. He pulled up his shirt to expose his bare belly and assumed a body-builder's pose. "Six three, one-eighty, abs of steel."

"More like butter," she said with an impish gleam.

"Butter?" He sounded wounded. "They're at least as hard as toast!"

"You better hit the iron, buddy."

Rose was something of a local heroine. Some considered her Joan of Arc reincarnate. Anointed leader of *SOB – Save Our Beach* – a resistance group fighting developers and politicians bent on plundering the oceanfront. Jonas Bigelow and Gunther Klum had persuaded her to run for mayor of Fort Lauderdale. Although her odds of winning were somewhere between nada and nil, she was campaigning hard. Despite her lissome figure – plainly apparent in her spandex shorts and butterfly T-shirt – Rose was no fragile flower. She had a clear-eyed steadiness about her that Brady found himself drawn to.

"You plan to wear that outfit at City Hall?" he said.

"Why not? Just because I'm mayor doesn't mean I'll be giving up the gym."

"Good. I won't have to walk far to complain."

She stood staring at him, hands on hips, not smiling. "Brady, you've got to earn the right to complain. You just stand back and let it all be."

He thought for a moment then snapped his fingers. "Springsteen? Right? *Jungleland.*"

Rose shook her head. "Yeah, right," she said and walked off to tend to a lumpy older woman who looked like it was her first venture inside a gym.

Brady went through his usual rigorous thirty minute routine of curls, bench presses, and belly crunches. Despite Rose's mockery, his daily run, swim, and workout at the Papillon kept him in decent enough shape for a man at the advanced age of forty two years. He was on his way out the door when Rose was finishing. The old lady looked like she'd just spent a half-hour on the rack.

"You must be related to a guy named Torquemada?" Brady said to Rose. "If by some remote chance you lose the mayoral election, I hear Guantanamo's looking for a new Grand Inquisitor."

She flashed a tart smile. "Very funny."

"See you later, Rosie."

"Is that a threat?"

"No. That's a promise."

Then he saw a cloud pass across her face. "Brady, what happened to the Pelican's Nest?"

In addition to being card-carrying members of *SOB*, Olga and Gunther Klum were regulars at the Papillon Gym. Brady told her that it looked like arson.

"Why would anyone hurt those sweet people?"

"The fire investigator doesn't think it was intended to harm them physically. But why someone wanted to destroy the motel, I have no clue. John McCarty's a good man. He'll get to the bottom of it."

Rose was standing at the door of a large greenhouse she'd had built on the rooftop overlooking the ocean. Even though she was a physical trainer, she had a Master's Degree in zoology, with a specialty in lepidoptery – butterflies. Hence, the Papillon Gym. Rose maintained the butterfly was the perfect symbol for a health club. A place people go seeking transformation, like caterpillars that mutate into exquisite winged creatures.

"Want to see something special?" she said.

"I've really gotta…"

"Follow me," Rose said, ignoring his balkiness.

Brady trailed her dutifully into the greenhouse. It was like they'd stepped into another world; a lush, verdant magic garden bursting with all manner of orchid, hibiscus, dahlia, and snapdragon representing every stripe of the rainbow. The air was redolent with exotic perfume. He inhaled deeply while scores of butterflies danced about, chasing one another from blossom to blossom, as blithe as the giggly children he had watched on the beach.

"The orange and black ones with white spots on their wings are Monarchs," Rose said, pointing to a pair fluttering among a cluster of honeysuckle. "The yellow and blacks are Tiger Swallowtails. Then there's the Zebra Swallowtails, the black and white ones."

Brady knew nothing about butterflies except that they were pretty and placid.

"What do you feed them?"

"They suck nectar from the flowers."

"Where are their mouths?"

"They eat through a proboscis that winds in-and-out, like a garden hose."

"That's gotta be tasty."

"No. Butterflies actually taste with their feet."

"How the heck do they do that?"

"Don't worry about it, Brady. Just take a look at my newest specimen."

Rose picked up an enormous creature with broad brown wings. It had white markings, a cream-colored body, and a red tuft on its throat as dense as fur.

"Wow! You're raising condors?"

"It's a Queen Alexandra Birdwing. The world's largest butterfly. Most Lepidoptera have wingspans of three-to-five inches. Queen Alexandra's are more than twelve inches across." She was holding it as gently as a newborn baby. "I had a dozen shipped here from New Guinea."

"He's absolutely beautiful."

"*She*," Rose corrected. "Beautiful, yes. But looks can be deceiving."

"How so?"

"This sweet little lady is as lethal as a black widow spider."

"I didn't know butterflies bite," Brady said with a trace of shock. "Do they bark, too?"

"They don't bark and they don't bite."

He snapped his fingers again. "King Harvest. *Dancing in the Moonlight*. Right?"

Rose looked at him down her straight, aristocratic nose like a school-marm glaring at the class clown. Brady looked back with genuinely feigned contrition.

"Sorry, Miss Becker. Sometimes I just can't control myself." He nodded at the giant butterfly. "How do they kill if they don't bite?"

"Queen Alexandras are poisonous." The giant insect fluttered in her palms. "Eat one and you die."

"Glad you told me. I was thinking about putting them on the Sea Shanty menu. They're bigger than chickens, you know."

"Don't be silly, Brady! *People* don't eat butterflies. Predators do. Mainly birds. When they do they die. It's a built-in defense system. Protects the species. You know, survival of the fittest. Darwin. Evolution."

"Didn't the Supreme Court declare evolution unconstitutional?"

"Right," Rose said, her face deadpan.

She released the immense butterfly and they stepped out of the greenhouse and back into the morning sun. He was standing close to her. She smelled fresh as new mowed grass.

"Well, Rose. Hate to cut and run from entomology class but I gotta go before my gumbo burns."

"See you later?" she said.

Brady was about to ask if that was a *threat*, but stopped cold. Rose was staring at him. Her eyes were serene as a forest at dusk and, for a heartbeat, their gazes locked.

He descended the stairs wondering what had just happened. He hadn't felt a connection like that with a woman since…*Victoria?* Halfway down he passed a muscular man approximately his height, but about ten years younger. Brady had seen him in the gym before. His long blonde hair and square jaw reminded him of the model Fabio, if he overlooked the work boots, cut-off shorts, and a dirty black tank top. Judging by his swollen biceps and deltoids, Fabio spent way more time pumping iron than Brady did. *Fanatic!* They nodded at each other and passed without a word. Something about the guy sparked a flash of wariness in Brady. What it was, though, he couldn't put a name to.

Bradys Run

CHAPTER EIGHT

NORMAN EPSTEIN COULD see his own death like it happened yesterday. He was sitting in his fiftieth floor penthouse office, head propped bleakly in his hands, oblivious to the magnificent day outside his window. Instead, his world was black as midnight as he watched himself take a slow motion swan dive off the balcony.

Epstein was a short man and slim as a knife with skin the shade of unbaked biscuit dough. With his oversized spectacles and shirt-pocket pencil holder, he could reasonably have been mistaken for a high school geometry teacher. Rather, he was CEO of one of America's fastest growing banks. When Sherwood Steele founded the South Florida National Bank five years before, Epstein was a midlevel manager at Steele's former bank. Despite his milquetoast personality – or perhaps because of it – Steele christened him captain of his new ship. He proved to be an inspired choice.

SFNB was riding the crest of Florida's spectacular real estate boom, financing huge condo projects, office towers, shopping malls, and many of the opulent homes that lined Fort Lauderdale's three hundred miles of waterfront. From his lofty perch he had an unfettered view of construction cranes soaring in every direction, most of them bankrolled by SFNB. It should have been a sight for Epstein to savor. Instead, he realized he was looking at the seeds of the bank's destruction – and his own. South Florida National Bank's ascension had been a product of the times. The rising tide had lifted all boats. But the tide had shifted. Epstein didn't need a Ouija board to tell him his ship was sailing straight into an iceberg. The bank was as doomed as the Titanic.

The boom had been powered by the same riverboat gamblers behind every economic bubble from *tulipmania* in the 17th Century to the *dot. com* frenzy of the 1990s. After the high tech balloon burst, real estate became the next big thing. Quick money junkies bought and sold property like day traders, borrowing hand over fist, flipping land faster than TV poker players flip cards. And everything came up aces. Prices shot to the stratosphere. Speculators raked in huge pots then dove back in for more, as if the gravy train would never end.

But Epstein had been counting the cards. The aces had all been played and the deck was now stacked with jokers. He'd done the math a thousand times. South Florida was about to be swamped with eighty thousand new condo units, most bought pre-construction by speculators. The market would soon be saturated, prices would plummet, and any day now the gamblers would, like rats, start jumping overboard leaving him to go down with the ship. South Florida National Bank was holding billions of dollars in bad paper. Much of it belonged to Sherwood Steele, who had treated SFNB like his own private piggybank.

The despair was eating Epstein alive. He'd kept the bank afloat by fudging, juggling, and outright fabrication. He knew, though, it wouldn't be long before he felt the hot breath of federal regulators. Like a cancer patient prays for remission, Epstein prayed for a miracle. But he didn't delude himself. Instead, he imagined again climbing onto the railing of his balcony and taking that last leap into thin air.

Bradys Run

CHAPTER NINE

WHEN MAX BRADY returned to the Sea Shanty after his workout the place was thick with the savory aroma of gumbo. He ducked into the tiny galley behind the bar and lifted the hood from a brimming black kettle, ladled out a spoonful of the chowder, and tasted.

"Perfect," he said to himself and switched off the rickety gas stove.

Brady began turning the TVs to ESPN for the lunch crowd, mostly men who worked on the yachts and dive boats at Bahia Mar Marina across the street. Later the *soggy dollars* would wander in off the beach in flip-flops and wet bathing suits, order fruity drinks, and pay with cash soaked in salt water. Late afternoon was mainly off-duty lifeguards and beach workers who drank beer and watched the technicolor sunsets from beneath the banyan tree in the Sandbox outside.

Spinning through the channels, Brady saw video of flames and smoke against a platinum sky. He stopped and turned up the volume. It was a report about the Pelican's Nest fire. There was a shot of Gunther and Olga – identified as *"the motel's longtime owners"* – standing by helpless as they watched the flames consume their home and business. Olga's head was leaning on Gunther's shoulder and tears were streaming down her face. When the video ended an attractive female reporter named Sylvia Sanchez appeared live standing before the now smoldering shell. Behind her, Brady saw John McCarty sifting through the charred rubble.

"Investigators say the blaze appears to be a case of arson," Sanchez said, "but they're baffled over why someone would burn down this motel. Gunther and Olga Klum are fixtures in this beach community and are clearly devastated by the destruction of the motel they have called home for three decades. I'm Sylvia Sanchez reporting live from Lauderdale Beach."

Just before noon, Brady opened the Sea Shanty's doors and let the pungent bouquet of broiling chicken wings and spicy gumbo drift like live bait out over the sidewalk. Within minutes he'd hooked his first customer. It was the guy from Rose's gym. Fabio.

"I know you," Brady said. Fabio tensed and examined him with wary eyes. Brady watched the man try to place him. "From the Papillon," he said finally.

The man's guardedness melted away and was quickly replaced by an engaging smile.

"I'm there every day," he said. "Usually afternoons. Had some free time this morning. Got my workout in early." He thrust out his hand. "Adonis Rock."

"Max Brady," he said, gripping Rock's hand an extra second, estimating him, taking his measure.

Brady detected something peculiar about Rock, just as he had on the stairs. He had brawny brown shoulders and the muscled chest of a trained athlete. But there seemed to be some anomaly, something off-kilter, maybe something absent. His eyes were vivid blue, but seemed a touch too close together. He was handsome, with a salient jaw and high cheekbones, but seemed a bit of a peacock. He could have been a fashion model or movie action hero, one of those powerful blonde Aryan types who don't say much but attract women like a cozy featherbed on an arctic night. There was something else, though. The *Semper Fi* tattoo on his forearm? The deep lines around young eyes? The guarded way he carried himself? Brady's antenna was picking up something, but the picture was fuzzy.

"Rose recommended your place," said Adonis Rock.

"Uh-oh. Now I owe her another margarita." Rock gave him a quizzical look. "Referral fee. I think she's up to twenty now. Good thing she's more of a *Shirley Temple* kinda girl."

"She doesn't need to drink," Rock said with a cool assurance that bordered on cocky. "That girl's a smoking piece of ass just the way she is."

Brady was taken aback. Crude talk about women was as common in bars as tequila shots. But a comment like that about Rose irked him. He wondered if it was macho bombast or if something was going on between her and Mr. Beefcake. Brady was surprised by his own reaction.

"Rose said you serve a nasty bowl of gumbo."

"It's what I do," Brady said, his voice flat, not gruff, but not congenial either. "Five bucks for a bowl and a beer."

"Sign me up."

By noon every stool at the bar was occupied. The jukebox was blasting The Eagles' *Take It Easy* and Adonis Rock was on his second bowl of gumbo when Jonas Bigelow rushed in looking exuberant as a kid on Christmas Eve. The spot next to Adonis opened up and Jonas grabbed it. Brady poured him a Sam Adams. The old man held up his glass and smiled, his eyes like blue beacons beaming in a parched desert.

"What's got you so fired up, Jonas?"

"Rose and I are going to City Hall to rip some new assholes in them bastards for being in the developers' pockets."

"Watch out you don't get hit with a libel suit."

Jonas exploded like a storm without warning. He bolted from the stool and thrust his face across the bar at Brady. "Sue, sue, sue! Is that the only pablum you lawyers know how to serve?"

Brady smiled. Despite his hair-trigger temper, Jonas was about as threatening as a furniture leg in the dark. He set a bowl of gumbo in front of him.

"Ex-lawyer," he said and pointed at the bowl. "And that's the only pablum I serve these days. That and side orders of saloon psycho-babble."

Jonas's tantrum came and went faster than a dust devil. He sat back down with a contrite smile on his lips.

"Max, I think Gunther and Olga are gonna need some psychic massaging. They're saying on TV that the fire was arson."

"I saw."

"I blame them sons-a-bitches in City Hall," Jonas said with another sudden burst of fury. Then he attacked his food.

Brady noticed Adonis Rock next to him continuing to eat with languid disinterest, not listening, or pretending not to. He presumed out of politeness. *Maybe he's not such a jerk.*

"I told you, Max," Jonas said between bites. "They've been trying to run us out. Now they're burning us out."

Rock rose to his feet. His second bowl of gumbo was only half finished, but he wiped his mouth, threw his napkin onto the bar, and pulled a thick roll of cash from his pocket. He skinned off a ten and two singles and nodded to Brady.

"Good vittles," he said. "As advertised."

"We aim to please. Y'all come back now."

Brady watched Adonis walk out, triceps rippling under his smooth gold skin, blonde locks falling down his back. Jonas turned and watched as well.

"Guy looks like that model."

"Fabio."

"Yeah, the guy on the cover of those potboilers Betty reads."

Brady grinned at him. "Did you know studies show women who read romance novels have sex twice as often as women who don't?"

"They must not have counted Betty," Jonas said with a chuckle.

Rock crossed the street and slid into a battered red pick-up truck with *Yardbird* painted on the side doors. He backed up and started to drive off when Brady saw him peer back over his shoulder at the Shanty. Then it hit him. He realized what it was his internal radar had been picking up.

"Big guy," Jonas said, gouging a spoonful of gumbo into his mouth. "Bet he gets tons of pussy."

Bradys Run

CHAPTER TEN

THE BIG ROOM had the feel of a *Star Wars* bar. It was packed with an odd assortment of characters, some in business suits, others in Bermuda shorts and polo shirts, and a band of twenty or so sporting cardboard hats crafted in the shape of mushrooms. They faced a horseshoe table at the front of the room. A man sitting at the center of the U picked up a gavel and slammed it down with a bang.

"This meeting will come to order," announced Mayor David Grand. "This is the Fort Lauderdale City Commission's final hearing on the Sun Palace."

David Grand was a thickset man with a bulldog face and a nose that looked like it had been pickled in whiskey. Grand fancied himself the consummate politician, often joking he was elected president of his maternity ward the day he was born. He was a master at the scurvy art of speaking ad nauseam about almost anything while saying absolutely nothing. As mayor he had not done much more than nothing. But he'd done it well. Particularly for the city's powerful development community. No surprise. They were his people. Grand had been a builder for thirty years. That was before the lavish support of his peers put him in office and kept him there almost eight years. Ever grateful, he had rolled out the city's red carpet for them, rubber stamping billions of dollars in new construction permits that had transformed the city skyline.

The Sun Palace was the latest. When it was approved – there was no *if* – the hotel/condominium would soar more than three hundred feet over Lauderdale Beach.

"The Sun Palace," Mayor Grand told the crowd, "is a proposed five star resort complex on A1A between Surfside and Cabana Streets. Today is the final vote on this excellent project. First we will hear comments. I am happy to see Mr. Robert Langston, the distinguished CEO of the Florida Millennium Group, developer of the Sun Palace. Mr. Langston?"

Robert Langston approached the podium, a tall, tanned, silver-haired man attired in an impeccable camel-colored suit, white shirt, and yellow tie.

"I used to know a guy named Langston," Jonas Bigelow whispered to Rose Becker. They were wearing mushroom hats, emblems that the beach and dozens of small mom-and-pop motels that had served tourists for more than a half century were being lost in the veil of shadows cast by the giant new towers. "Langston was full of applesauce. This guy is too. I bet he's got dollar signs stenciled on his balls!"

The CEO flashed a mouthful of white teeth that stood out like a Chiclet fence against his bronzed skin.

"Eighteen months from now," said Langston in silken voice, "the Sun Palace will open its doors as the finest hotel Fort Lauderdale Beach has ever seen. With four hundred rooms, three first class restaurants, and the largest swimming pool in South Florida, it will be a mecca for visitors from around the world. The Sun Palace will create hundreds of new jobs and pump tens of millions of dollars into the local economy. We see it as a win-win for Fort Lauderdale and the Florida Millennium Group."

"Thank you, Mr. Langston," Mayor Grand said. "In my opinion the Sun Palace will be a radiant gem the whole city will be proud of."

"Bullshit," someone yelled from the crowd.

"You're killing the beach," another voice shouted.

A babble of rebellious sound came from the mushroom people. Grand slammed his gavel on the horseshoe table.

"Silence!" he bellowed. A frosty stillness filled the room. "Anyone who speaks without being recognized will be ejected."

The mayor called on the head of the City Business Alliance, a tiny man with an egg-shaped cranium that reminded Rose of Humpty Dumpty, who bubbled about the Sun Palace like a mountain brook. Several more suits came forward from banks, labor unions, and tourism boards to praise the project before Grand ended the love fest.

"The time has come for the final vote on the Sun Palace," he said.

"Wait a minute," a mushroom shouted.

"This is a sham," echoed another.

"The fix is in," someone hollered. The mushroom people began chanting in unison: *"Fix! Fix! Fix!"*

"Quiet," the mayor yelled, red-faced.

Rose Becker lurched from her seat and sprinted to the front of the room, her toadstool hat swaying like a chef's chapeau.

"Public commentary is over," Grand snarled, his eyebrows arching like hackles on a cat.

"Those bootlicks aren't the public," she shot back. "*We* are the public! *We* demand to be heard."

Her fellow mushrooms howled their support.

"Take your seat, miss, or I will have you removed."

"Don't *miss* me, mayor," Rose said. "You know exactly who I am."

Grand bristled on his throne. "I know the newspapers call you Madame Butterfly! I can only assume because you're so flighty."

"She's the butterfly who's gonna fly away with your job," Jonas called out to more hurrahs. The chants started again. *"Fix! Fix! Fix!"*

The mayor looked down at Rose like a wrathful god, his front teeth biting his lower lip so hard they left two white marks. She seemed to delight in rubbing him raw as sandpaper. Grand removed his wire-rimmed spectacles and massaged red pockmarks on either side of his veined nose, then raised his palms in a cease-and-desist motion and waited for the hurly-burly mob to simmer.

"Okay, young lady," he sighed with a tone of resignation. "You've got two minutes. State your name."

She stepped to the pulpit. "Rose Becker, owner of the Papillon Gym, leader of the *SOBs*, and the next mayor of the City of Fort Lauderdale."

The crowd went wild. Grand scowled like a dog with a thorn in its paw. He hammered the table again.

"No campaign speeches," he said. "The clock is ticking."

"Fine," said Rose. "I'll get right to the point. Mayor Grand, you and your cronies are selling this city down the drain."

"That's outrageous," Grand shouted.

"Mr. Mayor, please do not infringe on my time." Rose gestured toward Robert Langston and the eggheaded fellow from the City Business Alliance. "You and your allies are turning Fort Lauderdale Beach into a shadow world. Every afternoon the sun disappears behind those twenty five and thirty story atrocities you've already allowed."

"If Madame Butterfly had her way," the mayor retorted, "we'd still be a mosquito infested swamp inhabited by Seminoles – and I don't mean FSU Seminoles."

"No, sir." Rose pivoted, turning her back on the mayor, and faced the audience. "I am not trying to turn back the clock. I'm trying to prevent a murder. Those behemoths they are building are killing the golden goose. Killing our beach. The thing that makes Fort Lauderdale such a magnificent jewel. But if the developers get their way, thanks to the undying assistance of politicians they've bought and paid for, our beach will soon be blanketed by more shadows than sunshine."

A stone-faced man was sitting to Grand's left. He wore a plaid jacket, a pencil-thin mustache, and a bad toupee. To his right was a woman with severe red lips, a snarl of copper hair, and a face with more wrinkles than a schoolgirl's prom gown the morning after. The troika composed the City Commission's power block. Mayor Grand, Commissioner Jarrett Griffin, and Commissioner Anita Plante controlled the five-member board by voting together on every issue. Thus, they controlled all development in Fort Lauderdale.

Jarrett Griffin cast a smarmy smile at Rose. "Miss Becker, thanks to world class hotels like the Sun Palace this city has become a tourist mecca. Do you realize we had ten million visitors here last year? They spent eight *billion* dollars. That's three times more than a decade ago."

"But these atrocities are turning the beach into a concrete jungle."

"These atrocities, as you call them, are paying the salaries of thousands of school teachers, policemen, and firefighters. That's fact."

"The fact is," Rose shouted, "the developers that you and Mrs. Plante and the mayor kowtow to are decimating our beach."

Grand's anger flared like fat dripping on a fire. "How dare you," he snarled. "I'm not in anyone's pocket."

Rose wouldn't back down. "Look at the numbers. Builders have pumped a quarter-million dollars into your campaign chest. I'd say they're getting their money's worth."

The mushroom hats jumped to their feet screaming invectives. Robert Langston's suntan seemed to grow several shades lighter. Humpty Dumpty's face was solemn as a death mask. David Grand looked like he was being poked with a cattle prod.

"That's it, young lady." He motioned toward the back of the room. "Officer Dent, get her out of here."

Rose shouted. "You can kick me out, Mayor Grand, but you can't shut me up."

An instant later she felt something clench her elbow. It felt like an iron claw. She winced and turned and gasped. A big man with thick-shoulders and a shaved head scowled at her. His lips curled, exposing nicotine stained teeth. The smell of old sweat surrounded him like stale perfume.

"Let's go lady," Officer Dent growled. He sounded like Darth Vader.

Rose shrank under his menacing gaze. "You're hurting me."

He pushed her toward the door and the mushrooms erupted in a chorus of boos. Jonas Bigelow, his face blue with rage, rushed to the microphone.

"We know your game, Grand. You're trying to run us out."

"That's absurd," the mayor said.

"Absurd? Who burned down the Pelican's Nest this morning?"

"I don't know what you're talking about," Grand hollered. But he was drowned out by the jeering of human fungi. He slammed his gavel and stood up, sputtering. "Ten minute recess. Officer Dent, I want the chambers cleared of all these, these, these toadstools. Then we'll approve the Sun Palace!"

Bradys Run

CHAPTER ELEVEN

BRADY WAS RINSING beer mugs behind the Sea Shanty bar when Captain John McCarty walked in and sat down. He attempted a smile, but his cheeks wouldn't participate.

"You look exhausted," Brady said.

"I'm ready for that gumbo."

Brady dried his hands with a dish towel. "Something to drink?"

"Why not? I'm off duty – finally. *Johnny Red.* Straight up."

Brady splashed an extra dollop of scotch into McCarty's glass. The fire investigator drained it in a single swallow, grimacing as the liquid seared his throat. Brady set a steaming bowl of gumbo on the bar.

"Bon appetit!"

McCarty tucked into it, shoveling a hearty spoonful in his mouth.

"Yum. Haven't eaten a bite all day."

"Plenty more in the pot. Compliments of the house."

"Trying to bribe the fire investigator?" he said from one side of his mouth, chewing with the other.

"Let's just call it friendly inducement."

It was late afternoon and the Sea Shanty was deserted, except for a man and woman wearing bathing suits in the corner, huddled over beers in hushed conversation. Mitch Ryder and the Detroit Wheels were on the music box singing *"Fe-fe-fi-fi-fo-fo-fum…"* A tall thin young man with a wild mane of straw-colored hair padded up to the bank of open windows and stuck a white nose smeared with zinc oxide into the bar.

"Gotta check out," the life guard Johnny Glisson shouted over the music. "Back in ten for a Tecate."

Brady stabbed the air with his thumb and turned back to McCarty. His glass was empty and Brady replenished it.

"So, John, what's the scoop? Solve the Pelican's Nest mystery yet?"

McCarty polished off the second scotch, again in a single mouthful, and deposited the glass on the bar. "You know the Klum's pretty well, right?"

"We're friends. They usually come in about this time every day."

"Do they have enemies?"

Brady jutted out his lower lip and thought for a moment. "Not that I know of. I can't imagine they do. Why?"

"Just wondering." Brady could see by the look in McCarty's eyes that he was feeling the warm glow the grog was stoking inside him. "The torch was definitely a pro."

He explained that the gas chromatograph analysis confirmed what he'd suspected. The accelerant was gasoline.

"The flammable favored by four-out-of-five firebugs, , according to *Arsonist Weekly*."

Brady looked at him with marvel. "Arsonists have their own newspaper?"

"My hunch about the hot plate was on the mark, too. Clean and efficient and gave the torch time to vamoose."

"What's the flashpoint for gasoline?"

"Flashpoint relates to a trigger, like a spark from a sparkplug. We're looking at kindling point, the temperature a substance ignites. For gasoline that's Fahrenheit four ninety five."

"Hotplates get that hot?"

"Not the models you'd find in motel rooms. Our guy brought his own. A *Biomega P-40*. Made for laboratories. We've got a half-dozen at the shop. They get up to seven hundred degrees, hot enough to fast-fry a steak. Soon as I saw it I knew the torch was a professional. He was long gone by the time the plastic container melted. When the gas ignited the flames sprayed everywhere. The studs in that building were perfect tinder. Fifty year old Dade County pine. Place went up like a box of matches."

Brady had been involved in arson investigations as a cop, but he'd never heard of using a hot plate to trigger a fire.

"It's not common," McCarty said. "The U.S. Arson Clearinghouse has a few cases on record. Mostly back in the early '90s. Over in Tampa. String of bar fires."

"They ever catch the torch?"

McCarty held up his empty glass. Brady hesitated. The two scotches were already doing their work. He didn't want McCarty driving off drunk, but the fire marshal was starting to unwind. A well-oiled tongue can be quite generous with its information. Brady poured another short one. McCarty eyed the glass and looked askance at him.

"At the time I was with National Fire Insurance," he said. "I'd been a firefighter. Me and my future-former wife were having problems. I thought it would help if I took a private sector job. The money was good and the hours more predictable. NFI had coverage on the Tampa fires. I was their man on the west coast of Florida."

"So, Sherlock," Brady said with a wry grin. "Did you crack the case?"

McCarty dispatched the *Johnny Walker.* "Never made an arrest. But I did identify the arsonist."

"Don't keep me in suspense."

"There was a local legend on the prowl around Tampa at the time. Real bad actor. Worked for Cisco Blas. Ever hear of him?"

"Blas? Sure. Hitman for Santo Magadinni, Tampa's Godfather. Old school mob. Shrewd, unpretentious, lethal as a cobra. Controlled drugs and gambling on the Gulf Coast. Big in Cuba before Batista fell. Tight with Meyer Lansky. Suspect in plots to assassinate Castro and JFK."

McCarty said: "When Santo died – of natural causes, by the way, without ever going to prison – the family rewarded Blas with his string of strip joints. Then, a few years later, somebody put a bullet in Cisco's brain. Ever hear of Crackhead Corrales?"

"Drug dealer?"

"Nah. Stone cold killer. Cisco whacked people for Santo. Crackhead whacked people for Cisco. But his real claim to infamy was as a torch. Cisco collected more than two million dollars from NFI when some of his joints went up in smoke."

"Crackhead?"

"Corrales was a pyromaniac. Scuttlebutt was he got off sexually setting fires. Liked to polish his rocket while he watched buildings go up in smoke. Good, too. I never could nail him."

"What's the connection to the Pelican's Nest?"

"Tampa newspapers called them the *Hotplate Fires*."

Brady raised an eyebrow. "Sounds like Crackhead's our guy."

"Nope."

"Why not?"

"He's on Death Row."

"For what?"

"Crackhead whacked Cisco."

Johnny Glisson walked in and took the stool beside McCarty. Brady pulled a cold Tecate from the cooler. Glisson was a lank, smooth-faced stringbean with a tall forehead and prominent Adam's apple. Every inch the beach boy. He was possessed by a festive spirit and loved to laugh and make merry. Lately he'd been picking Brady's brain about law school.

"Why," said Brady, winking at McCarty, "would you leave a job that requires you to sit on the beach every day and fend off nubile young girls in bikinis?"

"There's no future in it. I'm nothing but a sex object to those girls."

Glisson said it with utter sincerity. McCarty coughed out laugh.

"Everybody's got their cross to bear."

"Yeah, but in ten or twenty years that'll get old. Then what? I want more substance in my life."

"Well, then," Brady said with a straight face, "you've got time to think about it."

"Maybe I'll be a fireman."

McCarty lifted his glass to Brady, who reluctantly splashed in another shot. "You could do worse. Twenty-four hours on, forty-eight off.

Good pay, great benefits, retire after twenty five years at seventy five percent pension."

"Are there fire groupies?"

"You kidding? Women love guys with long hoses."

"Is that all you guys talk about?"

The three men looked up and their eyes widened. Rose Becker stood in the doorway, looking spectacular, long black hair pulled back tight, drawing their attention to her clean, perfect features.

"Why do men think their *hoses* are so much longer than they actually are?"

"Really?" said Brady. "And you know that from…personal experience?"

Rose's face turned radish red as McCarty and Glisson choked back laughter.

"No," she said quickly, "but girls talk."

Johnny moved down one seat and Rose took his stool. Brady placed a tureen of gumbo and bottle of water in front of her.

"Try this."

She tasted it and blinked. "Too hot." She stuck out her tongue and fanned it with her hand. He went into the galley and came back with another bowl. She took a spoonful and shook her head. "Too cold."

"Who are you? Goldilocks?" He fetched a third sample. "Try that."

"Just right," she said. Brady took a bow behind the bar. Rose kept speaking between bites. "Have you talked to Olga and Gunther?"

"Not since this morning. Victor says they disappeared into the guest suite. They're probably sleeping."

"Or grieving. Those poor people. Who would do such a thing?"

"Do you know Captain John McCarty of the Fort Lauderdale Fire Investigation Unit?" Brady said. "John, this is Rose Becker, a.k.a. Madame Butterfly. Our next mayor."

Rose turned to McCarty. "That means I will soon be your boss, captain. What can you report to me?"

McCarty leaned back and took his time evaluating her. "You've got my vote. All I can say, eh, Madame Mayor-to-be, is that whoever started the fire was probably paid. And my guess is it wasn't by the Klums."

Rose took a swig of water. "I guarantee you that. They loved the Pelican's Nest. They planned to spend the rest of their lives there."

The evening wore on and the party animals packed into the Sea Shanty like cattle at a feed lot. Music blared and conversation became hopeless. McCarty, Glisson, and Rose bid Brady farewell. On her way out the door, she turned and looked at him and their eyes locked for an instant. After she'd gone, he was left with the same dazed feeling he'd had at the gym earlier, which he found oddly unsettling.

He stepped to the jukebox and pushed A-12. Bruce Springsteen's raspy voice poured from the Bose speakers singing *Jersey Girl*. He reached behind the bar and cranked up the sound then walked outside and stood barefoot in the sand. The twisty banyan tree was wrapped in a garland of amber lights that cast a faint orange glow over the Sandbox. His mind was a million miles away. With Springsteen's throaty tones reverberating from the bar, he thought about his own Jersey girl. Victoria had been born and raised in Bayonne.

His friends told him his grief would ease with time, but the years had brought him little solace. Since she'd been gone his life had seemed as black and empty as deep space. The jagged pain never went away. Even so, it was all he had left of her to hang onto and he freely embraced it. He lived in dread that his memory of her would someday fade. That he'd somehow forget the ferocity of the love they had. Or, worse, that she would vanish from his memory altogether. Vanish into the mist of time, into the vast legion of the forgotten, all trace of her gone, like a second death. He reached up and absently ran his thumb over an inscription he'd carved into the banyan's bark the day he opened the Shanty. *Max & Victoria – Don't ever forget!*

Bradys Run

CHAPTER TWELVE

ADONIS ROCK WAS certain of one thing – the woman kneeling at his feet was nutty as pecan pie. She was dressed like a Roman slave girl in a sheer purple silk tunic, calfskin gladiator sandals strapped up to her knees, and a garland of rose petals adorning her blonde hair, which was braided to make her look like a vestal virgin from ancient times.

She looked up at Rock, sitting like a king on his throne, wearing a white toga, gold-plated crown, clutching an ornate wine goblet.

"Master," she whispered, "how may I serve you?"

She might have been batty, but he didn't mind, considering who she was. And it wasn't like they hadn't done this before. He did his best impression of Marlon Brando doing Julius Caesar in that old movie.

"What is it you have in mind, slave?"

She held up a bunch of fat white grapes. "Let's see what fun we can have with these, sir."

"Why not?"

Why not, indeed. Especially when the slave girl kowtowing before him was neither slave, nor girl, and certainly no vestal virgin. Far from it. At age forty five, she had long since lost the flower of pubescence. And she genuflected to no one, unless it was of her own choosing. She was, in fact, a woman of wealth and power. Her face was plastered on billboards and bus benches all over town. The newspapers called her *Queen of Fort Lauderdale Real Estate.* Yet, on this evening, Cherry Hampton was a most subservient woman.

Hampton peeled back Adonis's toga and her face flushed. He squirmed with anticipation as she raised the cluster over his abdomen and crushed the grapes between her palms. Translucent juice rained down on his masculinity and she massaged him with fingers as deft as a castanet dancer. His head fell back against the throne and his eyes closed. She looked at his face and her pupils flared.

"Does this please you, master?"

"Oh, very much."

She cupped him with her other hand.

"And this?"

Adonis opened his mouth to speak but, by then, he was beyond words.

He'd only known her for a few weeks. Jack Del Largo introduced them. Hampton lived in Mediterranean villa on the Intracoastal in one of those gated communities designed to cloister the patricians from the plebians. She needed some black olive trees removed. While Adonis toiled beneath a broiling September sun, Cherry kept vigil from her bedroom balcony, spellbound by the strapping young man brandishing his chain saw, bathed in sawdust and a profound sweat, black shirt glued to his rippling back.

Later, paying him, she said: "Why don't you go home and clean up and come back around eight."

He looked at her, hesitant. "For?"

"Theme night."

Del Largo had warned him about the whispers. Cherry Hampton, it was said, kept a harem of *boy toys*. The rumors were fuzzy – or they wouldn't have been whispered – but true. Cherry enjoyed the company of young men. She brought Adonis into her menagerie and quickly introduced him to the exotic enchantments of food and fantasia.

On their first tryst she'd dressed him in cowboy regalia – chaps, spurs, lariat and wide-brimmed Stetson, to her befeathered Indian princess – and taught him things he had never imagined. Despite her age, he was pleased to find she had kept the incursion of time in abeyance, thanks in large part to the miracles of modern surgery. Another night he was a football hero in helmet and pads while she played cheerleader, complete with artificially enhanced pom-poms. There had been a naughty nurse night, teacher's pet night, and Alice in Wonderland night. Tonight he was the Roman emperor and she his concubine.

"You know, Adonis," she said, caressing him with the grape lubricant, "you are the best man I've been with."

He smiled down at her. "Who have you been with?"

"Why do you ask?"

"Well, if you're comparing me to a bunch of nimrods, that's not exactly flattering. It's another thing if you've been with a few good men."

"What's a few?"

Hampton was a female Horatio Alger. She'd been born a poor girl named Cherisse Booker, but had clawed her way from the basement to the penthouse, thanks to her gift for kissing princes and turning them into frogs. She'd had three husbands. Each one richer than the last. And each had gone down in flames while she soared.

Her ascent began with the silk stocking lawyer George Bodine, who hired her at age eighteen as his legal secretary, despite her proficiency for typing and spelling roughly equivalent to that of a chimpanzee. Three months later Bodine, age sixty, divorced his wife of thirty years and flew Cherry to Las Vegas for a quickie wedding. Before their first anniversary he was dead of a heart attack and she was suddenly a very wealthy and not-so-grieving widow. Next came socially prominent blueblood Arthur "Flip" Whaley, whose uncanny gift for faking compassion had won him four terms in Congress. Alas, the FBI pinched poor Flip for pocketing lavish gifts from contractors to whom he'd shown genuine compassion. After Flip went to prison, Cherry became the third wife of big shot real estate magnate Brian Hampton, who tutored her on the fine art of the deal. Unhappily, Hampton had more zest for the boardroom than the bedroom and Cherry divorced him after only two years, ending up with most of what he had. She promptly opened her own white glove brokerage and, before long, Cherisse Booker Bodine Whaley Hampton was Fort Lauderdale's real estate queen.

On this night, though, she was a docile courtesan kneeling at her emperor's feet.

"Oh, master," she cooed. "The things you do to your worthless slave."

For Adonis, the hanky-panky had been kinky, but harmless, fun. And profitable. Cherry knew every deep-pocket in town and had induced many to hire him to trim their trees. Adonis had always had rich ambitions, but empty pockets. He intended to exploit Hampton for all she was worth – a frog who would be prince.

Bradys Run

CHAPTER THIRTEEN

IT HAD BEEN a long day and was well past midnight when Max Brady pedaled home on his bicycle. Dog-tired, he trudged through the yard back toward the dock and the Victoria II, his high-top sneakers sodden with night dew from the same grass blades that had soaked them eighteen hours ago. Before he reached the boat he noticed lights on in the house and entered without knocking. Victor Gruber was sitting in his wheelchair in the Great Room with Gunther and Olga Klum.

"Max," Victor said, "we were concerned about you."

"This is when I always get home," Brady said and flopped into a big soft chair that swallowed him like a man-eating plant. "You'd know if you didn't go to bed before the owls wake up."

Victor Isaac Gruber had a face no man would choose for himself. A wooly mastodon with an unkempt jungle of gray hair and the prodigious brow of a savant, he had sharp stabbing eyes, a bulbous snout, and weak chin, all of which fused into a bafflingly noble cast. Sitting in his wheelchair, Victor looked soft and spongy, but Brady knew him to be composed of the finest clay. Fifteen years before, a random shooting on the streets of Manhattan left him a paraplegic. He would have died in a pool of his own blood had a young police officer not happened by and kept him alive until paramedics arrived. Victor Gruber and Max Brady had been enduring friends ever since.

"You may not be aware of this, Max." Victor's voice was as resonant as a Stradivarius. "As your landlord, I always know when you come and when you go."

"I feel so much safer knowing that, Victor."

Gunther and Olga were sitting together on the sofa. The glow that normally lit their faces had been snuffed out. Gunther wore a vacant stare, like a shell-shocked soldier. Olga looked as though she'd been diagnosed with a terminal disease.

"Is Victor taking care of you? He loves nothing more than hosting good friends."

"Is there another kind?" Victor said.

"He's been incredible," said Olga in a lackluster voice. "We'd be lost without him."

"You are welcome here as long as you like," Victor said.

"Maybe we'll stay forever," Gunther said and they laughed, though with little joy. "Max, have you heard anything?"

Brady filled them in on the news from John McCarty. He remembered McCarty's question and asked them if they could think of anyone who would want to harm them. The Klums considered the question for about three second and shook their heads.

"I'd trade my right thumb to know who did it," said Gunther.

"McCarty doesn't think the torch was trying to injure you physically. The fire seemed to have been set so that you and your guests had ample time to escape."

"But why? Why?" Olga said. Her voice was frail, desolate, like a mother trying to comprehend the death of a child. A tremor wracked her body and she buried her face in her hands and sobbed. "It makes no sense!"

Victor was listening intently. His mind was precise as a Swiss watch. Before he was disabled, he'd made a vast fortune developing sophisticated software for Wall Street brokerage houses. After the shooting, he sold Gruber Systems and came away with a nine-figure bank account. Now he consulted for corporations like Google and Microsoft and lectured widely on subjects ranging from the Mathematical Theory of Computation to 20th Century philosophy. His tongue gave his lips a quick moistening.

"To paraphrase Bertrand Russell," he said, "philosophy begins with something so simple it's not even worth stating, and ends with something so absurd no one believes it."

"In this case," Brady said, "we're starting with an absurdity. To paraphrase Olga, the arson was senseless."

"It's difficult to reduce anything to a single truth," Victor said, his tone reflective. "Your friend Captain McCarty doesn't think the arsonist is a pyromaniac, or someone who starts fires out of sexual compulsion?"

"Correct," said Brady, watching his friend do his mental acrobatics.

"A professional job?"

"Yes."

"Apparently motivated by profit?"

"That's McCarty's hypothesis."

Victor scratched his chin and turned to the Klums. "Has anyone tried to purchase the Pelican's Nest recently?"

Gunther nodded. "Since beach property values began to skyrocket, yes, we've had some offers."

Olga looked at them through tear-fogged eyes. "We have no wish to sell. It's our home in paradise. We love living there. Money can't replace what we have…had."

"Anything serious?" Victor persisted. "A dogged suitor who refused to take no for an answer?"

Gunther and Olga gazed at each other in silence for several seconds, as longtime couples often do, their bond as much extrasensory as physical, like clairvoyants communicating without words. Gunther spoke for them.

"Early this year we had someone. We didn't know who. A real estate broker made the offer. She said she didn't know the buyer's identity."

"I think it was some kind of naked trust," Olga said uncertainly.

"Blind trust?" Victor asked.

"That was it. Blind trust. She came back twice, upping the ante each time."

"Her final offer was three million dollars," said Gunther. "It was breathtaking, even in today's market. But we weren't interested in selling. We said no."

Brady's rabbit ears were up now. He was annoyed at himself for not thinking of such a possibility sooner. As a cop he'd been a first-rate bird dog. A natural born detective. But that was years ago and his instincts had gotten as rusty as a junkyard sedan. *I need brain oil*, he thought. With enormous effort he extricated himself from the cushy jaws of the big chair, wandered into the kitchen, and plucked a Budweiser from the fridge. He returned to the Great Room and plumped back into the embrace of the cozy throne.

"Motels are bought and sold every week," he said. "No big deal there. Buyers are paying crazy prices."

"So three million might be insane," Victor said, eyebrows rising above the horn-rims of his glasses, "but not outlandish?"

"Correct." Brady turned to the Klums. "Who was the realtor?"

"Her name was..." Gunther said, but it didn't come. He looked to Olga. "You should remember her. You were quite impressed by her wardrobe."

"She was a woman of means," Olga said. "Elegant ensembles. Perfect hair. I've seen her name in newspaper ads. Sherry something."

"Cherry?" Brady said.

"Yes."

"Cherry Hampton?"

"That's her."

"The real estate queen," said Victor. "You know her, Max?"

He nodded. "She and some guy came into the Shanty a year or so ago. Got hammered on tequila shots. Said they were celebrating a big closing." He looked at the Klums. "Maybe that *naked trust* is still interested in your property."

Bradys Run

CHAPTER FOURTEEN

THAT NIGHT BRADY dreamed about his first encounter with Victoria. It was not romantic. Early morning on a cool spring day. Him jogging on one of the spiderweb of secluded foot trails that crisscrossed Central Park. Careening down a craggy escarpment near the *Shakespeare in the Park* amphitheater. A muffled scream from a clump of scrub brush. Following the sound. Finding a man and woman rolling in the undergrowth. Him tearing at her clothes, she kicking and clawing. Brady seized the man's collar, yanked him off her, and pinned back his arms. When he resisted, Brady twisted until he heard bone snap and the assailant fell writhing in the brush. He tended to the weeping woman. She was covered with dirt and dead leaves, her legs and arms lacerated and running shorts in tatters. Then he looked at her face. Milky skin, flaxen hair, rose-petal lips, eyes blue as windflowers. The face of an angel. He knew at once he'd made a monumental discovery. Like Newton identifying gravity. Columbus stumbling into America. John Marshall finding flecks of gold at Sutter's Mill. He was moonstruck.

Victoria Carter turned out to be a strong-willed, high-spirited young woman, a stately beauty with her head held as high as a queen. Six months later she left behind a cavalcade of heartsick suitors and wed Max Brady.

Victoria was a high-paid Wall Street bond analyst. Brady had just earned his law degree at City University of New York, turned in his NYPD detective shield, and embarked on a new career as a federal prosecutor in Brooklyn. They moved into a Greenwich Village co-op with dazzling views of the Empire State Building to the north and World Trade Towers to their south. She loved dancing and Broadway musicals; he loved the Knicks and Rangers. She loved museums; he loved exploring historic sites like Fraunces Tavern and the graveyard at Trinity Church. They both loved running in the park, discovering new restaurants, the neon glare of Times Square. Most of all, they made each other happy. Victoria was an eager, joyful lover and Brady had never known such bliss. They were a love song come to life. Two pulses beating as one.

Then, in the bat of an eye, it all disintegrated.

"Get out, Victoria. Get out."

"Max, I love you. Don't ever forget."

He sprinted across the bridge. Headlong into the black cloud. Into a sea of soot-bathed humanity. At Ground Zero the towers were gone. Their trellis façades standing like grisly tombstones. Paper blizzard swirling. Ankle deep volcanic dust. Hollow-eyed firemen spilling water on rubble. Frantic digging. Corpse after corpse. Disembodied arms and legs. Hundreds of ambulances. No one to save. When the house of cards imploded Victoria was on the ninety-fifth floor of the South Tower.

Brady spent days staggering through Lower Manhattan. Brandishing her photograph. Scouring every hospital. Clawing through the ruins cached in a membrane of gray ash. Kneeling in the rip-rap like a sinner begging absolution. Praying for a miracle. Praying she was alive. Trapped. Awaiting his rescue – again. Praying she would rise like a firebird from the cinders. But he knew. It was over. Their love song had come to a sudden dreadful end.

The grief was crushing. The towers may as well have collapsed on his soul. He couldn't stop envisioning Victoria in those last seconds as her world disintegrated. Was she in a dark stairwell desperately trying to escape? Was she cowering from the inferno when the rumbling began? Did she look into the doomed eyes around her? Did she reach out? Did she hold someone? Did she think of him?

Brady barely slept for months, incapable of wrapping his mind around what had happened. That she'd been taken from him. That he couldn't separate his private agony from the public anguish of so many human lives squashed like bugs on a windshield. He tried to imagine Victoria and three thousand souls rising from the heap, an army of angels in wait, ushering them to heaven's gate. Victoria was a *believer*. She *believed* in God and Heaven. He was a *hoper*. He *hoped* that stuff was real, but deep down *believed* they were fairy tales. Cotton candy for the soul.

Through it all Brady never wept, though he wanted to, tried to. But tears would not come. Misery would not release him. He never returned to work. Instead, he spent weeks holed up inside their apartment, alone with his memories. Occasionally foraying outside his hermitage to revisit places they'd been. Seeking respite where they'd walked and laughed and touched. Battery Park. The Gapstow Bridge in Central Park. The Ice Rink at Rockefeller Center. Fifth Avenue's Museum Mile. Places that still brimmed with remembrance of her. But nothing would dulcify the pain. His only solace was that, after a while, his heart simply turned to ice and he felt nothing.

Brady sold the co-op. He gave her family half the proceeds and half of the one-point-eight million dollar settlement from the Victim's Compensation Fund. He returned to his hometown of Fort Lauderdale, bought a sailboat, painted *Victoria* on the transom, and sailed toward the horizon with no plan to return. No plan at all.

For months he wandered the Caribbean, aimless as a blind bird, letting the wind push him where it might. Dropping anchor in secluded lagoons. Living off fish and conch. Avoiding human contact. Hoping the sun would burn away the impenetrable fog that encased him. His gloom so thick that at night he'd stand on the side of the schooner, clutching a rope from the mainsail rigging, and weigh whether or not to let go. Maybe he'd find her again waiting for him in the blackness.

The storm struck in the night, rising from the sea like old Poseidon from his lair, firing tridents of lightning. The Victoria bobbed like a cork in the nothingness. He lashed himself to the wheel while wave after wave crashed down. The schooner tipped over so far he could reach out and touch the sea. Then he felt something he hadn't since 9/11. He felt fear. Fear as immense as the wall of black water coming straight at him, cresting above the mast, sixty, seventy, eighty feet high.

It was only then, bound to the helm, helpless, the ocean about to devour him, that he finally wept. Not for himself. Not out of fear. But because, at last, he knew. He comprehended Victoria's terror in those final seconds. Felt her desperate will to live as the world disintegrated around her. With the wind screaming and the leviathan about to swallow him, Brady sobbed. The mountain of water drove him down, deep into a black hole, plunging him toward his own Ground Zero. And all he could think, the only thing that mattered, was that he wanted to live. Just as he knew she had wanted to live. His last thought was: *Victoria, help me!*

He awoke on a beach at sunrise. And he was elated. *Is this heaven? Where is Victoria? Victoria!* Then something that felt like meat hooks grappled him beneath his armpits and jerked him back to reality. Too weak to lift his head, he felt himself being dragged, his toes raking the sand as someone, something, pulling him down the beach.

His name was Luther. An old black man who lived with his black-and-white Capuchin monkey, Phoebe. They were on the windward side of Little Exuma, an out-island in the southeastern Bahamas. Luther had a tiny tiki bar he called the Sea Shanty that catered to tourists who happened by on rented motor scooters as they explored the island and searched for deserted beaches to skinny dip. They drank beer and rum and snapped photos with Luther and Phoebe, using his palm frond hut and the azure sea as backdrops.

Luther nursed Brady in a wooden shack behind the Sea Shanty. For days he lay hallucinating, half-dead, half-alive. Trying to reconstruct what happened. How had he escaped the blackness? How had he reached the beach? How had he cheated the reaper?

"It was her," Luther told him one night sitting by a driftwood fire, his lilting Bahamian patois as gentle as the light from the crescent moon dancing on the combers rippling ashore. "She pulled you from that ocean and threw you onto the sand, just as surely as fish can swim and birds can fly."

"I wish I could believe that, Luther."

"She be up there. She be watching over you. She always be there. She be your connection to the Supreme Being. Believe it, Max Brady."

He wanted to believe Luther. How else to explain his survival? For the first time in his life it would give him some evidence, some validation, that *something* was out there. Not anything he could see or touch or prove in a court of law. But something he could *believe*. That Victoria *was* out there someplace. That someday they might be together again. Someday. But not this day.

Brady's Run

CHAPTER FIFTEEN

WHILE BRADY DREAMED a gunmetal sky cast its evil eye on Fort Lauderdale. *Hurricane Phyllis* had shellacked the Yucatan Peninsula with one hundred forty mile per hour winds that whipped up behemoth waves and swamped the island of Cozumel, collapsing buildings and drowning dozens of inhabitants. Now the devil wind had South Florida directly in her sights. The forecast had the storm still forty eight hours out, but portentous gusts were already rattling the Sea Shanty's windows.

"*Phyllis's* advance guard," Brady said to Jonas Bigelow.

The Shanty hadn't opened yet and they were alone. The older man sipped black coffee while the younger man prepared for the day ahead, expertly wielding a long, black-handled, scalloped-blade knife, cleaving cubes of chicken, sausage, shrimp, and fish for the day's pot of gumbo.

"Goddamndest streak of weather I ever saw," said Jonas. "Four big hurricanes last year. Now King Kong's coming."

"Mother Nature getting even."

"For what?"

"Seventy-five degree February's."

"Goddamned global warming. We'll be ten feet under the Atlantic before those bastards wake up in Washington."

Brady smiled at him. Jonas was not one to hem or haw. He'd been a union man, a boilermaker from Pittsburgh, and could cut through bullshit faster than an acetylene torch. Ten years ago, he and his wife, Betty, moved to Fort Lauderdale and bought the Coral Reef Motel a block off A1A. Jonas brought with him a lifelong distrust of authority.

"Did you see this?" he said, glowing like a bullfrog with a belly full of fireflies.

He held up the front page of *The Lauderdale News*. Brady examined the headline: *Beach Activists Accuse Mayor of Collusion with Developers*. Dominating the page was a large color photograph of Jonas and Rose Becker in their mushroom hats, a mutinous grin on his face as he was being evicted from the City Commission chambers.

"Jonas, I'm gonna have to buy you that book on how to make friends and influence people."

"Fuck 'em. That double-dealing David Grand would've slapped me with a slander suit by now if what I said wasn't true."

Brady knew he was right. The mayor and his confederates were plundering the beach. It was as barefaced as the cranes looming over A1A. And the feeding frenzy wasn't likely to abate. Too many people were getting too rich. The construction of sun-blocking high rises was only going to get worse. Jonas knew it too.

"Mark my words, Max Brady. The bubble's gonna burst someday. But them sons-a-bitches ain't gonna be crying in their beer. Their pockets'll be stuffed and they'll be gone and the rest of us will be left scratching our heads wondering how we let them destroy our paradise."

Jonas had worked himself into quite a lather. His face was the color of a strawberry margarita. Brady was afraid he'd burst a blood vessel and decided to change topics. Specifically to last night's conversation with Olga and Gunther.

"Jonas, has anyone ever tried to buy the Coral Reef?"

He slapped at the air with his hand. "Somebody's always waving money under my nose. I tell 'em to screw off. I ain't going no place – not by choice."

"Anybody in particular?"

"I don't pay attention."

"The Klums said they'd been approached several times about selling. The offers all came from a female realtor. That woman they call the real estate queen."

Jonas cast a barbed eye at him. He tilted the coffee cup to his mouth, drained the last drops of sediment, and slammed the bar with the empty cup.

"Cherry Hampton," he growled. "Built like a brick shithouse. Snappy wardrobe. Nice face too, though I'd bet the Coral Reef she's had a nip and tuck or two."

Brady refilled his cup. "What's she like?"

Jonas hesitated and a shadow crossed his face. "Half angel, half she-devil."

"Come again?"

"All candy and flowers – on the surface. Fawning over me. Telling me what a dreamboat I am. Telling Betty we'd be living in the lap of luxury if we sold. Trying to sweet talk us out of the Coral Reef. My answer was always the same. No way, no how. Then, the last time she came by, the queen flashed mean."

"Oh?"

"It only lasted a second. I told her we weren't selling and that was final. I told her don't bother us no more. That's when the hell-cat bared her fangs. *'You better reconsider,'* she says, *'or you'll regret it.'* Cold as a witch's tit in a brass brassiere. Now, I'm tough as old shoe leather and proud of it. But the look on that woman's face gave me gooseflesh. Then in the blink of an eye she's sweet as honey again. But I seen it. No doubt about it. Behind them fancy threads and that shiny smile lurks a junkyard dog."

Bradys Run

CHAPTER SIXTEEN

CHERRY HAMPTON TOOK immense pleasure boasting to Adonis about the opulent deals she had cooking. A ten million dollar oceanfront *palazzo*. Multi-million dollar penthouses in the new towers downtown. Crackerboxes on the river selling for a million dollars, only to be demolished and replaced with *McMansions*.

"It's a home run, Adonis. Get in the game," she said, popping grapes into his mouth on one of their *theme nights*. Cherry was partial to grapes. "Wealthy retirees are moving here in droves. Donald Trump's the new paradigm. Morons are making fortunes."

Adonis began to think maybe his life didn't have to be one long bad dream lived out in a dingy room and paid for by deviltry. He began to see Hampton as a mentor. Someone to learn from and prosper. If only she didn't hurl those verbal pitchforks, as if he was too stupid to understand. *"Morons like you..."* The insults cut him, deeper than he let on. They made him feel unclean, insignificant. But, then, he'd felt that way as long as he could remember.

The notion had been planted in him by his gaunt, gray, Bible-thumping grandmother Nana Ruth. His mother's mother. Seeming to be without sin herself, she had dedicated her life to obsessing about the sins of her daughter, and her daughter's misbegotten son.

Adonis was born Donald John Rockwell, the bastard son of a boozy teenager drawn to boozy, abusive men. When Donnie was very young his mother was taken away in handcuffs by policemen. Why he did not know. He only knew it meant moving in with Nana Ruth. She was a hard woman with deep wrinkles around thin lips, lips he could not remember ever smiling. It was Nana Ruth who informed him he'd been born with a stain on his soul.

"Your sins will find you out, child," she taught him.

Every morning she woke him before dawn and they walked the six blocks from her small ramshackle house to a Catholic Church, Our Lady of the Rosary. They would sit in the front *stink*, as little Donnie called the pew. An old white-haired priest at the altar. Nana Ruth, her eyelids squeezed tight, bony white fingers kneading black rosary beads, withered lips in silent prayer, ardent prayer, perpetual prayer, for Donnie's soul. Leaning down, whispering urgently.

"You've been cursed, child." Then spitting on the floor, as though her tongue had been dipped in poison. *"Through no fault of your own, Donald. For your mother's sins. For my sin of bringing her into the world."*

The boy looking up at his grandmother, his big innocent eyes searching for something they were incapable of seeing, listening with ears that could make no sense of her words, except to register shock that Nana Ruth was a sinner.

"Your mother has indulged in fruit from the forbidden tree. Like Eve, she is guilty of abominations, of lust and greed, vanity and sloth. She has traded her soul for sex and drugs and alcohol. And, child, her sins are on your soul. My penance for bearing her is to save you."

None of it making an imprint until, later, in the dark cavern of Nana Ruth's curtained bedroom, sitting on her big soft featherbed, his feet dangling inches above a dark wood floor burnished by decades of caresses from her old bare soles. She with the big red leather-bound Bible on her lap, turning back the cracked cover, leafing through the dog-eared pages until she came to the picture, the vivid, ghastly depiction, her skeletal forefinger guiding his wide eyes to the hideous red creature, horned and winged and ringed by flames and wretched screaming faces, the image burned into his memory as indelibly as if the Bible had been a branding iron.

"The dark angel," she said, still whispering, like she was afraid eavesdroppers were hiding beneath the bed, and then she spit on the floor. *"Lucifer himself, prince of Hades, with whom you are cursed to spend eternity, with whom you will burn for all days. Not for your sins, child, but for the sins of your mother, and her mother. As surely as Cain slew Abel. Unless you are saved."*

The last time Donnie saw Nana Ruth was through the rear window of a moving car. His mother had returned, without the police this time, her hands uncuffed, and took him away. The old lady, gaunt and gray, standing on the doorstep of her dilapidated house, receding from view like a setting sun, her withered face no longer hard, but bathed in tears. He did not know much. He did not even know she could cry. Yet, with the intuition of an innocent he discerned, too late, that Nana Ruth was the one person in the world he could trust. The one person who truly loved him. And he too wept.

Nana Ruth died six months later. His final memory of her was a pine box descending into a dirt hole while he knelt nearby in the graveyard grass, vomiting, overcome by the saccharine scent of rotting flowers. That night he dreamed of the dark angel, red and pestilent, with its horns and wings, surrounded by flames and woeful, contorted faces. Seeing his own face now among them. And his grandmother's whispered admonition: *"Unless you are saved."*

Donnie heard nothing more of sin until he was fifteen years old. Living in a two room cockroach-infested apartment paid for by *gifts* from his mother's many male *friends*, sometimes several a day, visiting her for an hour or less at a time. One day one of them, a short, bald man with a massive potbelly, attacked Donnie in a drunken fury, pummeling him with fists and feet, screaming: *"You dirty little bastard, I will beat the living sin out of you."* Afterwards, when the man had collapsed and lay cataleptic on a threadbare brown twill couch that doubled as Donnie's bed, the boy bashed his head with a baseball bat.

Potbelly spent the next three weeks in a coma. Donnie spent the next three years in juvenile prison. It was a place, he quickly learned, where anything went, where down was up, black was white, bad was good. He slept in a long Quonset dormitory, side-by-side with twenty-three other delinquents. They were like one boy with two-dozen faces. Dead-end kids. The kind watchful mothers shield their children from.

The worst time was at night, lying in his bunk, the big room dark as a crypt. Desolate and utterly alone with his black thoughts. Not once did his mother visit, or write, or send a birthday card. He thought sometimes of Nana Ruth, her hard face now no more than a blurry spectral, cold and gray, like a hearth without fire, wondering if this was the Hades she had warned him of. Baffled, he lay there, desperate to find something, some strand to pull, some filament that would unravel the tangled labyrinth that was his life. He never found it.

Stripped of hope and illusion, Donnie spent three years pumping iron and learning about crime. At eighteen, he was released and joined the U.S. Marines, who exorcised whatever tenderness was left in him. Only the demons remained. After a two year stint he returned home to Tampa and worked a succession of low pay jobs. On the side he sold weed and snow.

Donnie began hanging out at The Ecstasy, a titty bar on Dale Mabry Strip renowned for its star attraction, *Vicki Vagg,* a busty redheaded dancer endowed with a remarkable talent for launching hardboiled eggs like bazooka shells from her vagina. Temptation was a constant at The Ecstasy, and if there was one thing Donnie could not resist it was temptation. Magnificently sculpted, he became quite the Cocaine Casanova. Women fluttered to him and his white powder like hummingbirds to sweetwater.

The Ecstasy was owned by the notorious gangster Cisco Blas, a jowly dark-featured man with a perpetual five o'clock shadow. Cisco's manager was Willie Corrales, an ex-biker known to everyone as Crackhead, though nobody dared call him that to his face. Corrales was short and skinny as a rope with muscles like swollen knots and the disposition of a wasp. Donnie had seen him thrash men twice his size. Crackhead took notice of the strapping crew-cut kid with *Semper Fi* tattooed on his forearm. Corrales had once been a leatherneck – for two weeks – before being booted from the Corps for beating the tar out of his Parris Island drill instructor.

"Hey, Marine," he said one day, "what's your name."

"Rockwell, sir," Donnie said, startled to be approached by the hard-bitten manager.

"How thick's your bankroll, Rockwell?"

"Thinner than a Cuban sandwich without the meat."

"Well, son, the way I see it an empty wallet ain't nothing but a useless slab of leather. I need a guy to work security. Interested?"

Crackhead took a fast liking to his new bouncer and before long Donnie had worked his way into the inner circle. Within a year, Cisco Blas made him manager of The Fifth, a blue-collar club whose dancers had considerably more miles on their odometers than The Ecstasy girls. Under his command The Fifth was soon raking in more money than ever, and so was Donnie. For the first time in his life he felt like he was on his way to finding the end of the rainbow. Then his luck reverted to form.

The IRS was squeezing Cisco for back taxes and he needed cash. One night he called Donnie to his office behind the stage at The Ecstasy. When he arrived Cisco and Crackhead were sitting in hushed deliberation under a harsh lightbulb hanging over a table at the center of the room. Vicki Vagg was in the corner loading her howitzer with *Grade A's*. Cisco barked across the room.

"Go stuff that thing someplace else."

Vicki picked up her egg carton and stalked out in a snit. Cisco stood and walked to the far end of the room. He removed a portrait from the wall – a nude woman painted on black velvet – and spun the dial on the safe it had been hiding. The door swung open and Donnie saw several stacks of cash. Cisco grabbed two. He tossed one to Crackhead and the other to Donnie.

"Ten grand each."

"For what?" Donnie said.

"Willie'll tell you," Cisco said and walked out.

Donnie looked across the table at Crackhead thumbing his banknotes.

"We're torchin' the Kitty Kat," he said.

"Why?"

Crackhead's face lit up in a rare smile. He was missing more teeth than a jack-o-lantern. He stuffed the cash in his pocket.

"Million dollars in insurance."

"I don't know anything about burning a building."

"Just do what I tell ya."

The Kitty Kat Klub was Cisco's largest joint. Located on a lonely country road in rural Thonotosassa on the outskirts of Tampa, it catered to rednecks in pick-up trucks from the orange groves and strawberry fields of west central Florida who were drawn to a club called the *KKK*.

Crackhead and Donnie arrived in separate cars at five o'clock the next morning. The bar had been closed for an hour and the place was deserted. By pre-arrangement the Kitty Kat manager had switched off the parking lot lights before he left. Crackhead broke the back door lock and showed Donnie how to set up hot plates and plastic milk jugs filled with gasoline. He instructed him where to splash accelerant and explained they'd have five minutes after they turned on the hotplates before the first explosion.

"Scram," Crackhead said when they exited the building.

But Donnie wanted to see the blast. He circled his car back just as the Kitty Kat blew. Fire and glass sailed in every direction and within minutes the bar was swathed in orange flame. Donnie spotted Crackhead's black GTO parked in the shadows a hundred yards down the road. He got out and walked up from behind. A few feet from the door, he stopped cold. *Jesus!* Crackhead was behind the steering wheel masturbating, as if the blaze was a XXX-rated bonfire licking at his balls. Donnie did a U-turn and hightailed it back to Tampa.

That summer they burned down four more bars, two of Cisco's and two owned by his chief rival, Gaetano *Tommy Bats* Battaglia. Between running The Fifth and his burgeoning career as an arsonist, Donnie was making more money than he ever imagined possible. Then his world turned to shit. He got popped on a cocaine rap. Cisco took a bullet to the head. And Crackhead was fingered for his murder.

Sitting on his throne one *theme night*, Adonis told Cherry Hampton his story while she knelt wide-eyed at his feet, like a proper slave, him remembering to forget the most incriminating parts.

"Oh, my!" she whispered, aghast and enthralled at the same time. "You're a convict!"

For their next fantasy tryst, Hampton made Adonis wear an orange jumpsuit she'd borrowed from her friend the Sheriff of Broward County. She donned a prison guard uniform and brandished manacles and a leather whip.

Brady's Run

CHAPTER SEVENTEEN

FOR TEN THOUSAND years, what is now Fort Lauderdale was a mosquito-infested swamp inhabited by the Calusa, Ais, Seminole, Loxahatchee and other small native tribes that lived off fish and game and roots. Not much changed until 1896 when Henry Flagler's railroad opened Florida's lower peninsula to the masses. Among the first to venture south was a visionary named Charles Green Rhodes, whose dream was to create an American version of Venice, Italy. Rhodes dredged miles of muck and mangrove, dug hundreds of canals, and built long slender fingers of loam which ultimately became the trellis upon which Fort Lauderdale grew.

Max Brady's Victoria II was floating on one of Rhodes's canals. Brady had another boat, a twenty-one foot Sea Ray moored beside the schooner. At mid-morning he cast off the Sea Ray's lines, turned the key, and the two hundred sixty-horsepower Mercury inboard cleared its throat and purred slowly down the waterway.

He steered into the Intracoastal and was immediately forced to swerve hard to starboard to avoid being rammed by a mammoth yacht. The Sea Ray rocked violently as a fat captain in starched white blasted an airhorn and shook his fist like a road-raged driver. The Intracoastal did remind Brady of Interstate 95 at rush hour. Boats were everywhere, churning the water like a washtub, leaving an oily sheen as iridescent as dragonfly wings.

Brady was born and raised in Fort Lauderdale. The town was encrypted in his DNA. But it had changed drastically since he'd grown up on New River. Back then it was a paradise. When he was twelve he saved up enough money delivering *The Miami Herald* to buy a little Boston Whaler powered by an old rebuilt fifty horsepower Evinrude. With the city's Venetian network of rivers and canals, he was like a kid with a car. Max was half-boy-half-fish, water skiing with his friends on the river, surfing beside the long granite jetty at Port Everglades inlet, scuba diving for lobster on the pink coral reefs offshore.

Those sun-drenched days shimmered like diamonds in his recollection, but they were gone forever. Skiing was now prohibited on the river. The waves had either shrunk or he'd grown too big to ride them. And the ocean reefs had been picked cleaner than a Christmas turkey. Brady felt a certain melancholy for town kids who would never know the wonderland of his youth. Now it was the playground of the rich and highfalutin.

Nothing epitomized the opulence more than the floating castles of the global aristocracy. Fort Lauderdale was the self-proclaimed *Yachting Capital of the World.* Winter was like spawning season for mega-yachts, as though they'd heard the siren's call and crossed the seas to multiply there. Empty docks were scarcer than virgins.

Brady steered toward Bahia Mar Marina to check out the glitzy new tubs that had come in. One stuck out above the rest. Too big to enter the marina, it was berthed at a quay on the Intracoastal. Its navy blue hull gleamed in the morning light. A helicopter sat on its deck and a dinghy the size of his Sea Ray hung from its stern. A retinue of crewmen were scrubbing and polishing. He slid in for a closer look and was rewarded when a redhead in a yellow bikini stepped on deck. Stunning didn't quite describe her. Her face and figure were almost taunting. She looked down and waved, as people on boats are wont to do. Brady never understood why, but he waved back anyway, wondering what moneybags owned the yacht – and the redhead. Then he saw Shangri-La stenciled in gold lettering on the blue stern. *Can't argue with that, pal, whoever you are!*

He guided the Sea Ray to the mouth of New River and rambled into the briny black tea of the serpentine waterway. He'd have known it by smell alone, its mudbank breath, fishy and algaeic, mingling with the faintly toxic belches of the Mercury. Most of the homes that once lined the river had been razed and replaced by swank palaces built, he couldn't help but think, by vainglorious men as monuments to themselves.

Brady tethered the boat to a seawall cleat behind a graceful white building called Stranahan House. Now a museum, it was the town's oldest structure, built in 1901 as a trading post by an Ohio settler named Frank Stranahan. If Fort Lauderdale's canals were its trellis, Stranahan House was the seed from which the city sprang. Which made Stranahan its father. Tragically, in 1929 poor Frank – depressed by a series of epic hurricanes that destroyed the local economy and left him destitute – tied an iron grate to his leg and jumped in the river a few feet from where Brady docked. *What does it say about a city,* he wondered, *whose patriarch drowned himself?*

It was a two block walk to downtown. When he was a kid the business district had been a dingy collection of two and three story brick buildings. Now it was a forest of steel and chrome stabbing the sky like giant stalagmites.

Tropical Tower trembled in the harsh morning sun, a sleek new forty five-story blade of glass. The entrance was dominated by a plaza with a large fountain surrounded by Jacaranda and Royal Poinciana trees. Office workers were lounging in the shade, smoking cigarettes, drinking Starbucks, and relishing the fresh October breeze. Brady took the express elevator to the top floor.

The doors opened onto a high-ceilinged room layed out like a wagon wheel. It had big arched windows and polished black marble columns. The perimeter was ringed by low onyx tables adorned with cut glass vases holding long-stemmed yellow roses, surrounded by posh contemporary chairs in warm greens and golds. Frosted glass lightboxes dangled from above, diffusing light so there were no shadows. Attractive young women bustled to and fro in pastel business attire. They seemed cold and impersonal. Brady got the sense they dispensed their attention by divining the net worth of visitors. In his T-shirt, frayed shorts, and black high-tops, he didn't even rate a smile.

At the hub of the wheel, inside a glass-walled office, Brady spied Cherry Hampton. She was wearing a pale yellow pants suit and standing before an easel propping up a canvas splashed with yellows, greens, and reds. *Jackson Pollock*, he thought, smug with himself for actually recognizing the artist's work. Backwash from all the Manhattan museums Victoria used to drag him to. *She'd be so proud!* He remembered her telling him Pollock paintings fetched millions. *Cherry's in tall cotton.*

Hampton was talking to a tall, asexual-looking brunette with no discernible curves. She looked up and noticed Brady staring at her and nodded to the brunette, who exited the office and made a beeline straight for him.

"Welcome to Hampton Realty," she said in a deep sepulchral voice that sounded like Nina Simone on testosterone. Her long straight nose could have doubled as a sightline for her gunbarrel black eyes. "I'm Deirdre."

"I'm Max," he said and shook her hand as she calculated him with cold precision. He sensed he didn't grade out too highly with her either.

"How may we help you today, Max?"

Deirdre exuded all the warmth of a Siberian winter. Brady decided to repel the arctic chill with sheer animal magnetism and summoned up a hearty, insincere smile. "I came to see Cherry Hampton."

"Do you have an appointment?"

"Thought I'd roll the dice," he said, nodding toward the glass room. "Looks like I got lucky."

Deirdre's dark brows gathered into a frown. She consulted a leather-backed planner cradled in the crook of her left elbow, perusing it for thirty seconds then scribbling for another half minute. Brady wondered if she'd forgotten he was there. Maybe his charm reservoir had suddenly gone dry. He made a mental note to check his charisma dipstick.

"I'm sorry," Deirdre said finally. "Ms. Hampton is booked solid. I'd be more than happy to help you. Are you a buyer or seller?"

"Neither. I'm here on behalf of the owners of a property Cherry was interested in."

"What property would that be?" she said. Her tone was apathetic.

"A beach motel."

Deirdre gazed at him for several seconds, her eyes dark and lifeless. He considered the possibility she was an android.

"Let me tell Ms. Hampton you're here. Perhaps we can arrange an appointment."

Deirdre returned to the command center. Across the room a leggy young agent in a minty-green suit led a prosperous-looking middle-aged couple into a room marked *Video Lounge*. Brady saw a big screen TV inside streaming shots of a waterfront mansion. Another woman dressed in a clingy peach pants outfit sat at the *Espresso Bar* chatting with a well-heeled older twosome. The stench of money was everywhere.

Brady turned and saw Hampton studying him through the glass. He doubted she would remember him, she being blotto the one time they'd met. She whispered something to Deirdre, who came back out.

"Ms. Hampton has a sales meeting," she said in her basso profundo, "but she can give you a couple of minutes. If you will follow me."

Deirdre led Brady into the glass sacristy. Hampton stood and greeted him with a three-act smile – teeth, dimples, eyes – one gone before the next appeared. He guesstimated she was in the late summer of life, but she was keeping a death grip on her salad days. Tight white skin, platinum hair elegantly pinned back, pearls the size of maraschino cherries hanging from her earlobes. As Jonas had observed, she'd undergone renovations, but it was quality work.

She extended a hand festooned with precious baubles. "I'm Cherry. Have we met, Mr. Brady?"

Brady remained stone-faced. "Sorry, Cherry. That line's been tried on me before. It ain't gonna get you anywhere."

The remains of her smile evaporated faster than dew in daylight. She blushed like a teenager, groping for a response. Brady broke into a grin.

"It's a joke, Cherry. People tell me I have a warped sense of humor."

"Oh," she said with an anemic smile, teeth only this time. "I suppose I walked right into that."

"Actually we have met. I served you and a gentleman at my bar last year." He pointed to the logo on his T-shirt. "Sea Shanty."

Hampton inspected him like she was trying to remember the name of someone she'd woken up beside the morning after.

"Oh, yes," she said vaguely. "That quaint little place down on the beach."

"*Quaint!*" Brady said brightly. "I like that. *Quaint!*"

Hampton motioned him to a contemporary orange chair that looked uncomfortable but felt like sitting on a cloud. She retreated to her chair behind the desk and saw Brady glance over her shoulder at the easel.

"You like my Pollock?"

"I'm sure it's beautiful, but I'm color blind."

"Oh," Hampton said with a disappointed expression. She peeked at her watch. "I wish I had more time, Mr. Brady. You wanted to talk about a motel on the beach?"

"The Pelican's Nest. Do you remember the place?"

Brady noticed her nostrils flare and a patch of red break out on the skin at her throat. She scratched the back of her hand like she had poison ivy.

"I've handled so many hotel and motel properties."

"The former owners tell me you made several offers to buy their place."

He saw a startled expression fill her eyes. "Former owners?" she said with alarm in her voice.

"Olga and Gunther Klum. A German couple."

"Of course. I remember them well. I hope you're not telling me they've sold. I can't imagine anyone making a more attractive offer."

"The Pelican's Nest burned down yesterday."

"Oh, dear." She said it like a piano player who'd hit a dissonant chord. "I saw something on the news about a fire, but didn't realize. I'm so sorry. It was such a lovely property."

Brady remembered Jonas's remark about the ice queen behind the smiling face. Hampton had lamented the Pelican's Nest's destruction, but said nothing about the Klums. She glanced at her watch again.

"I really must be going, Mr. Brady. Was there something specific?"

"The Klums wonder if you might still be interested in their property."

He detected her breath quicken for the briefest instant. "I'd have to speak to my client."

"My friends tell me you made a generous offer. Far above market value. Your client must have been very motivated."

"I'm a go-between, Mr. Brady. Clients have the prerogative to offer whatever they like. Frankly, the more they pay the larger my commission."

"I wonder why someone would make such an exorbitant offer."

Hampton rose abruptly and came around the desk.

"I'm sorry but I've got to run now." She stepped toward the door. "I'll speak with my client. Leave a number with Deirdre and we'll get back to you."

"By the way, Cherry, are we talking about the same client who made on offer on the Coral Reef Motel?"

Hampton froze in her tracks. Brady saw a faint shudder run through her before she stiffened and wheeled on him. Storm clouds billowed across the surface of her eyes.

"You don't sound like a bar owner, Mr. Brady."

He smiled. "I guess a leopard can't change its spots. In a previous life I was an Assistant United States Attorney. Before that I was an NYPD detective."

"Well, I'm not about to be cross-examined, not by a former federal prosecutor, or ex-New York cop, or leopard in bar owner's clothing." She looked him up and down. "If that's what bar owners wear. Good day, Mr. Brady."

She turned and walked briskly to the door, her high heels clacking like capguns on the black marble. Brady spoke to her back.

"The fire marshal says the Pelican's Nest fire was arson. I'm looking for a motive. Your client seems to have been motivated."

Hampton spun on him again. She was wearing her ice queen face and her fingers were buckled like cat's claws. "Why would someone burn down a motel they're *motivated* to buy?"

"Fair question. I'm just fishing for leads."

"Well, Mr. Brady, wet your line someplace else. This isn't New York City. Let our local authorities do their job. I'm sure they're quite competent."

"You're right. I'll pass the information to Captain McCarty at the Fire Investigation Unit. You'll probably be hearing from him."

Brady strode past her and out the door while she glared at him with eyes hard as rivets. He had to hand it to Jonas. He'd pegged her. Cherry Hampton was about as much fun as a burst appendix.

Bradys Run

CHAPTER EIGHTEEN

THE BELL HELICOPTER lifted off the deck of the Shangri-La, swung east out over the ocean, and zipped north low and parallel to the bleached ribbon of coastline. Thirty minutes later it touched down in Balmy Bay on the verdant lawn of the palatial Shangri-La Club. Sherwood Steele and Tiffani Bandeaux bounded from the chopper into a courtyard and past a large fountain filled with terra cotta nymphs launching cool mist into the warm air.

Mayor David Grand was waiting on the veranda of the elegant yellow Key West colonial clubhouse with its green tin roof. Commissioner Jarrett Griffin was beside him, wearing red and green plaid golf pants and a bright green shirt. He was smiling, his tongue protruding from the corner of his mouth, staring at Tiffani's bouncing breasts. She watched him watch her.

"Griffin reminds me of a dog wagging its tail," she whispered to Steele.

"Pet him on the head. I think he likes that."

"I would, but that rug looks like it bites."

"Jarrett, thanks for coming," Steele said. "David, nice to see you. How's Maisy?"

"*Grand*," said Grand, chortling at his threadbare joke.

"Welcome to the Shangri-La Club, gentlemen."

The Shangri-La was Florida's most exclusive golf club. It had but one member – Sherwood Steele. Every July 4th – Steele's birthday – invitations went out to a hundred or so movers and shakers to be his honorary guests for a year of golf, drink, and sumptuous meals – all free. Champagne corks could be heard popping all over South Florida. It wasn't the freebie that was so appealing. Rather, it was the cachet of being part of Steele's inner sanctum.

"I hope you brought your clubs," he said.

"We did, Sherwood," said Griffin, his eyes darting between Steele and Tiffani's chest. "We look forward to playing with you and Ms. Bandeaux."

"Unfortunately, Jarrett, I've got too much on my plate at the moment. If I start ignoring business to play golf I'll have to begin charging my guests." The politicians chuckled. Steele didn't. "I'll invite you gentlemen to be members when you get off the public tit."

"If things work out, Sherwood," said Grand, "that could be soon."

Steele glowered at the mayor with black, censorious eyes.

"Don't tear down the goalposts just yet, Mr. Mayor. The game's not over. I need you in office until the deal is done. And that's starting to look very iffy."

Grand's eyes got wide and his jaw dropped. "The deal looks iffy?"

"No. Your tenure in office."

The mayor started to laugh, but Steele's countenance hardened and an awkward silence filled the air. Grand traded a nervous glance with Griffin. The blood rushing in his ears was so loud he could barely hear himself speak. "I don't understand."

Steele half-laughed, as if the mayor had said something funny. "That cute little health club owner. The one the newspapers call Madame Butterfly. She could very well end up kicking your ass. I'd vote for her, if I didn't have so much invested in you."

The mayor's face grew as red and twisted as a Twizzler stick. He looked to Griffin for support but his confederate was staring down at the tassels on his white loafers with fervid interest. Grand swallowed hard.

"Don't worry, Sherwood. That dike's not going to beat me."

Steele flinched. "Dike? Are you sure, David? She seems very feminine." He glanced at Tiffani. "Sexy as hell, if you ask me. Smart as hell, too. That's a problem."

Griffin might as well have been deaf and mute. He hadn't seemed to hear a word. He certainly was making no attempt to defend Grand.

Then Steele slapped the mayor's shoulder and his tanned face broke out in an oily white smile.

"But enough politics for now. You fellows must be hungry?"

The tension broke like quicksilver. Grand's color returned. Griffin, apparently delighted with his shoes, beamed brightly. Steele led them into the clubhouse to a glass-walled room a nine iron from the eighteenth green. It was the course's signature hole, featuring a spectacular waterfall that cascaded into a moat surrounding the putting surface. Beyond, sailboats tacked back and forth on the Atlantic. Griffin noticed a table along the wall. It was lined with thick leather-bound volumes. He looked closer and saw they were loan documents. The spines were embossed with the names of Shangri-La resorts and the dollar amount of each loan: *Shangri-La Negril* – $420,000,000, *Shangri-La Grand Cayman* – $630,000,000, *Shangri-La Paradise Island* – $750,000,000. Griffin recalled Steele once describing his business philosophy: *"OPM, Jarrett. That's the secret. Other People's Money."*

A black butler dressed in white came in with a tray of hors d'oeuvres. Tiffani poured drinks and they picked at crab Rangoon and pickled Swedish shrimp as they looked out at the ocean and chatted pleasantly. *How're the kids? How's the dog? How about them Dolphins?* Griffin and Grand relished the bonhomie. The coin of their realm was access to power and Sherwood Steele was the most powerful man in South Florida. Bantering with him put them close to the flame. They'd be boasting about it for days. *"I was having lunch with Sherwood at the Shangri-La Club the other day and..."*

"David, I understand you're building a new house," Steele said.

"Yes siree, bob. Ten thousand square feet. Six bedrooms. Big theater. Big pool. Sauna. Our dream house. All thanks to you, Sherwood."

"Don't go there," Steele said, his voice drenched with reproach. "I warned you. No spending sprees."

"Not to worry, Sherwood. I took a page out of your book. I'm using OPM. Your Jewish banker arranged the loan."

The butler, whose name was Claude, made a slight bow.

"Excuse me Mr. Steele, Ms. Bandeaux, gentlemen." He spoke with a Jamaican lilt. "We have steamed Danish lobster tail sandwiches on brioche with lemon mayonnaise and tomato. On the side we have potato flaked prawns on a bed of asparagus."

"Sounds delicious," Steele said.

Claude set plates in front of each of them while Steele and Grand talked. Jarrett Griffin, waiting for an opportunity to jump into the conversation, contented himself by stealing not-so-furtive glances at Tiffani Bandeaux. When she looked up and caught him staring, he flustered and abruptly broke in.

"David, I don't know how you're going to live in that crackerbox. Ginger and I needed fifteen thousand square feet."

Claude stood impassive against the wall. Working for Sherwood Steele, he was used to the braggadocio of pretentious men boasting about fancy cars, fabulous yachts, and grandiose houses. *Like boys bragging about the size of their cocks!* He wondered if these vain men were happy.

"Sherwood," said Grand, "how's that palace you're building on the Intracoastal?"

"Slow. Had to fire two contractors already. It'll be another six months before I move in."

"You must be tired having to live on that dinghy," Griffin said with a laugh.

"Actually, Jarrett, I am. I'll be happy to get back on terra firma."

"What's your square footage gonna be?" the mayor said.

"Fifty thousand." Steele noticed Griffin twitch in the act of harpooning a prawn. "Two thousand more than Bill Gates."

"Wow, Sherwood, that's a big erection," Grand said, slapping Griffin on the back. "Kinda makes that little shack of yours seem like a crackerbox, don't it, Jarrett."

Claude fought to keep the smirk off his face. Steele sat back, his manicured fingers steepled at his lips, as if he was deep in prayer, while his inscrutable black eyes regarded the public servants. He nodded, almost imperceptibly. Tiffani stood.

"Gentlemen," she said, "I will leave you to your business."

She and Claude walked from the room, Griffin and Grand gawping at her all the way out. When they left they took with them the air of camaraderie. Steele sat forward, took a sip of club soda, and fixed his cold dark eyes on the men.

"My friends, I am concerned."

A pregnant hush fell over them as Steele's words sank in.

"Whadya mean, Sherwood?" Griffin said, a trace of goofy smile still lingering on his lips, like he wasn't certain if Steele was telling a joke.

"You are not delivering on your promise. You assured me that I would get the properties I require."

"You'll get them, Sherwood," Grand said.

"The election is one month away and I still don't have twenty five percent of the parcels."

"It's just taking longer than we expected," said Griffin.

"You two have been feathering your nests with my money. I expected results. You gave me your word."

"We'll keep our word," Grand said, his voice rising an octave.

"You can't keep your word if you lose the election."

Grand's nose had lit up like an automobile taillight. "I will not lose the election."

"No? Perhaps you haven't been reading the papers. Those beach people, including that *dike,* as you call her, are painting you as a developers whore."

"Sherwood, nobody believes that crap."

"I do. It's absolutely true."

Steele said it as placidly as if he was discussing Grand's golf game. The mayor nearly gagged on his lobster. He coughed for several seconds. When he finally regained his composure he stiffened.

"I resent that, Sherwood, considering our relationship."

"The truth's the truth, David. Let's be real. You are a whore." He turned toward Griffin, who recoiled like someone was pointing a gun at him. "You're a whore too, Jarrett. You two are my whores. Expensive, but whores nonetheless."

Grand's face was purple. "That's outrageous! It's not just about the money. We believe in your resort too. It will be good for the city."

"Rationalize graft any way you want. To paraphrase Shakespeare, though, a bribe by any other name is a bribe."

"Bribe is severe," the mayor sputtered. "I prefer the way you put it when we negotiated our, our, our…arrangement. It's more like a gift."

Steele's face was graven as carved stone. "I've deposited one million dollars into numbered Cayman Island bank accounts on behalf of each of you. I've promised to add two million more as soon as you come through. Do you really believe that is a gift?" Neither man responded. He leaned forward and shouted at them. "Do you?" Silence. "I expect a return on my investment. You lose the election before you deliver what you promised and I'm going be very unhappy." He let his words sink in before continuing. "You've never seen me unhappy. You don't want to."

Jarrett Griffin had been sitting wide-eyed and open-mouthed. His pencil-thin mustache was twitching and sweat was dripping from beneath his toupee. He finally found his tongue.

"That won't be necessary, Sherwood. We're gonna deliver for you."

"Keep your promises. When I close on the last piece of property and get my permits you each get another two million. *Or else.*"

Steele stood abruptly. He patted a napkin to his lips as he stared down at them, then walked out without another word. Minutes later, Griffin and Grand watched the Bell helicopter swoop out over the water, Steele's last words hanging in the air like gunsmoke. *"Or else…"*

Bradys Run

CHAPTER NINETEEN

"EXCUSE ME," BRADY said.

He was standing at a counter trying to catch the attention of a chubby-cheeked young man with a slightly green complexion who bore an uncanny resemblance to Jiminy Cricket, minus the hat. Jiminy was pecking at a keyboard ten feet away, pretending not to notice him.

"Hello?" Brady said a little louder. "I'm talking to you."

Jiminy finally stopped typing and let out a heavy sigh. He squinted up, his spectacles propped on the tip of his nose, his face pinched in a sneer.

"I'm very busy. What do you want?"

"I'd like to look at some property records."

The clerk rolled his eyes. "By name, address, or legal description?"

Brady considered the options. "Address."

Green man huffed and nodded toward a bank of computers across the room, then spoke slowly, as if Brady was too thickheaded to comprehend his words at regular speed.

"Pick one…Click *enter*…Read the instructions…It…is…idiot… proof."

Brady sneered back at him. *Pompous little shit!* He wished cricket-boy did wear a hat. He'd enjoy knocking it off.

"O...kay...thank...you," he said and crossed the room.

Cherry Hampton had not given him much to go on. He'd cast her a baited hook but she hadn't bitten. He decided to try a new fishing hole. Maybe he'd get a nibble trolling around the Broward County property records. When he left Hampton's office he walked three blocks west on Las Olas Boulevard, turned right at Andrews Avenue, continued to the county records center, and took an elevator to the fifth floor.

The doors opened on a vast, dimly lit room lined floor-to-ceiling with shelves of faded gray volumes stamped *Official Records of Broward County – Contracts, Deeds & Mortgages.* A long time ago, way back in his detective days, Brady spent countless hours rummaging through property registers. For his purposes, they contained a treasure trove of information about mobsters, drug dealers, and all manner of swindlers, charlatans, and degenerates. But that was a more innocent time. O.J. Simpson was still beloved, presidents could still enjoy a good cigar, and records were still kept on paper. Brady was techno-challenged. He didn't even own a computer, still holding out just in case they turned out to be a fad, like cell phones and color TV.

He sat down at an empty terminal and hit *enter.* Detailed instructions popped up on how to proceed. Jiminy was right. It *was* idiot proof. *Asshole!* He tapped in the address on Playa del Sol for the Pelican's Nest Motel. Within seconds the screen filled with green letters detailing the property's ownership history dating back fifty years. *Jeez!* His animus receded, slightly. Thirty years ago, Gunther and Olga Klum had paid two hundred forty nine thousand dollars for the motel. Two years ago, the Broward County Property Appraiser's Office had put its most recent evaluation on the Pelican's Nest – one point seven million. Cherry Hampton had offered the Klums three million dollars.

Brady returned to the counter and asked the clerk for a telephone book. He was more conciliatory this time and green boy complied without any wisenheimer comments. For the next hour, he entered the addresses of more than two dozen beach area motels and printed out their histories. When he finished he grabbed the sheaf of papers and headed toward the elevator, slowing at the front desk to mumble *"Thanks"* in Jiminy's direction.

Bradys Run

CHAPTER TWENTY

BY THE TIME Brady got back a small throng had congregated in the noonday sun outside the Sea Shanty, some hungry for lunch, some just antsy for the day's first beer buzz. For the next two hours they lined the bar like birds on a wire, Brady in constant motion, drawing drafts, splashing whiskey, shucking oysters, ladling gumbo.

The blitz didn't abate until mid-afternoon. Brady finally poured a black coffee and dropped the cache of courthouse documents on a table by a bank of open windows. The day was sunny and cloudless. A serene breeze was whispering in off the ocean. Across the street, a woman and little girl stood hand-in-hand on the beach in white sun dresses and floppy straw hats holding yellow balloons against the sea blue sky. A few paces away two teenage girls in bikinis were flirting with Johnny Glisson, sitting bronzed and regal on his lifeguard's throne. *Poor doomed sex object,* Brady thought with a grin.

He began shuffling through the papers and felt the familiar tingle of electricity he used to get when he wore a badge. *Thrill of the hunt.* He took a swallow of coffee, wishing he knew what he was looking for. A breadcrumb. A footprint. A flashing neon billboard. Something. Back in the day, Brady had had an internal sensor. He told Victoria it was his Geiger-counter. *"I get close to a bad guy, I can hear them tick, like they're radioactive.* " She'd let her blue eyes get big and round and tried to sound impressed. *"Max, that's such a gift."*

He hoped he still had the gift. After an hour sifting papers, though, he still hadn't heard the first tick. He glanced at the *Pabst Blue Ribbon* clock on the wall behind the bar to make sure *something* was ticking. He felt like he was trying to see through mud. He narrowed his eyes – all else invisible now – and scanned the documents again. Nothing. Then he did it again. On his third attempt he got a hit. He found one motel that had changed hands in the past year. Then he went through the stack again and found another. Before the next hour passed, he'd identified a half-dozen beach motels that had been sold over the past year. The prices were eye-popping, but that wasn't necessarily suspicious in the runaway real estate market. He kept reading. A few minutes later something flashed at the edge of his cerebrum. *What was that!* Something in the paperwork had sparked...*something*. A half-remembered, half-forgotten glimmer of...*what?* He closed his eyes and concentrated like a blind man trying to cross a strange room, searching his consciousness for something he could not see. Before he could throw a rope around it, though, a soggy dollar sauntered in and Brady's brainstorm burst like a soap bubble.

Bars had always been magnets for louts and buffoons looking to flex their beer muscles. During his time as saloonkeeper Brady had had to use physical force to evict more than one belligerent patron. This guy fit the bill. Big and lumbering, lots of tattoos, mean pitted face, bleary red slits for eyes. He wore a black leather vest decorated with Harley Davidson patches that did little to hide a belly that bulged like he'd swallowed his motorcycle helmet. Brady left his paperwork and moved behind the bar.

"What'll it be?"

"Bud Light," the newcomer said dully, not looking up.

Brady filled a mug and slid it to the man, who dipped his beak and inhaled the brew in a single breath. Within seconds his eyes lit up like someone had flipped a switch. He swiped a backhand across a foam mustache and pushed the empty stein back to Brady, who refilled it, hoping the guy would slake his thirst and go away so he could get back to his documents.

A minute later a sun-ripened blonde in a bikini wandered in. Blondes in bikinis were as common as coconuts on Lauderdale Beach. You had to be careful not to run them over. This one was a pedestrian beauty who perched herself on a barstool, lit a cigarette, and sat there doing a good impersonation of a dessert topping. Beer Muscles leered at her over the rim of his mug.

"How 'bout I buy you a Bud, honeybuns?" he said, punctuating his proposition with a loud belch.

Golden girl rolled her eyes, expelled a cloud of smoke, and turned away. It was a garden variety brush-off she looked like she'd practiced in a mirror. But Beer Muscles didn't look like a guy who spent much time in gardens. He began spewing a litany of epithets that would've made a Hell's Angel blush. Brady quickly interrupted him.

"Hey, buddy, we don't talk to ladies that way in here."

"Why?"

"It's uncouth."

"Fuck's that mean?"

"It means you ain't got no couth."

A constipated look crossed the man's face and Brady watched him strain to make sense of his words. After several seconds he gave up and went with the standard reply Brady was accustomed to hearing from patrons of his ilk.

"Fuck you!"

On another day he might have dusted off the behavioral psychology he'd learned at the police academy. Maybe try to reason with the guy. Persuade him to go outside and take a nice nap under a shady seagrape tree. But Brady was itching to get back to his courthouse papers. Besides, he was in no mood to play nice to a potty-mouthed goon. At first glance the guy looked dangerous. Brady knew the type, though. He sensed he'd go down in a stiff breeze. He circled around the bar. Before the big man could react, he grabbed his ink-stained right arm and jerked him roughly to his feet. The bar stool crashed to the floor. Beer Muscles didn't resist and Brady hustled him to the entry and launched him outside like the Sea Shanty was a Wild West saloon. The only thing missing was the swinging doors.

"That was gallant of you," the blonde said, batting her eyes at him.

"Can I get you something?"

"Mojito."

He made her drink and, invigorated by the dustup, returned to the window table. It dawned on him he hadn't concentrated on anything this keenly in years. It felt good. He was using parts of his brain he'd forgotten he had. He felt an eyelash from discovery, still trying to lasso the comet that had catapulted through his cranium a few minutes before. It was there someplace, like a back-itch just out of reach. Brady licked his left thumb and forefinger and began winnowing through the papers again. With the concentration of a diamond cutter, he scrutinized each page, each line, each word, over and over and over. Tedious work but, one by one, new kernels of information started popping out at him.

Before long he had identified a dozen motels sold within the past year, ten of them within a four square block radius of one another. The same four blocks as the Klum's Pelican's Nest and Jonas Biglow's Coral Reef motels. *Now we're getting someplace.* He stepped behind the bar and fetched a yellow legal pad and red felt-tipped pen and constructed a rudimentary chart.

Beach Motels

Name	*Address*	*Date of Sale*	*Seller*	*Buyer*	*Sale Price*

Brady entered the data from the ten motels in close proximity and stacked the documents for each in a separate pile, then scoured them for some kind of hook. He homed in on common denominators. The longer he looked the more he saw. Each property transaction was financed by the same lending institution – the South Florida National Bank. That was no big surprise. SFNB was Fort Lauderdale's hottest bank. Its headquarters was the tallest building downtown. Nonetheless, it was something. A breadcrumb, perhaps. Certainly worth noting.

An hour later, Brady's Geiger-counter started ticking. He felt the radiation before he saw the name. It was stamped on the back of the last page of all ten Contracts for Deed. He slapped a palm to his forehead. *Well, hello! Are you the footprint I've been looking for?* He sifted through the stack again until he'd confirmed his suspicion. Every transaction within the four square blocks was handled by the same real estate broker. *The ice queen herself. Cherry goddamn Hampton! So that's how you pay for your Jackson Pollock's and cosmetic enhancements.*

It wasn't long before a second name caught his eye. He recalled Jonas mentioning it once during one of his habitual rants about political shenanigans downtown. *"Jack Del Largo,"* he had said, spitting out the name like it was battery acid. *"Goddamn bagman!"* Del Largo was the closing attorney on all ten motel deals.

Then Brady's eyes were drawn to a single sheet of paper and his Geiger-counter started ticking like it was Three Mile Island. He realized it was the same document he'd been reading when Beer Muscles interrupted him. He read it once, then a second time, and his nerve ends began to twitch.

The *Driftwood Motel* on Sunset Street had been bought four months ago for one-and-a-half million dollars. Ten days later it was sold – for two million. Two weeks after that the property changed hands again – this time for three million dollars. The motel had doubled in value in less than a month – on paper. And each transaction was financed by the South Florida National Bank.

"I'll be damned," he said aloud. "A blinking neon billboard. A daisy chain!"

Brady had seen daisy chains before. A string of trades involving the same piece of property bought and sold over and over, the paper value building transaction by transaction like layers of candle wax dripping on a Chianti bottle. It wasn't just real estate. He'd prosecuted daisy chains involving penny stocks, heating oil, even Lamborghinis. The principal links in the chain were a willing seller, a willing buyer, and – most important – a willing bank.

He rifled through the paperwork again, following the trail of breadcrumbs, knowing now what to look for. Until each crumb grew into a footprint. Which grew into a neon sign. By the time he finished, he'd found the unmistakable tracks of four more daisy chains. He did some quick arithmetic and let out a long whistle. The collective value of the motels had artificially swollen by more than fifteen million dollars in a matter of months. The four block area was suddenly lit up like Times Square on a Saturday night.

Brady sat back, took a deep breath, and savored the moment. He'd always felt a certain elation at a time like this. Not a jumping up and down excitement. Quieter than that. More giddy. He'd stuck one shovel into the ground and unearthed a tantalizing nugget. He suspected he'd just discovered a buried treasure.

It was late afternoon. Moted yellow sunbeams slanted through the windows dancing with microbes of floating dust. Thirsty patrons were starting to stream in for happy hour. Brady served a few beers and whipped up a batch of frozen Margaritas, then returned to his document-strewn table. He leaned out the open window, rested his elbows on the sill, and breathed in the sea air. A blood-red sun loitering low in the western sky began its diurnal metamorphosis, splashing the horizon with an anarchic array of pinks, oranges, purples, and blues, creating a momentary masterpiece Jackson Pollock could only envy.

Not even the stained-glass sunset could quell the clamor coming from the papers spread out on the table. Brady sat down and combed the pages for the fifth time, or was it the sixth? One thing didn't add up. It was the same neighborhood, same bank, same realtor, and same lawyer, but different buyers. *Crown Resorts, Iguana Properties, Dover Holdings, Bishop's Gate Ltd., King Hotels, Ambassador Enterprises.* He searched for a common thread, but the documents didn't contain the names of individuals, officers, or stockholders. He noticed the buyers were all Delaware corporations based in Dover. Then he looked closer and realized they shared the same address. A post box in a *Mail 'R Us Store*. He saw they also shared the same corporate agent. He studied the name. *T. Bandeaux.* It didn't ring a bell.

Bradys Run

CHAPTER TWENTY ONE

"WELCOME ABOARD THE Shangri-La," Tiffani Bandeaux said. She was standing at the top of the gangplank in her yellow bikini, arms akimbo, posed like a *Sports Illustrated* swimsuit model. Norman Epstein gazed up meekly from the quay.

"Hello, Miss Bandeaux."

He was wearing a charcoal Brooks Brothers suit, black tie, and crisp white shirt, oozing all the solemnity of a mortician. Briefcase at his side, Epstein scaled the steps and shook Tiffani's hand, his eyes scrupulously averted from the abundant bosom staring him in the face like a pair of headlights on hi-beam. No easy task, him being several inches shorter than her.

Epstein tilted his head back, pushed his eyeglasses up the bridge of his nose, and looked into her green eyes. "I have an appointment with Sherwood. Did he mention it to you, Miss Bandeaux?"

"Please call me Tiffani." Her voice was sultry as steam. "Mr. Steele asked me to apologize. He's tied up in a meeting. He'll be flying back within the hour. He asked me to make you comfortable." She reached out her hand and took his. "Come with me, Norman."

She led him along the teak-planked companionway, everything spit-and-polish, the air replete with the astringent scent of fresh paint and varnish. Epstein followed, his eyes fidgeting up and down her back side, half-wishing she'd put on some clothes, half-wishing not. They entered a formal dining room dominated by a table approximately the size of an airport runway. It was covered with white linen, silver place settings, crystal stemware, and candelabras, ready for a state dinner to break out at a moment's notice. From there into the sprawling main salon with its plush leather furniture. A small square table bedecked with dozens of black and white stones for the ancient Japanese board game *Go*. And a cherrywood bar in the corner.

Tiffani stepped straight to the bar. A crudité tray was stacked with raw celery, broccoli florets, snow peas, sliced fruit, wedges of pumpernickel bread, and a bowl of green goop that resembled guacamole. She chose a baby carrot and dipped it in the green stuff and slid it between her lips.

"I'm a vegan," she said, nibbling slowly. "I hope you don't mind. Are you hungry, Norman?"

"Oh, go ahead, please," he said nervously. "I've eaten."

"Well, then, what will you drink?"

"Oh, eh, club soda would be fine, thanks, Miss…"

"Tiffani, remember," she said, flashing a white smile.

She circled behind the bar and bent over and pulled out two glasses from below the counter top. Flesh spilled from her bikini top like butter from a cup. Epstein looked away, as if afraid of being struck blind. She saw him and smiled.

"Norman," she said in a near whisper, "I know we haven't spent much time together, but I feel as though we're friends. Don't you?"

His brown eyes darted and his brow contracted forming three horizontal creases across his forehead. "Friends? Oh! Sure! Yes! Of course!"

"Would you mind terribly if I made a personal observation?"

"I, I, guess not."

She leaned across the bar toward him, her voice barely audible. "Norman, you are too tight. You seem to be under so much pressure. I would hate to pick up the newspaper someday and see – *Norman Epstein, bank president, dies prematurely of heart attack. Doctors blame stress.*"

Epstein looked at her with a flustered expression, seeming not to know quite how to respond. "I would hate that too," he said finally.

"So many people go through life without really living."

"Yes. I guess. I mean I suppose so."

Tiffani combed her fingers through her auburn hair, her décolletage jiggling like jelly confection demanding to be acknowledged. "Norman, I think it would do you a world of good to relax. Let your hair down."

Before he could catch himself, his eyes flitted down and stole a quick peek. A kittenish smile crossed Tiffani's face. She tilted her head and wagged a finger at him.

"I saw that, you bad boy."

Norman's face turned the shade of a fire hydrant. "I'm so sorry. That was incredibly vulgar of me."

"Vulgar? Don't be silly. That's my point, Norman. Here we are, two healthy adults, together on one of the most luxurious yachts in the world, embarrassed to enjoy ourselves."

Epstein felt beads of perspiration drip down the nape of his neck. "You, you, you are probably right," he stammered.

She stepped from behind the bar, handed Norman his drink, and collapsed onto a leather love seat, aligning her limbs theatrically with the grace of an accomplished actress. She patted the cushion beside her.

"Come, Norman. Lighten up! Sit by me."

For a vegan Tiffani seemed to possess robust carnivorous impulses. She looked capable of devouring Epstein in a single bite. He looked down at her, took a gulp of his drink, and erupted in a coughing spasm. Tiffani quickly pulled him to the love seat and slapped his back like a mother burping her baby.

"Norman, I'm so sorry! That wasn't club soda. I thought some vodka would relax you. I should have told you. Now I'm a bad girl?"

"No, no," he said, gasping to regain control of his epiglottis. "You're not bad."

A coquettish gleam came into in her eyes. She leaned into him, pressing her lip to his ear. "I've got a wonderful idea."

A lightning bolt shot up his through Epstein. He felt the soft cushion of her right breast against his left arm. Her skin was as smooth as a satin slip. "What?"

"Sherwood won't be back for another hour. Let's go relax in the Jacuzzi."

"Oh," he said and grabbed the lapels of his business suit. "I'm not really dressed for that!"

Tiffani squeezed his arm and stood. "We have bathing suits in every size." She pointed down the corridor. "They're in the dressing room. Pick one out for yourself and meet me in the hot tub in two shakes of a bunny's tail."

She tiptoed from the room, wiggling her bottom as she disappeared. Minutes later, Epstein emerged in red-and-white striped trunks. His skin was as pink and hairless as a newborn hamster. Tiffani was splayed out in the bubbling tub, eyes closed, flaming hair cascading like red water over her chest. She held a champagne flute in her left hand and a magnum of Dom Pérignon was cradled in an ice bucket beside the tub with two yellow ribbons strewn over it.

"Is that you, Norman," she murmured. "What took you so long?"

Epstein stepped into the tub and stood knee deep in the hot swirling water. He looked down at her, then at the yellow ribbons.

"Oh, my God!" he blurted.

Tiffani bolted upright. "What? What's the matter, Norman?"

"You!" He pointed at the yellow ribbons. "That's your bathing suit. You're naked."

Tiffani looked down at herself, then up at Norman standing there with his mouth agape. His skinny legs were quivering like fiddle strings.

"Oh, that. I just love the feel of the bubbles on my skin. I hope I'm not making you uncomfortable?"

She slid down into the warm water. Her breasts poked up through the froth like a pair of pink ballistic missiles – aimed straight at him. She looked at his bathing suit and smiled. "Oh! You *are* tense."

She closed her eyes again, waggled her empty flute in the air, and spoke in a voice wispy as a baby's breath.

"Norman, please be a dear and pour me another."

Bradys Run

CHAPTER TWENTY TWO

THE RED ROADMAP of David Grand's veined nose poked over the brim of a snifter holding three fingers of straight Kentucky bourbon. Bourbon is the quintessential American spirit. True bourbon is made only in the United States, distilled predominantly from sweet corn and aged, by law, in new charred oak casks. H`e'd ordered a Woodford Reserve, considered by many to be the benchmark of bourbons. It was certainly the most expensive. Sherwood Steele was paying, so why not? He swirled the glass to release the amber liquid's aroma and breathed in the smoky bouquet. His practiced snout picked up the scent of ripe banana with a trace of fudge and honeyed vanilla, residue from the oak barrel it was aged in. He tilted the glass to his lips and downed it in a single swallow. Jarrett Griffin sat across the table, his pinched face trained on Grand while his mind brooded over Steele's last words to them before he flew off.

"*Or else* what, do you think?"

The mayor closed his eyes, luxuriating in the burn of the whiskey cascading down his throat. Then he blinked back to the present and considered Griffin. "*Or else* we don't get our two million dollars?"

"*Or else* we go to prison?"

"Steele's not stupid. He knows if we go, he goes too."

Even after Steele's brusque exit, Grand and Griffin had stayed at the Shangri-La Club and played a free round golf. Now they sat on the clubhouse balcony overlooking the Atlantic and watched long crooked shadows slant across the verdant green fairways.

"Steele's got a lot riding on this," Griffin said. He held his glass close to his mouth like baseball catchers hold their mitts when they talk to their pitcher on the mound, just in case Sherwood staffed his club with lip readers. "If he thinks we fucked him I wouldn't put it past him to put out contracts on us."

The mayor leaned toward Griffin and whispered harshly. "Don't get paranoid, Jarrett! Sherwood may be a cut-throat businessman, but he's no killer."

A waiter came out carrying plates stacked high with barbecue pork, mango salsa, mashed sweet potatoes, and steins of Guinness. All courtesy of Sherwood Steele. They ate while, below, sprinklers bathed the lush eighteenth green, spawning mini-rainbows in the air.

"I think Sherwood is capable of more than you think," Griffin said.

"That's preposterous!"

"Preposterous? Who do you think was behind that fire at the beach?"

"The motel fire? The one that wacko in the mushroom hat, what's his name…"

"Bigelow?"

"…Bigelow was ranting about it?"

"Steele needs that property. It's part of his *'grand plan'*," Griffin said, using his fingers derisively as quotation marks. "And suddenly it burns down. You think that's a coincidence?"

"Jesus Christ!" Grand said. His corpulent cheeks had taken on the same hue as the sauce slathered on his pork.

"In case you haven't noticed, David, when it comes to money Sherwood's vicious as a pit bull."

Grand stopped stuffing his face for a moment and mulled Griffin's words. After a minute he seemed to come to some conclusion. "You're right, Jarrett. If we're gonna collect our two million we have to be just as ferocious."

"But how?"

"I'm no pit bull, but I do own one. Let's let him be our attack dog."

***

Two hours later Grand and Griffin were back in Fort Lauderdale standing in a tenth floor condominium overlooking Port Everglades inlet looking up at a man who towered over them.

Roscoe Anderson was the City of Fort Lauderdale's Director of Building Code Enforcement. He was what some would consider odd looking, with stooped shoulders, which is not uncommon among tall men, not enough hair to make a respectable Indian scalp, and eyes that pointed in opposite directions. He smiled down at his two visitors, who weren't sure which eye to look at.

"You certainly live well, Roscoe," said Griffin. "For a civil servant."

"Life is good – when it's Christmas all year round. Right, mayor?"

Before Grand could respond a foghorn droned in the darkness. They turned and looked out the window. A cruise ship was sailing between the harbor's granite jetties on its way out to sea. Its behemoth red smokestacks were as high as Roscoe's condo.

"*Queen Elizabeth II*," he said.

Griffin nodded. "I read somewhere she burns a gallon of diesel every six inches she moves"

"Magnificent, isn't she?" said Grand. "Over three football fields long."

"Almost as long as Codeman*,*" Roscoe said.

"Codeman*?*"

"My fishing boat." He looked at the mayor. "Thanks to friends like you, David."

"I was a good Santa to you, wasn't I Roscoe?"

"You were that. And now you're my boss." He saluted the mayor like he was a four star general. "What can I do for you gents?"

As Director of Building Code Enforcement, Roscoe had a well-earned reputation as a fetch-dog for builders. Always willing to come to heel for a snack. Which was why, even though the city paid him a respectable ninety thousand dollars a year, he could afford to live so lavishly in this million dollar condo, and own several investment properties, not to mention Codeman.

Grand had known him for thirty years. Once, when the mayor was still a contractor he built a one hundred-unit apartment complex. City code required four electrical outlets per room, but Grand had mistakenly installed only three. Anderson could have forced him to fix it, which would have cost Grand two hundred thousand dollars in labor costs and lost rentals. Instead, he slipped Roscoe an envelope stuffed with ten thousand in cash and the problem went away. Anderson saw it as performing a public service. He'd spared a respected businessman a draconian penalty. Tenants could move in on schedule. And the Roscoe Anderson Retirement Fund had been augmented. There were no losers. He liked it when everybody won. But something about this felt different.

"What can I do for you gents?" he said again with a nervous laugh.

Grand and Griffin looked at each other and a silent message passed between them. The mayor clapped Anderson on the shoulder and led him to a bar in the corner of the room while Griffin remained out of hearing distance.

"Roscoe, we go back a long way, don't we?"

"Back to the flood, mayor."

"That's why I've come to you, old buddy. I need your assistance. And if I get it this will be a very merry Christmas for you."

"Mr. Mayor," he said slowly, "what exactly are we talking about?"

Grand stepped to the bar and tore a sheet off a message pad by the telephone. He layed it on the glass top, picked up a pencil, and scrawled a number. He held the paper up to Anderson's face.

"Roscoe, I want you to imagine a dollar sign in front of that figure. Then imagine depositing it in that numbered Cayman Island bank account I'm guessing you have."

The building inspector stared at the paper for several seconds and his strabismal eyes began to oscillate in their sockets like BBs in a funnel.

"We need a grenade thrower, Roscoe. Are you our man?"

The Code Enforcement director smiled. "Like I said, what can I do for you fellas?"

Brady's Run

CHAPTER TWENTY THREE

JOHN McCARTY AMBLED into the Sea Shanty late in the afternoon. His white fire investigator's shirt was mottled with black smudges.

"You look like Pig Pen," Max Brady said.

"Usually do this time of day," said McCarty, his soot-soiled face lit in a wan smile. "Got any wings?"

"Coming right up."

"Hotter the better."

"You've got a real yen for hot stuff. Beer? Or maybe you'd prefer a *Blazing Saddle*?"

"What's that?"

"Blackberry brandy, one hundred fifty one-proof rum, and a match. Tastes like a flamethrower."

"Sounds delish, but a coupla *Rolling Rocks* will do me fine. Then I'll be ready for the pillow. Been working a three alarm since before dawn."

"Fire seems to be a real steady business," Brady said. "Good for job security."

"Somewhere in America today a house catches fire every forty-five seconds."

"You oughta let that place burn down before somebody gets hurt."

"You might be surprised to know the Great Fire of 1666 destroyed half of London, but only killed eight people?"

Brady slid a frosty green bottle of Rolling Rock across the bar. "You're a walking, talking Encyclopedia of Conflagration."

"Max, you're showing your age. Encyclopedias are so yesterday. Now it's all about Google."

"What's a Google?"

Brady stepped into the tiny galley behind the bar and fetched McCarty's five-alarm wings. Baseball playoffs were underway on the TV overhead. The screen against the far wall showed a pencil-necked meteorologist in an ill-fitting suit giving new coordinates on *Hurricane Phyllis.* The storm had taken a dogleg right and was five hundred miles out in the Gulf of Mexico coming hard and fast straight at South Florida.

"Maybe she'll turn again," McCarty said. "If not, we've got two days."

"Plenty of time to batten the hatches."

The weather geek was saying *Phyllis's* winds were blowing at one hundred fifty miles an hour. Brady felt a chill run through him. He looked at McCarty. He'd already finished his wings. Brady had never seen anyone down a plate so fast.

"Hungry?"

"Not anymore." McCarty quelled the inferno in his maw with a swig of *Rolling Rock.* "If you had a little more cleavage, Max, you could give Hooters a run for its money."

"Think I'd look good in orange short-shorts?"

Three young women strolled in wearing bathing suits and assorted shades of skin. One was dark as a macadamia nut, but her friends looked like they'd been marinating in ragu sauce. Brady and McCarty cringed. Abstaining from sunscreen was the cardinal sin of most vacationers. These girls would atone in their own private hell. God forbid anyone touch them tonight. Tomorrow their skin would blister. The next day they'd itch like crazy. By the time they got home they'd be peeling like paint on a scrapyard car.

Brady stepped around the bar to their table. "I'd strongly suggest a heavy coat of aloe," he said to the lobster girls.

"Will you rub it on?" the brown girl asked, beaming at him like he'd just brought her a dozen roses.

She was a local girl. Her name was Cheryl. She'd been in the Shanty many times before. Cheryl didn't wear a wedding band and seemed like a girl who never would. She had all the right parts, but they didn't quite fit together into an attractive woman. She'd made it clear to Brady more than once that, if he was interested, she was available. Overtures like that were not uncommon. They usually came from tourist girls who'd come to town looking for some carefree vacation love but came up empty and were willing to settle for a roll in the sheets with a tall, handsome barkeep.

"I'm sorry," he said to Cheryl, "but a rubdown could lead me to violate my vow."

She looked at him uncertainly. "Vow?"

"Chastity."

"What?"

"I'm a Benedictine. You know, a monk."

The girls stared at him, mouths agape, then burst into laughter like Brady was the funniest guy in the world.

"You've got quite a set up here," McCarty said when he returned to the bar.

"I have a firm rule," he said with a smile. "No fooling around with patrons." His face turned serious. He leaned across the bar. "By the way, I found some things you should know."

He told him about the string of motel transactions he'd dug up at the courthouse, including the daisy chains. All in a four square block area. And how the Klums and Jonas Bigelow, whose motels were in the same tract, were being pressured to sell their motels. Both by real estate queen Cherry Hampton who happened also to be the realtor on the daisy chain deals. He recounted his visit to Hampton's office.

"I told Cherry she'd be hearing from you."

"Do you really think she might be a connected?"

"She wasn't exactly tickled by my questions."

"I'll give her a call," McCarty said then stood up and examined himself in the mirror behind the bar. He straightened his disheveled shirt and wiped the soot stains from his face. "Meanwhile, as the self-appointed goodwill ambassador for the City of Fort Lauderdale, I am obliged to perform my civic duty and make these young ladies feel welcome."

"I thought you were ready for bed."

A modest smile shone on the fire investigator's face.

Bradys Run

CHAPTER TWENTY FOUR

WHEN THE RED Jaguar pulled up, Olga Klum was sifting through the charred remains of a life gone up in smoke. Through tear-misted eyes she had managed to salvage a few relics, family photographs, a diamond necklace Gunther gave her on their twenty fifth wedding anniversary, a ten-inch tall porcelain of a nude woman, circa 1870, willed to her by her mother in Düsseldorf.

Olga watched in dismay as a striking blonde woman in an elegant chartreuse pants suit climbed out of the sports car and walked directly toward her. She felt as raggedy as an abandoned garden. Hair wrapped in an old scarf, no make-up, eyes punctuated by dark half-circles. She wanted to hide.

"Mrs. Klum, do you remember me?" Olga looked at the woman like she was from another planet. "I'm Cherry Hampton."

"Oh, yes," Olga said numbly.

"I want you to know how terribly sorry I am about the fire." Hampton said it with feigned compassion, a talent she'd acquired from husband number two, Flip, the crooked Congressman. "The Pelican's Nest was such a lovely motel. It's a great loss to the beach area."

"That's very kind."

Hampton's eyes swept the property. A demolition team was feverishly trying to clear debris before *Hurricane Phyllis* reached South Florida. An old man was shuffling like a sleepwalker around the flotsam-filled pool. She was startled to realize it was Gunther Klum. The last time she saw him he'd been a strapping, robust man. Now, stooped and spiritless, he looked like a lost soul. She turned back to Olga, who was primping wild strands of hair.

"Mrs. Klum, I'll be quick. I spoke to a Mr. Brady. He is a friend of yours?"

"Max? Yes, a very dear friend."

"He indicated you and your husband might be interested in selling this property now."

Olga gazed at her for several seconds, dazed and lethargic, as if she was medicated.

"We haven't decided," a man's voice said.

Hampton turned to find Gunther staring down at her. His cheeks were covered with silver stubble and his countenance was droopy, like the bones of his face were rubber.

"Mr. Klum, I was deeply sorry to hear about the fire."

"Thank you. We're waiting to hear about the insurance money. And a man from the city came by about an hour ago."

"Who was that? If you don't mind me asking. I know a lot of people."

Gunther thought for a moment. "I think he said his name was Anderson."

Hampton was buoyed to hear Roscoe Anderson was on the case. "What did Mr. Anderson have to say?"

"That it could take us two years, or maybe three, to get the permits and rebuild."

Gunther's lax eyes and listless manner encouraged Hampton. He looked like a beaten man. "That's an awfully long time. What are you going to do?"

Klum draped his left arm around his wife's shoulders. "We don't know."

"I see. Well, then what I have to tell you may come as good news. After Mr. Brady's visit I spoke to my client who, you may recall, was quite avid about buying your motel."

"Who was that again?" Gunther said.

"I'm sorry, he has asked me not to identify him at this time. Of course, he was disappointed when you declined his previous offers. He hoped you might reconsider."

"Reconsider?"

"Well, it's actually an incredibly generous proposal. Quite frankly – and I hope you won't repeat this – I don't think it's a wise business decision on his part. I told him as much. But he's the client. He wants to offer you the same amount he did before the fire."

Gunther looked at her dully for a long moment, then his eyes widened.

"He's still willing to pay us three million dollars? Just for the land? But that makes no sense."

"I agree, Mr. Klum. That's to your benefit, though. I assume your insurance will pay the cost of rebuilding the Pelican's Nest – regardless of whether you actually rebuild."

Gunther's blue eyes narrowed. "How would you know that?"

"Standard coverage. Based on the square footage and current construction costs, I estimate you should collect at least one million dollars."

"I see you've been doing your homework," Klum said, watching her closely now.

"My client is a very sophisticated businessman. He ran some calculations. He assumes you also have loss of income insurance to compensate you for a certain period of time. That's typically one year. My client estimates that should amount to another half million dollars."

"Around that."

"Which means if you sell you will walk away with four point five million dollars." Hampton's face was bright as a full moon. "I'd call that a home run."

Klum took a deep breath trying to calm his pounding heart as he absorbed the numbers.

"What do you say, Mr. Klum? My client is eager. He'd like an immediate answer."

"Well, this is very sudden. I don't know what to say. We'll have to think about it."

Hampton scrutinized Klum's weary face. The bombshell offer had plainly rocked him.

"Look, this storm is supposed to hit us tomorrow. With luck it won't be as bad as they're predicting. My office should be reopen the day after tomorrow. Can you give me an answer by then?"

Olga had slid out from Gunther's arm and walked off to continue foraging through the ruins. He watched her crouch down and wipe ashes off something and wondered if she'd found the diamond earrings that matched the necklace he'd given her.

"Yes," he said in a subdued voice, "I think we can let you know by then."

Minutes later Hampton was behind the wheel of her Jaguar driving south on A1A. She lit a cigarette then punched a number on her cell phone.

"I just left them. There's no way in hell they'll turn it down. It looks like a go."

Bradys Run

CHAPTER TWENTY FIVE

BARBRA STREISAND WAS belting out *On A Clear Day (You Can See Forever)* over the patio speakers. Jesse Rosinski turned his eyes to the gloaming sky and decided his experiment wasn't working. Not that he really expected it to. *Hurricane Phyllis* was coming and not even Babs was going to stop her.

Rosinski was a tall, thin man with a shaved head and bushy mustache. He dipped a net into the swimming pool of the Dew Drop Inn, a prim, immaculate, salmon-and-white Caribbean-style bed-and-breakfast. The inn's web site touted it as *Where the Boys Are,* the title of the iconic Spring Break film about Fort Lauderdale. When it came to the Dew Drop, though, the words carried an entirely different connotation.

At the moment, the motel's only blemish was a vagrant clump of Jacaranda leaves blown into the water by a tempestuous wind. Jesse scooped out the soggy foliage and deposited it in the cuttings bin just as a man walked through the front gate.

"*Gooood* day," Jesse said in his most congenial voice. "Welcome to the Dew Drop Inn."

The visitor wore dark slacks, white shirt, and a skinny black tie. Not standard attire at the Dew Drop. Nor was his surly expression. He handed Rosinski a card.

Roscoe Anderson
Code Enforcement Director
City of Fort Lauderdale

"Oh, that sounds exciting," said Jesse, inspecting the card. "Do you enforce *secret* codes? I love James Bond. That Daniel Craig is a real man, if you get my drift."

Jesse could see revulsion scroll across Roscoe Anderson's pasty face, even with his bollixed eyes. He was tempted to say: *Get over it already! It's the 21st Century, for God's sake!* But alarm bells were ringing in his amygdala, the fight or flight portion of the temporal lobe. He bit his tongue.

"No, it's not like James Bond," Roscoe said. His voice was cold as a meat locker. "And it's no secret. The laws in this city are very public. You have disregarded them."

Jesse felt queasy. *I told Bill!* He tried to avoid Anderson's eyes and flipped his hand toward an open door on the second floor.

"Let me get my partner. He handles all the paperwork. He's upstairs changing bed linens. I'm the gardener. And the pool boy. And I tend bar at happy hour every evening. *Do drop in!*"

Anderson glanced impatiently at his watch. "Hurry up and get your boyfriend."

Bill Weiss ran down the stairs barefoot in a red Speedo and muscle T-shirt. Shorter than Jesse, he had close-cropped black hair and arms as thick as fence posts. He thrust his hand out to Anderson. The code enforcer slapped a yellowed document into his palm.

"I've got bad news for you...boys. You owe the city a lot of money."

They'd met when Bill was a Broadway dancer in *A Chorus Line* and Jesse worked wardrobe. It was the first steady relationship for either man and they were happier than they'd ever been. They decided to forsake the Great White Way for a more serene life in the sun. So they pooled their savings and bought the Dew Drop Inn. At the closing, the City of Fort Lauderdale demanded they sign an agreement to fix several code violations. That was August 25, 2001. Two weeks later – just as they were opening their doors – America exploded. People stopped traveling, stopped taking vacations, stopped spending money. Bill and Jesse put off the promised renovations and the work was never done.

"You promised to install hurricane windows and put on a new roof within six months of signing that document, or begin paying a fine," said Roscoe. "I've highlighted the amount."

Bill scanned the paper until he found the figure. Suddenly he couldn't breathe. "A thousand dollars a week! You must be kidding!"

"I don't joke. As of today, your fine adds up to two-hundred-ten thousand dollars. I expect you're looking at another hundred fifty grand to replace the roof and windows."

Bill clenched his arms, trying to hold himself together. "That's three-hundred-sixty thousand dollars," he said weakly. "You can't do that. You'll destroy us!"

"I can do that," Roscoe snarled, "and I will. Here's the deal. If the work's not completed in thirty days, I'm going to shut you down."

Jesse listened in horror. He and Bill had about as much chance going up against the city as a butter knife in a bayonet fight. The code enforcement chief knew it too. Jesse detected a harsh glint of pleasure in Anderson's left eye.

"You cocksucker," he said.

"Cocksucker? Roscoe said, turning toward the gate. "I thought that was your department, mister. Or whatever you are."

Bradys Run

CHAPTER TWENTY SIX

MAX BRADY DIDN'T need a weatherman to tell him *Phyllis's* cyclopean eye was trained on Fort Lauderdale. It felt like judgment day. Towering black thunderheads galloped across the sky like horsemen at the apocalypse. The ocean roiled and wind gusts were launching grains of beach sand through the air like millions of tiny needles.

A1A was deserted and Brady didn't expect much business today. Instead, he was whipping up provisions for the Sea Shanty hurricane party. The bar's shutters rolled down as easy as a garage door, so he'd button up later. Victor's house was being secured by Charles. He had only one other concern.

When he stepped onto the roof, Rose Becker was perched on a ladder fastening window guards to the roof of her greenhouse. He paused for a moment to admire her taut calves before announcing himself.

"Reporting for duty," he said and saluted. "What can I do?"

Rose looked down. Her black ponytail was whipping in the wind and she wore a bemused expression on her face. "If you'd like, you can move the benches into the shed."

"Sir, yes, sir," he said with another salute.

Brady hoisted benches, barbells, and exercise mats into a metal storage shed while Rose harvested dozens of chimes jangling like clusters of cacophonous grapes. They secured the shed doors then inspected the greenhouse one last time. Rose's flashlight cut through the murk illuminating hundreds of butterflies fluttering erratically, like a swarm of bats fraught with foreboding.

"Why don't they call them *flutterflies*?" Brady asked.

"In colonial days most butterflies were yellow. Colonists believed they were witches who turned into winged creatures and flew around stealing butter."

"Fascinating! Do you think your butterflies have butterflies in their stomachs because they know the storm is coming?"

Rose shined the light at him. His face was a picture of sincerity. "Brady, where do you come up with something like that?"

She turned and stood in the dark, backlit by the flashlight beam. Coils of black hair dangled like delicate corkscrews at the hollow of her neck. Brady could see her long eyelashes and the soft follicles of hair on her cheeks and had to fight off a sudden impulse to lean over and kiss the white arc of her throat. Rose turned and caught him staring. A curious expression came across her face. Brady couldn't tell if she was happy or sad, or something in between. She opened her mouth to speak, but the words seemed to stick in her throat. Then she flicked off the light and the spell was broken.

"How about a power shake?" she said.

"I could use one."

"You earned it."

"Happy to be of service, madame," he said and bowed.

"Hey, what happened to the salute and *'Sir, yes, sir'*?"

"Suddenly you don't seem like a *sir*."

Bradys Run

CHAPTER TWENTY SEVEN

THE SHANGRI- LA'S big main cabin seemed to shrink under Norman Epstein's fitful pacing. He was sweating like a sprinkler had gone off inside his Brooks Brothers suit. His once-crisp white shirt was sticking to his skin like flypaper.

Epstein was in the midst of an extreme bout of self-flagellation that would have warmed the cockles of Carmelites everywhere. His brief splash in the Jacuzzi with Tiffani Bandeaux had been stupid and self-ish and could have destroyed his family's happiness. Maybe not Eva, his wife, who was incapable of real joy. But his kids. He would rather die than see that happen. He vowed never to be so self-indulgent again. Then he heard the helicopter. A minute later Sherwood Steele rushed in.

"Norman, I'm so sorry. I got stuck with a roomful of architects and engineers. Gotta spoon feed them everything I want or they'll screw it up. I hope Tiffani was good company."

Steele saw Epstein's flushed face and sweat-soaked shirt. He looked like a man hanging from a ledge by his fingernails.

"What's the matter, old friend? Everything okay with Eva?"

"F-f-fine, Sherwood. Fine."

"You're a lucky man to have a woman like her. And those beautiful children? Barry, what's he now, ten? And Sarah? A real kewpie doll! She'll be fighting off the boys before you know it."

Epstein stepped to a porthole. The scene outside looked like the end of the world was near. Black clouds racing overhead, palm trees undulating wildly, the Intracoastal chock-a-block with vessels pitching through rancorous black water on their way to safe harbor.

"That damned storm's getting close," Steele said, retreating behind the bar. "Didn't think Hendricks could land the chopper on deck. He was a Special Forces pilot in Afghanistan. Put her down soft as a head on a pillow. How about a drink, Norman?"

"No, I don't want a drink," Epstein snapped.

"Norman, it can't be that bad."

"It is bad, Sherwood. Very bad. We're in big trouble."

"Who's in trouble? You? Eva?"

"You know goddamned well who's in trouble. I'm in trouble. You're in trouble. The bank is in trouble. Everything. The whole thing is going to collapse like a house of cards."

Steele stood behind the bar swirling a glass wand in a flagon of vodka and ice. He could smell fear like a jungle animal and right now Epstein had the scent of a man in panic. Steele poured the translucent liquid into crooked-stemmed martini glasses, dropped an olive into each, and handed one to Epstein.

"Pour this into your think tank, Norman. You'll see things in a whole new light."

Epstein slammed the glass on the bar. Vodka splashed over the rim onto his hand like a wave breaking onto rocks.

"Sherwood, this is beyond serious. Everything's disintegrating. I'm juggling the books like they're chainsaws. I can't do it anymore. It's a miracle the auditors haven't caught us yet."

"Relax, Norman. Drink your drink. It's going to be okay. I've got a plan."

"Sherwood, you've got to find cash. *Fast!* You've got to start selling assets."

"No, no, no, Norman. That's out of the question."

"You must!" Epstein's voice was becoming manic. "This boat's gotta be worth fifty million. You've got another twenty tied up in that mansion you're building. And the country club could bring at least thirty million, maybe forty."

Steele sipped his martini with the calm assurance of a man who never entertained doubt. "Norman, you don't get it. Perception is power. I liquidate and I become a laughingstock. If that happens the project crumbles."

Epstein collapsed into a chair, head down, running his fingers through still-wet hair. "Sherwood, there's nothing left to do. If you don't come up with a lot of cash immediately, I've got to call in your loans."

Steele stood in the middle of the room glowering down at the banker. He wedged an olive between his white teeth, cleaved it down the middle, and plopped the remains back into the icy liquid. Epstein raised his dismal face, seeming on the brink of tears, but shrank under Steele's hot glare.

Sherwood spoke in a low flat tone. "Norman Epstein. You poor bastard! I *made* you! And now you try to *fuck* me?"

"I have no choice, Sherwood."

"You were lending money to Cuban fucking boat people when I found you. I made you CEO of the hottest bank in the hottest market in America. You own a beautiful home. You pamper your two fat kids and that hag wife."

"How dare you call Eva a hag."

"Well, if she's not now, she will be."

Steele picked up a remote control, jabbed a button, and shades descended on the cabin windows. A large white screen slid down against the far wall. He pointed the remote like a laser weapon at a box hanging from the ceiling. A beam of light shot out and an image popped onto the screen. Epstein's mouth dropped open.

"I see Tiffani *was* good company," said Steele.

The banker's eyes widened to the size of silver dollars as he watched Tiffani naked in the hot tub. He saw himself shed the red-and-white striped bathing trunks and engage in some brief foreplay followed by a bout of spirited coupling. Steele fast forwarded through the video like he was searching for highlights in a football game, slowing when the splashing became particularly paganistic, turning up the volume when he grunted or she groaned. Every minute felt like a lifetime to Epstein, yet he couldn't turn his eyes away. Steele finally shut off the homespun porn show and the window shades ascended.

"Norman, you are a revelation!" he said with an unpleasant laugh. "Beneath that meek bean-counter façade dwells the heart of a wild stallion!"

Epstein sat wilted, his head drooping, as though his neck couldn't support the weight of what his eyes had just seen. Tiffani Bandeaux walked in without knocking, serene as a cloudless sky, attired in white boat pants and tailored navy blazer, her hair dry and coiffed, her make-up immaculate. She strode past Epstein like he was invisible and handed Steele an envelope, then exited without a word.

"Don't feel bad, Norman," said Steele, trying to sound sympathetic. "Tiffani could turn a drag queen into a raging heterosexual. No man alive could resist her charms." He dropped the envelope on the coffee table in front of Epstein. "That's your copy. Eva might enjoy it. Show it to her. Maybe it'll make her horny. Maybe she'll perform some of the same tricks on you that Tiffani did. God knows you need the relaxation."

Epstein looked at the envelope, then at Steele staring down at him with cold-eyed consideration, a crooked smile frozen on his oily face. Norman stood and faced him, the veins in his throat bulging like cords.

"You bastard," he said with all the menace he could muster. "You're blackmailing me?"

Steele nonchalantly sipped his martini. "Come on, Norman. You just had the most incredible fuck of your life. Something you'll remember till the day you die. You should thank me for that."

"You rat. You snake. You…"

"Let's keep the analogies to a single species. I prefer mammals but, if you must, reptile rather than rodent. Lizard or crocodile would do."

"How about rat snake, Sherwood? Nothing's lower than that."

Steele stepped over to the chair and layed a hand on his shoulder. "Calm down."

Epstein pushed him away. "Don't touch me, you sonofabitch! I'm not going to settle down. I won't be blackmailed. I'm calling in those notes today."

Steele snatched the envelope from the table and waved it in his face.

"Do that and by sundown this will be all over the World Wide Web. Every member of the bank's Board of Directors will be e-mailed a copy. So will Eva. They say adultery is the easiest sin to commit but hardest to forgive. Is that what you want, Norman?"

Epstein's face was white as his shirt. He fell back in the chair and began to sob. Steele glared at his bank CEO with undisguised loathing. He handed him his handkerchief. Epstein wiped his face and blew his nose, continuing to snivel.

"Get a grip on yourself, Norman," Steele said gently. "All is not lost. I told you. I've got a plan. It will save me. It will save you. And it will save the bank. Trust me!"

Bradys Run

CHAPTER TWENTY EIGHT

"TRUST ME, MR. JONAS," said Delbert Tanner. "You don't have to worry none about no flying cannonballs."

Long experience had taught Jonas Bigelow he *could* trust his Jamaican handyman. Bigelow was standing in the courtyard of the Coral Reef Motel considering a cluster of coconuts dangling like green bowling balls from a palm tree. He felt the ground tremble from one of the massive gray swells crashing onto Fort Lauderdale Beach a half block away. The Atlantic was flexing its muscles in earnest.

A minute earlier Jonas had hollered over the whistling wind. "Delbert, I'm afraid these coconuts are gonna fly around like cannonballs."

A husky man with skin the color of a coffee bean, Delbert was hurling aluminum lounge chairs into the swimming pool and watching them drift lazily to the bottom where they would ride out *Hurricane Phyllis*.

"I wouldna be worryin', Mr. Jonas," he said.

"Damnation, Delbert! When you say *Mr. Jonas* you make me sound like a colonial plantation owner. It's *Jonas*."

"Yes, sir, Mr. Jonas."

"Jonas!"

"Sorry. Da wind ain't gonna budge dem coconuts. Dey ain't comin' down till dey good and ready."

A white car with a yellow license plate pulled into one of the parking spaces in front of the motel. A tall bald man got out wearing a white shirt, thin black tie, and dour face.

"This guy's from the city, Delbert. He should know." Jonas turned to the newcomer. "Glad you stopped. I was wondering if we need to cut down them coconuts."

The city man looked at Jonas and Delbert without responding, then handed Jonas his card. The old man decided on the spot he didn't like the guy. He examined the card. *Goddamned bureaucrat!*

"What can I do for you, Mr. Roscoe Anderson?"

"I'm here to deliver this notice," Anderson said with cold efficiency. He handed a white envelope to Jonas, who looked at it for some clue as to its content.

"Looks important. You gonna keep me in suspense or do I have to read it?"

"What it says is that you made illegal improvements to your property without obtaining proper permits."

Bigelow regarded Anderson like he was an irritating rash. He *had* made renovations to the Coral Reef. A new swimming pool, a new air-conditioning system, and a paint job that changed the motel's color from lemon yellow to turquoise and pink. Delbert and a cadre of Jamaican laborers did most of the work at half the price of companies listed in the Yellow Pages. Jonas had intentionally disregarded the permit process. *And apparatchik's like this cock-eyed bastard.* If the city busted his balls, he reasoned, he'd pay a small fine. No big deal.

He waved the papers at Anderson. "You throw this applesauce at me *today*?"

"I thought you'd want to know." Roscoe's voice was sodden with insolence. "As of this minute, you are shut down."

Shock registered on Jonas's face. "What? Is that some kinda threat?"

"No threat. You are out of business until you fulfill your obligations under Fort Lauderdale City Ordinance Number 10-6752."

Bigelow's first impulse was to punch the cheeky bastard. *Maybe straighten them eyeballs!* But he looked at the card again and decided it was no time to lose his temper.

"Explain to me *Mr. Roscoe Anderson*," he said, spitting out the name, "what in God's name is Ordinance Number Ten dash whatever the fuck you said?"

Anderson didn't flinch at the old man's wrath. Bigelow was a toothless tiger. The more indignant he got, the more Roscoe relished his task.

"It's all in the letter. Suffice to say you didn't obtain permits for the work and, under the law, you must re-plat."

Re-plat was a dirty word to Jonas. Anderson was saying he'd have to re-survey, re-record, and re-register his land with a complete legal description and detailed map. His friend, John Benson, had been forced to re-plat last year when he renovated the Seabreeze Motel. It took him more than a year and cost thirty thousand dollars. Now this pencil pusher was telling him he was being shut down, maybe for a year?

"Don't think I don't know what you're doing," Jonas said. "You city sonsabitches are trying to squeeze us little guys outa here."

"It's been fifty years since this property was platted," Anderson said. "When you make major improvements, Ordinance 10-6752 requires re-platting."

Jonas shouted over the rising wind. "You didn't shut down the Seabreeze."

"He had proper permits."

Jonas stared in disbelief. Behind him, Delbert Tanner stood listening with growing alarm. Bigelow's face was red and his head shaking.

"You *ain't* shutting me down," he shouted.

"That's what you get, Mr. Bigelow, for breaking the law."

Jonas lunged and almost had his hands on Anderson's throat before Delbert thrust out his burly brown arms and wrapped him in a bear hug.

"No, Mr. Jonas. They'll arrest you and put you in jail. It ain't worth it."

Jonas tried to break loose but Delbert was too strong. He kicked at Anderson, who backed out of reach as Bigelow sputtered futilely.

"I'll kick your ass you, you, you…fucking *mandarin!* I'll go to the newspaper. I'll go all the way to the goddamned White House. You ain't runnin' me out! Do you hear me? I ain't goin'. Get the hell off my property!"

Anderson had already opened his car door and was gone before Delbert released Jonas. He drove two blocks, pulled off the road, and dialed a telephone number.

"That old madman's flaky as a pie crust. He ain't like the queers. I don't think he's gonna go quietly."

Bradys Run

CHAPTER TWENTY NINE

THE SEA SHANTY hurricane party was a screwball tradition spawned by three straight years of major hurricanes. Outside it looked like Dante's *Second Circle of Hell,* the one where souls guilty of the sin of lust are condemned to be battered about for eternity by violent storms.

Three hundred miles to the south *Hurricane Phyllis* was clobbering Cuba. But her leading edge was already unleashing angry bands of wind and rain on Fort Lauderdale. Pitchforks of lightning were flashing across the sky. The Atlantic was a lawless cauldron. Tugs boats were chugging through a riot of foam, nuzzling up to tankers and cruise ships, and prodding them into Port Everglades.

At the same time, a dozen or so members of the beach's lunatic fringe were assembled inside the Shanty for Max Brady's soiree. For some reason, the genesis of which none of them seemed to recall, they were armed with a vague notion that they could mollify Mother Nature by toasting her with mass quantities of firewater. At least it was better than a human sacrifice. And, even if it didn't work, it was a good excuse for a party.

Thunder rumbled over the sound of the juke box blaring Creedence Clearwater Revival's *Who'll Stop the Rain.* A gale hit the building like a kidney punch, producing ripples in the lamp-shaped glasses into which

Brady was pouring a concoction of rums, liqueurs, and juices that he called *Liquid Lunacy*. He set one on the bar in front of Rose Becker.

"For Madame Butterfly. Drink enough *Liquid Lunacy* and you'll forget all about *Phyllis*."

"Or just not care," said Rose, who rarely allowed alcohol to cross her lips. The storm bashes had become one of the few exceptions. She took a sip and cringed. "Jesus, Brady, this stuff's lethal."

"Like your power shakes?"

"My power shakes never killed anybody. Can you say the same about your *Liquid Lunacy*?"

By six o'clock the Shanty was a pain-free zone, a muddle of staccato voices, raucous music, and the shrill whistle of rowdy wind. The only people not taking part in the revelry were Bill Weiss and Jesse Rosinski from the Dew Drop Inn, who sat at the end of the bar with faces as long as stretched taffy. Everyone liked the two men, even Jonas, who had once been an unrepentant homophobe. After he got to know Bill and Jesse his feelings changed.

"Aw, let 'em be," Jonas said recently to one his lodgers at the Coral Reef who had been railing about Fort Lauderdale's small patch of gay beach. "I was born left-handed. They were born queer. So what? They ain't hurtin' nobody."

Jonas had downed several *Liquid Lunacies* and was getting as blustery as the weather. He shouted over the music: "What are you two plotting down there? Join the party."

Bill and Jesse reluctantly slipped off their barstools, eyes downcast, and stepped to the center of the giddy circle of merrymakers. Jesse was wearing a sad grin while Bill gnawed his lip.

"We have an announcement," said Jesse.

"Don't tell me you guys like women now," Jonas said.

"Nothing *that* appalling." Jesse looked at Rose and Sunny Regan. "No offense."

"None taken," Rose said. "Brady, shut off that record machine so we can hear."

"Sir, yes, sir, Madame Butterfly," he said with a salute and pulled the plug.

"I think you've been drinking too much of your profits," Rose said.

"Profits?" He sounded more than a little lubricated. He held up a glass of *Liquid Lunacy*. "I'll have you know I'm not making a plugged nickel on these tasty treats?"

"That's why you're our favorite mixocologist," Jonas said.

"Mixologist," Sunny corrected.

They raised their glasses and Brady took a deep bow. Through the window the late afternoon had taken on an eerie yellow hue. Palm fronds were rolling down the street like Texas tumbleweed. The wind's fury filled the bar.

"This is bittersweet," Jesse said at the center of the room. His voice broke and Bill wrapped an arm around his shoulder. "We love you guys…"

"Hey, none of that," said Jonas, provoking nervous laughter.

"Don't worry, Jonas," he said. "We do love you guys, and girls, and we love Lauderdale Beach. But we've sold the Dew Drop."

"No way!" Rose blurted.

"They made us an offer we simply *couldn't* refuse," said Bill, doing Vito Corleone in drag.

"But you guys love the inn," said Amy Bremer. She and her husband Bob owned the Sunset Beach Motel.

A tear trickled down Jesse's cheek. "It was either sell the place, or lose it."

Bill explained how the city had hit them with an enormous fine and demanded expensive improvements that made keeping the Dew Drop impossible.

"We were trapped in a corner, " said Jesse.

There was a lot of head shaking and hugs, the others trying to comfort Bill and Jesse. Jonas remained on his stool, glowering, deep in thought.

"Just a minute," he said finally. "Who was this code enforcement prick?"

"He was a prick," Bill said. "He was so cold, like he enjoyed ruining us."

"What'd he look like?" Jonas said. "Tall, bald, cock-eyed bastard?"

"That's him," Jesse said. "Roscoe something. Do you know him?"

Jonas took another slug of *Liquid Lunacy*. "Son-of-a-bitch is a rotten apple, that one. A bad man. He's screwing with me too. Came by today. Says I'm shut down. I told him to fuck himself. Woulda punched out his headlights if Delbert hadn't held me back."

Gunther and Olga Klum listened intently. The party was the first time they'd laughed since the fire and it had been a relief not to think about their own decision.

"We may be selling too," Gunther said.

Rain pinged the windows like pebbles on a tin roof. Brady could see the spindly palms bending like willows on the beach across the street.

"The offer is enormous," Gunther said. "With the insurance money we'll walk away with a fortune."

"The realtor said we'd be hitting a touchdown," Olga said.

"Grand slam," said Gunther.

"Home run?" Brady said.

"That was it," said Olga.

"Who was the realtor?" Jesse asked.

"A woman. She made offers to buy the Pelican's Nest in the past," Gunther said. "Max, we told you about her. She said you spoke to her."

"Cherry Hampton," said Brady, exchanging glances with John McCarty.

"She was the one who made the offer to us, too," Bill said.

"Who were the buyers?" said Jonas.

"She wouldn't say," Gunther said.

"Us either," said Jesse. "Said it was a blind trust."

Rain was coming in buckets now. Haphazard blasts of wind were striking from every corner of the zodiac. Brady glanced at the TV and saw *Hurricane Phyllis* was still over Cuba blowing at one hundred thirty miles per hour now.

Rose said: "Does anyone think this is a coincidence?"

"No such thing," said Jonas. "It's no fluke these boys were forced to sell after a visit from the same city man who's trying to muscle me."

"What will you do, Mr. Bigelow?" Johnny Glisson asked.

"Young man, nobody's running me off this beach. As you'll discover someday, life's too short. I've done the arithmetic. You get maybe thirty thousand days on this earth, if you're lucky. That's eighty two years, which really ain't nothin' but a tick of the big clock. I've used up all but a couple thousand of my allotted days. And, believe me, that ticking's getting louder all the time." Jonas punctuated his sermon with a melancholy grin and another swallow of Brady's elixir. "I ain't afraid of dying. But I'm goin' with sand between my toes. When that sonofabitch Beelzebub swallows me, I'm gonna give him a hellish case of heartburn."

They absorbed Jonas's soliloquy in silence. Then *Hurricane Phyllis* roared like a lioness and the room snapped back to life. Brady realized it was black outside.

"Well, my amigos, we'll have to solve this puzzle another day."

There was reaching around of arms and wishing each other safe passage. Rose was the last to go.

"Why not ride out the storm at Victor's?" Brady said. "He'd love to have you. And his house is solid as the Rock of Gibraltar."

Rose looked at him and he saw her eyes flicker like a candle. She spoke hesitantly.

"I gotta go, Brady. If my cat has to go through this hurricane all by herself she'll go crazy."

Rose hugged Brady, holding him a nanosecond longer than a casual embrace. She smelled fresh as a bar of Ivory Soap. As she pulled away, her black hair swept his face. The scent lingered on his cheek long after she disappeared into the storm, without a backward glance.

Bradys Run

CHAPTER THIRTY

WHILE BRADY rolled down his hurricane shutters and secured the Sea Shanty, *Hurricane Phyllis* was carving a swath of devastation across Cuba. Radio Havana reported a seventeen-foot storm surge had flooded littoral regions. Scores of coastal dwellers were drowned before communications from the island were severed.

A capacious wind exploded just as Brady was climbing into his Jeep. He slammed into the vehicle and was almost knocked off his feet. The rain was coming sideways. For all the good they did the wipers may as well have been trying to sweep elephants off the windshield. The five minute drive home took twenty.

Brady finally tucked the Jeep safely in Victor's garage and walked around back. The wind had reached gale force. Charles – always vigilant – came out and helped him brace the Victoria II and the Sea Ray with davits, dock whips, and heavy rubber fenders.

When he entered the house, his wet clothes were clinging to him like plaster. It was past midnight by the time he got a hot shower and changed into dry togs. The night ahead promised to be bruising. He poured a cup of black coffee and joined Victor, Charles, and the Klums in the Fun Room, as Victor called it – a windowless, high-ceilinged room with black walls, reclining theater seats, and a one hundred fifty-inch movie screen, perfect for watching DVDs and Dolphins games, as well as being the safest room in the house.

One of the local TV meteorologists, Bryan Norcross, was dissecting *Phyllis*. Brady sipped his coffee and thought about Rose home alone with her cat. *Or is she?* He wondered again if there was something between her and the tall blonde bodybuilder. He sighed and Victor looked over at him.

"*Phyllis* has crossed Cuba and is moving northeast at a very rapid forward speed of twenty eight miles per hour," Norcross was saying. "On this track the center will make landfall in the Florida Keys during the next few hours and cross southern Florida later this morning. Winds are now one hundred thirty miles per hour, making this a strong Category Three hurricane."

Phyllis was a whopper. Brady thought back to his boyhood, curled up in a blanket inside his family's dark, shuttered house, listening to the bloodcurdling howl of the winds. Hurricanes were thrilling then, like roller coasters and vampire movies. They didn't seem so romantic anymore.

Olga nestled close to Gunther, her head on his shoulder, legs folded beneath her, looking small as a frightened child.

"This waiting reminds me of the horror stories my mother used to tell me about Düsseldorf," she said. "June 1943, hiding in the dark, listening to the RAF bombers, hundreds of them, night after night, until they'd reduced the city to rubble."

"Like the Pelican's Nest," Gunther said, tenderly caressing her blonde hair. "War is the most destructive force on earth. But hurricanes are the most powerful. Both, I think, are the work of the devil."

"Actually, Gunther," said Victor, "the word hurricane derives from *huracan* – the Taino Indian word for evil spirit. The Taino's probably got it from the Mayans, who called their storm god Huraken." The other three listened, never ceasing to be amazed by Victor's encyclopedic brain. "And you're right, my friend. Hurricanes are the most pernicious force in Mother Nature. Cold-blooded whirlwinds without mother, spouse, mercy, or spite. Quite simply, they are moving mountains of wind, water, and heat. Over the past two centuries they've killed two million people."

Not to be outdone, Brady said: *"The Herald* had an article today saying Category Two 'canes possess enough energy to power the entire world for two hundred days."

The Klums stared at him blankly. "Speaking of energy," Gunther said, "I have none left. Are you ready to sleep, my love?"

Olga nodded and smiled at Victor and Brady with sleepy eyes and bade them goodnight. Charles came in with a thermos of fresh coffee and tray of sandwiches, cookies, and snacks, and also retired for the night.

Once they were alone, Victor said: "So, our friends have decided to sell their property?"

"I can't blame them," Brady said. "The money is staggering."

"A *touchdown*?" Victor said with a chuckle.

"Grand slam," Brady said smiling, then his features hardened. "Victor, something fishy is going on."

"How so?"

Brady trusted Victor Gruber more than anyone on earth. After Victoria died it was his delicate counsel that kept him from going mad. One night he sat outside the bedroom where Brady had sequestered himself.

"My dear friend," he said through the locked door, *"try to understand that you are enduring heartbreak beyond expression. Life is as fragile as wafer. Victoria may be gone, but she will always live on in your memory. As long as you exist, she does also."*

As the wind brayed, Brady described for him the picture that had emerged in the last two days. The Klums deciding to sell the Pelican's Nest. Bill and Jesse giving up the Dew Drop Inn. Both after visits from a city code enforcement officer, the same one threatening to shut down Jonas. Add to that, the property records showing ten other beach motels sold the past year. Cherry Hampton the realtor in each case. The buyer anonymous. Not to mention the daisy chain of sales inflating their values.

"And all these motels are clustered in the same area?" Victor asked.

"Four adjacent blocks. If the pattern continues, I would expect Jonas to get another visit from Hampton soon."

"It sounds like someone is trying to corner the market on beach motels."

"Whoever it is, they've got money to burn."

"And very bad manners," said Victor.

The wail of the wind was palpable now, even in the soundproof room. Brady wondered anew how Rose and her cat were faring, and if they were alone. He sighed again.

"Victoria?" said Victor.

"What?" Brady said, yanked from his reverie.

"You're sighing like you did after Victoria left us. I assumed you were thinking of her."

Brady had not discussed his feelings for Rose with anyone. He wasn't even sure what they were.

"I have been thinking about Victoria."

"Oh?" said Victor, his aerial up.

"I feel like I may be betraying her."

Victor scrutinized his friend with keen eyes. "How so, Max?"

"There's a woman. I think I'm developing a crush on her."

"Crush? You sound like a lovesick school boy."

Brady waved his hands in the air and spoke with an exasperated tone. "I don't know what to call it, Victor. Victoria is the only woman I've ever really loved. I still see her face and hear her voice and smell her smell like she's standing next to me. This woman is nothing like her."

Victor rubbed his chin and sat in deep thought for some time.

"My friend," he said after a while, "you of all people should understand that in the long tunnel of history billions of women have walked this earth. They are God's most precious gift to man. Yet there has never been an identical set of lips or eyes or breasts among them. Women are as unique as snowflakes and few have been as rare or impossible to forget as Victoria. The odds of you finding another like her are, well, less than microscopic."

"I know, I know, I know," Brady said, massaging his forehead with his fingertips.

"Whoever it is, Max, do not feel guilty. You are a very healthy, very vital man. You've been alone a very long time. Frankly, I'm surprised this hasn't happened sooner."

Brady and Victor sat silently for a long time listening to the tempest outside.

"Do I know the young lady?" Victor said.

Brady nodded. "Rose Becker."

Victor clapped his hands in obvious delight. "I should have guessed. Madame Butterfly! Excellent. Someone with an appreciation for such exquisite creatures must have impeccable character."

"She does have that."

"She's also got pizzazz. She sparkles like the Hope Diamond."

"That too."

"Are you in love her?"

"I don't know, Victor. What the hell is love, anyway?"

"My dear Max, if you *think* you love her, you *do*. Love is, after all, a state of mind."

"I'm pretty certain Rose feels a lot more affection for her butterflies than she does for me. Besides, I'm fifteen years older than her. What would she want with an old man like me."

"Fifteen years is nothing," Victor said. "You're in excellent condition – for a man your age."

"Thanks for the backhanded compliment."

Victor laughed very hard.

They kept vigil until three in the morning when Brady's head fell back against the reclining leather seat and he yielded to the blackness. As the wind raged outside, he felt his mind lift away like a magic carpet. Inexorably, he was returned to the flames and smoke and horror where his soul had been in bondage since that day.

"Get out, Victoria. Get out."

"Max, I love you. Don't ever forget."

Sprinting across the bridge, straight into the black cloud, into the sea of soot-bathed humanity, the paper blizzard, the volcanic dust, the dazed firefighters, digging frantically, pulling out corpse after corpse, disembodied legs and arms. But then something remarkable happened.

The black dream evaporated and Brady found himself standing on an alabaster beach, the sun trembling overhead, its diamond light sparkling off the backs of dolphins cavorting in the turquoise surf. Sea birds floated on a delicate breeze. A single white cloud drifted on high. Two women stood beside the water, hand-in-hand, wearing floppy hats and white sun dresses, holding yellow balloons against the sapphire sky. Waves lapped gently at their feet and they giggled like the best of friends. He walked up slowly behind them and they turned to greet him. It was Victoria and Rose. They were smiling at him. A wondrous white mirage with golden borders. Victoria wrapped her arms around his neck and gently kissed him, her mouth on his, warm and soft and real. Then Rose did the same. Then the three of them embraced.

Bradys Run

CHAPTER THIRTY ONE

THE SLEDGEHAMMER CAME down at six in the morning. *Hurricane Phyllis* unleashed her fury like a juggernaut from hell. Power failed thirty minutes after the big blow struck. Charles cranked up the generator, so they had a refrigerator and television for weather reports, as long as the cable lasted.

They watched the show from front row seats in Victor's sunroom. The house was equipped with hurricane-proof windows that had been tested by firing two-by-four inch wood studs into them at one hundred fifty miles per hour. *Phyllis* was blowing at one hundred thirty, so they felt relatively safe. The first tree to go was a big mango across the canal. Then the metal frame of a screened pool patio collapsed and blew apart like a tinker toy. Minutes later a power pole keeled over into the swimming pool. Its high voltage lines convulsed in the water like black mambas in a vat of acid. A house roof blew off. The mast of a sailboat snapped in half. Brady kept an anxious eye on the Victoria II. He could see the mast pitching violently in the white-capped waterway while the Sea Ray seesawed beside her. Rain water was oozing under the French doors like a liquid poltergeist.

Phyllis was a fast woman, moving at close to twenty two miles per hour. After three relentless hours, without warning, the sound and fury died. The sun shined, the sky turned blue, and the air grew as silent as a formation of swans at three thousand feet. It all felt unreal, deceptive, like a counterfeit day. It was the eye of the storm.

Radar images indicated *Phyllis'* front side was far more malevolent than her aft. The worst, it seemed, was over. An hour or two more and the storm would be gone. Brady ran to the dock and secured the boat whips and repositioned the fenders. Across the canal people milled about, laughing, drinking cocktails, chatting with neighbors like they were at a backyard barbecue. He hollered at them to get back inside.

Minutes later the eyewall passed and the whirlwind breathed once more. The Victoria II vanished behind a blinding sheet of rain. Trees gyrated like they were possessed by evil spirits. A flying tree limb crashed into the window. Olga shrieked and buried her face on Gunther's shoulder. The French doors began to rattle. Before Brady could react, they blew open. Wind and rain rushed into the room. The curtains blew straight up and stuck to the ceiling. He bound from his seat and fought his way to the doors. Slipping and sliding, he managed to force them shut, then collapsed back into his chair, wet as a clam, thinking: *This is the goddamndest storm I've ever seen!*

A mile to the east, the protective panels on Rose Becker's greenhouse clattered ferociously. Inside, hundreds of butterflies flailed about like a hive of angry hornets. The wind blasts grew more savage until a single plank ripped off the top gantry and the glass shattered.

On Sailboat Bend, the mammoth tree in Jack Del Largo's front yard was doing its own delirious tango. Its massive canopy of limbs and leaves captured the wind like a sail and thrust relentlessly until the trunk snapped near the ground and the giant toppled.

A black-hooded figure staggered down Sunset Street, lurching like a drunken sailor from street sign to car bumper to telephone pole. A furious gust hit him with a haymaker, knocked him to the ground and he blew like a leaf down the pavement. When the gale slackened he hugged the ground, then began crawling, turtle-like, inch-by-inch, until he reached a concrete wall. He clambered to his feet and pulled himself forward hand-over-hand. As he reached the entrance to the Coral Reef Motel, another vicious squall forced him to his knees. He stayed down and crept on all fours to a door marked *Office* and began pounding.

"Help!" he hollered. "Help me!"

His shouts were strangled by the wind and it took several minutes of banging before the knob turned from the other side. The door opened a few inches. Jonas Bigelow yelled through the breach.

"What in hell are you doing out there?"

"Help me!"

"What kind of fool is out in this storm?" Jonas muttered as he unlashed the chain lock.

The door flew open and the black clothed man lunged at him. The old man's knees buckled and his lips curled in horror. A pair of powerful hands clutched his shirt front and before Jonas knew what was happening he was wrenched out the door. The hooded man bashed his face against the concrete wall until he sagged to the ground.

Betty Bigelow was in her pajamas, disabled and in bed in their upstairs apartment.

"Jonas?" she called out weakly. "What was that? Jonas?"

With Betty bedridden most of the time these days, the Bigelow's decided not to cut-and-run every time a storm hit. They'd been hitting so often. And the Coral Reef was strong as a bomb shelter. They felt safe here.

Betty looked out the floor-to-ceiling bay window of their bedroom toward the courtyard downstairs. She'd been keeping her eye on the palm trees, terrified a coconut would break loose and fly through the glass, despite Jonas's assurances otherwise.

"Jonas!" she yelled, more insistent, her voice laden with dread now. Then she saw something outside. A dark figure was moving across the courtyard. Betty squinted. It looked like a large black man. "Oh, my lord! Is that Delbert? Jonas! Delbert's outside in the storm!"

Jonas didn't answer. *Where is that man? The bathroom?* Then she was struck by a chilling thought. She yelled at the window, as if he could hear her.

"Jonas? Is that *you*? You damned fool! What are you doing out in this storm? I am going to brain you, Jonas Bigelow."

Betty struggled from the bed and put her nose to the window pane. She was trying to see through the rain when a palm frond blew into the glass. She tumbled backward, hit the bed hard, and caromed onto the floor. Something snapped and she felt as if she'd been stabbed in the hip with a white hot knife. Betty squeezed her eyes shut and saw fireworks. She had never given birth but imagined this is what the pain felt like. She inhaled sharply and tried to think like a women in labor. *Breath, breath, breath.* The burning diminished.

"Jonas!" she cried in a frail voice.

Her head flopped back against the mattress. She opened her eyes and looked out the window. Jonas was still moving against the wind. *What is he doing?* He approached the swimming pool and now she saw he was dragging something. It looked like a sack of potatoes. She forgot the pain and pressed her forehead to the window. *What is that?* It hit her like a thunderclap. *That's not Jonas.* Jonas was the sack of potatoes. He was on the ground being pulled by his collar across the courtyard by a large black man.

"Oh, my God!" she cried, frantic. "Jonas! What's happening? Who is that? Why is he doing that to you?"

Betty whimpered as she watched her husband tugged, thrashing and twisting. But the big man didn't let go. He pulled Jonas to the pool, lifted him off the ground, and slammed him hard onto the six-inch high concrete buttress surrounding the water. Betty could see Jonas writhe in agony.

"He's hurt!" she screamed. "My Jonas is hurt! Why are you hurting my husband?"

Jonas tried to lash back at his assailant. A gust knocked the black figure to the ground. Jonas struggled to get to his feet but the dark man grabbed him and forced his head into the water. Betty moaned like a wounded animal. Jonas's legs jerked wildly and he lifted his left arm, desperately trying to hack at the other man. Then his arm froze like a statue in mid-air. A second later, Jonas sank limply into the pool.

Sitting on the floor, weeping pathetically, Betty lurched for the telephone on her bedstand. Through her tears she punched 9-1-1. When she put the receiver to her car the line was dead. Betty rubbed the wetness from her eyes and looked out the window. The dark figure was gone. Then a horrifying thought. She crawled across her bedroom to the door. The hot knife twisted in her side. She slammed the door and turned the lock, then inched back to the window on hands and knees. Jonas was floating like a dead fish, face up in the pool with rain pouring into his open mouth.

Brady's Run

CHAPTER THIRTY TWO

PHYLLIS DEBARKED FOR five hours before she bid South Florida bon voyage and sailed off into the Atlantic. By early afternoon the sun was smiling down like a happy face from an endless blue sky scrubbed clean by the storm, eclipsed only by all the frowny faces on the ground.

The hurricane left an epitaph of utter disaster. Thousands of power poles snapped like matchsticks. Trees uprooted by the tens of thousands. Countless houses shorn of roof tops. Millions without electricity.

Miraculously, Victor Gruber's property was almost completely un-scathed. A downed Royal Poinciana tree, a few roof tiles blown off, the swimming pool a terrarium thick with leaves and branches. The Victoria II and Sea Ray were still afloat.

After everyone counted fingers and toes, Brady hopped in his Jeep and headed toward the beach. Police had set up a blockade at the Las Olas Bridge. An officer walked up, his visored cap pulled low over his eyes, head tilted back, chin jutting out. It was Dan Mason, the young officer with Popeye forearms who patrolled the beach area.

"Hey, Mr. Brady," he said "Everything okay at the Shanty?"

"On my way to find out right now, Dan. How's it look over there?"

"It's a mess. Lots of downed trees. The beach road is buried. Some guy drowned in a pool. God only knows why he was swimming in the middle of a hurricane. Good luck."

Mason slapped the Jeep's hood and waved him through. He entered the war zone. The Intracoastal's seawalls were lined with dozens of capsized boats and sailboats with splintered masts. Palm trees stood like Indians shorn of their headdresses, fronds gone, yet coconuts remarkably still in place. Several buildings had been stripped of their paint by beach sand being blasted at them at one hundred thirty miles per hour.

The Sea Shanty appeared unmarred from outside. Brady rolled up the shutters and unlocked the door. Water had seeped in and the floor was soaked. The power was out. He'd stocked up on ice before the storm but there was no telling how long the electric would be off. He made a mental note to get Victor's back-up generator before his food spoiled.

Brady stepped outside and looked up toward the Papillon Gym. Rose had been on his mind since he awakened. He wasn't big on dream interpretation, but last night's apparition had left him oddly euphoric. An old Patti Loveless country song kept playing in his head: *Who knows how love starts. I woke up with you in my heart. Timber I'm falling in love.*

"Anybody home?"

"In here," a voice said. It came from the greenhouse. Brady saw the protective panels had blown off and several pieces of glass were gone. Rose stepped out. Her face was tracked with tears.

"What's wrong, Rose."

She shook her head mournfully. He looked past her. The greenhouse was a farrago of shattered glass, tumbled foliage, and dead butterflies. Rose held out her palm. She was holding a limp, still Queen Alexandra Birdwing.

"They're all gone," she said, her voice thin and tremulous. "Some of the Monarchs and Swallowtails survived, the ones that didn't escape. But the Queen Alexandra's were too fragile."

She had lined up the furry cadavers like victims of a terrorist bombing.

"I'm so sorry, Rose. You'll find more to replace them."

She nodded tearfully. Brady had never seen anyone weep over butterflies.

"Do you want me to take them to the beach and give them a proper burial?"

Rose swabbed her eyes with her shirt sleeve. "No thanks. I want to do a necropsy on them."

"You're welcome to store them in my cooler downstairs," he said. "Just do me a favor. Wrap them up. I don't want them staring at me every time I reach for a beer."

She gave him a weepy smile. "I promise. Thanks, Brady."

He helped her finish cleaning out the greenhouse. He replaced the broken glass with spare panes she had stored. He pulled out the exercise benches, barbells, and weights. An hour later, the Papillon was ready for business. They moved the butterfly remains downstairs to the Shanty and Brady put them into a cooler. They'd be good there for a few days.

"Don't feed them to your customers," Rose said. "They might not appreciate it."

Brady was relieved to see her laugh and decided to ask the question that had been on his mind since last evening.

"How'd you and your friend make out last night?"

"My friend?" she said, eyebrows arched quizzically. He studied her face long enough to pacify his angst about Adonis Rock. His spirit soared.

"Your cat."

"Oh, we missed the storm. Fell asleep watching movies. When I woke up it was sunny."

John McCarty walked in dressed in shorts and a navy blue T-shirt with a Fire Investigation Unit logo.

"Am I interrupting anything?"

"Sorry, sir, we're closed for business," Brady said.

"I'm not looking for a drink," McCarty said. "Still too woozy from all that *Liquid Lunacy*."

Brady and Rose laughed, but McCarty's face had a grave cast.

"What's the matter, John."

"I just got a call from a detective friend at the PD. Something bad has happened."

Bradys Run

CHAPTER THIRTY THREE

SOME PEOPLE HAVE a talent for sniffing gold under mountains. Adonis Rock could smell his fortune laying across Jack Del Largo's driveway. It was camouflaged as a tree. It had fallen onto the front of his house, smashed the roof and blocked all egress and ingress. Del Largo stood in the yard flapping his arms like a pelican on a piling, the armpits of his shirt saturated by half-moons of sweat.

"Do you believe this hunk of fucking firewood? I should have had you take it down last week."

"Too late now," said Adonis.

"Well, I need this out of here immediately, if not sooner. My wife…"

As if on cue, Marla Del Largo rushed around the corner of the house like she was rounding third base, cigarette dangling from her mouth, red wine tippling from the glass in her hand.

"This is a *disaster!*" she said with drama queen ado.

"Hello, Mrs. Del Largo," said Adonis.

"Thank God you're here," Marla said. Copper hair poked out from under her turquoise scarf and large lovebird earrings swung furiously from her lobes. "How fast can you get this monstrosity out of here?"

He spent several minutes surveying the mammoth trunk, marveling at the enormity of the prostrate leviathan. "Two days," he said.

"Oh, thank you. Our son's wedding is Saturday. We've got to fix that gashed roof, too."

"It was a major hurricane, Marla," Del Largo said, "I think our guests will understand."

"Jack Del Largo, that roof better look as good as new by Saturday or I will make the remainder of your life a living hell."

She wheeled around and stalked off, leaving an exhaust trail of cigarette smoke and splashed wine. Adonis had no doubt she could make good on her threat.

Del Largo frowned darkly. "When can you start?"

"I can be back with my gear in two hours."

"Three thousand, right?"

Adonis frowned and shook his head. "Sorry, Jack. That was then. It's ten thousand now."

"That's fucking highway robbery."

Adonis reached into his pocket, pulled out his cell phone, and held it up to Del Largo's face. "Supply and demand, Jack. I've got a dozen desperate voicemails from customers screaming for help – immediately. Thanks to *Phyllis*, demand for my services presently exceeds supply."

"Screw you," Del Largo said, his cheeks turning the shade of raw meat. "I'll get someone else."

"Good luck. Every tree service in South Florida is swamped."

"You son-of-a-bitch!"

"That's ironic, Jack. I drown an old man on *your* orders and you call *me* a son-of-a-bitch?"

Del Largo's eyes grew round as saucers. "Goddamnit, keep it down," he said, swiveling his head left and right. He stepped in close to Adonis, inhaling in rapid gulps, His shoulders were heaving like he'd just finished a long run. "You did it?" he wheezed. "It's done?"

"You owe me sixty grand."

Jack's red face turned ashen. He recoiled from Adonis like he was a leper. Del Largo had committed more sins than he could count; bribery, blackmail, adultery. But the enormity of this overwhelmed him. He immediately wanted to go back in time. Undo his deed. Cancel the contract. If he could do a Lazarus and raise Jonas Bigelow from the dead he'd have done it. Anything to cleanse the blood from his hands. That, though, was the thing about murder. There were no do-overs.

Del Largo's body began to quake. He staggered to the fallen tree and dropped onto his hands and knees in the grass. Adonis stepped over and put a hand on his back. Del Largo's shirt was stretched tight as sausage casing over his spongy, trembling flesh. Adonis pulled away quickly, disgusted, while the fat man retched, loud and pitiful.

After several minutes, Del Largo yanked a handkerchief from his pocket and wiped his mouth and wet eyes. He pulled himself to his feet and stumbled toward the front door, waving weakly at Adonis to follow. The windows were shuttered and the house flickered with dozens of candles. Adonis followed him to the study. The lawyer locked the door and stepped to the wet bar. He poured a large shot of bourbon, belted it down, and then splashed more whiskey into two glasses. He handed one to Adonis and wilted into his big leather chair and swilled the second drink. His eyes closed and his head fell back, revealing the white bulges of his triple chin. Adonis thought he'd passed out.

"Jack?"

Del Largo opened his addled eyes and stared into space. "Sorry. I guess I'm tired. Up all night."

"Where's my money, Jack?"

"Money? Oh, yeah. What was it? Fifty, right?"

"Sixty. Fifty plus ten. Remember?"

Del Largo remembered. He'd told Steele the hit would cost one hundred thousand dollars. The other forty would help pay for the wedding.

"Right. Sixty grand. I don't have it now."

Adonis leaned toward him. "Don't fuck with me, Jack." His voice dripped with menace.

"I don't keep that kind of cash around here," Del Largo said. He opened his desk drawer, removed an envelope, and threw it across the desk. "Here's twenty-five. If the bank opens tomorrow I'll get you the rest then."

Adonis thumbed the money, then stood and stepped toward the door.

"What about the tree?" Del Largo said.

He stopped and looked back at the lawyer. "What about it?"

Del Largo hesitated and then nodded.

"Okay, ten thousand, you bastard. You haul away the wood and get rid of the stump in two days. If the yard's not spic-and-span, I'm only paying five. Deal?"

"Deal," Adonis said and walked out, thinking: *Nitwit's got no clue!*

Bradys Run

CHAPTER THIRTY FOUR

GIANT ROLLERS STAMPEDED the shore like a herd of thundering stallions. *Phyllis* was gone, but she'd taken gluttonous gulps of sand from Lauderdale Beach. A1A was buried under dunes piled high like snow drifts after a blizzard. Brady, Rose, and McCarty circumnavigated back streets strewn with a hodgepodge of dross and detritus. Brady felt like the world had turned topsy-turvy, as if the sun had risen in the west, or night had fallen at dawn.

The Coral Reef Motel was ringed with yellow crime scene tape. Police cars, a crime scene investigation van, and an EMS truck clogged Sunset Street, along with TV news units and dozens of gawkers. Brady saw a white sheet stretched over a human form beside the pool. Rose saw it too and tears began dripping from her eyelashes like raindrops from a leaf. Brady struggled to retain his own composure.

McCarty introduced him to Captain Ron Register, a tall, ramrod straight, gray-haired man who was the supervising homicide detective. Register shook Brady's hand and lifted the yellow tape.

"Professional courtesy," he said. "I'll want to ask you some questions later."

"Whatever you need, captain."

Like the rest of the city, the Coral Reef looked like it had had a bad haircut. The courtyard was a tangle of broken tree limbs, vagabond roof tiles, and assorted debris. A paramedic stood beside the body talking to a uniformed cop and a woman wearing a white lab coat.

"Hello, Belinda," McCarty said to her.

"John," she said with a surprised smile.

Belinda was an attractive Latin-looking woman with braided brown hair. She held a clipboard embellished with a casserole of black ink jots, scribbles, and diagrams of a human body. McCarty hugged her and Brady got the impression they were more than business acquaintances. She was clicking a ball point pen nervously in her ringless left hand.

"Belinda, this is Max Brady," McCarty said and gave each a quick rundown on the other's curriculum vitae. She was Belinda Boulanos, a Broward County Assistant Medical Examiner. "Max was a close friend of the victim."

"My condolences, Mr. Brady," she said in the practiced manner of someone who'd made a career of death. "Would you like to look at the body?"

"*Like* is probably not the right word. But yes, if it's okay."

Boulanos squatted down and pulled back the sheet. Brady and Captain Register leaned over the body, but McCarty kept his distance, as if afraid to catch his own death. Brady had to force himself to look. Jonas, so vibrant and alive hours ago, now lay silent and still, a novitiate in that mysterious, ethereal congregation of the departed. He might have been mistaken for a sleeping man, if not for his purple face and open eyes as blank as the margins of a book. His forehead was disfigured by large abrasions. The right side of his face was covered with black lumps, like it had been garnished with Beluga caviar. Brady noted scrapes on his feet and legs. His body was bloated, a condition he was all too familiar with from his NYPD days, having helped fish more than a few floaters from the East River.

Boulanos said, "We'll likely find the official cause of death to be cardiac arrest due to hypoxia and acidosis precipitated by water inhalation."

"That's drowning to you and me," Register said.

"But it's also clear he suffered severe blunt trauma pre-necrosis," Boulanos added.

Brady stood up and turned away from Jonas's body toward the motel office.

"Where's Betty?" he said with a trace of alarm.

"Broward General," the police captain said. "She was in pretty bad shape."

"Assaulted?"

"Shock. And a broken hip. She was apparently watching through the upstairs bedroom window while her husband was being murdered. She injured herself falling back against the bed."

"My God!" Brady said. "Can she identify the perp?"

"Mrs. Bigelow says a black male dragged him across the courtyard and pushed his head into the pool. We found traces of blood on the wall outside the office door. It looks like the killer knocked and when Mr. Bigelow answered he pulled him out, slammed his head into the wall, and dragged him to the pool."

Brady looked at Belinda Boulanos. "When?"

"I estimate between 8 a.m. and 10 a.m."

"Height of the storm," said Register. "The wife tried to call 9-1-1 but the phone was out. She couldn't move. She sat there for four hours looking at him floating face up in the pool. A Jamaican guy found him. Says he came by after the storm passed. Delbert Tanner. Claims he worked for Bigelow."

"Jesus! Delbert can't be a suspect. He would never have hurt Jonas."

"We'll see. But I doubt it too. He waved down a cruiser. Seemed pretty shaken himself."

Bradys Run

CHAPTER THIRTY FIVE

ADONIS ROCK HEFTED the big Stihl chainsaw from the bed of his truck. He felt like a poker player sitting on pocket aces and looking at the biggest jackpot of his life. All he needed to do was to pull off the bluff. Carve up the tree and haul it away before Jack Del Largo got wise.

Adonis knew trees. It was his fantastic good luck Del Largo did not. The second he saw the magnificent hardwood he knew it was a bonanza waiting to be had. A big-leaf mahogany, the world's most prized – and pricey – wood.

Buck Mayfield had taught Adonis all about mahogany. They met at Citrus Correctional. Mayfield was doing life for shooting a guy he caught *"eatin' at the Y,"* as he put it, the *"Y"* being the junction where Buck's wife's legs met. Before that Mayfield spent twenty years grading lumber in North Florida sawmills. He would regale Adonis for hours on end about the lustrous burgundy hues of Brazilian cherry and the lush chocolaty tones of black walnut. But Buck got a special light in his eyes when he talked about mahogany. Its curly interlocking grains, its rich mottled pinks and reds, the exquisite texture that made it the preferred wood for violins, pianos, and the finest furniture. Most of all, mahogany reaped a huge bounty. Buck would say: *"Why do you think the Amazon rainforest is shrinkin' down to nothin', Donnie?"*

Mahogany trees were rare in South Florida. Adonis had seen a few in the older parts of town, most planted in the early 20th century. After he saw Del Largo's tree, he contacted a factory in Virginia that specialized in high-end mahogany furniture. He gave the manager the dimensions.

"If the wood's good," the manager said, "and you get it here, it might bring a hundred."

"A hundred what?"

"Thousand."

"Dollars?"

Adonis was flabbergasted. He considered removing the tree for free if Del Largo signed over rights to the wood. Then *Phyllis* hit. If it meant he could bleed another ten grand out of the fat fuck, he was happy do so. He'd stopped at *Temporary Labor* on Broward Boulevard and hired two brawny Jamaicans. They'd arrived at Sailboat Bend just as Del Largo was driving off. He leaned out the window of his silver Mercedes SL 500.

"Marla's mother's house in Lighthouse Point has electricity. I'll put up with the old shrew for a couple of days if it means AC and TV."

"What about my money?" Adonis said.

"Don't sweat it. You'll get your money."

Yes, I will, Jack, Adonis thought as Del Largo drove off. He pressed a red button and the big chainsaw hiccupped to life. It coughed blue smoke until it caught its rhythm and began screaming at one hundred decibels. With the Stihl's forty two-inch blade and eight-point-four horse power engine, he could delimb the tree and cut it into logs faster than fifty Paul Bunyan's. By dark they'd pared it into ten sections, each ten feet long. The next morning Adonis would pull out the stump. A log picker was coming to lift the wood onto a flatbed. By midnight he'd be in Virginia.

It was dark by the time he dropped off the Jamaicans and – after two days of little to no sleep – he was eager for bed. Then he cursed. He realized he'd left his chain saw sitting on the stump in Del Largo's front yard and backtracked to Sailboat Bend. When he arrived a little red sports car was parked in the driveway. Adonis grabbed his saw, threw it in the truck bed, and was about to drive off when he heard someone shout.

"Hey, handsome!" It was a woman. He turned and saw the blonde bombshell engaged to Del Largo's son. She sprang from the doorstep and pranced through the truck lights in cut-off jeans and a tube top. Daisy Duke in the flesh. Not the modestly-endowed, dark-haired Daisy in the TV rendition. This was the big-breasted, bleach-blonde version from the movie. She ran up to his door and eyed him like a cat stalking a canary.

"Remember me?" she said with a seductive smile.

"Raymona the blushing bride."

"Adonis the bush trimmer," she laughed.

"Arborist."

Raymona smelled like she'd been drinking eggnog with plenty more nog than egg. He saw a brunette woman reclining against the house door like a biker chick leaning back on a sissy bar.

"That's Mandy, my maid of honor," Raymona said, waving her over. "We came to soak in the hot tub. There's no electricity but the water's still warm. And the bar's stocked. And my future mother-in-law's got enough candles to start a forest fire."

"Sounds like good clean fun," Adonis said.

He reached to turn the ignition key as Mandy crossed in front of his headlights. He could see she enjoyed some of the same prominent attributes as the bride-to-be. Mandy walked straight up to Adonis's window.

"What else you got, sweet meat?" she said.

"Excuse me?" he said with a puzzled look.

"You heard me. I said what else you got. Besides those big muscles and that pretty face?"

Raymona giggled. "It'd be oodles of fun if you joined Mandy and me so we can find out."

"Find out?"

"What else you got, silly."

"I don't think your fiancé would approve," he said, aghast to hear himself rebuff such a proposition.

Raymona pouted like a little rich girl whose daddy refused to buy her a pony. "Well, John Junior ain't here, is he? Mandy was gonna throw me a bachelorette party, but that damn storm blew the roof right off *Chippendale's* and ruined everything."

"I have a great idea," said Mandy. "You can be our *Chippendale* boy."

Without warning, Raymona yanked down her tube top and her left breast sprang out. Adonis gaped at the women. A pair of silicone strumpets. Inviting smiles on their lovely faces. Raymona's prodigious tit hanging out. Petunias begging to be plucked. Just the way he liked his women. Wild, drunk, and dumb. He took a deep breath and climbed from the cab, sure of only one thing. *This is a big mistake!*

Bradys Run

CHAPTER THIRTY SIX

THE FOURTH FLOOR of Broward General Hospital looked deserted when Brady got off the elevator. No hustle-bustle, no nurses bearing bedpans, no sound at all. Brady had a sudden urge to shout: *"Friends and enemas, where have you gone?"* Instead, he turned right and quickly discovered the source of silence. At the main desk, a covey of doctors and nurses was clustered around a small television watching The Weather Channel.

"Do you believe this?" a male nurse in green scrubs said.

A heavyset black nurse was sitting behind the counter scribbling on a chart. "No, no, no. I'm sorry, baby. I still ain't got power at my house from *Phyllis*. I ain't havin' no new hurricane."

"Excuse me!" Brady said, leaning over the counter. No one paid him notice.

The Weather Channel's meteorologist was announcing the formation of another major storm that was tracking straight for South Florida.

"I feel like I'm dodging bullets in a freakin' shooting gallery," the male nurse said. "These hurricanes are like jets lined up on the glidepath into Lauderdale airport. They keep coming one after another."

"I had to wait in line two hours this morning just to get gas, and I'm a doctor," said a young man in blue scrubs with a stethoscope hanging from his neck. "What'd they name this one? P for *Phyllis*. I'm guessing Q for *Quincy*."

"R for *Rollie*," the green scrubs nurse said, wagging his finger at the TV. "The weather man just said they don't use Q-names. U, X, Y, or Z either."

Brady banged a bell on the desk. "Excuse me!"

The male nurse looked at him. "Can I help you."

"I'm looking for Betty Bigelow."

The nurse looked up at a white board hanging over the desk. It was strewn with blue scribbles showing the names of patients and their room numbers.

"Bigelow – four ten," he said, pointing down the hall.

Room 410 had the usual assortment of monitors, wires, IV poles, and blood pressure cuffs. The bed nearest the door was occupied by an ancient white-haired woman who might have been asleep, or she might have been dead. Betty was in the bed by the window. Her eyes were open but they were staring into middle space, as barren as dry lake beds. Her grandmotherly face was framed by a tangled forest of gray hair. She looked like a ghost who hadn't quite died yet. He whispered.

"Betty."

She turned her head toward him but showed no sign of recognition, as if she was blind.

"What?"

"Betty, its Max."

"Max?" she said. "Max, Jonas is dead."

She seemed fragile as a snowflake. Her lower body was encased in a cast and her feet and legs were levitated with straps inches above the mattress.

"I know, Betty," he said and patted her bony hand. "I'm so sorry."

Her hands were folded on her chest, her thumb and forefinger absently twisting her wedding band. "It's okay," she said. "I sold the Coral Reef."

"What?" Brady said, stunned. He wondered if she was hallucinating.

"Two million dollars. Enough for assisted living. Jonas wouldn't hear of it. *'Elephant burial grounds!'* he calls them. But Eleanor says they're very nice."

"Eleanor?"

"My sister."

Like Jonas, Betty had always been razor-sharp, funny, engaged. Now her mind seemed mired in molasses. He reached down and entwined his fingers in hers. Her skin was diaphanous as rice paper. Beneath it he could see a spiderweb of blue veins.

"Betty, who bought the Coral Reef?"

She shook her head grimly and began to weep. "That woman. Jonas didn't like her. He didn't trust her. But what was I to do, Max? Jonas is dead."

Brady wanted to ask Betty about Jonas's murder but she looked so frail and desolate he decided to let her rest. Then, as if reading his mind, her grip constricted and she erupted. Choking with rage, tears rushed down her cheeks.

"That black man threw poor Jonas around like he was a rag doll. I screamed at him to stop, but he kept hurting my poor..." Her words were drowned in sobs. The maze of wrinkles and creases on her face channeled the tears like aqueducts.

"Betty," he said when the storm passed, "can you describe the black man who hurt Jonas?"

She looked up at Brady with vacant surprise, as if she'd just noticed him. After a moment she spoke in a tiny, spiritless voice.

"Black man? He was big. All black. Black pants. Black hood."

"Did you see his face?"

"Face?" she whispered.

Just then a large brown-skinned man walked into the room wearing a black ball cap with the letter *"J"* stitched on its bill. Startled, Brady's knee-jerk reaction was that this was the killer returned to finish the job. He positioned himself between Betty and the intruder. Then the man removed his hat.

"Mister Max," he said. "It's me, Delbert."

"Oh, Delbert," Brady said and let out a sigh of relief. He shook Delbert's hand. "I didn't recognize you. How are you?"

"I had nightmares last night." He spoke in a low Jamaican cadence so Betty wouldn't hear him. "About Mister Jonas in that pool. I can't get it out of my head."

"We're all very sad, Delbert. It's good of you to visit Betty."

They gazed down at the bed. She looked as abandoned as a waif, her pilot light about to flicker out.

Brady leaned down and kissed her forehead. "Get some rest, sweetheart. I'll be back to see you."

He was halfway down the hall when Delbert called after him.

"Mister Max. I wanted to tell you sometin' dat been eatin' at me. Dat city man dat came out da day before da storm. I just couldn't help but tink he was tryin' his hardest to drive out Mister Jonas and Miss Betty."

"Why do you say that, Delbert?"

"Can't say why," he said shaking his head. "Just a feelin'. My momma always said I had a sense about people. Bein' born with da veil over my face."

"Veil?"

"Da afterbirth. Placenta. Momma said I see tings other folks don't. I had a bad feelin' about dat city man," Delbert said, his emotion rising. "Mister Jonas almost punched him. I can't help tinkin' that's connected to him bein' dead."

Bradys Run

CHAPTER THIRTY SEVEN

A MUFFLED CONCUSSION rent the air like a sonic boom and Adonis Rock felt the ground shiver beneath his feet. A cloud of acrid blue-gray smoke rose from the dirt as the immense stump of Jack Del Largo's mahogany tree was liberated from its earthly bonds.

Adonis was forced to resort to explosives when, just after dawn, he realized his Stihl chainsaw was as useless as a one-armed clock trying to remove the stump. The tree's roots were thicker than giant octopus tentacles and so many had taken such a deep grip of the gummy black loam below that freeing the stump with the saw would take all day. Maybe two. He'd planned to be in Virginia by midnight. That wasn't going to happen. Adonis was livid.

Then Vincent Jumper came to the rescue. Jumpy was a roly-poly full-blood Seminole with a long black ponytail, straw cowboy hat, and a toothpick hanging perpetually from his lip. Like Buck Mayfield and Dantrelle Peppers, Adonis knew Jumpy from Citrus Correctional, where he'd done time on a marijuana rap. He owned a log picker and Adonis had called him to lift the mahogany logs onto the flatbed he'd rented. Jumpy slid out of his truck at eight o'clock that morning. Within minutes he'd prescribed an antidote to Adonis's conundrum.

"The cavalry has arrived, homes."

"Well, then you better get your red ass outa here before they fill it with lead," Adonis snapped at him, his anger by then boiling over.

"Don't get pissy, pale face, or that bleached blonde scalp of yours will be hanging from my rearview mirror."

Adonis broke into a self-effacing grin and the two men hugged. The Indian examined the stump and gave a sagacious nod.

"Homes, you need to blow that bitch."

"What with, my nose?"

"Jumpy's got just what you need."

Jumper walked back to his truck and returned with a rectangular wooden container the size of a bread box. He pried off the top to reveal a dozen red paper-covered sticks the size of Jack Del Largo's stogies.

"Jesus!" said Adonis. "Dynamite?"

"Hell, no, white man. That shit's too volatile. Look at it cross-eyed and it'll blow your ass to kingdom come. This shit's trinitrotoluene."

"What the fuck's that?"

"TNT, homes. Safe as a pussy cat. Very stable. Just don't eat it or you'll be pissing red."

"And you know that from personal experience?"

"You don't wanna know, bro. Trust me."

"Where the hell'd you get that shit?"

"Don't ask. Just pony up a grand and your troubles are over."

"A grand! I don't need the whole fucking box, Jumpy. One stick'll be plenty."

"Tough titty said the kitty. All or nothing."

Adonis paid him and the TNT worked like magic. With Jumpy's able assistance, he had the stump and mahogany logs stacked onto the flatbed by noon. A dozen Guatemalans were already swarming over Del Largo's roof like a colony of army ants, replacing the smashed red Spanish tiles. Jack had had to call in some big favors to get enough workers to fix it so fast in storm ravaged South Florida.

A white van pulled into the driveway with *Weddings by Aldo* painted on the side. A tall skinny man dressed in white vaulted out, eying Adonis as he minced toward the house. Adonis watched him watch him, thinking: *They'd love his bony ass at Citrus.*

"Aldo!" Marla Del Largo shrieked. She rushed from the house to meet him, a panicked look on her face. "I still don't have *RSVPs* from a dozen guests. The gazebo hasn't been delivered. Are you sure we should go with the oyster Melrose damask linen?"

Aldo sighed melodramatically and kissed her on both cheeks.

"Tranquilize, my child! Remember Aldo's first rule? On your special day, let *Aldo* worry, and you just *pay*! I guarantee it will be flawless. *I'll* call the guests. And *I* nixed the gazebo. It would block that luscious view of Sailboat Bend. We'll go with a trellis instead. And the oyster damask with coordinating chair covers and organza sashes will be exquisite. Trust Aldo, darling!"

Aldo tipped his sunglasses down a long thin nose and looked over his shoulder. His face twisted like rubber and his tongue glanced over anemic lips.

"Who *is* that fabulous thing? When I drove up I thought I was looking at Fabio*!*"

Marla was fanning herself furiously with a paper plate. "That's Adonis. He cuts down trees. But you are right, Aldo. He is fabulous."

Aldo watched her wave her paper plate. "You seem as turned-on by him as I am."

"Hot flash, darling. Don't stand too close. I may spontaneously combust at any moment. Oh, and Jack wants to know why you ordered *Veuve Clicquot* instead of *Dom Pérignon.*"

"Because that's what you pay Aldo to do," said Aldo, looking up to inspect the Guatemalans' progress before flitting toward the house with Marla.

Del Largo's silver Mercedes pulled into the driveway behind the wedding van. He labored to extricate himself as his wife and the wedding planner vanished into the house.

"Those two seem to think I'm a goddamned ATM machine," he growled.

Del Largo inspected the yard and then wagged his finger at Adonis to follow him. As they walked through the house Adonis averted his eyes from the bathroom with the Jacuzzi, where he'd been till the wee hours. Raymona and Mandy were nowhere in sight. He hoped they stayed that way.

"Here's the balance due on the..." Del Largo said, not finishing his sentence.

He threw a manila envelope on the desk. Adonis opened it and examined the currency. Del Largo owed him thirty five thousand dollars for Jonas Bigelow's murder, but he was too exhausted to count. It looked close enough.

"I'm paying for the tree by check," Del Largo said, writing as he spoke. "Tax purposes."

It's all good! Adonis thought, not arguing. He handed Del Largo a piece of paper.

"Sign this, then, Jack."

"What's that?"

"Standard contract. Tax purposes. IRS is gonna wanna know where the ten grand came from."

Del Largo snorted and scrawled his signature without reading the document.

"Where are you dumping the wood?"

The question caught Adonis off guard. He studied the fat face across the desk, but detected no sign of suspicion.

"County landfill off State Road 84. They grind it into mulch and give it away. Costs a few bucks, but I'll cover it," he said, waving the check.

There was a knock on the door and a burly young man with messy-chic black hair came in. He looked like he pumped iron, but his body was swollen, not chiseled like Adonis.

"Adonis, this is my son, Jack Junior. Jackie, Adonis here trims trees."

Adonis stood and offered his hand. "Congratulations."

"Huh?" Jack Junior said, barely acknowledging him.

"On your wedding."

"Yeah, sure, whatever."

His dismissive tone enraged Adonis. *I should bitch slap the spoiled fuck right in front of his daddy.*

"You're a lucky man," he said instead. "Raymona's red hot."

Jack Junior turned and faced Adonis for the first time, his eyes icy and his fists balled.

"What did you say?" Then he noticed Adonis's rippling biceps and his glare was replaced by a wary expression. "How do you know Raymona?"

"Oh, she and I had a long talk last night," he said, leaving out the part about: *While I was banging her brains out!*

Jack Junior rushed around his father's desk. He tried to puff himself up in front of the larger man but he looked like a Bulldog confronting a Bullmastiff.

"You did, did you? Why the fuck are *you* talking to *my* fiancé?"

"Chill, Junior," Adonis said with a smile, pleased to get a rise out of the pompous marshmallow. "We were cleaning up. She and another girl, Mandy I think her name was, came by looking for you. She couldn't stop talking about how excited she was." *But not about you, you fucking pussy.*

Jack Junior was still processing what he'd heard when Adonis grabbed his hand and shook briskly before he could respond.

"Good luck, pal," he said and walked out. *You're gonna need it.*

Bradys Run

CHAPTER THIRTY EIGHT

ROSCOE ANDERSON KNEW the day was going to be a ball-buster the minute he walked into his office. The telephone was ringing and his voicemail was jammed. In *Phyllis's w*ake, Fort Lauderdale was still staggering like a punch drunk palooka and Code Enforcement would be swamped all day.

I'm getting too old for this shit! he thought. Adding to the misery index was another hurricane heading his way. And forecasters were predicting a relentless barrage of tropical storms for years to come. It was time to get out. Why not? He'd socked away a hefty nest egg in a numbered Cayman Island bank account. He had a million in equity in his condo. And he owned several rental properties that had mushroomed in value during the real estate boom. Now David Grand had handed his walk-off home run.

Roscoe had squeezed the faggots into selling the Dew Drop Inn. And the German couple was sure to follow. Jonas Bigelow was a tough old nut, but he'd slap him around until the man broke. Anderson suffered no guilt pangs. *Like scraping gum off a shoe. When the money comes in, I'm gone.*

Anderson heard a knock at the door. He looked up and tautened. A tall lean man in a T-shirt and tattered khaki shorts filled his doorway. Despite the outfit, Roscoe detected an element of authority.

"Who are you?"

"Brady. Max Brady."

"Whaddya want?"

"Whaddya got? Pony rides? Bonbons? Topless bathing beauties?"

"No, but I got a word of advice. Don't be a wise ass."

"I got news for you, Roscoe. That's five words."

"Listen, mister, I'm up to my keister in crocodiles. Tell Jen at the front desk what you need. She'll send you to the right place."

The telephone rang and Anderson answered quickly, apparently hoping his visitor would go away. But when he hung up Brady was still there.

"Look, buddy, are you deaf?"

Anderson's bifurcated eyes were darting this way and that and Brady was trying to get a fix on which one to address.

"I've got questions," he said, deciding for no good reason to talk to his left eye. "You're the only one who can answer them."

"I told you I don't have time."

Roscoe seemed as irascible as a wet cat. Brady wondered why. Maybe he was just an overworked, underpaid bureaucrat. Or maybe it was more basic than that. Maybe he just hadn't gotten layed lately.

"Have you seen today's newspaper?" Brady said.

"Paper? I haven't had time to take a dump."

Brady threw a copy of *The Lauderdale News* on Anderson's desk. He pointed at a headline in the lower right corner of the front page: *Beach Activist Murdered During Storm.*

Roscoe blinked. He picked up the paper, inspected it hastily, and tossed it back across the desk. He wore an incongruous smile that reminded Brady of a grin he'd seen once on a guy in a silk-lined box.

"That's a shame," Anderson said, his voice softer now.

"Did you visit Jonas Bigelow the day before he was murdered?"

"Who are you?"

"I'm an assistant United States Attorney, retired." Brady mumbled the last word, hoping his résumé would impress Roscoe more than it had Cherry Hampton. "Mr. Bigelow was a friend of mine. If you don't want to talk to me I'll pass your name along to the Broward County State Attorney."

Anderson's tongue poked nervously between thin gray lips, like a moray eel darting from a rock.

"Look, mister…"

"Brady."

"Mr. Brady, I visit a dozen property owners every day, five days a week. This week it'll be seven days. So what?"

"How many are murdered hours after you threaten to shut them down?"

"The hell I did," Roscoe said, a bit too quickly.

"I hate to nitpick, Roscoe, but if you were under oath I'd already have you indicted for perjury."

Anderson stretched his hands out plaintively, like a man feeling for raindrops. "What are you implying? That I had something to do with this old guy's death?"

"Just trying to find out who murdered my friend."

"Look, I enforce codes. He had code violations. Check the record. My *t*'s are all crossed and my *i*'s dotted."

"Tittled."

"What?"

"The dot over the *i*. It's called a tittle."

Annoyance rippled across Roscoe lackluster countenance.

"Look, I'm sorry your friend's dead, but I was doing my job. End of story."

"How about the Dew Drop Inn?

"What about it?"

"And the Pelican's Nest?"

"Jesus, mister, you ask more questions than a four year old."

Brady scrutinized Roscoe's body language. He looked like he was mainlining caffeine, squirming in his chair, folding and unfolding his legs, tapping his pen on the desk like it was a snare drum. The telephone rang again and Anderson lunged for it like a starving man for a sandwich. *Saved by the bell.*

While Roscoe talked, Brady ambled around the office taking inventory, the bureaucrat watching him warily. Red-and-black city code books were perched on a ledge behind his desk. A taxidermy of an eight-foot blue marlin was mounted on the far wall. Beside it a photograph of Roscoe standing next to a sleek Seafox fishing boat that looked about forty feet long. The name on the transom said Codeman. Brady guessed it was worth a couple hundred grand. He wondered what the pay grade was for a city *codeman*. He ducked inside a tiny bathroom in the corner. A dirty hair brush sat on the sink ledge and the toilet seat was adorned with three drops of urine. When Brady came out Anderson was hanging up.

"What is this all about?" he said, his defiant tone returned.

"It's about why you are turning the screws on the mom-and-pop motels by the beach."

"Look, don't come in here and tell me how to do my job. I've been doing this thirty years. Now get the hell out of my office."

"You a baseball fan, Roscoe?"

Anderson looked confused. "I catch a few Marlins games. What that's got to do with anything?"

"You haven't gotten wood on a single ball I've thrown so far. You're batting zero in the truth department. That means you're either a liar or a fool. I'd bet even money on both."

Anderson shot from his chair and leaned across the desk.

"I said get the fuck outa here."

Brady held his ground, standing calmly, looking back at Roscoe's left eye. "Look, something stinks around here. I'll wager another couple of bucks that it won't take a bloodhound to track the skunk right here to your door."

Anderson rushed around the desk with a savage look on his face, but by the time he got nose-to-nose with the taller, fitter Brady his fury had deserted him.

"Do I have to call security?"

"I got a better idea, Roscoe. Call a good lawyer."

Bradys Run

CHAPTER THIRTY NINE

ADONIS ROCK WANTED to pluck out his eyeballs and soak them in ice water. It was just past midnight and he'd barely slept in four days when he navigated the flatbed off Interstate 81 in Staunton, Virginia, and pulled into the Shenandoah Valley Designer Furniture mill. Three hours later he was back on the road, heading south with a brown paper bag stuffed with $100,000 in cash. Adonis knew the mill manager had fleeced him, in return for paying cash. The mahogany was worth more. Much more. But it was also more money than he'd ever possessed in his life. Much more.

Now he felt like a leaf floating on the sea, drifting without control, propelled by the current of time and events, his thoughts as tangled as a kelp bed. He was operating in a state of drug-induced hypnosis. Plying himself with Red Bull, cigarettes, and crystal meth. His speed-addled brain was swirling with a goulash of fire, wind, trees, cash, dead men, and big-breasted girls.

He made Atlanta by nine o'clock in the morning and pulled into a twenty four-hour strip club on the I-285 loop. The *Peachtree Revue* was a skank joint that catered to truckers horny enough or lonesome enough to pay five bucks for a bottle of Bud served by broken-down jezebels with track marks and puffy midriffs. A double sawbuck procured pretty much anything else.

Adonis ordered a steak and bottle of champagne and celebrated his nouveau riches by playing big-rig philanthropist, liberally tucking tens and twenties in thongs and garterbelts. The *Peachtree* girls thronged to the deep-pocketed stranger like sows to swill.

"Y'all need a lap dance, honey," said one shoat-faced junkie with bottle-red hair, rubbing herself against him. "Ya need to work off that big piece a meat you just 'et."

She reminded Adonis of stale cake. Still, her belly was sort of flat and the cottage cheese on her legs was negligible.

"Darlin'," he said, "I'm needin' more than a lap dance."

Adonis booked a room in the abutting *Peachtree Inn,* which came with the stink of stale cigarettes and pubic hair in the bathroom sink. Dixie, the redhead, called a friend, who arrived with a bag of cocaine. Adonis gave her twelve hundred dollars and the coke kept the three of them going until late afternoon. The whores were still asleep when he left at six that evening.

Bradys Run

CHAPTER FORTY

IT WAS HIGH noon and the sun was singing a sultry serenade in the indigo sky. The beach road was still buried under a blanket of yellow sand, making Max Brady's bikini run a toilsome slog made infinitely more arduous by the total absence of bikinis or, for that matter, anyone in a bathing suit. Inevitably, his eyes were drawn to the quicksilver sparkle of the teal sea. After three miles, with nothing to egg him on, he hit the brakes, took an avaricious lungful of air, and plunged into the surf.

A languid breeze tiptoed across the water soft as cat's paws. Brady floated on his back and let the lazy tide carry him down the beach while questions sloshed around his consciousness like random waves. *Who torched the Pelican's Nest? Who killed Jonas? Who's trying to drive out the motel owners? Who's behind the daisy chain?* Too many questions, too few answers. It wasn't long before his meditations strayed to Rose. Brady had no answer on her either. He wasn't even sure of the question. He did notice, though, that the mere act of thinking about her always seemed to make him feel light and airy.

He drifted at tortoise pace. The only flutter of life he encountered was a diamond-shaped stingray as wide as a kitchen table that flapped gracefully beneath him. Thirty minutes later he was lateral to the Papillon

Gym. He looked up at the rooftop but was disappointed to find no trace of Rose.

Bulldozers were plowing sand drifts off A1A. Men with shovels and brooms were clearing the sidewalks. Brady dodged them crossing the road and made his way to the Sea Shanty. His electricity was back, but beach traffic was as scarce as bikinis. Even so, he decided to whip up the usual gumbo and wings. He was chopping onions and listening to the Weather Channel's latest coordinates on *Hurricane Rollie,* which was now a Category Two storm with sustained winds of one hundred miles per hour.

"When you peel onions you should chew gum."

Rose Becker was standing at the doorway in her butterfly T-shirt and shorts. Brady felt his mood brighten.

"Why's that?"

"Keeps you from crying. By the way, you gonna help me tie down again?"

He gave a deep bow. "But of course, madame. As always, I am at your service."

"How gallant," she said, bestowing a wide smile upon him.

Brady detected a new light in Rose's eyes. Inviting? Enticing? He couldn't tell, but he suddenly felt like a tongue-tied teenager suffering from a terminal case of puppy love. The best he could muster was: "That's me. Sir Galahad in the flesh."

"Hmmm." She leaned against the door jamb, arms folded, shaking her head. "Gym's open. Come on up, old timer."

Old timer! The balloon in Brady's head burst so loud he thought she had to hear it. Rose suddenly seemed very far away, as if he was looking at her through the wrong end of a telescope. *What was I thinking?*

"I really shouldn't strain myself, being so near the grave."

Rose laughed. *She really is Torquemada reincarnate,* he decided.

"Quit feeling sorry for yourself, Brady. You've got a good forty years in you. Maybe fifty – *if* you take care of yourself."

"And if I don't?"

"I'll kick your ass," she said and laughed again.

"Nice to know you care," he said, shamelessly fishing for some token of affection. She spurned the bait. Brady could swear she was reading his mind. He changed the subject. "How's the campaign, Madame Butterfly?"

"Ugly as an old man's toenails. I'm afraid I'm coming off as a waspy bitch. Mayor Grand is spreading word I'm a lesbian."

"Has the city ever had a Lebanese mayor?"

"*Lesbian.*"

"How did he know?"

"I thought it was obvious. I'm so butch!"

"I don't think you're a bitch."

"*Butch!*"

"Such a waste," he said, resorting to absurdity to regain his equilibrium.

Rose laughed again. It felt like a warm caress. He motioned toward a bar stool and offered her a cup of coffee. The election was only two weeks away. Between the campaign, the storm, the gym, and Jonas' murder, Rose looked bone tired.

"It'll be over soon and then you'll be mayor."

She rolled her eyes above the cup brim. "Fat chance!"

"Rose, you're only twenty seven. You've got plenty of time to be mayor. But don't give up yet."

"Believe me, Brady. I have no burning desire to be mayor. I was recruited to run, you may recall. It's not about me. It's about saving the beach."

"Somebody's got to be hearing you."

Rose sipped her coffee and shrugged her shoulders. "Actually, it's not as bad as I'm painting it. *The Lauderdale News* endorsed Grand, but I think *The Miami Herald* is going to back me. At least they've been devoting more ink to my candidacy. And the *shadow world.* Unfortunately, it took a fire and a murder to get their attention."

"Artful phrase, shadow world."

"Why, thank you, Brady. But I think it's too little too late."

"Well, speaking for myself, I think this city needs a Lebanese mayor."

"You'd love that, wouldn't you?" she said with a smirk and walked out.

Bradys Run

CHAPTER FORTY ONE

JACK DEL LARGO'S face was as red as the Costa Rican strawberries, surrounded by pyramids of Italian cannoli, Swiss chocolate éclairs, and French almond petit fours, arrayed on the Viennese dessert table.

"Why in hell do we need ten waiters, five bartenders, two chefs, and a sous chef?" he snarled at his wife. "Not to mention five valets, a photographer, videographer, and ten-piece band?"

Jack shoveled a forkful of ginger peach mousse with apricot icing into his mouth.

"Does it taste as good as my baking?" his wife asked.

"Pencil shavings taste better than your baking, Marla."

"Oh, Jack. Really."

"What's this costing me? Fifty bucks a slice?"

Del Largo was shouting over *Jada McDonald and the Sunshine Riders* singing *Love Shack* while dozens of guests gyrated around the pool.

"Jack," said Marla. She was fluttering a red-and-black Flamenco dancer's fan, fighting off another attack of menopausal pyrogenics. "Please spend some time with Raymona's family. I think they feel left out."

"Fuck 'em," Del Largo said, snapping at her like a wet towel. "They didn't put up a fucking penny! They're lucky to be invited."

"Get over it, Jack!" Marla said and stalked off.

The wedding had gone off without a hitch. Blue cloudless sky, bells pealing, bride and her maids in horse drawn carriage crossing the old swinging bridge over Sailboat Bend. Raymona, breathtaking in a white silk gown that emphasized her abundant attributes, calla lily bouquet in hand, walking down a white-carpeted aisle dusted with red rose petals. Two hundred members of South Florida's Social Registry looked on from Del Largo's sprawling lawn against the elegant river backdrop. Raymona and John Junior, in charcoal tailcoat, uttered their vows and embraced. A flock of white doves and a thousand butterflies were released into the air.

Marla sobbed while her husband glared, mostly at Raymona's extended family. Ray Berger – Raymona's father – in rumpled blue jacket, blue jeans, and Budweiser T-shirt. His third wife, Minnie – who was anything but – in garish flowered dress and Minnie Pearl hat minus, mercifully, the dangling price tag. His first wife, Raymona's mother, Bonita – which means *beauty* and who was anything but – attended with her fourth husband, an unshaven auto mechanic with grease under his fingernails. Also on hand, an assortment of brothers, sisters, half-sisters, step-brothers, and unkempt cousins. *Goddamned Beverly Hillbillies*, Del Largo thought. The Clampetts on one side, the Drysdales on the other.

Afterwards, Raymona made the rounds, her diamond ring sparkling on her finger like a five-carat lie, John Junior in tow, holding open a white satin money bag into which guests deposited envelopes of cash.

Del Largo was still gobbling mousse and quaffing a flute of *1995 Veuve Clicquot La Grande Dame* when Ray Berger walked up with both fists wrapped around Budweisers.

"I gotta give you credit, Ray," Del Largo said, speaking to his new in-law, trying to placate Marla.

"What's that, Jack?" Ray said with an amiable smile.

"You are loyal."

Ray stared back blankly until Jack motioned to his T-shirt then to the beer cans in his hands.

"Oh, yeah," Ray said laughing, "I do love my Vitamin B."

"Vitamin B? B for beer?"

"*B* for Budweiser, Jack. But I guess you could say *B* for beer. I prefer longnecks," Ray said, holding up the cans. "But, hey, it's free!"

"Tell me about it." Del Largo took a slug of champagne, grimacing like it was vinegar. "I hate to bring it up, Ray, but it is traditional for the bride's family to pay for the wedding. Or at least *something*."

Ray looked at Jack and took a long swallow from one of the Buds.

"Well, Jack, now that you mention it, I feel a little bad about that. Times is tough lately. I got a lotta mouths to feed, what with all the kids and the grandkids. Don't even talk about the alimony I'm payin' to wives one *and* two. And I'm still gettin' bills from Minnie's stomach staplin'."

Del Largo shook his head, his jaws clamped shut.

"I was gonna offer to barter, Jack."

"Barter? What kind of barter?" Del Largo said, not even trying to hide his disdain.

"I was gonna offer to get rid of that big tree that fell on your house. Woulda sold the wood and split the profit with you. But I drove by the other night and it was gone. I guess he who hesitates is late."

"Lost," Del Largo said, then under his breath, "*idiot*!"

"Whatever," Ray said. "Anyway, I figure the tree probably paid for the whole wedding anyways, so it's not like its comin' outa your pocket."

"Ray, that Vitamin B you're swilling has gone to your head," Del Largo said and started to walk away.

"Yeah, I bet that mahogany fetched a pretty penny."

Del Largo stopped in his tracks and wheeled on Ray, his eyes hard as buttons. "Mahogany?"

Ray smiled like he'd just found a twenty dollar bill in an old coat pocket. He drained one of the Buds and crushed the can in his fist.

"Hell, Jack, you didn't even know, did you?"

Ray turned toward the hors d'oeuvre table and called to a burly young man piling food on a plate.

"Jack, you met my son, Billy Ray? Raymona's big brother?"

Del Largo nodded to Billy Ray, but didn't offer his hand.

"Jack, I know you think we're a buncha yokels," Ray said with an affable glint in his eyes. "But everybody's smart about somethin'. Billy Ray here's smart about trees. He's a landscaper. Real worker bee, ain't ya son?"

"Sunup to sundown, daddy," Billy Ray said without a shred of hubris.

"He's got all the saws and grinders and such to take out a tree as big as you want. Son, you're gonna get a kick outa this. Jack here had a giant mahogany tree in his front yard."

"I seen it, daddy. When we drove by to see where Raymona's been spendin' all her time."

"Well, that tree tipped over in the storm. I was gonna offer Jack here to cut it up for free. You know, as our part of the wedding cost. But you was so busy and everything after the storm. Then it was gone."

Billy Ray looked at Jack and smiled with innocent admiration.

"Golly, Mr. Del Largo, I bet that tree paid for this whole wingding. You shoulda called me, daddy. I'da come runnin'. We'd be rich."

"That's the joke, boy. Jack here didn't know it was mahogany, did you, Jack? I bet you had somebody haul that wood away without makin' a nickel."

Del Largo's face had turned deep scarlet. Ray was beaming. Billy Ray's mouth was wide open. Both of them looking at him like *he* was the hayseed.

"That's a dang shame, Mr. Del Largo," Billy Ray said with childlike sincerity. "Mahogany's worth its weight in gold. You mighta got upwards ninety or a hundred."

A relieved expression came onto Del Largo's face. "A hundred dollars?"

Billy Ray laughed. "No. Thousand. A hundred *thousand* dollars."

Del Largo felt like a ball-peen hammer was tap dancing on the back of his skull. He stalked off with an audible growl, grabbed another flute of *Veuve Clicquot,* and plopped down next to a dripping dolphin ice sculpture, shoulders hunched, his face now the color of chili pepper.

On the other side of the swimming pool David Grand and Jarrett Griffin strolled up to Sherwood Steele who was standing poised like a rooster, puffing a brown cigarette, thumb hooked to the watch pocket of his white suit.

"Gentlemen," Steele said with not quite a nod.

"Sherwood," said Grand, a troubled expression on his face. The mayor was sipping his fourth or fifth Old Raj martini – he'd lost count – his red varicose nose sweaty and swollen. "We've got to talk."

A waiter came up with a fresh tray of martinis. Each man took one and they walked down to the river and sat on a bench facing Sailboat Bend. The mayor scanned the lawn, making sure they were out of earshot. Grand recounted an agitated telephone call he'd gotten from Roscoe Anderson.

"So what?" Steele said, rolling his cigarette urbanely between his thumb and forefinger.

"Some guy shows up on Roscoe's doorstep," Grand said. "He starts cross-examining him. Talking about the old man's murder. The Pelican's Nest fire. The Dew Drop Inn. Making noise about Anderson driving out motel owners. Making all kind of innuendoes. Says he's going to the State Attorney. Roscoe's scared shitless!"

"And this is who?" Steele said.

"Owns a bar down on the beach," Jarrett Griffin said. "Sea Shanty. Apparently was a cop in New York City, then a federal prosecutor. Max Brady's his name."

"Don't worry about it," Steele said, nonchalant, taking a slow sip from the clear cocktail.

The revelers had imbibed an enormous witch's brew of intoxicants and, like a cauldron over a flame, the celebration was coming to a boil. Raymona was at the center of it all, spilling out of her wedding dress on the dance floor. Mandy staggered through the crowd, downing flute after flute of champagne, hugging and kissing every man and women she encountered.

Grand hostess Marla was making the rounds. Flapping her fan. Laughing and chattering with the Marshals, the Bakers, the Griffins, and the Grands. She came upon Tiffani Bandeaux in rapt conversation with Eva Epstein as they nibbled lobster mango canapés. Tiffani was wearing an emerald gown that looked like it had been painted on. Eva sat beside her, dowdy by comparison; almost sexless, identifiable as a woman only by her dress and a barely perceptible swell of bosom. *A thoroughbred sharing oats with a nag,* Marla thought, inspecting Tiffani, wondering how much pain went into making a body like that.

Norman Epstein stood a safe distance away – he hoped – squirming, pensive, his eyes frozen on his wife and the woman he betrayed her with, trying to decipher their body language, only to be jolted by a sharp slap on the shoulder.

"Don't look so frightened, Norman," Sherwood Steele said.

The banker recoiled like Steele was a rabid dog. "Don't touch me, you blackmailer."

"Norman, I'm hurt. I thought we were friends."

"So did I," Epstein said and walked off.

Jada McDonald and the Sunshine Riders broke out into U2's *Vertigo.*

"Slam!" Mandy screamed, overcome by the throbbing beat.

Within seconds the patio became a mosh pit. Bodies banging wildly. Tuxedoed men and women in elegant gowns crushing and groping like jungle savages. Their prodigious alcohol intake coalescing with the pulsating music, filling the air with a sexual frenzy. The hysteria reached a crescendo when Mandy sprinted screaming across the dance floor and catapulted herself into the swimming pool. She sank like an anchor, her platinum dress wafting up over her head. Within seconds, the other bride's maids plunged in to rescue her. They hauled Mandy out of the water, sputtering, laughing riotously, and dragged her into the house, barely able to keep her feet, reeking of alcohol.

"Nobody light a cigarette," said Gina Perini. "Mandy'll burst into flames."

They helped her into the bathroom and peeled off her sopping gown. Mandy was half-naked when she pointed at the Jacuzzi.

"Helluva party in there the other night," she said, giggling.

"What party?" said Gina.

"Raymona's bachelorette party."

"You are such a silly goose," Gina said, removing Mandy's undergarments.

She pulled down her panties and noticed a red blotch on Mandy's left buttock cheek. It looked like a birthmark. Gina was confused. She, Mandy, and Raymona had been cheerleaders together at Stranahan High

School. They'd showered together every day for years, Gina secretly admiring the figures of her better-endowed friends. She did not recall Mandy having a blemish on her bottom.

"I am not a shilly gooth," Mandy said, her neck swiveling like a bobblehead doll.

"You are too," Gina said. She bent down, her wide eyes inches from Mandy's ass. "Raymona didn't have a bachelorette party."

"Did too. Right there."

Mandy hiccupped. She felt the room begin to swirl.

"Mandy, where did you get this hickey?"

"Hickey?"

"You've got a monkey bite on your butt. Who exactly was at this bachelorette party?"

Mandy closed her eyes, trying to make the room stop moving. "Just me and Raymona." She giggled again. "And Chip."

"Chip?"

"Chip Chippendale." Eyes still closed, a smile was painted on her pretty face. "Hunky. Big muscles. Big everything! Kept us up all night. Or did we keep him up? I dunno!"

"You and Raymona were in the Jacuzzi with a *man*?"

"Sssshhhhh!" Mandy hissed and fell to the floor, laughing hysterically. "Don't tell anybody we were naked. John Junior'll be pissed."

Jack Del Largo sat in purple rage, his blood pressure rising with every drip of the dolphin ice sculpture beside him, downing glass after glass of champagne, pouring kerosene on the wildfire raging inside him. Standing in the middle of the inferno was Adonis Rock. *A hundred grand! That motherfucker's fucking with the wrong fucking guy!*

"Mr. Del Largo! Mr. Del Largo!"

Aldo the wedding planner, dressed in white, speedwalked heel-to-toe across the lawn. He stopped in front of Del Largo and placed his hands on his hips.

"We're ready for your toast. Followed by the cutting of the cake. And then the surprise grand finale." Aldo pointed his right pinky toward Sailboat Bend, where a black barge had anchored. "Mark my words, Mr. Del Largo, this was an inspired idea. It's going to make this the absolute wedding of the year!"

"Yeah and cost me another twenty grand." Del Largo said acidly. He rose unsteadily, bracing himself on the ice sculpture, and made his way to the stage.

Gina Perini emerged from the house and was intercepted by her boyfriend, Rick Begatta, one of John Junior's groomsmen. He dragged her onto the dance floor, but Gina was too distracted to dance. She whispered something in his ear and Begatta stopped gyrating. Vic Amato, John's best man, was sitting off the dance floor a few feet away. Begatta leaned over and mumbled something to him. Vic shot out of his chair like he'd been stung by a bee.

"What should we do?" Begatta said.

"I don't know, Rick."

"If it's me," Begatta said, "I wanna know."

On stage, Jada MacDonald was speaking into the microphone. "Now, here's the proud papa, who must love his son a heck of a lot to pay for this shindig. Give it up for the one, the only, Mr. Jack Del Largo."

Del Largo climbed onto the stage to boisterous applause. He forced a smile onto his face, reminding himself that his guests were a cornucopia of capitalism. The collected worth of those gathered was probably two or three billion dollars. Del Largo stretched his arms toward them in a grandiloquent embrace, looking in his tuxedo like a portly penguin with its wings spread.

Across the yard his son, the groom, leaned against a palm tree on legs as wobbly as a newborn colt. John Junior had been drinking hard all day. The first whiskeys had exploded in his head like July 4th firecrackers. Now his brain was a mucilaginous blob of goo. He was so drunk his friends were razzing him about not being able to consummate his marriage.

He grabbed his crotch in defiance. "Don' worry 'bout me. I got what Raymona needs."

John Junior cackled and a globule of whiskey dripped from his mouth. Vic Amato and Rick Begatta came up behind him. Without a word, they seized his arms and pulled him off to a dark corner of the yard. They didn't notice his father raising his champagne glass to the crowd.

"What the fuck you doing," the young Del Largo said to his groomsmen. "We're gonna cut the cake."

"Maybe not," said Vic.

Del Largo was speaking to the crowd. "Thank you all so much for being here on this most special day for our family. Marla and I are so pleased you are able to share this blessed event with us. You know, I've learned many things in my lifetime. We all know that money and big houses and beautiful yachts are important. That's no secret to anyone here. But I've found that *the* most important thing in life isn't money or possessions. No, my friends, the single most significant thing in life is love. And we are here today to celebrate the love between two young people..."

A loud crack rang out from the far end of the pool. It was followed by a high-pitched shriek. All eyes turned from Del Largo. Raymona was holding a hand to her face while John Junior teetered belligerently over her.

"You bastard!" she squealed.

"You goddamned whore!" he shouted. "Fucking another guy *in my house* two days before our wedding!"

John Junior slapped Raymona hard across the cheek. Then he grabbed her by the hair and hurled her into the swimming pool. Billy Ray Berger came up fast from behind him. He spun around his brand new brother-in-law and slammed a fistful of bunched knuckles square into John Junior's nose. Blood gushed and the groom fell into the pool next to his wife. Within seconds the wedding party erupted into free-swinging, fist-flying throwdown. The Clampetts versus the Drysdales.

Out on Sailboat Bend the barge master mistook the melee for his cue and pushed a button. Fireworks began bursting in the night. The sky erupted into brilliant blues and reds and greens. On shore, men in black ties flailed away. Women in floor-length gowns pulled hair and ripped at each other's clothes. Ray Berger took a swing at Jack Del Largo, who ducked, and caught Jada McDonald on the jawbone, prompting the *Sunshine Riders* to join the donnybrook. Marla climbed onto a table, imploring her guests to stop fighting. Someone crashed into the table and Marla toppled onto the four-tiered white cake. The Wedding of the Year had turned into a horror movie. Within minutes, flashing red lights were racing across the old swinging bridge with sirens blaring.

Bradys Run

CHAPTER FORTY TWO

MAX BRADY MISSED the old Orange Bowl. He and his grandfather used to drive to Little Havana for Dolphins' games back in the day when Don Shula, Bob Griese, and Larry Csonka ruled professional football. The stadium was rickety, but the grandstand hung out over the gridiron like a balcony and eighty thousand delirious fans could dominate a game by the force of sheer bedlam.

The Dolphins' glory days were over. The 21st Century team was a shadow of its former self. The stadium it inhabited reflected the team's mediocrity. The seats seemed miles from the field and fans didn't play the essential role they once had. Not that Brady much cared. His zeal for sports quelled after Victoria's death.

Since moving to Florida, though, Victor Gruber had become a rabid Fins fan. He owned season tickets and once or twice a year cajoled Brady into joining him for a game. On this Sunday they went early, set up a grill, cooked hotdogs and hamburgers, and split a six-pack of Pilsner Urquell, the heavy Czech brew Victor insisted was the world's finest beer. Brady pushed Victor into the stadium to the wheelchair section just beneath the skyboxes on the west side of the field.

The Dolphins were playing the hated New York Jets, whose insufferable green-and-white-clad fans were being embraced by the locals with remorseless scorn. Brady expected fisticuffs to break out some time during the game. But by the fourth quarter Miami was up 34-10 and the crowd was placid, at least compared to the Orange Bowl days.

The clock was moving slower than a nonagenarian pushing a walker. Brady lost interest in the field action and began scanning the luxury skyboxes for a vicarious glimpse of life among the privileged class. The sign in the box directly behind the wheelchair section identified the owner as *Woulfe Brothers.* Brady knew the name. The big daddy of South Florida construction companies. Its wolf-head crest was plastered all over the high-rises going up on the beach. The company lair held a couple dozen people. Unlike Brady and the commoners in the cheap seats, attired in T-shirts and shorts, the muck-a-mucks were decked out in their Sunday best. Brady scoured the faces, curious to see if he recognized any. One looked vaguely familiar. He leaned over to Victor and motioned toward the skybox.

"Who's the guy with the fat red face?"

Victor spun his chair around and looked up. "That's David Grand, your mayor. Rose's adversary. The man next to him with curly blonde hair is Harvey Woulfe, the builder. I've seen him speak downtown."

"Who's the ice cream vendor next to him? He doesn't look like he loses much sleep worrying about money. More to the point, who's the woman next to him?"

Victor studied the man in the white suit. Then, like Brady, his eyes were drawn to the woman.

"I don't know the young lady, but the gentleman is Sherwood Steele, the luxury resort tycoon. He owns Shangri-La."

"Looks like he owns a spectacular redhead too. She looks even better in a bikini."

"I'm sure you're correct," Victor said.

"What is it about money that attracts beautiful women?"

"Perception, my friend. Nothing to do with reality. Money has the power to turn a pygmy into a colossus. Many women find that quite magnetic. Of course, the lack of money has also transformed goliaths into midgets." Victor pulled out his cell phone and pointed it toward the skybox. "I take it you are familiar with the beautiful young auburn-haired lady?"

"I've seen her around. What are you doing?"

"I thought Rose might like a picture of her opponent cozily ensconced between the city's two biggest building magnates."

Bradys Run

CHAPTER FORTY THREE

LITTLE DONNIE ROCKWELL was playing in the woods with Georgie Ingles and Tommy Patrick. At age nine, they were the big kids in the neighborhood. Donnie was only six and looked up to Georgie and Tommy like older brothers. He was always trying to impress them.

"Watch me climb to the top," he shouted.

He scaled a giant oak tree, scampering like a monkey from branch to branch. He was nearing the apex when he heard Tommy yell.

"Snake!"

Georgie bawled. *"Python!"*

"It's slithering up the tree. Run!"

"No, don't go you guys!" Donnie screamed. *"Tommy! Georgie! Come back!"*

They didn't listen and Donnie was left trapped in the oak, overcome by a black panic. He could feel the python slithering up the tree toward him. He screamed as loud as he could, hoping someone would rescue him. Then he heard loud banging. *It's Georgie and Tommy! They're killing the snake.* Relief coursed through him. The noise grew louder. Then he heard a voice.

"Open the goddamned door!"

Adonis Rock awoke with a start and shook his head. He was stupid with sleep and whiskey and cocaine. He opened one eye and grappled to get his bearings. *Where the hell am I?* Wherever he was, it was black as a mausoleum. He smelled disinfectant and realized he was back in the *Rat's Nest.* Then everything came flooding back. *Fire. Wind. Rain. Tree. Hookers. Money. A dead man floating in a swimming pool.*

"Open up," the voice bellowed.

Shut the fuck up, Adonis thought, too tired to speak. The red crystal display on the digital clock beside his bed read 12:00. *Noon or midnight? Did I sleep twelve hours? Or twenty four?* He tumbled from the bed, using the wall to hold himself up, and tripped to the door. He twisted the knob and was stabbed in the eyes by blinding white light. The door burst open and a man bowled into him like he'd been shot from a circus cannon.

"Motherfucker!"

They tumbled into the wall like dice on a craps table. Adonis slid to the floor and sat there with his eyes closed, too tired to look up, definitely too tired to fight. He finally forced open his left eye. Jack Del Largo was standing over him, snorting like a dyspeptic rhinoceros.

"You ripped me off!" he shouted. "*And* you screwed my son's wife!"

Shit! Adonis thought, remembering the big-breasted blonde. *Raymona. I knew that was a mistake.* He couldn't speak. Or lift his head. He wanted to go back to sleep, his python dream forgotten.

"You son of a bitch!" Del Largo said. "I pay a hundred grand for a wedding and the marriage is over before the goddamn reception. Then I find out you conned me on the tree."

Jesus! One minute Jack's harmless as a Cub Scout, the next minute he's Mike fucking Tyson.

Adonis tried to muster his strength. It was no use. With his eyes closed again he mumbled up at Del Largo. "Hey, Jack, listen man, them bimbos practically raped me."

Del Largo looked down at him. He was seething, but didn't argue. He knew Raymona would stray sooner or later. This was about three years sooner than he expected, though. John Junior was devastated. Worse, Marla had come completely undone. She'd been shamed before

South Florida's glitterati. After the police left their house last night she wept uncontrollably.

"I'm a laughingstock. I'll never be able to show my face in this town again. We have to sell the house and leave Fort Lauderdale, Jack. *NOW!*"

Del Largo stood over him yapping like a small dog. "You knew that tree was mahogany. And you had the balls to charge me ten fucking grand!"

Adonis listened, eyes still closed, and shrugged his shoulders.

"Hey, Jack, what can I say. Buyer beware. We had a deal."

"What deal?"

"Look at the contract. Any wood I haul away is mine. You signed it. I can't help it you don't know a mahogany tree from your big fat ass."

"What did you get for it?" Del Largo demanded.

Adonis tilted his head up and squinted. *You fat fuck! So fucking smart! Outfoxed by a tree trimmer!*

"A hundred.

"A hundred?"

Adonis's face lit up in a smug, bleary smile. "Thousand. One hundred thousand dollars."

Del Largo wailed like his scrotum was being squeezed by hot tongs. "That's my money. I want that money. Do you hear me?"

Adonis shimmied his back up the wall until he stood, teetering, face-to-face with Del Largo. "Jack, I got one thing to say."

"What's that?"

"Screw yourself! You ain't gettin' a penny."

Adonis lurched at him. Del Largo backpedaled and tripped over a chair. He fell hard onto the bed and the frame buckled and crashed to the floor.

"Shit!" he panted, wheezing like an asthmatic. "My back!"

Adonis was wide awake now. His right arm shot out faster than a snake fang and grabbed him at the base of his third chin. He squeezed. Not hard. Not soft. Just enough to throttle his breathing. Del Largo's eyes bulged and he made the puling sound of a strangling man. Adonis put a finger to his lips and spoke in a serene, almost soothing voice.

"Shush."

Del Largo obeyed and Adonis's grip slackened. The big man lay splayed across the bed, breathing hard, drool trickling from the corners of his open mouth down his flabby cheeks. Adonis jerked him savagely to his feet. He pulled him to the door, opened it, and thrust Del Largo into the harsh morning light.

He stumbled into the Rat's Nest parking lot and stood bent over, hands on knees, gasping for air. After a minute he tried to speak, but it came out sounding like a frog's croak.

"You're going to pay for this," he said. "Nobody fucks with Jack Del Largo."

"I just did, Jack. Don't ever bother me again," Adonis said and slammed the door.

Bradys Run

CHAPTER FORTY FOUR

A BAREFOOT ROSE Becker was standing on the low white wall that curved along the sidewalk bordering Lauderdale Beach. A gaggle of bathers had gathered around her, their toes dug into the sand, blanketed by the shadow of *The Aztec*, a thirty-story condominium-hotel under construction across the street. Rose raised a bullhorn to her lips.

"We've become a *shadow world*," she blared. "Monstrosities like *The Aztec* are blotting out the sun. The beach looks like a piano with more black keys than white."

An elderly man with a deep tan was listening, holding a metal detector in his arms. "You are exactly right, young lady," he said. "If you don't get here by two in the afternoon these days you can miss the sun altogether."

Rose nodded toward him. "That's because Mayor Grand has abdicated his responsibility to the people of this city and sold out to the developers."

"Go girl!" shouted a woman with two small kids at her feet. "Tell it like it is!"

Sylvia Sanchez, the TV news reporter, was covering the event. A cameraman stood behind her with his lens pointed over her shoulder. Sanchez held her microphone toward Rose.

"Ms. Becker, Mayor Grand has raised twenty dollars in campaign contributions to every one of yours. How can you possibly compete against that kind of money?"

"Where do you think Grand's money is coming from, Sylvia?" Rose shot back.

A confused look crossed Sanchez's face. Reporters like to ask questions, not answer them. Rose did wait for a response. She pointed a finger at *The Aztec*.

"I'll tell you where. Ninety percent of his money is coming from developers, contractors, and big hotel companies. The same people who are making fortunes building these monstrosities and destroying our beach. It's all about money."

The crowd responded with spirited ovation.

"You've got my vote," the old man said.

"Mine too," said the young mother.

"Me too," said another voice.

Rose looked down and saw Max Brady. She rolled her eyes.

"Thanks for your support," she said to the scattering crowd. "And remember, be an *SOB*. Save Our Beach from the shadow world."

Two skinny teenage boys in baggy bathing suits walked up carrying boogie boards.

"Hey, lady," said one. He had shaggy blond hair. "You're way too hot to be a lesbo."

Rose hopped down onto the sidewalk in front of them.

"Thanks for the compliment boys, I think. Now go play in the water. Watch out for jellyfish."

"Hey, lady," Brady said, "you're way too hot to be a mayor."

"Thanks." She nodded toward the boogie boys. "If you hurry you can catch up with your friends."

"I'd rather listen to you give speeches."

"Too late. You should have gotten here sooner."

"Never too late. What do you need? Money? Advice? A Madame Butterfly banner hanging outside the Sea Shanty?"

Brady had gotten back from the Dolphins game and gone for a jog down the beach when he came upon Rose. He'd never seen her speak in public. She made an alluring candidate in her cut-off shorts and SOB T-shirt. And he liked her fire, raging against the political machine.

He abandoned his run and walked back down the beach with her. They skimmed stones and splashed their bare feet in the warm surf. Rose's long black hair rustled in the soft sea breeze.

"Did you know," he said, "that the Atlantic is saltier than the Pacific?"

"Really? Did you know that all seven continents are wider at their north ends than the south ends?"

"Did you know nine-out-of-ten women instinctively turn to their right when they walk into a department store?"

"Did you know men are six times more likely than women to be struck by lightning?"

"Okay, okay," he said. "I give up. You know more than me. You win."

They both laughed. Then Rose's face hardened.

"What's going on, Brady? Do the police have any leads on Jonas's murder yet?"

"Not many, from what John McCarty tells me. But I think if we can identify the Pelican's Nest torch we'll be closer to knowing who drowned Jonas."

She cast an inquisitive look at him. "We?"

He shrugged. "Jonas was my friend. So are Gunther and Olga. I owe it to them to find whose doing this."

"It's nice to see you are finally engaged in more than hawking beer and ogling girls in bikinis."

Brady looked at her, searching for a smile, but Rose's face was solemn.

"You know it drove Jonas crazy," she said.

"What did?"

"That you wouldn't get involved in our fight to save the beach. You grew up here. This is your sand more than any of ours. You, of all people, should want to protect it."

The afternoon sun was sinking behind the high-rises. The shadows had already crept down to the water line. Brady kicked an ankle high wave as it rolled onto shore.

"Look, Rose, you're the Joan of Arc. I'm no crusader."

"What exactly are you, Brady?"

"You're apparently the expert on me." His voice was brusque, defensive. "I'm the beer merchant. The guy who admires pretty girls on the beach. That's who I am."

Rose frowned at him and he instantly wanted to retract his words and respeak them in a more amicable tone. She shook her head slowly, like she was trying to muster the nerve to say something. Finally, she spoke with a gentle, almost motherly inflection.

"Brady, I know about you. I know about your wife. I know how she died. I can only imagine how painful that was for you. And is still."

He didn't respond or look at her. His face twisted. He'd never spoken of Victoria's death with Rose, or anyone, except Victor. The subject had always been off limits. He certainly wasn't prepared to talk about her now. His insides began to churn and his legs grew weak. She reached over and touched his elbow.

"I'm sorry for your heartache. Victor told me she was an extraordinary woman. A beautiful woman. I know you loved her deeply. Maybe more than you'll ever love another woman. But I think the day your wife died you gave up living too. I suppose I understand. That was then, though. This is now. She's gone. You're not. Come back to the living, Brady. You could be happy."

He gazed out at the horizon thinking about Victoria. Her flaxen hair, her lush lips, her joyful sensuality. A mile offshore a half dozen cargo ships sat at anchor awaiting berths in port. Beyond them a single shaft of sunlight broke through a chute in the clouds, shining like a laser beam on a patch of sea just over the earth's curve.

He turned and looked at Rose. She was wordless now, her face sphinxlike. He sensed she too was thinking of Victoria, or the ghost of a woman she'd never met. Rose looked up at him. Then, without another word, she handed him her bullhorn and took off running. He watched her lope down the beach, her legs long and athletic, her feet leaving graceful *S*-shaped inscriptions in the sand.

Brady knew Rose was right. Victoria's death had sucked the life from him, like the marrow from his bones. The pain had always been too black for him to bear. He locked it in cold storage. *Freeze it or die!* He might as well have died. The last years had been an emotional flat line. Working, joking, at times even laughing, yet his soul as numb as a paralytic's limbs. Devoid of joy, love, passion, hate. Victoria's specter was all that kept him going. A secret notion, a quite delirious notion, he knew, that she – or at least her spirit – was with him still, watching over him, protecting him, like a guardian angel. Waiting for that day when Father Time would wield his scythe and they'd be together again.

It occurred to Brady that he'd slept through the spring and summer of his life. Now it was autumn and he felt a stirring inside. An awakening. As if he was coming out of a coma. And the reason was Rose. *Come back to the living!* Was it possible? *You could be happy!* He remembered his dream. Embracing Victoria and Rose on the beach. Was that Victoria stamping Rose with her imprimatur? Was she telling him to be happy? Or was it just an empty hallucination? Wishful thinking.

By the time he got back to the Sea Shanty Brady felt like a family of fiddler crabs was crawling around his innards. He thought he might be sick right there on the sidewalk. Two doors down, at the entrance to the Papillon, Rose was sitting on the curb watching him, her face as glum as the color purple.

"Sorry, Brady," she said as he walked up. "I crossed the line."

He handed her the bullhorn. "Can I buy you a beer?"

Rose looked at him with somber eyes, as if she'd hoped to hear something more.

"I've gotta get upstairs. Yoga class in five minutes."

"Will you keep teaching yoga and Pilates when you're mayor?"

"Why not?" she said with a slight smile. "Whip the whole city into shape."

Her smile lightened Brady's mood. "That should be your campaign poster. I can see it. You, dressed up like Uncle Sam, pointing your finger. The caption will say: *'Madame Butterfly! She'll whip YOUR CITY into shape!'*"

"Hmmm, you might have something, Brady. You should be my campaign manager."

"I'll come up later. We can discuss strategy in the sunshine – while we still have some."

An hour later, he shoved a few *Sam Adams'* into an ice bucket and scaled the stairs to the rooftop. Rose was sitting at the center of a circle surrounded by a dozen middle-aged women leading them through *asanas,* as he remembered her calling yoga positions. She was wearing black spandex, her arms stretched in front of her, her legs lifted, her back tilted to form a *V*, as limber as a Twyla Tharp dancer.

"This is the *boat pose*," she said, "Stay steady on your sit bones and hold. Wonderful for core strength and abdominals."

Brady pulled up a chair, ocean on one side, Intracoastal on the other, Rose in the middle. He admired her physicality, gracefully balanced on her tailbone, holding the boat pose while her students grunted and strained. It struck Brady that she was a remarkable woman. Beautiful, smart, passionate, and only twenty seven. He felt prehistoric.

"You could have joined us," she said when the class ended.

"I'd be afraid of breaking something."

"Ah, give yourself credit. You're not *that* old. What are you – fifty?"

"Ouch! You shouldn't tease men about their age. We're sensitive – especially around beautiful young women."

"No need to be sensitive. To be honest, I'd say you're in fantastic shape."

"For an old man."

"For any man." Her smile was as warm as the late day sun. "You just need your chakras cleaned."

"Excuse me?"

"Energy centers. I sense your chakras are clogged. You seem to have a lot of anger."

"Me?" he scoffed, conjuring a happy face. "Fun-loving, devil-may-care Max Brady? Angry? Nonsense!"

"Could be a past life. Perhaps you were a hangman. Or a grave digger. Or an assassin. Whatever, your chakras need cleansing."

"You paint such a pleasant picture. What are you a chak-jock?"

"Very funny."

"You pulling some kinda chakra-con?"

"It's all about the meaning of life." She had a twinkle in her eyes and he wasn't sure if she was playing with him. "Don't you know the meaning of life?"

"The meaning of life," he said, "is to live."

Rose's face was daubed by the gentle glow of the paling sun. She gazed at him for a long moment. Her eyes were as blue as the nucleus of a flame. Her lips were painted in a half-smile as inscrutable as a DaVinci portrait. Impulsively, he reached over and touched the back of her hand. He regretted it at once, as if he'd punctured an invisible bubble between them. To his astonishment, though, Rose took his hand in hers and squeezed. The effect was electric.

He said: "You're trying to decide what to make of me, no?"

"How can you tell?"

"I'm reading your chakra."

She stifled a laugh. "Get outa here."

"You should know something about me, Rose. I can read people. It's like I have ESPN."

"ESP?"

"No matter. All I know is I could make a fortune as a poker player."

Rose turned toward the east and looked out at the ocean. It was an exquisite autumn afternoon. A group of teenage girls and boys were frolicking in the shallows a few yards off the beach. A flock of pelicans glided lazily over their heads. She turned back to him and spoke in a voice as downy and weightless as falling snow.

"What *should* I make of you, Max Brady?"

He was thunderstruck. He knew at once that a door had just opened abruptly on his life. It may have been the most consequential door he'd ever stood before. Rose on one side, Victoria's ghost on the other. He could stand pat, stay where he'd been these many years, alone, emotionally insensate, he and his lost love, less tangible than a rainbow. Or he could walk through that door to Rose. He did not delude himself. If he chose her, he fully expected to be spurned. She was so young and beautiful. Why would she ever want to be with him? The thought was absurd. But it was time to find out. One way or another, he wanted to know. Then he could move on with his life. He took a deep breath and stepped into the void. He spoke in a hushed voice, as if he was afraid to wake someone.

"You could take pity on me."

"Pity?" she said with a confused expression. "For what?"

"For being a forty two-year-old man madly in love with a twenty seven-year-old woman."

Brady's heart was beating like a tom-tom. Rose sat silent for what seemed like an eternity. She stared at him, then back out at the ocean. The teenagers had stopped splashing and were paired off into couples, embracing in the warm water. A pelican nose-dived into the green sea and surfaced with a fish squirming in its long bill. Brady searched her face. The quivering late day sun had produced a halo around her head and he had the sensation of gazing at an angel. She ran her fingers through her long black hair and turned back to him. Brady noticed, for the first time, flecks of gold in her blue eyes, shimmering like the sun on a sylvan pond. She smiled a tender smile and spoke in a drowsy voice.

"Pity me, too."

"Pity you?" Now he was puzzled. "For what?"

"For being a twenty seven-year-old woman utterly in love with a forty two-year-old man."

She leaned toward him, her mouth so near he inhaled her breath.

"Poor child," he whispered and touched his lips to hers.

Bradys Run

CHAPTER FORTY FIVE

A MOB OF picketers rushed David Grand's white stretch limo as it coasted to a stop in front of the downtown City Centre. The red-faced mayor lumbered from his car to chants of *"Shadow world! Shadow world! Shadow world!"* Grand, his jaws clenched, trudged through a forest of placards emblazoned with incendiary phrases. *Cronyism! Sell Out! Government in the Sunshine, Not in the Shade!* Passing cars honked and drivers raised fists in solidarity with Rose Becker and her army of supporters.

"Shine a light on the *shadow world*," Rose shouted.

"Yeah, shine a light on the *shadow world*," a man's voice repeated. It was Max Brady.

Grand grunted like a man with a bad case of heartburn and fled into the building to a chorus of *"Mayor Rose!"* and *"Madame Butterfly for Mayor!"*

The mayor felt safe inside the shiny, spangled City Centre. He was with his people, his base, here to introduce the Greater Fort Lauderdale Chamber of Commerce *Businessman of the Year.* The catcalls outside were soon washed away by rousing applause.

"Ladies and gentlemen," Grand said from the podium, "I have the great honor to introduce a man I've known since he was a boy. I knew his father and, I must say, the apple hasn't fallen far from the tree. But the tree is yielding many more apples these days."

While Grand paused for a smattering of polite laughter, Brady slipped into the rear of the ballroom. He stood against the back wall, unnoticed, and let his eyes sweep the audience. At a table up front he spied Cherry Hampton's platinum coiffeur. Toward the back he noticed a heavyset man who looked familiar. It took him a minute to connect the scowling face to a photograph in this morning's newspaper. *The Miami Herald* headline trumpeting: *"Society wedding ends in fireworks, fisticuffs, flashing lights."* The article identified Jack Del Largo as a local attorney and *political insider*. Brady remembered Jonas Bigelow's blunter description. *Bagman!*

"The Chamber's *Businessman of the Year*," Mayor Grand was saying from the stage, "has been building offices complexes, condominiums, and luxury resorts in South Florida, the Bahamas, and throughout the Caribbean for more than twenty years. Nobody has done it better. *Forbes* lists him as one of the hundred wealthiest Americans. He founded the dynamic South Florida National Bank. He owns the most exclusive golf club in America. He lives on the biggest yacht in the yachting capital of the world. He's building a mansion on the Intracoastal that, I'm told, will make Bill Gates' house look like a garage apartment. Oh, and I think he invented hot water. Most important, he's donated millions of dollars to children's education, battered women, and to beautify our fair city. Everything this man does is big. That's why it is such an honor for me to salute the Greater Fort Lauderdale Chamber of Commerce *Businessman of the Year* – the man from Shangri-La – Mr. Sherwood Steele."

The crowd rose in unison and lavished Steele with stirring applause. The *Man of the Year* waved grandly, resplendent in his trademark white suit and white smile set off by a deep tan and tongue of black hair licking his forehead. Steele basked in the adulation of South Florida's power elite. Every man and woman there was ready to eat from his hand if he asked.

The truth was, though, that the people who filled this room did not love or respect Steele. But they did fear him. He was their Great White Gordon Gekko and they were willing to attach themselves to him like remora if it meant getting pieces of his scraps. They also knew that sharks often swallow the fish that feed off them. The people now exalting Steele were fully aware he would fill the water with their blood if it suited his purposes.

"Friends, colleagues, fellow South Floridians," Steele began, as cool and smooth as a mountain lake. "I honestly am not worthy of such a great honor, but thank you nonetheless."

He spoke with the assurance of a man who expected his likeness to be cast in bronze someday. He talked about his father, his bank, his wealth, his philanthropy, his greatest deals, and his Shangri-La franchise. He mentioned a number of people in the ball room, including David Grand and Harvey Woulfe.

"And, finally, I want to thank my major domo. She is literally my right arm. Without her I would be lost. Miss Tiffani Bandeaux."

A woman stood up at a table at the front of the room. She turned and waved as the crowd clapped. Brady felt like he'd been poked in the ribs with an electric prod. Tiffani Bandeaux was the stunning redhead he'd seen on the big blue yacht the other day. And in the Dolphin skybox beside Steele yesterday. And now she was blowing kisses at him and the audience. *T. Bandeaux* was also the name on the documents he'd dug up at the courthouse. *T. Bandeaux* was the business agent for the secretive Delaware corporations that were buying up the beach motels.

Brady walked out a side door to a courtyard and sat beside a fountain in the shade of a Jacaranda tree. Chin in hands, he tried to sort through the jigsaw puzzle. The key pieces, it seemed, were in the City Centre at this moment. Cherry Hampton. Jack Del Largo. Tiffani Bandeaux. Sherwood Steele. *Man of the Year*. Developer. Founder of the bank that financed the motel deals. The same bank that made the daisy chain loans. Now it turns out Steele's *"right arm"* was also the front person for the recipients of those loans. *"I don't believe in coincidences,"* Jonas had said. Was it possible someone inside the ballroom was responsible for his murder? It was hard to fathom.

Brady, though, was having a tough time concentrating. His thoughts kept turning to Rose. Trying to grasp what had happened. How his life had taken such an extraordinary turn in a matter of hours.

Last night she'd worn a sleeveless saffron dress that italicized her narrow curved hips and toned bare arms. The two of them looking out at the Atlantic from the balcony of the *Casablanca Café*. Dim candlelight, nibbling calamari and yellowfin tuna, quaffing carafes of wine, hands cupped together on the table, staring into each other's eyes like love-struck adolescents.

"Promise me," she whispered.

"Anything."

"No secrets. Never leave anything unspoken between us."

"Yes. I swear."

Ambling back barefoot on the beach, two soft shadows against the mirrored sea, ushered by a full-faced October moon waltzing gracefully atop the liquid dance floor. Across the beach road, hand-in-hand, past crowded sidewalk tables rippling with genial chatter. More drinks at the *Elbo Room.* Sweaty dancing in a wild crush of corybantic revelers. Then to Rose's rooftop. Spiriting yoga mats into the greenhouse. Making love in the ambrosial mist. Embraced by the breathless hush of butterflies until the silver moon sank into the ocean. Brady felt brand new. As if reborn. Euphoria was coursing through him like a drug.

The ballroom doors crashed open and he was torn from his reverie. The crowd streamed out. It wasn't long before Sherwood Steele emerged. Tiffani Bandeaux was on his arm wrapped in a lush white fur that looked like it had once belonged to a member of some endangered species. They moved like matinee idols on a red carpet. Every eye riveted to them. So reverential Brady half-expected the crowd to genuflect. Mayor Grand, Harvey Woulfe, and Jack Del Largo followed close behind, like good dogs, or bad reputations. They were flanked by a big ominous looking man with a shaved skull who seemed to be missing the body part that normally connects the head to the shoulders.

"Sherwood!" Brady called out.

The cluster turned as one. Steele flashed a wide smile. His white teeth reminded Brady of razor wire glinting in the sun. He had never seen Steele up close. It was clear he enjoyed his celebrity, like a postulant in the Church of Trump.

"Congratulations, Sherwood," he said. "Quite an honor."

Steele's eyebrows arched like two question marks, trying to put a name to the face.

"Thanks," he said uncertainly.

"Miss Bandeaux." Brady extended his hand, searching her face for flaws, finding none. "It's a pleasure to see you again."

"Have we met?" Tiffani said with a slightly confused expression.

"Not formally, but it doesn't take an elephant to remember you on the deck of that yacht. And I've certainly been seeing your name a lot lately."

She stood assessing him like a string of expensive pearls.

"Oh?"

"On a fistful of motel deeds. Some changed hands two and three times in a matter of weeks. Remarkably, prices shot up every time. Values inflated tens of millions of dollars. Oh, and Sherwood, your bank made the loans. Don't you find that, what's the word – *curious?*"

A clumsy silence ensued. Tiffani turned to Steele. His smile had frozen but his eyes were burning like cinders. Brady got the sense Steele wore white to cloak a black heart. A vulture masquerading as a dove.

"Can I assume you represent Mr. Steele in that capacity?"

"You shouldn't assume anything, Mr...."

"Brady. Max Brady."

A look of recognition came over Steele's face and his smile mutated into an arctic glare.

"Brady," he said. "Ex-New York cop. Ex-federal prosecutor."

"Doing your homework, are you Sherwood?"

"Why are you wasting my time?"

"Somebody murdered a friend of mine. And burned out another."

"What's that got to do with me?"

"You and Miss Bandeaux secretly bought their properties, along with a slew of other motels. All in the same four block area." He glanced at David Grand. "Thanks to a whole lot of coercion from the City of Fort Lauderdale. I thought you could give me some insight."

Brady felt Steele's malignant eyes lock on him like a sniper with his prey in the crosshairs. A dozen other eyes glowered in his direction.

"A little knowledge can be a dangerous thing, Mr. Brady," Steele said.

"Dangerous to who? Or is it whom? I can never remember."

"Sir, I am a very busy man. I don't have time for this nonsense. If you have questions, please address them to my lawyer."

Steele turned and he and his entourage started to walk away.

"Jack Del Largo's name is on the documents too." Steele stopped again. "I'm just curious, Sherwood. What are you up to down on the beach? All that buying and selling. Using your bank to jack up prices artificially. Motels burning. Old men dying."

Brady was having fun. He felt like a cop again. A torero waving his red cape. Interrogating his suspect. Taunting. Badgering. A grimace rippled across Sherwood's face like wind across water.

"Are you accusing me of something?"

"I hope I'm not being vague."

Steele moved in on him, his oily face inches from Brady's, and jabbed a finger into his chest. "Be careful what you say, my friend."

Brady smiled broadly. "Does this mean we're pals? Think I can get a ride on your big blue dinghy."

"Mister, you are playing with fire."

"You mean like the Pelican's Nest?"

"Be careful or you'll get burned too."

"Or drowned?"

Steele was about to say something when Jack Del Largo stepped forward, a hard look on his fleshy face.

"Sir, if you don't get away from Mr. Steele this minute I will go to the courthouse and get a restraining order against you."

Brady had a sudden urge to tweak the lawyer's pudgy nose and boink him on the head, his Moe to Del Largo's Curly.

"Have at it, Jack. While you do, I'll be calling a pal of mine at FDIC. He might like to know about a certain someone using the SFNB as his own private piggy bank."

Brady's words echoed through the corridor. Steele and the others scowled at him. Then Mayor Grand spoke up.

"Officer Dent."

The big bald guy stepped forward. Brady had pegged him as a plain-clothes cop, probably Grand's bodyguard. Dent was six inches shorter than Brady but had sixty pounds more beef. He stood in close and looked up at him, his eyes black as wormholes in fetid fruit.

"Who are you?" Brady said.

The big man nodded at the mayor. "I'm his friend," he said in a trombone voice.

"What's the matter?" said Brady. "Couldn't find a tarantula?"

"Step back, brother. I'd hate to have to roust a badge." Plainclothes prodded him with his ample stomach. Brady stood stock still and was rewarded with a gust of day old whiskey breath.

"No offense, *brother*," he said, "but you're toilet water ain't making it."

Officer Dent's lips curled in a ruthless smile. He glommed onto Brady's arm with a hand the size of a ham hock.

"You're gonna get more grief than you want, fella. Back off."

"I hate to be a pain in the neck," said Brady, "but I notice you don't have one."

"That's enough," Sherwood Steele said.

His face was a mask now, severe, inexplicit, betraying no emotion, like a Royal Guardsman standing sentinel. He turned on his heels and marched off, his clutch of hangers-on in tow.

"Watch your back, brother," Officer Dent said and followed the others.

Brady watched them walk off, rubbing his arm and wondering what bitter fruit might sprout from the seeds he'd just sown.

Bradys Run

CHAPTER FORTY SIX

JOHN McCARTY NAVIGATGED his red Fire Investigation Unit van through the twists and turns of State Road 16, adjusting his window visor to block the blinding slats of sunlight coruscating through groves of tall loblolly pine. Max Brady sat in the passenger seat. It was nearly noon by the time they pulled through the stone gateway into the Florida State Prison.

Ringed by thirty foot concrete walls garnished with guard towers and concertina wire, the penitentiary was the hell-hole-home of fifteen hundred men, half of whom were serving life sentences and were likely to die here. McCarty and Brady entered through the red brick administration building.

"We've been expecting you, Captain McCarty," said a guard in a brown uniform from behind green steel bars. He signaled another uniform in a glass booth who threw a switch and a set of bar doors rattled open.

Brady and McCarty emptied their pockets, stepped through a metal detector, and signed waivers promising not to sue the State of Florida in the event one of them was shot, shanked, or otherwise molested. Another guard walked in who looked like he'd been assembled at the Abrams tank factory.

"I'm Officer Don Parker," he said, jangling a lanyard of big keys. He jammed one into a lock and rotated severely. "I'll be your escort."

McCarty held out a red and white carton of Marlboro cigarettes. "We brought this."

"I'll give it to him for you," Officer Parker said and took the package.

Three sets of bars clattered open and shut before Brady, McCarty, and their chaperon entered the main prison. They walked down a wide corridor with institutional beige walls and floors shiny enough to eat off. The building vibrated with an undercurrent, like giant pistons churning in the bowels of a powerhouse. Inmates in light blue shirts and dark blue pants with white-striped legs stepped aside as they passed. Many with arms so swollen from pumping iron that Brady wondered how they combed their hair. They came to a set of black steel doors and Officer Parker waved at a camera in the corner. A lock snapped.

"Gentlemen," he said, "welcome to the most dismal address on earth."

Death Row was a long dark catacomb of the living dead. Brady felt like he'd entered a parallel universe utterly devoid of joy. Even the air was bleak. The only evidence of an outside world was a splinter of blue sky visible at the top of a high concrete wall that ran the length of the cell block. Barred cells six feet wide and nine feet deep lined the corridor. Each contained a bed, sink, toilet, and a man in an orange V-neck shirt. Florida's roster of condemned currently stood at three hundred twenty. All of them, Brady noted, had sad, haunted eyes. Officer Parker stopped at the third cell from the steel door. A black inmate sat inside chewing a sandwich.

"What's for lunch, Bennie," he said.

"Baloney and cheese," the prisoner said. He held it up for them to see. "Governor send my pardon yet, boss?"

"Not yet, Bennie."

"That's a hurtin' thing," said Bennie.

"Any day now."

"I know that's right."

Under his breath, Parker told Brady and McCarty that Bennie had robbed a 7-Eleven and decided to murder the three women working there. The whole thing was recorded by security cameras.

"He's scheduled for execution next month."

"Sounds like he's still got hope," said McCarty.

"His lawyers claim Bennie's retarded and shouldn't be executed. Who knows? Florida's number one in overturned death sentences. It gives these guys hope. For most of them, though, it's false hope."

They had agreed that Brady would do the talking. The fire marshal stood back out of sight when they stopped in front of a cell halfway down the block. Brady was surprised when he saw the prisoner sitting on his bunk. The cold-blooded killer was a jagged little man with a hard, square face that resembled a clenched fist. He looked up at them with dark, bulging chihuahua eyes that twitched back and forth between the two like metronomes. Brady realized why McCarty called him *Crackhead.* A deep purple crevice zig-zagged like a lightning bolt across his forehead. *The Harry Potter of hitmen,* he thought.

"Looks like the San Andreas Fault," Brady whispered to Parker.

"Somebody cracked his skull with a baseball bat when he was a kid. Long before there was even a drug called crack. But don't call him Crackhead."

"Who the fuck are you?" Willie Corrales said.

His voice was startlingly raspy voice coming from such an elfin man.

"You don't know me, Willie," Brady said. He poked a hand through the bars. "I'm Max Brady."

Crackhead ignored his hand. "You a cop?"

"Not exactly."

"Fuck's that mean?"

"Ex-cop."

Officer Parker stepped to the bars and held out the box of Marlboros. "Mr. Brady brought you a gift, Willie."

Corrales took the cigarettes and threw them on the bed, his jumpy eyes darting up and down Brady.

"You trying to pin a new rap on me? Stick me with another ten years? Maybe you ain't heard. My life expectancy ain't that long."

"No, Willie. I'm here about your copycat."

Crackhead bit into his own baloney and cheese sandwich and took a sip of black coffee from a green plastic cup. A handful of potato chips and a Dixie Cup filled with syrupy canned peaches sat untouched on the tray. He chewed with his mouth open. Brady had seen better teeth on a Halloween pumpkin.

"What's this copycat bullshit?" Crackhead said. "I got no copycat."

"Somebody's been torching places and leaving your autograph."

"You know so much, tell me something."

"Willie, you were the master. The Picasso of pyros. Hotplates and gas jugs. That was your M.O. Somebody's ripping you off. Forging your signature."

Crackhead didn't respond, but Brady detected a flicker of recognition in his bug eyes. Corrales put down the sandwich and twisted one of his gray cadaverous fingers. A knuckle cracked like a dry twig.

"John McCarty put me onto you."

"McCarty? McCarty? I know a McCarty. Insurance prick."

"No more. He's a fire investigator in Fort Lauderdale. Somebody torched a motel there last week. McCarty said it was like déjà vu all over again. The hotplate reminded him of you. But you were here. He figures you must've taught the torch your technique. Like an apprentice."

"A pyro tyro," said Crackhead and let out a harsh cackle that segued to a hacking cough.

"What'd he say?" Officer Parker asked. "What's a *tyro*?"

"Novice, you moron," Crackhead said between coughs.

"Watch your mouth, Corrales, or I'll pull him outa here."

"What do I care?" He rubbed the fissure on his forehead. "I'm on Death Row for a murder I didn't commit."

Crackhead's teeth clacked like a man in an ice house. He tore open the Marlboros and reclined on his bunk, coffee cup in one hand, cigarette in the other, legs crossed like a man of leisure. The only thing missing was a red silk smoking jacket. Corrales was skinny to the point of emaciation and seemed to have an advanced case of emphysema. Brady suspected Mother Nature would snuff him out long before the executioner.

"Whaddya wanna know and how bad you wanna to know it?"

"The motel belonged to friends of mine."

"That ain't worth two bits to me."

Crackhead maintained a tough façade, but he reminded Brady of a caged dog desperate for adoption before the euthanizer arrived.

"You wanna escape the needle, Willie, you gotta cut a deal. Your problem is you've got empty pockets. Your only currency is a secret. Whoever burned that motel may also have murdered another friend of mine. Help me find him and I'll do what I can for you."

Crackhead finished the remains of his coffee and took a long reflective drag on the Marlboro, as if the smoke was fuel for his memory.

"What if I told you the guy you're looking for is the sonofabitch who put me here?"

"I'd find that very interesting."

The condemned man sat silent for a minute sucking on his cigarette. He was in no hurry.

"Let me tell you a story," he said eventually.

"Okay," Brady said, a surge of energy shooting through him.

"No names. You help me, maybe I help you."

Brady nodded. "Fair enough. Let's have it."

"I used to work for a guy..." Crackhead began.

"Cisco Blas," Brady said.

"I said no fucking names!"

"Sorry. No names."

"Let's call him Mr. Smith. He owned a string of businesses around Tampa Bay. Fucking goldmines. Cranked out more cash than the U.S. Mint. A hundred dancers, er, employees. Not skeevy bitches. Tight, clean, college girl-types."

The steel door at the end of Death Row crashed shut. The sound was still echoing when an inmate several cells away erupted into a wild spate of inarticulacy.

"Shut the fuck up, Hastings," Crackhead shouted. Hastings apparently didn't hear him because he kept up his incoherent ramblings. Crackhead turned back to Brady. "Customers swarmed in from St. Pete, Sarasota, all the way from Orlando. I had twenty five-thirty guys working security. No thugs. Mr. Smith wanted a class operation. One guy I hired was a big kid who used to hang out at our main joint. I'll call him Frank. Pretty boy. Vain as a swan. But girls buzzed to him like bees to pollen. Said he was hung like a pony. I started him working the door. Mr. Smith took a liking to the kid. Gave him one of his smaller joints to run."

Crackhead flicked ash into his coffee cup, took a deep draw, and coughed out a pearly cloud.

"Frank was always pestering me about doing more. There were bullshit rumors I burned things. Started maybe by your prick pal, McCarty. Anyways, this Frank kept at me. Said he'd do anything. So the time came when I needed help on a job. I taught him some things and he came along with me a few times. I ain't sayin' what, but he did okay.

"I got to like the kid. But he was stupid. Banging all the dancers, I mean, employees. Taste for nose candy. Sold a kilo of coke to an FDLE snitch. I went to see him at the Hillsborough County Jail. He was looking at a fifteen year minimum. Scared to death. Frank had muscles, but he wasn't hard. Kept saying he was gonna end up some buck's poodle. Then outa nowhere he hires this lawyer, Paul Coleman, Esquire. Big-ticket cocksucker in Tampa. Way outa Frankie's pay grade. Frank ain't got no money and Coleman don't do no charity. Next thing I know Frankie's out on bond, Mr. Smith's got a bullet in his brain, and I'm gettin' pulled over on Dale Mabry Strip. Cops find the murder weapon in my trunk. Know right where to look. Frankie cops to jaywalking or some venial fucking sin and gets six Hail Mary's and eighteen months at Citrus. I end up here till the end of days."

Crackhead sat looking at Brady. He ran a finger again over the purple gulch on his forehead.

"Sounds to me like Frankie did Cisco, I mean Mr. Smith, and set you up."

He rolled his eyes to the ceiling of his cell. "Caught that, did ya?"

"Maybe I can help you get some payback."

"I get my own payback."

"Give me a name. I'll see if we can do something for you in Tampa."

"Do something and get back to me," Crackhead said and turned his back on Brady. "I gotta get some rest. Bridge club meets in an hour."

Bradys Run

CHAPTER FORTY SEVEN

ADONIS ROCK'S CHROMOSOMAL circuitry was as embedded with madness as stink in skunks. His mother was a drug addicted prostitute who'd gone to an early grave, destitute and alone. The father he'd never known had been declared criminally insane and, so far as his son knew, or cared, was dead or locked up in some asylum. Adonis was cruelly aware of his genetic gremlins. He'd certainly committed his share of insane acts. None more crazed than shooting Cisco Blas.

He was still haunted by the image of Cisco's brains splattered on the wall like sausage-and-pepper marinara. He thought about it every day, just as he thought about Crackhead Corrales sitting in his cell waiting for the executioner. But he'd had no choice.

Adonis had been looking at hard time on a coke rap. Three years in juvy prison was enough to teach him he'd never survive a fifteen year stretch in an adult pen. Late one night, Paul Coleman bailed him out of Hillsborough County Jail after he promised to pay him twenty five thousand dollars cash. As soon as he was free Adonis drove straight to The Ecstasy.

The club was closed and he found Cisco alone in his office sitting at a table puffing a stogie, a bare lightbulb casting harsh shadows across his coarse assassin's face. With smoke wafting from his nostrils, he listened to Donnie beg for twenty five grand.

"It's either that, Cisco, or I end up at Union Correctional. That's the Rock. You know what happens there. This is life and death."

Cisco listened quietly, grazing the tip of his cigar against the table lip, scraping ash onto the floor.

"I wanna help ya, kid, but things've changed. This cocaine knock puts me in a bad spot. Fucking beverage agents got a real hard on for me. Looking for any reason to jerk my liquor licenses. What do I do with a dozen titty bars that don't serve whiskey? You understand?"

Donnie stood looking down through the blue haze at him. "Cisco, you know me. You know you can trust me. I'll pay you back. Whatever vig you say."

"Sorry, kid. No can do. Gotta cut you loose."

Cisco rose from his chair and walked to the back wall. He removed the black velvet nude and spun the dial on the wall safe. He pulled the door open and reached inside. His hand came out holding a stack of cash. He peeled off several bills and handed them to Donnie.

"Here's five grand. I hope it helps, but that's all I can do. You fucked up."

It wasn't nearly enough and, in a flash, Donnie devised a mad plan. He had a .22 caliber Smith & Wesson tucked in his waistband. When Cisco turned to replace the bundle of cash to his safe, Donnie pulled out the pistol, stepped quickly behind Blas, and fired a single shot into the back of his skull. Blood sprayed from his head like oil from a gusher. Cisco went down without a whimper. Donnie stood studying the dead man at his feet. Fascinated. *Like swatting a fly.* Then a shiver ran through him. An image flashed in his mind of a little boy and a hard, gray, unsmiling old woman. They were sitting in a church. A white-haired priest was at the altar mumbling prayers. She leaned over to him and whispered. *"You've been cursed, child, as surely as Cain, who slew his brother Abel."*

Donnie grabbed the cash from the open safe and walked calmly from The Ecstasy. Outside he counted the loot. It turned out to be forty thousand dollars. He drove to Crackhead's apartment in Ybor City, the old Spanish section of town. His black GTO was parked outside.

Donnie found the key Corrales kept hidden in a magnetic box under his back left fender. He unlocked the trunk and planted the gun beneath the spare tire. Then he called Coleman and told him Cisco had been hit and he knew who did it.

Coleman cut a deal with prosecutors. Donnie got eighteen months at Citrus and Crackhead went to Death Row. The lawyer kept Donnie's name out of the Blas case. But Donnie knew that Crackhead knew it was him. He did his time in segregation.

After his release Donnie quietly settled in Fort Lauderdale, grew his hair, bleached it, and fabricated Adonis Rock. But, even in freedom, he remained a caged man. A prisoner to his inner demons. The specter of Crackhead followed him like his own shadow. Just the thought of him left Adonis bathed in sweat. He was constantly looking over his shoulder. Avoiding dark places. Wedging matches into his door jambs at the *Rat's Nest,* like he'd seen done in the movies.

Now, flush with cash for the first time in his life, he planned to kiss the flea bag goodbye. Get out of Florida. Go someplace Crackhead, or his minions, could never find him. Start a new life. Find a woman. Maybe even have a kid. Be the father he never had.

The night after Jack Del Largo's angry intrusion, Adonis went out on the town and spent some of his mahogany money getting wasted on champagne and cocaine. It was near dawn when he got back to the *Rat's Nest.* Despite his condition, he instantly noticed the match he'd jammed into his door frame was on the ground. *Crackhead!*

Silent as daybreak, he circled around back and squeezed through a hole in a ficus hedge that separated the motel from the parking lot of a *Burger King.* He peered in the window. Someone was sitting in the black Naugahyde reclining chair in the corner. He was a grown man who gave the impression of a ramshackle boy. He was watching a *Beavis & Butthead* cartoon on TV. An automatic pistol was balanced on his knee.

The trespasser was sitting with his back to the small kitchenette. Adonis had stuffed a match into the rear door, too. It was still there. He tested the knob. Locked. Noiselessly, he inserted his key and pushed the door open, careful not to rattle the glass jalousies. A dopey laugh was coming from the next room. *This nimrod's dumber than Butthead!*

The apartment was as dark as a grotto and reeked of human gas. Adonis kept a sawed-off baseball bat on top of the refrigerator. He grabbed it and inched toward the doorway. The intruder's legs were stretched out on the recliner. His left hand was hanging off the arm rest a few inches from the gun.

He waited for Butthead to hee-haw again, then stepped swiftly into the doorway and smashed the bat down on his forearm. He heard bones shatter with a sickening crunch and Butthead wailed in agony. Adonis grabbed the gun and swung the bat again hard, catching him square in the mouth. Three of Butthead's teeth tumbled into his lap and blood spurted from his face like it was shot from a squirt gun. A scarlet string of spit as thin as a cat's whisker yo-yoed from his swollen lips. The man waved a hand at Adonis like he was flagging down an oncoming car, pleading with him to stop. Adonis stepped into the kitchen and found a dish towel, returned, and threw it in Butthead's face.

"Don't bleed on my chair."

Butthead sobbed feebly. Adonis snatched the front of his shirt, yanked him from the chair, and threw him face down onto the floor. He larruped the back of his knees with the bat. Butthead brayed again.

"Stop! Please stop!"

"Did Crackhead send you?"

The man whimpered and Adonis smashed his left heel.

"Aaahhhh! No more! Please! "

"Answer me. Did Crackhead send you?"

"I don't know any crackheads," he grunted, "'cept a coupla guys down at the Greyhound terminal."

"Tell me. Crackhead Corrales. Willie Corrales. Did he send you?"

"I don't know anybody named that. I swear."

Adonis was relieved. He believed the guy. Crackhead would never have sent this numskull.

"Okay, Butthead – you don't mind if I call you Butthead?" He whacked his ass.

"Shit! Shit! Stop! Please stop!"

"Why should I? You break into my room and sit here waiting to blow my brains out."

Butthead rolled onto his back and held up his arms. His left fore-arm dangled like a snapped tree limb. His lower lip was swollen like a Ubangi tribesman's.

"Listen, mister," Butthead sputtered in a pitiful lisp. "I ain't no kill-er. Please don't kill me. I don't wanna go to Hell."

"You may not go to Hell, but you're gonna do a long stretch in Purgatory if you don't tell me who sent you."

"Okay, okay. Just don't hit me no more. It was some guy. I don't know his name. He paid me to scare you, that's all. I wasn't gonna kill you."

Adonis smashed Butthead's right knee as hard as he could and heard something pulvcrize. The intruder screamed. Adonis could see a glint of silver from the fillings in his back teeth.

"I hope stupidity ain't contagious, because you're dumb as a stump. You expect me to believe that shit? Who sent you?"

He raised the bat again. Butthead pleaded through his broken mouth. "No! Please! No!"

Adonis felt his fury mounting. "Listen to me. It don't matter to me one goddamn bit whether this bat cracks your head, or your head cracks this bat. You lose either way. Now tell me who sent you or I'm gonna spill your pea-*fucking*-brain all over the floor."

"Okay! Okay!" Butthead momentarily gagged on his own blood. "It was some fat guy. He didn't tell me his name. He gave me a thousand dollars cash. And your address."

"You're lying!"

"I ain't. Don't hit me! It was a short, fat guy. He looked rich. Drove a Mercedes. A silver Mercedes."

"Jack Del Largo?" Adonis said with shock in his voice.

"He told me to shoot you. But I wasn't gonna, mister, I swear. I was gonna give you a beat down. Scare you some. But I ain't no murderer. I never killed nobody in my life."

Fucking Jack Del Largo! Adonis thought. He felt a surge of barbar-ity shoot through him. *That motherfucker!*

Butthead dropped his arms and turned his head to the side. Pliant. Gutless. It was an act of cowardice. As if he was conceding to his own death without a fight. Red rage exploded inside Adonis. He loathed weaklings.

He raised the bat over his head and swung down with all his strength. Butthead's skull burst like an overripe tomato. A crimson geyser spewed from his temple and he began to shudder violently. Adonis watched, spellbound. While his uninvited guest convulsed on the floor like an epileptic, a peculiar, almost carnal thrill coursed through him. After a minute, Butthead's death throes ceased and he lay still, bathed in his own gore. His eyes were open wide, as if he was astonished by his sudden end. He reminded Adonis of a mackerel on a bed of shaved ice.

Bradys Run

CHAPTER FORTY EIGHT

FORBIDDING BLACK CLOUDS had erased the sun from the sky like chalk from a chalkboard when Brady and McCarty pulled onto Interstate 95 and headed for Fort Lauderdale. The further south they traveled the faster the weather deteriorated. Radio updates said *Hurricane Rollie* was twenty four hours from landfall and blowing at one hundred ten miles an hour. Brady's thoughts drifted inevitably to Rose. He was as beguiled by her as a drunkard to drink. He wished he was with her now, up on her rooftop, helping her gird for the storm.

"What did you think?" McCarty said from behind the wheel.

Brady reluctantly abandoned his daydream. "Did you know when President Eisenhower created the interstate system he stipulated that one out of every five miles of highway had to be dead straight."

"How come?"

"So they could be used as airstrips in times of war?"

"That's very enlightening. But I meant Crackhead."

"Crackhead?" Brady's musings about Rose were fast replaced by an image of the flinty little hangdog sitting in his cell. He laughed to himself about Corrales's final words before they left him. "Did you know there are six hundred-billion possible hands in a game of bridge?"

"Yuck, yuck!" McCarty said. "What do you think?"

"I think he was lying. They don't have a bridge club on Death Row."

"Come on, Max. Be serious. What do you think?"

"I think Crackhead knows who burned the Pelican's Nest and murdered Jonas."

"I doubt he'll talk unless we can convince the Tampa prosecutor to offer some kind of deal."

Brady looked at McCarty. He felt a genuine bond with the arson investigator. He was smart and a straight shooter. They'd known each other casually for several years, but in the last few days had developed a real rapport. They were roughly the same age and temperament and seemed to share similarly warped senses of humor. Brady thought McCarty would make a good friend.

"John," he said, suppressing a smile, "what kind of investigator are you?"

McCarty gave him a bruised look. "What do you mean?"

"Crackhead gave us the name."

"He did? I didn't hear that."

"He might as well have."

"How do you figure?"

"Elementary, my dear Watson."

"Sherlock Holmes never said that."

"Bogart never said 'Play it again, Sam,' either. So what? Here's what you do…"

Minutes later McCarty was on his cell phone to Deborah Jameson at the Broward County State Attorney's Office. She was handling both the Pelican's Nest arson and Jonas Bigelow's murder investigation. McCarty told her about their visit to Death Row and asked her to contact the prosecutor in Tampa.

"The guy who fingered Corrales was facing a coke rap. His lawyer was a guy named Paul Coleman. The snitch did eighteen months at Citrus. That should get a name."

Jameson said she'd do what she could and get back to him. An hour later McCarty's phone rang. They were doing eighty miles an hour through Indian River County between Vero Beach and Fort Pierce. Orange groves lined both sides of the highway as far as the eye could see, broken only by large swathes of real estate where citrus trees had been plowed and burned to make room for instant new residential communities with names like *Captain's Landing* and *Seminole Lagoon.*

Jameson apologized for taking so long.

"Long!" McCarty replied, glancing at Brady. "I didn't expect anything today."

The prosecutor said she spoke to a man named Bill James, the Hillsborough County State Attorney, who handled the Blas murder. She told him about their conversation with Corrales.

"Will he cut Crackhead a deal?"

"He didn't seem impressed," Jameson said. "He sure as hell isn't going to reopen the investigation."

"Tough luck for Crackhead."

"I'm sure he deserves to be right where he is."

"He's probably got some notches on his gun," McCarty said. "And he did torch a lot of buildings he was never brought to justice for. But he didn't kill Cisco Blas."

"If you're correct, John, Mr. Blas was dispatched by a con named Donald John Rockwell, DOB 3/21/74. Served eighteen months on a three year rap at Citrus for sale of a controlled substance, to wit cocaine."

"Address?"

"None. Released without parole. Part of the deal for snitching."

"How about a mug shot?"

"Check your cell phone after we hang up."

"Huh?"

"I sent you a picture mail."

"You can do that?"

"Come on, John. Do you know what century this is?"

McCarty hung up and handed his telephone to Brady.

"See if you can find a picture on this thing."

It took Brady ten minutes but a mug shot finally popped up on the cell phone screen. Brady took one look and his stomach turned like he'd swallowed a piece of spoiled meat.

"Jesus H. Christ!"

Bradys Run

CHAPTER FORTY NINE

JACK DEL LARGO didn't notice the fat raindrops popping on the glass-covered footbridge like egg yolks on a hot skillet. The only thing on his mind was a large tumbler of iced vodka he hoped to be sipping as soon as possible at the Blue Martini Lounge. He crossed the downtown span over Third Street and entered the courthouse parking garage.

When he reached his silver Mercedes he pressed a button on his key chain and the door lock chirped open. By the time he detected movement at the corner of his eye, it was too late. Before he could react, Adonis Rock rushed up and clubbed him over the head with his sawed-off baseball bat, still covered with Butthead's blood and brains. Del Largo went down hard on the oil-stained concrete.

Adonis grabbed him by the nape of his neck and dragged him two parking spots away. He reached under his armpits and, with a loud grunt, lifted him off the ground and thrust him into the bed of his pickup truck. Del Largo was starting to regain his senses. Adonis trussed his wrists and ankles with duct tape and affixed another strip across his mouth. Then he reached over and lifted a blue tarp.

When he whacked Butthead, he hadn't considered what to do with the corpse. He quickly discovered cadavers were more trouble than a roomful of ex-girlfriends. Now Del Largo lay face-to-bloody-face with his late, unlamented *hitman,* whose bewildered eyes were staring straight at him.

"Look familiar, Jack?"

Del Largo's eyes grew wide with alarm. He shook his head frantically. Muffled sound came from under his muzzled mouth. Adonis slapped his face hard.

"You fucked up, Jack. You fucked up bad."

He slammed Del Largo's head on the truck bed one more time and pulled the tarp over them both.

Bradys Run

CHAPTER FIFTY

"IT'S ME," BRADY said into the telephone.

"Me?" said Rose Becker. "Me who?"

"You forgot already? The guy you woke up beside – *this morning!*"

John McCarty looked sideways with raised eyebrows. A bashful grin was etched on Brady's face. McCarty nodded approvingly. They were still on Interstate 95 approaching the Sunrise Boulevard exit at Fort Lauderdale.

"Oh, *that* me," said Rose.

"That's a relief," Brady said. "For a minute I thought I'd dreamt it."

"That was no dream, old fella."

"Ouch! Tough love!"

"You're a tough guy."

"Well, this tough guy needs a favor."

He gave Rose a rundown on the lead he and McCarty had gotten on the Pelican's Nest arsonist, and maybe Jonas's killer.

"That's great!" Rose said.

"Not that great."

"Why?"

"You're not going to be happy when I tell you the suspect's name."

"Who?"

"I need his address."

"Why would I have his address?"

"He works out at the Papillon Gym."

"No way. Who?"

"Fabio."

"Adonis?"

"His real name is Donald John Rockwell. I have his mug shot. It's about six years old. His hair was short and dark, but it's the same guy.

"There's gotta be a mistake. He's such a nice guy."

"I knew he'd done time."

"How did you know that?"

"ESPN."

"Brady, why didn't you tell me?"

He hesitated. He'd spilled his heart to her less than two days ago. He didn't want her thinking he was some kind of green-eyed paranoiac. But they'd vowed – no secrets.

He winced. "To be honest, I thought there was something between you and him."

"What do you take me for, Brady?" He could hear the dander in her voice. "I have a firm rule. No fraternizing with patrons."

"Does last night qualify as fraternizing? Do I need to find a new gym?"

The telephone went dead and Brady thought she'd hung up on him. *Our first argument?* But, a minute later, she was back.

"He lives at the *Cat Cay Motel*. I think that's that dumpy little dive behind the Burger King on US 1. "

"I know the place, just south of 17th Street Causeway. Listen, Rose, this guy's bad news. He may have murdered two people."

"Two? Who besides Jonas?"

He told her about Cisco Blas in Tampa.

"My god, Brady. I can't believe it. I've got goosebumps."

"You had goosebumps last night, too."

"Not *those* kind, wise guy."

"Listen to me, Rose." His voice was serious now. "If he comes in, keep your distance. He's an ex-con. A *real* wise guy. He'll pick up on your vibes. And call me as soon as you can. And Rose?"

"Yes, Brady."

"Remember what I told you last night?" he said, glancing at McCarty, who looked straight ahead, pretending not to listen.

"Yes."

"That still goes."

"I hope so. It's only been one day."

Bradys Run

CHAPTER FIFTY ONE

ADONIS ROCK'S DILAPIDATED pick-up truck wheezed onto Alligator Alley and headed west into the Florida Everglades. He punched 102.7 on the FM radio in time to hear Rick Shaw, the disc jockey, announce that *Hurricane Rollie* would make landfall around midnight.

Twenty miles later he wheeled onto a narrow rutted dirt rise that ran through wild sawgrass as far as the eye could see. Steep ditches bordered the trail on either side. The black water was populated with alligators floating benignly, like armored logs.

The truck bounced down the scalloped path, bombarded by terse, relentless rain bursts. His wipers were oscillating at full throttle. At one point he had to jump out in a downpour to open a rusty gate with creaky hinges. A mile later he braked on a stony mound covered with scrub grass as coarse as the hair on an elephant's back.

When Jack Del Largo regained his senses he processed several bits of data – each more terrifying than the last. He was lying in the middle of a dirt road. The sky was nightmarish. And his nostrils were filled with the stench of…? *Shit!* He quickly realized the reek was coming from a hairy naked ass staring him in the face. Something was protruding from the ass. It had a fuse attached which was sizzling like a trick candle on a birthday cake.

"Jack, you're awake."

Del Largo strained to turn his head, but could barely move. His arms and ankles seemed to be superglued together. He looked down toward his feet. He was still wearing the gray pinstriped suit jacket he'd donned this morning with a blue Oxford-cloth shirt and red embroidered silk tie. But, except for black knee socks, from the waist down he was buck naked. And something else was off beam. His ass cheeks were contracting spasmodically. He felt a sharp aching in his rectum. He took that to mean he either had to take a mastodonic dump or he was being butt-fucked with a baseball bat. Then he looked at the furry fizzling haunch inches from his face and the horror took his breath.

"It's me, Jack," Adonis said, stepping into his field of vision. He reached down and ripped the tape from Del Largo's mouth.

"Shit!" he cried out, pain and panic vibrating synchronously in his throat. "You! What have you done? Where am I?"

Adonis waved his arm like a tour guide. "They call it the River of Grass, Jack. The Florida Everglades. Nobody for miles. Just you, me, and a bunch of hungry gators. Oh, yeah, and Butthead. But he don't count."

Adonis leaned down and grabbed the legs attached to the ass in Del Largo's face and began dragging.

Del Largo mewled like a frightened dog. "Why are you doing this to me? *What* are you doing?"

"What I'm doing at the moment, Jack, is disposing of Butthead."

"Butthead? Who the fuck is Butthead?"

"Don't be coy, fatso. He's your hapless hitman."

"What hitman? What are you talking about?"

Adonis had dragged Butthead's body thirty feet down the path. He stopped, dropped the dead man's legs, snatched him by the hair, and wrenched his head around one hundred eighty degrees. Del Largo stared straight at the bloody pulp of Butthead's face. The lifeless, befuddled eyes seemed to speak to him. *"You didn't tell me this would happen!"*

"Remember now, Jack?"

"Adonis! I swear to Jesus I didn't hire him to kill you."

"Come on, Jack. He made a death bed confession."

Adonis spun the dead man around so his ass faced Del Largo again.

"See that thing sticking out of Butthead's butthole? Die-no-mite! In four minutes he's gonna be blown into a thousand pieces of gator bait. That's what happens when you fuck with me."

Del Largo looked around but saw only truck wheels, cattails, and the endless dirt road. He began to scream.

"Help! *Help! Please help me!*"

Adonis grinned like a gargoyle. "*Help! Please help me!*" he mocked in a shrill voice. "Yell all you want, Jack. Nobody's gonna hear you."

Adonis picked up the dead man's feet and continued dragging him. A hundred yards down the trail he dropped his feet. He nonchalantly used the fuse burning in Butthead's ass to light a cigarette and then walked back. When he reached Del Largo he leaned down and picked up a string.

"Jack, this fuse is attached to a stick of *die-no-mite* crammed up your poop-chute. Just like the gunpowder suppository I gave Butthead. Watch what happens. You're next."

Seconds later, Butthead erupted in a great ball of fire. His carcass burst apart like a watermelon dropped from a ten story rooftop. Del Largo and Adonis flinched at the concussion. Then nuggets of raw flesh began raining down on them like manna from Hell.

"*Aggghhhh!!!*" Del Largo squealed. He began flopping like a fish on a rock, trying to dislodge a glob of bloody tissue that had embedded in left ear.

"*Goddamn!*" Adonis shouted, laughing as he kicked a lump of Butthead off his boot. "Guess I didn't move him far enough away. Looky there, Jack."

The ditchwater was roiling with alligators surging for morsels of Butthead, like blue-haired senior citizens at an early bird buffet. A brawny black ten-footer scuttered up the steep incline with alarming swiftness. It snapped its jaws down on a severed arm, with the hand attached, and vanished back into the water, an amphibious lion to its den.

Pregnant black storm clouds barreled across the sky like an invading army. Adonis tried to imagine the sun shining above the gloom. He puffed on his cigarette until it was red and touched it to the split end of the fuse sticking out of Del Largo's rump. It sputtered to life and began to sizzle. A turkey buzzard swooped from its perch on a barren pine and gorged on Butthead carrion.

"Jack, you've got five minutes before that vulture starts feasting on your blubber."

Del Largo's voice quivered like a pubescent choirboy. "Adonis, I was only trying to scare you."

"It didn't work, though, did it, Jack *fucking* Del Largo? Now I'm sending you to hell."

"If you kill me, Adonis, you'll be sorry. You'll regret it for eternity."

"I hate to inform you, Jack, but eternity ain't gonna last that long."

Adonis drew a vial from his pocket, turned his back to the galing wind, and sprinkled a line of powder on the back of his hand. He snorted, shook his head, and within seconds, the cocaine was working its sorcery.

Del Largo began to weep. Adonis stared down at him with a mix of exhilaration and outright loathing. He now had as little regard for human life as a slaughterhouse executioner had for cows or pigs or chickens. Cisco's killing had haunted him. But drowning the old man hadn't cost him a minute's sleep. And the thrill of watching Butthead die bordered on the erotic. Looking down now with glazed eyes at the obese lawyer sniveling at his feet, Adonis felt godlike.

"Jack, Jack, Jack! It's truth time. No lies. You've got four minutes. Tell me what this shit's all about."

Del Largo turned his head and tried to look up at him. "If I tell you," he said, stifling a sob, "will you put out the fuse?"

"There's only one way to find out, Jack. But you better hurry. The sand's almost run outa your hour glass."

Del Largo lay in the dirt emitting a high-pitched whine that sounded more animal than human, like a horizontal hippopotamus. Adonis reached down, seized his ankles, and started dragging.

"If you're gonna lay there cryin' like a little girl, I'm hauling your lard ass down the road and waiting for the fireworks."

"Please, no."

"Jesus, Jack," Adonis said, breathless, "you've let yourself go. You need to lose some weight. Hey, I got just the thing. *Adonis Rock's*

Die-no-mite Diet. I'm thinkin' about a book. I bet it'd make millions. A real home run, don't you think, Jack?"

The fuse kept burning even as a cloudburst spit down on Del Largo's head and fleshy cheeks.

"Okay, okay," he said, near hysterical now. "I'll tell you. I'll tell you everything. Just take that thing out of me."

Adonis kept pulling. "Not till I hear the whole story."

"We're buying up beach property. For a luxury resort. Some motel owners refused to sell. We had to persuade them. That's why I hired you. Now please let me go."

"That ain't all of it, Jack. Who paid for me to burn that place and kill that guy?"

"I can't say. Attorney-client privilege."

Adonis laughed out loud. "I gotta give you credit, Jack. You got ethics. Protecting your client all the way to the gates of Hell. Hope he's paying you a bundle, because in two minutes you're gonna be finger food for them hungry reptiles over there."

He dropped Del Largo's legs fifty yards past the spot where Butthead had blown up and wiped beads of sweat from his brow.

"I guess this is it, Jack," he said. "Pleasure doing business. Thanks to you, I'm rich. Don't think I don't appreciate it. Adios."

Adonis began to walk away, leaving Del Largo laying half-naked, the lit end of the fuse snaking relentlessly toward his anus.

Nearly mad with panic, he cried out. "His name is Sherwood Steele. He's my client. He put up the money to pay you."

"Sherwood Steele?"

"The billionaire. Lives on a big yacht at Bahia Mar. The Shangri-La. You've heard of Shangri-La?"

"The vacation places?"

"He's got his entire fortune riding on a Shangri-La resort on Lauderdale Beach. He's desperate. He'll be ruined if he doesn't get the property he needs. That's what this is all about. For God's sake, Adonis, take me to Steele. He'll pay you a lot of money. Whatever you want. I swear to Christ."

The fuse kept burning. Adonis stopped twenty paces from Del Largo and laughed.

"Jack, I think I *am* gonna take you to your Mr. Sherwood Steele."

"Oh, God, thank you, Adonis," he said, sobbing. "I knew you'd do the right thing."

"Yep, Jack. After that *die-no-mite* blows, I'm gonna find your fat head and show it to Sherwood Steele. Whaddya think he'll pay to avoid the same fate?"

Del Largo pleaded like a mendicant monk begging for alms. "Oh, no, please, Adonis, please."

"You got one minute. If I was you, Jack, I'd be making peace with my maker. Maybe you got enough time to save your black soul from damnation."

Del Largo felt the fuse inch up his leg, scorching his skin as it crawled. He shook his lower body, trying to dislodge the dynamite. He squeezed his rectum, trying to force it out. Nothing worked. He looked around madly. *Roll down the slope into the water. Kill the fuse.* Frantic now, he rotated his body, snorting like a truffle pig.

Adonis reached the truck and looked back. He pulled out his vile, sprinkled another line on his hand, and sniffed.

"Ya ain't gonna make it, Jack," he said, laughing. "Too fucking fat."

The burning fuse singed Del Largo's upper thigh and he knew Adonis was right. He stopped bucking and lay on his stomach in the dirt, his body trembling uncontrollably, babbling an inchoate language with no structure or syntax, like he was channeling the spirit of a dead Indian chief.

"Nice knowin' ya, ya fat fuck! You shouldn't have fucked with Adonis Rock!"

Del Largo lifted his head off the dirt and, as if a wizard had waved a magic wand and shouted *Abracadabra,* he was suddenly on a blue tropical island, lean and hard, eating papaya beneath a swaying palm, a beautiful young native girl nestled beside him.

"Jack," she whispered in his ear, *"my beautiful Jack!"*

Bradys Run

CHAPTER FIFTY TWO

TIFFANI BANDEAUX'S MILKY skin glistened like polished ivory in the hot tub froth. She was entwined with Norman Epstein, who was enraptured to be in the embrace of such a glorious creature. He licked her white skin, sucked her pink nipples, squeezed her voluptuous flesh. In his wildest fantasy he'd never imagined anything so sensual, so salacious, so euphoric. Then Epstein felt a tremor – and it wasn't in his loins.

A fierce squall was buffeting the South Florida National Bank Building. He tapped his computer pause key and looked out the window. Five hundred feet below, bumper-to-bumper traffic jammed the roads like an endless funeral procession – evacuees fleeing the beach.

Epstein was sitting alone at his desk in the fiftieth floor executive suite. Bank employees had been sent home early ahead of the gathering storm. The CEO had taken the opportunity to lay the photograph of his wife and two children face-down on his desk, insert a disk into his laptop, and watch his romp with Tiffani, yet again.

In the days after Sherwood Steele blackmailed him, Epstein had locked himself in his office, bewildered, distraught, a whipped dog licking his wounds. His impulse to leap off his balcony was more seductive than ever. Then he watched the extortion footage. Then he watched it again, and again, over and over, until a curious thing happened. His depression was eclipsed by obsession. Tiffani was the most magnificent, hedonistic woman he'd ever known. Their tryst had been the pinnacle, the zenith, the absolute apogee of his sexual life. And he couldn't get enough of it. He'd been reliving it every chance he got since then.

Epstein pecked the keyboard and they popped back onscreen, naked as Adam and Eve, his soft pink body tangled with the ravishing Amazon, groping, grunting, splashing, stirring up a mini-tsunami. Solar flares shot through him and his breath was getting erratic when a loud knock startled him. The door swung open and a tall, lean man stood in the void. Epstein slammed the laptop shut and looked up with the face of a penitent schoolboy.

"Who are you?"

Max Brady didn't answer. He sensed he'd barged in at an awkward moment.

"We're closed," Epstein said.

"I'm here to see you."

Brady stepped to the desk and extended his hand, which Epstein ignored, as Crackhead had the day before. *Sniffy prig,* he thought, wondering if he played bridge.

"Who are you?"

"Max Brady, ex-assistant U.S. Attorney."

"What do you want?"

Brady wasted no time on preambles. "I've got bad news, Norman. I know what you did."

Epstein shuddered. The color drained from his face. To Brady he looked like a man who'd just envisioned his own death.

"What do you mean?"

"For starters, you and Sherwood Steele have been looting your own bank."

"I...I don't know what you're talking about."

"Norman, this was easier to crack than a Rubik's Cube. You geniuses left a paper trail a blind man could follow. Mensa's gonna be pissed."

He waited for a response. Epstein just stared at him, mute, scared. He looked ready to collapse like a two dollar umbrella.

"Did you guys think you'd get away with those daisy chain loans? Stealing millions with the swipe of a pen – and I do mean *swipe!* What do you think the FDIC will do?"

At the mention of the federal bank regulator Epstein's spine seemed to stiffen.

"Who the hell are you?" he demanded again.

"I told you, Norman. But I haven't told you the trouble you're in. It gets worse. Much worse!"

The banker mustered a last bit of bravado. "Like what?" There was a trace of defiance in his voice.

"Let's start with arson. Ever hear of the Pelican's Nest Motel?"

"That's ridiculous," he said and coughed dryly into the palm of his hand. Brady took it to be one of those involuntary hacks people make when they lie.

"Ridiculous? Well, then, try murder on for size."

"Murder?" Epstein said the word with twenty four-carat shock. "What murder?"

"The name Jonas Bigelow ring a bell? Coral Reef Motel?"

"Coral Reef?"

Brady watched him put the pieces together. His face transformed by degrees until a shiver ran through him like an arctic zephyr. Brady noticed the downturned picture frame on Epstein's desk and lifted it.

"Put that down."

"Nice looking family," Brady fibbed. "Do them a big favor, Norman. Come with me to Deborah Jameson at the State Attorney's Office before you get sucked into something far worse than you can imagine."

A mawkish expression spooled across Epstein's face and he seemed to wither. Brady felt the building sway. He looked out the window. Hard rain was pelting the glass. *Rollie* was coming fast. The sky was fertile with doom. Epstein stood abruptly. Brady was surprised at his size and wondered if he bought his suits in the boy's department.

"Get out of here," the banker said.

"Norman, you're in way over your head. Sherwood Steele is going down. Save yourself before it's too late."

"Get out!" He said it with a big voice for a small man. "You are trespassing. Get out!"

Brady shrugged and turned to leave. At the door he looked back over his shoulder and pointed.

"By the way, Norman, you're fly is unzipped."

Bradys Run

CHAPTER FIFTY THREE

ADONIS ROCK WAS saved by a squall. He was getting ready to turn his pick-up into the *Rat's Nest* when a sudden rainburst strafed U.S. 1 and forced him to hit the brakes. He squinted through the dripping kaleidoscope of his windshield and saw yellow crime scene tape stretched across the motel entrance. Red and blue lights were dancing in the deluge.

Adonis drove past the motel, wended his way onto Miami Road, and backtracked until he found a spot in a Miami Subs parking lot across the highway with a clear view of the *Rat's Nest*. The rain had stopped as abruptly as it started and he could see cops swarming over the motel. A CSI van was parked in front of his room. Uniforms were streaming in and out. He screamed.

"Fuck!"

There was really no other word for it. The possibility that the police were wise to him had never crossed his mind. He'd stashed his hundred thousand dollars of mahogany cash in a brown paper bag on top of a ceiling tile above the kitchenette. He pounded the steering wheel with the palm of his hand. *What the fuck happened? Was it that fat fucking Jack?*

Adonis thought about Del Largo. Scarcely two hours ago he'd been squirming half-naked on the swamp road. The fuse spitting sparks, crawling relentlessly toward the TNT rammed up his ass. Wretched, incoherent, spewing gibberish. Going out like the coward he was. To Adonis's amazement, though, a hush fell over him. He lifted his head and turned toward Adonis. No more tears, no more pleading, no trace of fear on his face. His expression peaceful, tranquil, almost content. *Saying his last Act of Contrition,* Adonis thought. *Trying to salvage his black soul. Nana Ruth would be proud, Jack. Too bad that birdshit don't fly.*

Then Jack Del Largo exploded. The blast was earsplitting. More gruesome than Butthead's. Body parts flying in every direction. Fleshy tissue falling from the sky. Adonis dodging a shower of meat and bone. The concussion passed and the boom evaporated over the sawgrass with a cloud of acrid blue smoke that dissipated in the wind. Adonis ran down the dirt path, outracing an eight-foot gator for the trophy.

He found the head in a stand of cattails at the base of the abrupt slope, half-in-and-half-out of the ditchwater. It was neatly detached just below his multiple chins. Adonis leaned to his right and opened the flaps on a bristol box on the seat beside him. It had once contained Chinese food. Now it was a cardboard catafalque. He looked down at the chalky face flecked with dirt and grass and blood, staring up at him like a wax-work bust frozen at the instant of detonation. He had the look of a man who hadn't expected to die so young.

"Was it you, Jack?" Adonis said. "Did you blow the whistle on me?"

Del Largo peered back fixedly, offering no assistance to his assassin. Adonis doubted the lawyer had turned him in to the police. As much as he hated him for the mahogany, and the daughter-in-law, he had nothing to gain by it. Nonetheless, the walls were closing in. He racked his brain. *Who? Sherwood Steele? The old man's wife? Did they find something in the fire?* Then it came to him. He closed the box flaps and shifted the pick-up into reverse.

A crew of Haitian workmen was boarding up the walled Mediterranean villa when he arrived. He parked on the cul-de-sac and lifted the cardboard box off the seat. The dirty rag he'd layed beneath it was soaked with blood. He tucked the box under his arm and followed a winding flagstone footpath to a set of varnished oak doors and entered without knocking.

Voices were drifting through the house. He followed the sound into a high-ceilinged room filled with furniture that looked too expensive to sit on. Beyond that was a sunroom with a view of the Intracoastal. He found her standing there, her back to him, watching a big flat-screen TV hanging from the wall. A news anchorman was narrating over a grainy mug shot.

"A Fort Lauderdale man, Donald John Rockwell, an ex-convict who goes by the alias Adonis Rock, is being sought by police as a person of interest in the investigation into a beach-area murder and an arson fire."

Video of the *Rat's Nest* popped on screen. Cops were parading in and out of Adonis's room. There were shots of the assorted hookers, winos, and hamburger flippers who boarded there. File footage came up of the Pelican's Nest fire and Jonas Bigelow's murder scene. The next shots caused Adonis to wince.

"Police raided Rockwell's room at a flop house on U.S. 1 today. They say they discovered blood and a large quantity of cash..."

"Mother fuckers!"

Cherry Hampton nearly jumped out of her skin. She spun around and her expression went from shock to horror to panic. She looked like she'd seen Satan incarnate. She backpedaled toward the door. Adonis charged across the room and grabbed her yellow jacket lapels.

"Cherry baby."

"Adonis."

"You betrayed me."

"No! I...I didn't."

He squeezed her white unlined cheeks between his calloused palms and lifted her ear to his mouth. "Don't lie to me," he whispered. "This ain't fantasy night."

"Stop joking, Adonis."

"If I'm joking, Cherry baby, why are you so scared?"

"I'm not afraid." She saw white powder coating the follicles of his nostrils. "You startled me, that's all."

"Do you think I'm here to hurt you?"

"Of course not, Adonis." She tried to smile, but the tremble of her chin exposed her. "Not after all we've been through."

He laughed and released her and walked across the room to the bar. He poured a whiskey.

"Why are the police looking for you?"

"Don't play dumb, honey."

"Did you really drown that old man?"

His red-rimmed eyes crinkled sardonically. Hampton had never seen him like this. They'd spent nights living out the most torrid fantasies in this very room. Performing intimate acts with each other that few could imagine. Now *Fabio* had morphed into *Frankenstein*.

"Don't pretend you don't know what I've been doing for you. And Jack. And Sherwood Steele."

"I don't know anything about murder." She inched toward the front door again, gauging the distance, praying she could make it outside before he got to her. The Haitians had machetes. They would protect her from this madman. "If there's been killing, it's between you and Jack. I'm not involved. I don't want to know anything."

Adonis laughed harshly. Calculating her with maniacal eyes. Her heaving chest. Her sallow, fearful face. He knew she cared nothing about him. He'd been no more than a plaything. One of her *boy toys*. She'd throw him to the jackals in a heartbeat.

"Speaking of Jack," he said. He nodded toward the cardboard sarcophagus on the floor. A dark puddle had collected beneath it, like the broken yolk of a red egg. "Say hello."

Hampton spun and sprinted for the door but he was on her before she reached it. She let out a shrill scream brimming with hysteria. He slapped her hard across the face. She sagged to the floor like a deflated balloon. Adonis grabbed a fistful of platinum hair and dragged her across the room to the box.

"Open it!"

"No. Please, Adonis," she begged, weeping now. "Let me go!"

"I said open it!"

He pulled back the flaps and shoved her face down. It took Hampton several seconds to absorb what she was seeing. She jerked away and began ululating like the mother of a dead child at a Baghdad bombing.

A projectile of vomit shot from her mouth. Adonis released her and let her retch on the floor.

"You pig," he shouted. When she finished gagging he grabbed her by the hair. "Here's what we're gonna do, Cherry baby. We're gonna play your favorite game. Master & Slave. I'm master and you're slave and you are going to do exactly what I tell you. Say 'Yes, master.'"

She didn't respond. He kicked her in the ribs. She grunted and curled into fetal position, tears streaming down her cheeks.

"Yes, master?" he said again.

"Yes, master."

"Good, slave. Now I'm going to let you give me one hundred thousand dollars."

Hampton's tears stopped like someone had turned off a spigot. She looked up at him in disbelief.

"What?"

He slapped her face. "Wrong answer. You're not playing the game right. Let's try again. Say 'Yes, master.'"

"Are you insane? I'm not giving you a hundred thousand dollars."

This time he punched her. Hampton's cheekbone shattered under his fist. Her head struck the marble floor with a thud.

"Do I look like a dog begging for a bone?"

"You bastard! You murdered Jack. You murdered that old man."

Vengeance infected Adonis like a virus. He snatched her by the hair again and wrenched her to her feet.

"Tell me about Shangri-La, Cherry baby."

"What about it?"

Adonis nodded at the box. "Before he lost his head, Jack said Sherwood Steele bankrolled the fire and the old man's hit. Jack said he's trying to build some resort on the beach. Tell me what you know?"

"You're putting too much powder up your nose."

"What is it worth to you to save that tight little ass of yours?"

"You're going to prison, if you don't die first – *master*!"

"The pharaohs used to bury their slaves with them when they croaked. If I die, my kinky, twisted little slave, you are coming with me."

"Get your filthy paws off me, scum."

Hampton spit out the words then reached back and swiped her left hand at him. Her manicured fingernails clawed his face. Adonis felt a sharp sting. He touched his fingers to his right cheek. They came away bloody. Hampton backed away, but he was too quick. He seized her blonde head in his powerful hands and in one swift motion wrenched it one hundred fifty degrees to the left.

A silent scream lit her face and she crumpled to the floor like an imploded building. Adonis stood swaying drunkenly. He stared, waiting for her to move. When she didn't he crouched down to revive her, but Hampton's eyes were as vacant as a Greek statue.

Adonis staggered to a gilt mirror hanging on the near wall. He barely recognized the man staring back at him. His eyes were wild and addlepated. Three crimson talon tracks stretched from his earlobe to his chin, like Indian war paint. Then the man vanished and he saw a little boy sitting on a bed. His feet were dangling above a burnished brown floor. He was peering wide-eyed at a cracked red leather Bible. An old lady sat beside him, her bony white finger pointing at the vivid painting of a red horned monster ringed by flames and wretched screaming faces.

"The prince of Hades," she whispered. *"Where you are cursed to burn for all days. Unless you are saved."*

Adonis spoke to the mirror: "You shoulda prayed harder, Nana Ruth."

Bradys Run

CHAPTER FIFTY FOUR

FOR THE SECOND time in a week, Rose Becker was stowing away barbells and exercise benches when she heard a familiar voice.

"Reporting for duty, sir."

She turned and found Max Brady saluting.

"Sir?"

"Madame…sir?"

Most of the equipment was already secure, but Rose had yet to shutter the greenhouse or lock down her juice bar.

"I've hooked up a generator downstairs," Brady said. "You should move your perishables to the Shanty."

"Thanks, I'll take you up on that, old fella."

He wagged his forefinger at her like a stern schoolmaster. "You are a bad girl. I may have to spank you."

"Do what you must, *sir.*" She leaned forward and pressed her lips to his. "I'm just trying to get a rise out of you."

"You're doing a fine job."

A look of alarm came into Rose's eyes.

"What about Adonis?"

"His goose is cooked. They've got his face plastered all over television. The police will pick him up soon, if they haven't already."

Brady filled her in on his visit with Norman Epstein and how he'd squeezed him on Sherwood Steele.

"Steele is very close to David Grand," Rose said.

"I saw them together at the Dolphins game. Victor took a picture for you."

"Could Sherwood Steele actually be involved in all of this?"

"Someone said once that behind every great fortune lies a great crime."

"Honoré de Balzac," she said. "*Le Père Goriot*."

His eyebrows arched. "Not bad for a foxy fitness guru-zoologist-lepidopterist-mayor-to-be."

"Did I mention my undergraduate degree is in French literature?"

"I knew there was something I liked about you."

Day was fast being swallowed by darkness, ushered by ever more gusty winds. They finished securing the gym and greenhouse then cleaned out the juice bar and brought everything down to the Sea Shanty. Brady stored the food in his cooler. He held up a plastic baggie containing the remains of the giant Queen Alexandra Birdwing butterflies.

"You gonna send these to a taxidermist?"

"I still want to do a postmortem."

"Sounds like a blast, but dissecting frogs in ninth grade biology made me woozy."

"You're such a softy," Rose said and kissed him.

"Keep that up and…"

"Shush!" she said, and kissed him again.

Bradys Run

CHAPTER FIFTY FIVE

FLYSPECKS OF WHITE light blinked in the violent night outside the big window. Even that bleak spectacle was more preferable to Sherwood Steele than of the trumpet of perdition sitting across the table.

"I will not participate in murder," Norman Epstein said.

"Keep your voice down."

His black shark eyes cast a fitful glance around the rooftop lounge of the Pier 66 Hotel. Only two other tables were occupied and the few staff members on duty were busy closing down for the storm. Even so, the room felt full of ears. Most of the hotel's guests had evacuated the venerable sixteen-story Pier. Renowned for its cylindrical architecture and revolving lounge, Pier 66 provided a dazzling three hundred sixty-degree panorama of South Florida. Tonight that vision was dire, but not as alarming as Epstein, who was wringing his hands like it was doomsday.

"Why don't *you* just shut up," Epstein said in a mutinous whisper. The bartender swiveled his head in their direction.

"Norman, nobody's gonna pin a murder on you."

"Haven't you been listening, Sherwood? This Brady character already has."

"Keep it down, goddamnit!"

Epstein rubbed his forehead like he was trying to force the guilt from his conscience. "I'm done. Finished! I shouldn't have let you go this far."

"So, what is Eva going to do when she sees you and Tiffani on the sex tape?"

"Oh, I think she'll have more pressing things to worry about."

Epstein abruptly rose to his feet.

"Where are you going?"

He didn't respond. Instead, he pivoted on his heels and headed for the exit.

"Goddamn you, Norman," Steele muttered.

He threw cash on the table and followed the banker down a lushly carpeted hallway and out a heavy metal door to a balcony. Rain was coming in sheets and a shrill wind was blowing off the ocean. Steele looked north toward Bahia Mar. The Shangri-La was only a short distance up the Intracoastal, but the monsoon blinded his view.

Epstein stood at the balustrade facing downtown. Swollen teardrops of rain spattered his glasses, mutating the scattered skyline lights into hallucinogenic patterns. He swept a finger like a windshield wiper across the lenses until his muzzy vision cleared, wishing he could make Steele vanish as simply. Even with the storm raging, he felt Sherwood's breath on the back of his neck. Epstein turned and faced his adversary, a shadow standing against the wall like a hand-puppet in a projector light. A red cigarette ember glowed in the murk.

"Norman," Steele said, raising his voice over the wind, "I've got a serious problem."

"No shit, Sherwood," Epstein said with a short, mad laugh. "You have no idea."

Steele paused momentarily, unnerved by Epstein's tone. His banker was falling apart. Sherwood felt something alien to his senses – fear.

"What are you talking about?"

"You shouldn't have started killing people. You wanna show Eva the video, Sherwood? Go right ahead. But know this. When I go down, so do you."

Epstein turned and faced downtown once again. He could feel the chilled iron rail against his bare palms. Steele took a long drag on his cigarette and exhaled with suppressed fury.

"Norman, do you know you're problem? You're spineless as an amoeba. That's a fatal flaw."

Epstein emitted an outlandish cackle. "Fatal? What are you going to do, Sherwood? Put out a contract on me too?" He leaned over the rail and stared at the ground two hundred feet below. "My life is already toast."

"I'm not going to kill you, Norman. Don't be so melodramatic." He flicked his cigarette butt past Epstein's ear over the balcony. Norman spun around again, his eyes so wide and wild that Steele hastily altered his tone. "This is gonna work out, my friend. Trust me. I've got it under control."

Epstein threw back his head with a harsh laugh. "You don't have anything under control anymore, Sherwood. Least of all *this*."

Dread gripped Steele's insides. "What *this* are you talking about, Norman?"

"*This* this, you mother fucker."

Epstein swung around, seized the handrail, and launched himself over the balcony into thin air. Steele rushed forward, stretching desperately to get a hand on him, but the banker plunged into the yawning blackness, his face to the sky, looking straight up into Sherwood's eyes, his lips drawn back in a bizarre smile. Halfway down, the wind caught him and buffeted him like a bingo ball. His body flipped, twisted, and ricocheted off the hotel's wall until he crashed through the first floor roof sixteen stories below.

"Holy shit!" Steele said, staring down at the jagged hole Epstein had vanished into.

He staggered back from the railing into the shadows, his mind reeling. His eyes darted left and right, searching for witnesses. He didn't see any. He rushed down the emergency staircase to the ground floor, avoiding human contact, and burst out an emergency exit into the merciless night.

He caromed through the parking lot, trying not to rush, trying to look innocent, whatever that looked like. He found his car, blundered inside, and sat for several moments drenched and trembling. Hysteria spread inside him as the reality of his situation sank in.

"I am fucked!"

Bradys Run

CHAPTER FIFTY SIX

ADONIS ROCK WRESTLED his pick-up truck through the relentless downpour into Bahia Mar Marina and crept, sluggish as a snail, to the Intracoastal. He climbed out of the cab, the cardboard box gathered under his arm, and was instantly saturated by hard, cold rain. He lurched through explosions of wind to a floating concrete dock.

The Shangri-La looked asleep. Her windows were dark and there were no signs of life. Bumpers hung like boxing heavy bags every ten feet along its navy blue hull. Adonis walked the length of the dock, crouching into the driving rain, until he saw a shard of light seeping through a crack in a shuttered porthole. He climbed six steps to the deck and inched down the teak gangway, clumsy as a sot on a bender. When he reached the hatch he turned the handle. It wasn't locked. He opened the door and slipped inside.

He stood motionless as a marble sculpture and listened. The only sound was the wind and bullets of rain raking the window shields. Water dripped from his hair, face, and clothing onto a deep white rug that looked like the fur of some kind of animal. He moved furtively down the passageway, through a gymnasium, a Jacuzzi room, and into a huge salon with a fully stocked bar and movie screen. The size and splendor of the vessel was breathtaking.

Adonis heard a noise come from astern and stepped lightly toward it. He pressed a taut hand against the cabin door and pushed. A woman was sitting in front of a darkwood vanity applying mascara. She was naked. When she raised her arms he could see the swell of her full ripe breasts. A satiny cape of auburn hair hung down her back to her buttocks. Her face was framed like a portrait in the looking glass. He had never seen a more beautiful woman.

"I could be happy just being your mirror," he said.

Tiffani Bandeaux looked up and gasped at his reflection. She wheeled around to face the rain-drenched intruder. His arms and chest were massive and his left cheek had three red claw marks. Her eyes grew wide and her face froze, like she had swallowed a fishbone.

"Who are you? What are you doing here?"

"Where is Sherwood Steele?"

"He's not here. You shouldn't be either. Please go!"

She removed a green caftan from the back of her chair and threw it around herself, then faced him defiantly, as if to prove she wasn't afraid. His glassy eyes feasted on the lush anatomy beneath the clinging gown.

"You are absolutely incredible."

"Get out or I'm going to call the police." Tiffani took a step toward the door but Adonis took two steps and seized her arm with a grip as unyielding as a shackle. "Get your filthy paws off me." She slapped his face and realized at once she'd made a mistake. He twisted her arm until she cringed. "Stop. You're hurting me."

Adonis pulled her from the small room down a hallway to the main salon, showing no anger, as if in a daze.

"Where is Sherwood Steele?"

"He's going to be back any minute."

"Good."

Adonis reached out and tore open her robe.

"What are you doing? Stop it. Stop."

She tried to cover her exposed flesh with her hands but, without warning, he punched her in the face. She slammed into the wall, slid to the floor, and sat in a stupor, the signature of his knuckles imprinted in blood on her cheek. She touched it and began to shriek.

"Shut up," he said, towering over her, oddly tranquil. "I gotta tell you, angel, I ain't myself today. I've done some crazy shit that's freaking even me out. You keep up that noise, I'm gonna do something bad again. Shame to waste such a sweet slice of pie."

Tiffani cowered on the floor, whimpering, her arms folded across her breasts. Adonis yanked her to her feet and threw her onto the couch.

"We might as well enjoy ourselves while we wait for your husband."

"Sherwood's not my husband."

"Good. Married woman ain't nothing but trouble."

Bradys Run

CHAPTER FIFTY SEVEN

GUNTHER KLUM RAISED his glass in the air.

"To Jonas Bigelow," he said.

"To going out with sand between your toes," said Johnny Glisson.

"Here, here," the others repeated and tipped their glasses in a farewell toast.

The Sea Shanty hurricane party was winding down. Brady hadn't planned on a gathering, but the others hadn't gotten the memo. Late in the afternoon, with *Hurricane Rollie's* breath getting husky, the usual gang – minus Jonas – converged on the Shanty for a liquor-laced requiem. The mood was as melancholy as dead flowers.

"Here's to catching the bastard who killed Jonas," Bob Bremer said.

"I'll drink to that," said Jesse Rosinski.

They kept making toasts. At some point Brady described the visit he and John McCarty made to Crackhead Corrales and how it had led to Donald Rockwell, a.k.a. Adonis Rock.

"He comes in for coffee," Sunny Regan said. "I thought he was a male stripper."

"Let's turn on the news," McCarty said. "Maybe they've caught him."

The TVs were tuned to the Weather Channel. Brady clicked them over to a local station. A meteorologist was giving an update on *Rollie*.

"The eye of the storm is currently over Eleuthra in the eastern Bahamas," he said in a sonorous tone. "At its current pace *Rollie's* leading edge should reach our shores in about four hours. Hurricane hunter aircraft have measured winds near the eye wall at one hundred twenty miles per hour. All residents in low lying or beach areas are being advised to move inland immediately."

"We're driving straight from here to Kissimmee to stay with my brother," Amy Bremer said. "We'll come back tomorrow. I just hope the Sunset Beach is still here."

"We're going to ride it out at the Dew Drop," Bill Weiss said, his hand on Jesse's shoulder. "One last adventure before we go. It'll be exciting."

"Not too exciting, I hope," said Brady.

"Are you coming back to Victor's?" Olga Klum asked.

Before he could answer, Rose said: "Brady is staying with me." She smiled. "In case of emergency."

The Shanty fell silent. All eyes turned to the two of them. Bob and Amy Bremer grinned at each other and Sunny nodded sagely. Johnny Glisson lifted his glass.

"Here's to emergencies," he said and winked at Sunny, who tried and failed to suppress her own smile.

The weatherman tossed to an anchorman, who reported on the day's second biggest story. "The manhunt continues tonight for the suspect in a Fort Lauderdale murder. Donald John Rockwell, who goes by the alias Adonis Rock, is a suspect in the drowning murder of seventy five-year-old motel owner Jonas Bigelow last week during *Hurricane Phyllis*. He is also a person-of-interest in a fire that destroyed another beach motel. Police say they're not aware of a motive for either crime. But this afternoon investigators discovered blood and a large quantity of cash in a room rented by Rockwell at the *Cat Cay Motel* on U.S. 1."

"That son-of-a-bitch," Gunther said. "I just want five minutes alone with him."

"Darling," said Olga, "you've seen him at the gym. He's half your age. And all muscle."

"The police will take care of him," McCarty said. "He'll get what's coming."

"In other news," the anchor continued, "the body of one of Fort Lauderdale's most prominent real estate tycoons was found in her home today. Police suspect foul play."

"Holy smoke!" Bill Weiss said as the victim's photograph came on-screen. "It's her!"

"Cherry Hampton's body was found in her sprawling waterfront home this afternoon. Police say her neck had been broken. The forty five-year-olds death is being treated as a homicide."

"It's got to be Rockwell," McCarty said, dialing his cell phone. "Deborah Jameson…"

McCarty was in the midst of alerting the prosecutor about Adonis's possible link to Cherry Hampton's murder when the anchorman dropped another bomb.

"A well-known Fort Lauderdale attorney is reported missing." A photograph of Jack Del Largo flashed on the screen, followed by video of his Mercedes, found abandoned in a downtown parking garage.

"*Jesus!*" Brady said. He tapped McCarty on the shoulder and pointed at the TV.

"This just in, Deborah, Jack Del Largo's missing. I'd add him to Rockwell's hit parade."

They watched the report about Del Largo's disappearance until a commercial came on.

"What the hell is going on?" Jesse said.

"I don't know who's more dangerous," said Amy Bremer, "*Rollie* or this madman."

"We're not sticking around to find out," her husband said and stepped toward the door. "We're outa here, my friends. Hope to see you tomorrow. Y'all stay safe."

The Bremers gave hugs to everyone and left, followed in short order by the others.

"Sunny," Johnny Glisson said on his way out the door, "maybe I should stay at your place – in case of emergency."

Sunny looked at the others, then at Johnny, and they walked out into the rain.

"I didn't hear her say no," McCarty said.

"Who could resist that line?" said Brady.

Bradys Run

CHAPTER FIFTY EIGHT

SHERWOOD STEELE PITCHED onto the deck, gasping erratically, jelly-kneed, quivering like a hypoglycemic short on sugar. The Shangri-La heaved beneath him. He gripped the gangway rail and peered south into the stormy blackness. He could barely make out the tubular silhouette of the Pier 66 Hotel, standing like a giant corn cob with only a few stray kernels of light still glowing. He tried to locate the balcony Norman Epstein had plummeted from moments before, but the rain was too impenetrable for sight.

Steele's initial panic had subsided, replaced by a perverse exhilaration. An exquisitely corrupt euphoria, as if he'd been bathed in blood at a pagan orgy. He replayed the image of Epstein going over the rail, smiling up surreally, like an enraptured suicide bomber an instant before martyrdom. Steele could not muster a scintilla of remorse for Epstein. He was glad the worm was dead. His mood was one of liberation. Standing precariously in the whipping wind, his normally immaculate black hair now a soggy bird's nest, he considered whether he might qualify as insane. *I don't care.*

Steele was overcome by a sudden craving for Tiffani. He stepped inside and made his way to the main salon. She was lying on a couch, covered by a blanket with her face turned away. He shook the water off himself and looked closer to see if she was asleep. Several seconds passed before he noticed the duct tape covering her mouth.

"What the…"

He bounded to the couch and yanked the throw down to her waist. She was naked and trembling like a wet cat. Her wrists were fettered with tape. A bright red bruise discolored her left cheek and her face was engraved with tear tracks. She turned her head and stared up at him, but her eyes looked dazed and incapable of focus.

He leaned down to remove the tape. "Who did this?"

A voice rang out from behind him. "You must be Sherwood."

Steele spun around. A tall man with a mane of wet blonde hair stood at the bar. He held a pistol in one hand and a half-empty bottle of Chopin vodka in the other.

"Who are you? What do you think you're doing?"

"You should know me, Sherwood. I'm the guy who's been doing your dirty work."

Steele gaped at him with a mixture of astonishment and fright.

"What the hell are you talking about?"

"Don't pull that shit," Adonis said. He kicked the cardboard box across the floor. "Jack tried to fuck me, too. Look at him now."

Steele stared at the box for a moment then, reluctantly, bent down and lifted the flap. He sprang back in horror and Adonis burst into derisive laughter. He set the vodka bottle on the bar and reached into his back pocket.

"The human flesh is so fragile, don't you agree, Sherwood?" He held up a red stick of TNT. "Strategically placed, one of these can transform a man – or woman – into a thousand pieces."

Steele's exhilaration of a few moments ago was gone. "You goddamned animal. You murdered Jack Del Largo? You blew him up?"

"Jack betrayed me. So did Cherry."

"Cherry Hampton?"

Adonis's lower lip jutted out in mock remorse. "Gone too, I'm afraid. Too bad. We had a lot of fun." He waved his pistol at Tiffani. "Your girlfriend's next. And that's really too bad. She's got a dynamite ass." He laughed again. "No pun intended."

He came around the bar, his weapon trained on Steele, and stepped to the couch. He rolled Tiffani onto her side and yanked the cover off her completely. A red tube was protruding from her rectum with a three-foot fuse attached.

"You bastard!" Steele said. "Take that out right now."

"If I do, Sherwood, it's going straight up your Hershey highway. But maybe you'd like that."

Tiffani let out a muffled groan. Steele looked down at her. The flawless demigoddess seemed more like a bruised piece of fruit to him now.

"Why are you doing this? What do you want?"

"It's simple, Sherwood. I lost a lot of cash today. You're gonna re-place it."

"Cash? How much cash?"

"One hundred thousand dollars."

"I don't have that kind of money here."

Tiffani thrashed on the couch. Extruding a muted cry, she shook her head back and forth. Adonis leaned down and ripped the tape from her mouth.

She gasped for breath then began sobbing. After a moment she looked up at Steele. "Goddamn you, Sherwood. That monster raped me. Kill him. *Kill him!*"

Steele gazed at her, his mouth agape. Adonis shrugged his shoulders.

"Rape is a little harsh, don't you think? You barely resisted."

"You pig!" Tiffani screamed in full-throated fury. "You had a gun to my head."

"That was just a prop. To add a little spice. Cherry taught me that one. Besides, I just couldn't pass up a honey pie like you. And you sure were squealing like you enjoyed it."

"I did like hell. *Scum!*"

"You got a sassy mouth on you, sweetie," Adonis said. He reached down and poked at her lips with the TNT stick. She turned her face and swatted him away with her bound hands. "You like to play rough. I like that. But we can discuss our sex life later, honey pie. Right now we've got more important matters. Like my cash." He waved his pistol at a stool by the bar. "Sit down Sherwood."

His face devoid of emotion, Steele obeyed. Adonis followed him. He spun the stool around and jerked Steele's arms roughly behind him. Steele let out a small yelp. Adonis duct-taped his hands and then went around the bar and set down his gun. He pulled a vial from his pocket and sprinkled a line of cocaine on the polished glass top. He leaned over, pressed a finger to his left nostril, and snorted with his right.

"Fuck yes," he said, squeezing his nose between thumb and forefinger and sniffing.

He lifted the top off an onyx box sitting on the bar, pulled out a brown cigarette, and ignited it with a lighter shaped like a hammerhead shark.

"Cute," he said and stepped back to the couch. He flicked the fish again and the fuse attached to the TNT protruding from Tiffani's bottom started spitting sparks. "Whaddya say, Sherwood. We gonna do business? Or is your girlfriend going to pieces?"

Tiffani squirmed, frantic. "Put that out right now," she screamed.

Adonis slapped her bare bottom with a loud crack. "Careful, honey. You're gonna burn that nice leather couch."

Steele watched Adonis through the black craters of his eyes, like a rat calculating a piece of cheese, wondering if he bit whether he'd get a chance to swallow.

Tiffani wailed, on the edge of hysteria. "Sherwood, make him put it out. Make him stop."

"Yes, Sherwood, make me stop. But first show me the money... or I detonate your honey." Adonis laughed maniacally at his ghoulish rhyme.

Steele, his eyes locked on the burning fuse, finally spoke up. "I have a proposition for you."

"What proposition?"

"I want you to do a job for me."

"You mean *another* job," Adonis corrected.

"Do what I want and I will pay you twice you're asking price."

"Two hundred grand?"

Steele nodded at the wick attached to Tiffani. It had burned down to a stub. Adonis reached over, snuffed it with his fingertips, and jerked out the TNT. Tiffani grunted once then moaned. He held the stick up to Steele's face.

"Screw me, Sherwood, and this is going up your rear end. And it ain't coming out."

Bradys Run

CHAPTER FIFTY NINE

BY THE TIME John McCarty left the Sea Shanty, artillery bursts of wind and rain were exploding every few minutes. The whirlwind *Rollie* had already dispensed its hell on the Bahamian archipelago. An hour before, the eye of the storm had passed over the tiny isle of Bimini, submerging its main settlement of Alice Town under giant waves and storm surge. The front edge of the hurricane had catapulted into the Atlantic and was now hurtling across the fifty-mile stretch of open sea between Bimini and Fort Lauderdale.

Brady and Rose buttoned up the bar, rolled down the window shutters, and hooked up the generator so it would be ready to crank on after the storm passed.

"Your place or mine?" he said.

"Mine," Rose said. "Remember, in case of emergency."

"I love emergencies."

"And my cat."

"I love cats."

"I know what you love."

"Did you know," he said, "that some lions mate fifty times in one day?"

"I hope you're not suggesting…"

"I am man, hear me roar."

"Don't start thinking about Guinness world records, old boy. I prefer quality over quantity."

The din outside was more muscular than ever. She wrapped her arms around his neck and drew him to her. The sensation of her lips on his was exquisite. Brady flashed back to the first time he kissed Victoria. A warm summer night on a footbridge in Central Park. The city as backdrop. Lights reflecting off the water. A fairytale setting. This was more like a war zone, but no less sublime.

"Are you happy, Rose?"

"What's better than happy?"

"I don't know. A peppermint ice cream cone?"

"Well, then, I'm as happy as a double scoop of peppermint. How did this happen, Brady?"

"To quote the great philosopher Patti Loveless: *Who knows how love starts. I woke up with you in my heart. Timber I'm falling in love.*"

"Who's Patti Loveless?"

"A girl who sings love songs."

"What is love anyway?"

"Are we playing *Jeopardy*? I'm no philosopher but, whatever love is, I've got it. Bad."

"Me too," she said and kissed him again.

The door to the Sea Shanty burst open and a tall figure rushed in. A black hood was draped like a monk's cowl over his head and a pistol was attached to the end of his arm. Before Brady could react the intruder threw the weapon like a fist at his temple. He felt like he'd been shot with a taser. He stood paralyzed, swaying like a skidrow drunk. His brain was suddenly working in slow motion. He watched the hooded invader hurl a second blow that caught him square on the jaw. A bright light flashed behind his eyes and he sank to the floor.

Brady awoke like a bear coming out of hibernation. *Why,* he asked himself idly, *am I sleeping on the floor?* His vision was as distorted as a funhouse mirror. His eyes meandered around the room like a pair of robotic cameras with someone else at the controls. They settled on the warped outline of his old surfboard hanging on the wall. Loud droning filled his ears, like a colony of bees had built a hive in his head. The wind squalled outside, unleashing a High C note that stabbed the pain receptors behind his eyeballs. He squeezed his lids tight for several seconds, trying to recalibrate his senses, then lifted his head and squinted toward the far end of the bar. Someone was sitting on a stool. It looked like Rose. Her eyes seemed to be swimming with tears. *Why is Rose crying?* He swiveled his head until he came eye-to-eye with a hollow black barrel. Behind it, a man was holding a gun.

"I didn't know you two were together," he said, pulling off his hood and wiping the weather from his face.

Brady heard the voice but the words were being channeled to a part of his brain that had no clue what to do with them. At the same time, another corner of his cerebra was clear as crystal.

"Wewwo Noddie," he said. *What the hell was that?*

The gunman laughed. Raindrops sprinkled off him. "You've been drinking too much of your stock."

Brady giggled. *He thinks I'm drunk!* He wanted to close his eyes and take a nap, but a voice in his head told him he might miss something important. *What? Rose? Rollie? The gun guy?* He raised himself awkwardly into lotus position, like one of Rose's yoga students, and smiled up at her seeking approval. Her eyes remained dark and wet. He steeled himself to form his next words.

"Hewwo, Donnie."

"You know my real name?" Adonis said.

Brady's senses were regrouping like a school of fish after a shark had swum through it. Gradually, Adonis's face came into focus. Brady was struck by how much he'd aged since they met just a few of days ago. His features were drawn and his eyes had a deranged cast, underscored by deep black shadows. Brady spoke again, slow and deliberate.

"Crackhead told me all about you. Said to say hi."

"How is Crackhead?"

"Having a bad life. He blames you."

"That's a good one. Throw Crackhead in a pit with eleven snakes and you got a dozen snakes."

There was no view in or out of the Shanty. The metal shutters were clashing like cymbals with every peal of wind. Adonis jerked his pistol at Brady to get up and move next to Rose. He struggled to his feet and staggered to the bar. Rose threw her arms around him and squeezed tight. Her brow was wrinkled, her eyes teary pools. He could hear her teeth grinding. He touched his fingers gingerly to the spot on the side of his head where Adonis's gun butt hit him and discovered a knot large enough to fill an egg cup.

"Crackhead says you're the snake, Donnie. Says you murdered Cisco Blas, not him."

"Cry me a river. Willie deserves no sympathy. He earned his ticket to Hell."

Rose took a damp towel from the bar and swabbed blood from Brady's eye. "How about Jonas?" she said. "What did he do to deserve being murdered?"

Adonis shrugged. "What can I say, Rosie? I had a job to do."

"And Cherry Hampton?" said Brady.

"How the hell'd you know about her?"

"It's all over TV. So is Jack Del Largo."

"*Jesus!* Good news travels fast."

"What's your plan for us?" Rose said.

He smiled at her. "Honey, let's just say you won't be getting old and wrinkly."

Brady thought he saw an anticipatory drool escape the other man's lower lip.

"Don't we get a vote?" he said. He raised a hand in the air. "Rose and I vote no on your plan. We win two-to-one. Game over."

"You're a barrel of laughs, Brady. But this ain't no democracy. And it ain't a game. You don't get a vote." Adonis scanned the bar. "Whaddya got to drink?"

"We're closed," Brady said.

"You're about to be closed forever."

The Shanty pulsated with latent violence. Brady glared at Adonis like a blood enemy. The hollow black eye of Adonis's pistol glared back at the center of his chest. A gust of wind shrieked like Mariah Carey hitting an eighth octave. Rose slid off her stool and stood between Brady and the gun.

"How about a power shake?" she said to Adonis. "For old time's sake."

"Perfect. I haven't eaten all day." He lowered the pistol and examined her. "You know, Rosie, I am gonna miss that cute little fanny of yours."

"Are you leaving us Adonis," she said. "Or Donnie, or whoever you are?"

"Just make the shake, unless you gotta go upstairs for the fixings."

"Everything's here."

"Then do it. Try anything funny and I pop a cap in your boyfriend."

Rose stepped behind the bar while Adonis watched Brady through eyes as thin and cold as coin slots. For lack of anything better to do, Brady shot him a mystified look.

"What's this all about, Donnie? You torch a motel. You murder a motel owner. You kill Cherry Hampton. I'm guessing Jack Del Largo, too. What's going on? Or do you even know?"

"Business."

"Come on, Donnie. You're no Vito Corleone. Who sent you here? Sherwood Steele?"

Adonis stared at him, a glint of admiration in his eyes. "You're good, Brady. You shoulda been a cop."

"I was."

"No shit?"

"No shit."

"You musta been good."

"It was a breeze. I liked to crack two or three murders every morning then sip mimosas for lunch."

Rose flipped on the blender and the room was filled with a piercing scream.

"Terrible weather we're having," Adonis shouted over the maelstrom.

"So what's Sherwood Steele up to?" Brady said.

"Greedy bastard's got it goin', don't he? Incredible yacht. Amazing bitch. Everything he touches turns to gold."

"Inspirational. But why's the greedy bastard paying you to drown old men and burn motels?"

"That's top secret."

"I can keep a secret," Brady said, crossing his heart. "Cross my heart."

"Shortly before Jack's, uh, let's just call it his…"

"Untimely passage?"

"I like that. Before his untimely passage Jack said Steele's planning to build some big super-resort on the beach."

Rose slammed a tall glass onto the bar and poured a gelatinous pea-green substance into it from the blender. Adonis's eyes lit up like candles.

"Rosie, baby, I'm gonna miss your power shakes."

"You already said."

"I said I'd miss that perky little ass of yours. I might miss your shakes even more."

"I'm flattered," she said and slid the glass across the bar. *"Skoal!"*

"What's that supposed to mean?"

"To your health."

"All things considered, Rosie, that's very thoughtful. Now, come on out here." He gestured with the pistol. She came back around the bar and nestled close to Brady, as if drawing strength from his touch. Adonis took a big swallow of the power shake. It left a green mustache on his upper lip. "Delicious, Rosie. I gotta get your recipe."

"I'll write it down. You can pick it up next time you're in for a workout."

"You're quite the comedian too, Rosie. You two are a pair of quip-sters. Regular Al and Peg Bundy's."

"So?" Brady said. He was completely alert now, redirecting the conversation. "Sherwood Steele is having people killed over a resort? That's insane."

"Who's to say what's crazy?" Adonis swirled the green goop and took another quaff. "Guy's got megabucks. Must know something."

A wind bomb detonated outside and the building vibrated.

"Donnie, you're future's about as bright as a snowman in May," Brady said. "The cops have your name. *Names.* Your picture's splat-tered all over TV. I'd advise you give me that gun and cut a deal for yourself before it's too late."

"Now you sound like a goddamned prosecutor."

"I was."

"No shit?"

"No shit. Give up Steele or you and Crackhead are gonna be bunking next to each other on Death Row. Trust me, it's not a happy place."

"Why would a prosecutor cut a deal with me?"

"No offense, Donnie, but you're the scumbag *de jour*. Nobody gives two shits about an ex-con tree trimmer. Steele's the big fish."

Adonis let out a loud belch. "He's a fucking whale."

"Whales are mammals, Donnie. Steele's more like a tuna."

"Sturgeon's a big fish."

"Okay, so Steele's a sturgeon." Brady remembered he wasn't conversing with Stephen Hawking. "Deborah Jameson at the State Attorney's Office would love to get her hooks into him."

Adonis's face had taken on a pallid hue. He burped again. Brady and Rose exchanged furtive glances. Adonis moved behind the bar, laid down the pistol, and removed a vial from his pocket. Brady's muscles were taut as piano wire. Adonis sprinkled a white line on the bar, leaned over, and sucked it up his nostril like an Oreck vacuum. Brady coiled. He was about to spring when Rose squeezed his knee. She gave him a queer smile and shook her head. Adonis tilted his head back and snorted.

"You guys wanna hit?"

"I don't do drugs, Adonis," said Rose. "You shouldn't either. Maybe you wouldn't be in this fix."

He wiped the remaining powder off the bar with his forefinger and rubbed it into his gums. Beads of sweat were popping out on his forehead. His stomach growled loud enough to be audible even above the uproar outside. A queasy grin came onto his face.

"You're right, Rosie, but I'm celebrating. This is independence day for me."

"Do you really think you're going to get away?" Her voice had a scolding edge. "How many people have you killed?"

"At least four," said Brady.

Adonis looked at him with surprise. "Four?"

"Cisco Blas, Jonas Bigelow, Cherry Hampton, and Jack Del Largo."

Adonis picked his pistol off the bar and waved it dismissively. "Who's counting, anyway?"

His voice was weak, his face pale and bloodless. His chin fell to his chest and a stray tuft of wet hair flopped down over his eyes.

"It's so tragic," Rose said with unvarnished sincerity. "You were such a nice guy."

"Do a few murders make me a bad person?"

"You can't unring a bell, Adonis. Let Brady help you before they hunt you down like a rabid dog."

Adonis's face quivered and his lips curled grotesquely. Brady was straining to bolt. Rose pulled back his arm like the reins on a racehorse. Adonis doubled over and a green gusher spewed from his mouth. Rose held Brady for another heartbeat. Adonis convulsed again and collapsed behind the bar. She released her grip.

"Now!"

He shot from his chair, seized a stool, and rushed around the bar. He lifted it over his head just as Adonis looked up. He pointed the gun and squeezed the trigger. Fire spat from the barrel the same instant the stool smashed his head. Brady felt white hot pain explode inside his shoulder and flew backwards. The barstool shattered. Rose ran behind the counter and picked up a broken leg. Adonis's gun was lying on the ground. He was rolling in his own blood and vomit, groaning and retching loudly, his face covered with blood. He saw her standing over him and growled.

"You poisoned me, bitch!"

She brought the chair leg down on his skull with a grunt and he curled into a ball on the floor. Brady was on his back in the corner. Blood was spurting from his left shoulder. Rose grabbed a fistful of napkins off the bar and pressed them into the wound.

"We have to get out of here, Brady." She pulled him to his feet and they lurched across the room toward the door.

"What did you put in that shake?" he said.

"Two Queen Alexandras."

"Should have used three."

Rose pushed the door and the seething wind sucked it open. Then she turned and gasped. Adonis had regained his feet. He was propped up behind the bar, his face a hideous mask of dripping blood. He raised the pistol and pointed. Brady saw him and pushed Rose out the door. He dove after her into the blackness just as the gun exploded.

Bradys Run

CHAPTER SIXTY

HURRICANE TIFFANI HAD reached Category Five intensity when Sherwood Steele found her in her stateroom. She was stuffing her suitcase, furious. The welt on her cheek was purple now. Black rivulets of mascara streaked her face and her hair was a wild tangle of red. The femme fatale was a raging madwoman.

"Tiffani, what are you doing?"

"Getting out of here. Away from that psycho…and *you.*"

"*Me?*"

He was thunderstruck by the loathing in her voice.

"That son-of-a-bitch rapes me. Sodomizes me with dynamite. And you promise to pay him two hundred thousand dollars!"

"I did it to save you, Tiffani. He was going to blow you to kingdom come."

He reached out to touch her. She turned on him like a feral animal.

"You're in shock, Tiffani. Come inside and sit down. Have a drink."

"*A drink?* You bastard. Why don't you take me to a hospital? Why don't you call the police?"

"You know I can't call the police."

Steele knew he was teetering on a tightrope with no safety net. Push too hard and she would go over the edge – him with her. He reached out once more, but she retreated.

"Get away. Do you hear me?"

Tiffani was as tall as Steele and when he grabbed for her again, she rushed forward and rammed him into the wall. A mirror crashed to the ground and shattered.

"Don't you ever touch me again or I will kill you!"

Steele didn't know what to do. Worse, he didn't know what Tiffani might do. He ran to her stateroom and into the bath, opened the mirrored medicine cabinet, and found a vial of Xanax. Maybe sedatives would calm her. When he returned she was gone.

"Tiffani," he shouted over the tumult outside. There was no response.

Steele scoured the boat. She wasn't in the staterooms, the gymnasium, or the main salon. Then he heard sniffling and followed the sound to his office. Tiffani was kneeling in the corner in a rain jacket. She was shivering. Tears drizzled down her bruised cheek. She had pushed away a heavy teak Louis XIV tea chest from behind Steele's desk. Now her fingers were spinning the dial on the floor safe.

Steele's fear turned to anger. "What the hell do you think you're doing?"

Tiffani reached her right hand into the jacket pocket and pulled out a small handgun. She pointed it at him.

"Stay away or I swear I'll shoot you."

"Where did you get that?"

"You don't need to know. You just need to stay back."

"Get away from the safe. You're not going anywhere." He extended a shaky palm full of blue pills. "You're in shock. Take one of these. They'll make you feel better."

Gun in hand, Tiffani watched Steele with wide, primal eyes. "Don't come any closer."

Steele backed away. She held the pistol in one hand and continued twisting the dial with the other. The safe clacked and she swung the door open. She reached down, fished out a stack of cash, and stuffed it into a black leather shoulder bag. Then another and another.

"What are you doing?" he said, his alarm rising. "That's a half million dollars. I need that cash. Once I pay Rock we'll be home free. Listen to me, Tiffani. Everything is going to be fine."

Steele lunged at her and the gun discharged. Even in the storm, the blast reverberated like a clap of thunder. A tendril of blue smoke curlicued from the muzzle. Tiffani knelt with her mouth open. Steele stared at her with surprised eyes. Then he looked down. A pimento circle was growing at the center of his white shirt just below the sternum. Tiffani saw a flicker of comprehension in his eyes, as if he was mesmerized by the sight of his life leaking away. Without a word, he collapsed.

She froze, breathless, waiting for him to stir. He didn't move. She crawled across the room. He was belly-up on the white llama-skin carpet. Tiffani lifted his wrist. She felt no pulse and jerked her hand away. She leaned close to his mouth. He wasn't breathing. She looked into his eyes. They were open but blank, like a shark's, staring off at the end of time.

Tiffani shuddered and let out a convulsive sob. Sherwood Steele was dead and she'd killed him. It wasn't possible. It couldn't be real. Her eyes stayed riveted on his still form for several stunned seconds, refusing to believe, waiting for him to move. Then the wind bayed outside and the boat rocked and she snapped out of her stupor. Numbly she crept back to the safe and finished gorging her bag with bundles of cash. Then she went to a mirror and repaired her tear-streaked face. Without another glance at Steele's lifeless body, she picked up her moneybag and walked off the Shangri-La into the storm.

Bradys Run

CHAPTER SIXTY ONE

EVERYTHING WAS HAPPENING in milliseconds. Brady plunged out the Sea Shanty door just as Adonis Rock's gun detonated. He wasn't sure if it was a bullet or *Hurricane Rollie,* but something slammed him face down onto the cobblestone street.

He clung to the stone pavers with his fingernails. A torrent as swift as a Colorado rapid was surging down the road. Pellets of wet sand and water were stabbing him in the face. He tasted salt and realized the water wasn't rain but wind-blown sea. He lifted his head. The tufted tops of coconut palms were dancing madly. He didn't see any trace of Rose.

Across the road, a green metal electric box as big as a Volkswagen was anchored into the sidewalk. A ferocious gust plucked it off the ground and hurled it directly at him. It crashed into the ground inches from his head, bounced like a rubber ball over his prone body, and smashed into the Shanty's front window shutter.

Out of nowhere, a childhood nursery rhyme popped into his head. *"Jack be nimble, Jack be quick..."* There were times to stop and make a stand, and there were times to run. This was a time to run. His mind screamed: *Go!* He pushed off the ground. Searing pain shot through his left shoulder. He collapsed and his face smashed into the cobblestones. *So that's how it feel to be kicked by a mule.*

Brady forced himself to disregard the pain. He braced his right arm, pushed himself to his feet, and started running. His legs were liquid and aloof, as if they belonged to someone else. He guessed Rose had fled upstairs to the gymnasium. She was probably calling the police. He was about to follow her when an enormous burst of wind drove him to his right, away from the ocean, away from the Papillon. He made a hasty choice he hoped he wouldn't regret. He turned straight back into the gale, straight back toward the Shanty. When he passed the door he saw Adonis still inside, leaning against the bar. Blood was streaming from his forehead and he looked barely able to stand. He saw Brady and a demonic grin crossed his face. The look of a stone cold killer. The vision galvanized Brady.

Gun in hand, Adonis stumbled toward the door. Brady sprang forward like a panther. The glass door to the Papillon was unlocked. *She's up there.* He yanked it open and ducked inside just as a shot rang out. Glass shattered behind him. He blundered up the stairwell. The walls were awash in blood-red light cast by an exit sign. He banged into solid concrete. His left shoulder arched in agony. *That must be how it feels to be poked by a branding iron.* When he reached the second floor landing, another bullet ricocheted off cement and steel. Brady risked a quick peek over the rail. Adonis was propped against the disintegrated glass door.

"Give up, Brady," he hollered, his voice echoing up the stairwell. "I'm gonna kill you and your girlfriend."

"Don't bet on it, Donnie. I'd run if I was you."

"Sorry. No can do. Nothing personal."

Adonis raised his gun and fired again. The slug sparked off the steel banister and struck Brady in the left thigh just above his knee. The impact spun him half around and he collapsed. His leg was on fire. A runnel of blood streamed down his calf and into his high-top. Rose came to his mind. He hoped she'd gone to the roof and climbed down the back fire escape to safety.

Adonis yelled from below. "I'm coming for you, Brady."

He gripped the railing, dragged himself to his feet, and kept climbing. To his surprise the initial pain subsided. *Adrenalin.* Brady reached the top of the stairs and rammed his right shoulder into the door. It burst open and he lurched through the void. He was immediately bowled over by a wind blast. He knelt on the rooftop and shouted.

"Rose! Rose!"

No answer. He staggered to his feet and fought his way toward the greenhouse. Rain was coming like a black blizzard. Breathing was almost impossible. Brady felt like he was drowning on a battlefield of wind and water. At that moment gills would have served him better than his lungs. He hoisted his shirt up over his mouth and nose and shielded his eyes with his good arm. The chain link gate to the fire escape was unlatched and swinging wildly. *She's gone*, he thought, relieved.

Brady careened to a short wall overlooking the beach road and looked down. There was no sign of Rose. Down the beach red and blue police lights were flashing, but too far for the cops to have heard the gunfire.

Lightning cracked in the black sky like a sheet of white glass shattering. The sea alighted for a split second and he gasped at the terrifying freeze-frame. *If hell has an ocean,* he thought, *it looks like this*. He was perched three stories high – looking *up* at an enormous crest of black water barreling straight at him. It was as tall as the Caribbean wave that sank the *Victoria*. It rolled in with breathtaking speed. Over the beach and through an echelon of spindly palms and exploded on the road. Brady felt a concussion and white foam burst like frothy shrapnel all the way to the rooftop, covering him.

With Rose gone to safety, he moved to flee down the fire escape. He took one step but his left leg gave out and he collapsed to the ground. He looked up in time to see Adonis come through the door onto the roof. Brady rolled back into the shadow at the base of the wall. He could feel his heart pounding against his ribcage. The downpour made visibility gauzy. He could just make out Adonis stumbling against the wind. He was coming straight at him. One hand was fending off the rain while the other gripped his pistol. A colossal squall hit. The wind unzipped Adonis's black jacket and tore it off him, ripping the pistol from his hand. The gun skidded across the wet concrete. Adonis fell to the ground and crawled toward his weapon.

Brady had his chance. He sprang from the shadows and landed on top of the outstretched figure. Adonis grunted but gathered his strength.

He rammed an elbow into Brady's left shoulder, momentarily para-lyzing him. He shoved him off, got his hand on the pistol, and rolled onto his back. Brady yanked his leg as he pulled the trigger. The bullet nicked his right earlobe. He tried to scramble backwards but slipped and slammed into the fire escape gate. He ended up in sitting position, face-to-face with Adonis. The killer regained his feet and stood, tottering, his weapon trained on Brady.

"Give up, Donnie," he shouted. "There's no escape."

Adonis grinned down malevolently. "Wrong, Brady. I'm about to be gone with the wind."

"Turn in Sherwood Steele. It's your only chance. Kill me and you lose all hope."

"Sorry, Brady. You gotta go. You're my home run."

"Home run?" Brady laughed harshly. "You're about to strike out forever."

Adonis raised his gun. The greenhouse door blew open and a tor-nado of butterflies exploded in his face. Rose vaulted out behind them, shrieking like a banshee. Adonis recoiled and she hit him with a cross-body block. The impetus propelled him into the wall.

He quickly righted himself and smashed the butt of his gun on top of Rose's head. She collapsed like a puppet that's strings had been severed. He pointed the gun down at her. Brady shot to his feet and rammed the crown of his head straight into Adonis's solar plexus. Brady fell to the ground while Adonis teetered on the wall, his head and torso hanging over the edge. He flapped his arms like a big bird on a small perch, frantically trying to regain balance. Then *Hurricane Rollie* intervened with a furious gust. Brady saw a startled look in his eyes. Then a grin of resignation. Then he tumbled backwards over the precipice.

Bradys Run

CHAPTER SIXTY TWO

BRADY SCRAMBLED ON his knees to Rose and lifted her head. She was unconscious but alive. An indescribable wave of relief washed over him. Blood was streaming from her scalp. He had to get her to a hospital. He needed medical attention too, for at least two bullet holes. He held her in the hollow of his arms, stroking her wet face, filled with profound awe at her reckless daring. She had saved his life. He shouted over the howling wind.

"I swear to you Rose, I will never leave you. Never! I'll love you until the day I die."

A voice responded. "That'll be sooner than you think, Brady." It wasn't Rose.

He scanned the rooftop. There was no one. Then he stood and looked over the wall and his blood turned to ice.

Six feet down, Adonis lay flat on his back, spread-eagle on a narrow ledge. His eyes were open and the gun was still in his hand – pointed straight up at him. He fired. Brady ducked in the nick of time.

Alarm bells clanged in his head. He bent down and gathered Rose in his arms. Pain bolted through his wounded shoulder. He ignored it and mustered the strength to throw her over his good shoulder. With a bullet in one leg, he limped as fast as he could to the fire escape. Another shot rang out. The bullet clipped the chain link gate a millisecond after he passed through it.

Brady fled down the escapeway and emerged onto the beach road and collided with a wall of wind. He nearly went down but managed to keep his feet. He began hobbling toward the flashing red and blue police lights down the beach. He'd taken only a few steps when the ocean surged across A1A and caught him knee-deep in a riptide. Wind and water scissor-tackled him and he fell hard.

The violent rush of sea retreated as fast as it came and Rose's unconscious body was torn from his arms. Brady regained his feet and stumbled after her. A gunshot rang out. He looked back. Adonis was a hundred feet away, running pell-mell straight for him.

In the opposite direction Rose was being sucked out to sea like a piece of driftwood. He raced headlong into the blackness and got his hands on her just before she was pulled under. Then he looked up and electricity shot up his backbone. Another monster wave was coming fast from the darkness. This one larger than the last. Adonis was twenty yards away coming for them with pistol raised. Fear gripped Brady like a vise.

He heard a voice ask him a question. *Do you want to die?* The answer came in an instant. *If I die, Rose dies.* He lifted her and turned and, out of nowhere, everything began moving in slow motion. Brady was overcome by a dreamy tranquility that bordered on euphoric. For a split-second, he wondered if he was already dead. The big wave was still moving at him, but at a snail's pace. The roar of the wind was as hushed as snow falling on a forest. It occurred to him that his mind was moving so fast his senses had been altered. He felt like he was watching himself in a movie. Then he thought of Victoria. After his boat sank that stormy night in the Caribbean, Luther told him she had saved him. *As surely as fish can swim and birds can fly.* He looked down at Rose.

"Victoria, please don't let her die!"

He heard a gunshot. It came from close range, but he didn't feel an impact. He leapt up onto the low white wall that ran along the beach. It was now a seawall. There was no beach. The sand was flooded with ocean water. Adonis screamed, only feet away now.

"I got you, Brady! You're a dead man!"

Death seemed to have them between its teeth and was about to bite. He jumped down and staggered straight toward the giant wave. He floundered to a gangly coconut palm and wedged Rose between himself and the tree. Black water loomed overhead like the heel of an angry god. He wrapped his arms around the trunk, filled his lungs with air, and held on for dear life.

Adonis was ten feet away when the wave crested. Brady could see his face frozen in a macabre simian sneer. He pointed the pistol and fired. Brady felt wood splinter into his fingers on the other side of the tree. Adonis looked up, his face savage, and thundered at the sea like a maniacal Old Testament figure, his roar captured by the wind. Then the wave struck.

Brady felt like an elephant had fallen on him. The weight of the water crushed the air from his lungs. Ocean rushed into his mouth, his ears, his nostrils. He was suffocating and had to fight a desperate urge to breath, praying the surge would recede swiftly.

Rose regained consciousness underwater in total blackness and began to convulse. She couldn't know where she was or what was happening. She panicked as she fought for her life. The tension was more than Brady's bullet-torn shoulder could bear. Rose started to slip away. He knew if he let go she'd be pulled out to sea. With his right arm he spun her around, pressed his mouth to hers, and expelled the little air still left in his lungs. They remained locked together for what seemed like eternity. Finally, he felt her body slacken. Then all went black.

Bradys Run

CHAPTER SIXTY THREE

THEY WERE TRAPPED underwater longer than their lungs could possibly withstand. His lips pressed against hers. Trying to force every centimeter of breath he had into her. Knowing neither of them could last. His only consolation in those final seconds that he would die in the embrace of the woman he loved.

After what seemed like an eternity, Brady felt the water begin to rush back toward the sea. He held the tree with all his might until the tide ebbed below his head and he breathed again. Rose did not. Her mouth was open and her jaw slack. Her body was like rubber. She showed no sign of life.

Adonis was nowhere to be seen, but the wind was seething harder than ever. Brady disengaged his arms from the coconut tree. He lifted Rose and blundered toward the road. They tumbled over the low wall onto the sidewalk.

Brady flashed on something Johnny Glisson once told him. The most effective technique for resuscitating drowning victims was the Heimlich Maneuver. With Rose in his arms, he propped his back against the concrete and pulled her onto his lap. As the gale blew and torrential rain lashed them, he wrapped his arms around her and clasped his fists together below her ribcage. He thrust upward into her stomach cavity.

Four thrusts every ten seconds, Johnny had said. Once. Twice. Three. Four times. Water came out her mouth with each thrust, but she didn't breathe. He did it again. And again. Each time more urgent. No reaction. Enraged, he screamed over the wind into her ear.

"You will not die! Do you hear me, Rose? You will not die!"

He thrust again. And again. Nothing. He began to feel very empty, like the blood was draining from his body. He kept trying, but inside he knew. It was happening all over. First Victoria. Now Rose. The only women he'd ever loved. Gone. What had he done to deserve this? What abominable sin had he committed? He felt himself dying. Not his body, but his soul. He had been spiritually comatose for so long. Then Rose came along. *You could be happy*. And he had been, for one brief moment. But he could not survive this. He did not want to survive. Not without her. It was too much. He wasn't strong enough. No one could be. He kissed her throat one last time, clenched his fists, and jerked upward with every ounce of strength he had left.

Sometime later, a police car found them. Dan Mason was at the wheel. They were huddled at the base of the wall. Silent. Still. Mason recognized them and dreaded what he'd found. They were dead. He was certain of it. He climbed from his vehicle and ran to them. He touched Brady first. He opened his eyes. Then he nudged Rose. She did the same. They both smiled.

"Hi, Dan," said Brady. "Think we can catch a ride?"

Bradys Run

CHAPTER SIXTY FOUR

MASON SUMMONED AN ambulance and they were rushed to the emergency room at Broward General Medical Center. The pistol whipping had left Rose with a lacerated scalp and Grade III brain concussion. Brady's leg wound was clean but his shoulder was a mess. An orthopedic surgeon was called in at the height of the storm and spent six hours mending his shredded rotator cuff.

The next morning, a magnificent rainbow arched over the Atlantic. *Hurricane Rollie* had come and gone. Before it left, though, it had taken another huge bite out of Lauderdale Beach and left its own legacy of downed trees, severed telephone lines, and widespread power outages.

Providentially, only one building had been destroyed. Donald Rockwell's broken body was found by salvage workers in the rubble. Belinda Boulanos performed the autopsy and surmised the leviathan wave had apparently crushed him into the sand and propelled him into the low white wall, snapping his spine. Helpless, he was thrust across the beach road and into the pit of one of the new high rises under construction where he was wedged, alive but helpless, between two columns of steel rebar. The water pressure had been so intense it cracked a beam and the steel and concrete skeleton collapsed. After Rockwell's broken body was removed, the contractor, Harvey Woulfe, promised the tower would be rebuilt and tourist-ready by next season.

Police were faced with a daunting task. Bodies of prominent citizens kept popping up. At the Pier 66 Hotel, a female desk clerk in the first floor lobby heard moaning. She looked up and saw blood dripping from the ceiling. Firefighters were called to the scene and found Norman Epstein lodged in the rafters. He was still alive. They were able to get the bank president in an ambulance, but he died en route to the hospital. Not, though, before whispering Sherwood Steele's name into a paramedic's ear. Detectives interviewed the bartender in the revolving rooftop lounge. He recalled overhearing Epstein argue with a man he recognized from the news.

"That big shot developer," he said, "Sherman Stevens."

It was a busy night for Dan Mason. After he attended to Brady and Rose, he was dispatched to the Bahia Mar Marina where he saw lights coming from inside the Shangri-La. He pounded on the door. No one answered. He walked along the gangway banging on portals but no one stirred. Then, through a crack in a shutter, he saw a leg on the floor. Mason found an unlocked door and entered the vessel. Sherwood Steele's body was lying near an open floor safe. Jack Del Largo's severed head was in the main salon. The next day's headline read: *Jack-In-A-Box Found on Death Yacht*.

Two days later, Tiffani Bandeaux was arrested at Hartsfield Jackson International Airport in Atlanta boarding a flight for San Jose, Costa Rica. She blamed Adonis Rock for the murders of Sherwood Steele and Jack Del Largo. Adonis was also determined to have done in Cherry Hampton and Jonas Bigelow. As for Butthead, his identity was never determined, chiefly because he was never reported missing. It seemed no one knew he was dead.

After Deborah Jameson unraveled the whole sordid affair, Tiffani cut a deal and turned state's evidence against Mayor David Grand and Commissioner Jarrett Griffin. They, in turn, gave up Roscoe Anderson. All three men pleaded guilty to bribery and official misconduct. Each was sentenced to seven years in prison. Bandeaux got four years. The South Florida National Bank was taken over by federal regulators, who auctioned off its assets to Wells Fargo.

Brady was released from the hospital after three days. Rose, her head still bandaged, drove him back to the Sea Shanty. The place had been devastated by the storm. *Rollie* snapped off the front door and rain and storm surge had flooded the place. McCarty, Gunther, Olga, Jesse, Bill, Sunny, and Johnny Glisson all pitched in and mopped up the water and sand. Brady's blood and Adonis' butterfly-laced vomit had been washed away.

"Wow!" Brady said when he saw it. "The place looks good as new."

"Too bad you don't, old fella," said Rose.

"You're not going to start that again, are you?"

Rose kissed him.

"I guess when you're mayor," he said, "you can say whatever you want!"

"Actually, no. I dropped out of the race this morning."

"What? And give in to the *shadow world*?"

Rose explained that she had gladly bowed out after the governor appointed City Commissioner Liz Donnelly interim mayor to replace David Grand. Donnelly had opposed Grand's kowtowing to developers and promised to introduce legislation to limit buildings east of the Intracoastal to no more than five stories.

"So you're political career is over before it begins?" Brady said.

"Not quite," said Rose. "The governor appointed me to serve out the remainder of Liz Donnelly's commission term."

"Great. Does that mean you'll be able to fix traffic tickets?"

"No favors."

"How about fraternizing with constituents?"

"Hmmm. I'll take that under consideration."

"Congratulations Commissioner Butterfly."

"Somehow congratulations don't quite seem in order. Not after an arson, a bank failure, and six dead bodies."

"Almost eight," he said, "counting us."

Four weeks later, on a brilliant blue morning, Brady cast off lines and sailed the Victoria II out of Port Everglades and into the Atlantic. His shoulder had healed with amazing speed and he felt strong enough to sail. He navigated thirty miles due east until all signs of land vanished beyond the arc of the ocean's rim.

Brady let the schooner scud before the wind like a kite without a string. Where she ran mattered not. He was on a treasure hunt. The bounty wasn't under the sea. Or on it. In fact, he wasn't sure where it was. Or even what it was. If it did exist he suspected it was probably inside him. Some kind of inner bearing was the treasure he sought. So much had changed. He felt like his heart and mind and soul, his entire being, had been transplanted into a different man. He needed to chart a new point on the sextant for himself.

For three days he tacked back and forth alone across the horizon. Swinging on deck in his hammock. Swimming in the bottomless sea. Sitting on the bowsprit dangling his feet over the water while dolphins skittered playfully ahead.

All the while he contemplated everything that had happened since the day Victoria was stolen from him. The years of emotional narcosis. The fire. Jonas's murder. The ferocity of nature. His own brush with finality.

As the sun set on the third day, the western sky mutated into a cosmic symphony of pink, purple, and finally blood red that kissed the heavens before turning inexorably black. Brady found himself surrounded by a sonata of eternal light. He gazed up at the moon's pearly face smiling in a sea of stars. He wondered if Victoria was up there in infinity waiting for him. He believed now without reservation that she had saved his life that stormy night in the Caribbean. And that she had been the guardian angel who protected he and Rose from Adonis the night they survived.

For the first time since 9/11, Brady felt as if he'd put together the pieces to his puzzle. Standing at the wheel, he finally felt at one with the vast sea. And with himself.

He ducked into the cabin and came back on deck with an urn. It held dirt and ashes he'd collected at Ground Zero. It was the closest he ever came to finding Victoria's remains. Brady climbed up onto the bowsprit and released her to the sea. Then he tacked the schooner westward and headed back toward land, toward civilization, toward Rose.

About the Author

Joseph Collum is the recipient of more than 100 major journalism awards during his career as an investigative reporter, including the Alfred I. duPont-Columbia University Award, two George Polk Awards, five Investigative Reporters & Editors Awards and a dozen Emmy Awards.

His reports have led to a Congressional inquiry into elder care, saved the lives of people denied adequate medical care, prevented hundreds of low income homeowners from being evicted, and led to the imprisonment of dozens of corrupt public officials.

Collum was the first reporter in America to expose the widespread practice of racial profiling (the Oxford English Dictionary credits him with coining the term "racial profiling"). His final journalism assignment was at Ground Zero on September 11, 2001 and the days immediately following the collapse of the World Trade Towers. His account of the tragedy is excerpted in the book *Covering Catastrophe*.

After retiring from journalism following 9/11, Collum returned to his childhood roots in Fort Lauderdale, Florida to write books. His novel *Brady's Run*, a murder mystery set in Fort Lauderdale, was published in 2009. The sequel, *Et Tu Brady*, was published in 2013. *The Black Dragon: Racial Profiling Exposed*, the true story of the invention and fight to end the practice of racial profiling, was published in 2010. His next novel, *A Bullet for Brady*, will be published in 2014.

Collum and his wife, Donna, are the parents of four sons, Peter, Simon, Spencer and James.

Visit Joseph Collum on the Web at www.josephcollum.com or contact him at josephcollum.author@yahoo.com.

Made in the USA
Charleston, SC
24 September 2013